Praise for novels of

RACHEL LEE

"Attention grabbing...this well-rounded story
is sure to be one of Lee's top-selling titles."
—*Publishers Weekly* on *Something Deadly*

"Rachel Lee is a master of romantic suspense."
—*Romantic Times*

"Rachel Lee takes readers on a sensational journey
into Tami Hoag/Karen Robards territory."
—*Publishers Weekly*

"An entertaining romantic suspense
that stars two wonderful lead characters."
—*Midwest Book Review* on *A January Chill*

"A magnificent presence in romantic fiction.
Rachel Lee is an author to treasure forever."
—*Romantic Times*

"Lee crafts a heartrending saga."
—*Publishers Weekly* on *Snow in September*

"Rachel Lee delivers a highly complex thriller."
—*Publishers Weekly* on *Wildcard*

RACHEL LEE

THUNDERSTRUCK

MIRA®

MIRA®

ISBN 0-7783-2121-5

THUNDERSTRUCK

Copyright © 2005 by MIRA Books.

The publisher acknowledges the copyright holder
of the individual works as follows:

IMMINENT THUNDER
Copyright © 1993 by Susan Civil.

THUNDER MOUNTAIN
Copyright © 1994 by Susan Civil.

www.MIRABooks.com

Printed in U.S.A.

CONTENTS

IMMINENT THUNDER

To Leslie Wainger and Isabel Swift.
You both know why.

Chapter One

The midnight breeze had turned soft with the hint of thunderstorms and the scent of the nearby bay. It filled the night with the restless rustle of leaves in the old live oaks. Spanish moss swayed eerily before it, creating dark, rippling curtains of shadow. Mixed with the swish of the leaves and the sigh of the breeze was a distant, low rumble.

From the west came the approaching thunder of a storm and the flicker of sheet lightning, an ominous promise. From the north, too, there came a louder rumble, a more distinct thunder and a sharper flash of light, as bombers practiced on the military reservation. Both storms had their own kind of eeriness, the one wholly natural, the other wholly unnatural.

Just as Honor Nightingale pulled into her driveway, beneath the sagging shoulders of a row of old oaks, a thick cloud scudded across the moon, swallowing the last bit of illumination. The night abruptly devoured everything beyond the yellow beams of her headlights. It was a wild, beautiful night, she thought. The kind of night that always made her want to kick off her shoes and run barefoot through the grass like a frisky colt.

She pulled up to the detached garage that sat behind her ramshackle house and shoved the car door open, pausing to draw a deep breath of the northwest Florida air. Nowhere else on earth had nights like these. Nowhere else could you smell the sea and the thunder on a breeze as soft as silk and satin.

Climbing out of the car, she smiled to herself and threw back her head to soak it all in. The wind caught at her blue hospital scrubs, snatching the fabric and molding it to her trim body. Laughing softly, she turned her head a little and let the breeze tug her hair free of its pins and whip the long, dark strands around her. It was a beautiful, beautiful night, she thought, and for just this little while she felt free of all the sorrows that had haunted her for so long.

The wind suddenly whipped around her, feeling cold and damp, and snatched the car door from Honor's hand, slamming it shut. Damn—her keys were locked inside. She absolutely didn't want to cope with that right now. She had just come off a grueling shift as triage nurse in the emergency room, it was well past midnight, and not a light had been visible in any house along the dirt road leading to the highway.

And then she recalled the damaged screen on the kitchen window beside the back door, the window with the loose latch she had discovered only yesterday. With a little patience she could probably jiggle the darn thing open. If worse came to worst, she could break the glass. So what was she standing here dithering for? Giving a last toss of her head in the breeze, she stepped toward the back porch.

And froze.

She wasn't alone. How she knew that, she couldn't have said. But suddenly her heart was in her throat and she was paralyzed by the absolute conviction that someone was watching her from the house. Her house. The house with the torn screen and the loose latch on the back window.

Holding her breath, she sorted through the possibilities with lightning speed, the same speed that often meant the difference between life and death in the emergency room. The house up the road to her right was closer, but it was deserted. The house to her left was occupied by some kind of recluse. She'd lived next door to him for a month and hadn't seen him once, but Millie Jackson, who lived up near the highway, said he was some kind of military man who just wasn't sociable.

So okay, he probably wasn't a serial killer. He was probably some soured old warrior who would—

A thump. Distinctly, despite the rustling of leaves and the distant rumble of bombs and thunder, she heard a soft thump, as if something had been bumped. From the house. From her house.

That did it. Without another second's hesitation, she whirled and took off for the recluse's house. Whatever kind of crazy he was, he couldn't be as bad as someone who would be waiting inside a house for a woman alone after dark. No way. She'd seen too many women in the emergency room who'd come home to find a creep waiting for them. She didn't need to imagine a thing. She *knew*.

A holly hedge separated the two properties. The recluse might have preferred to let it grow into a forest, but someone had kept it neatly trimmed, so she was able to leap it with the grace that had made her a champion hurdler in high school. She covered the expanse of his yard like the wind and flew onto the porch without her feet touching a single step.

If the door had been unlocked, she probably would have barged right in, but the door was locked, which was probaby the only thing that saved her from getting a knife under the ribs. Or maybe not. Later she was never really sure that her neighbor would have done such a thing without checking out the situation first, though he definitely wanted her to think so.

She definitely thought so when, after thirty seconds of her hammering, a mountain of masculinity opened the door and greeted her with the ugliest-looking hunting knife she had ever seen. It was, in fact, exactly like the one her father had had. Recognizing it, she relaxed just a hair.

"In my house!" she gasped. "There's someone! Someone broke in...."

Recluse or not, the man was quick. He threw open the screen door and dragged her inside. "Where is he?"

"He was—he was watching me from the back window when I got home. The screen is torn and the latch is loose.... I heard a sound...."

She was talking to the air. Beyond the screen door, the night whispered of coming storms, the cicadas screeched as if the world were normal, and the air smelled like the sea.

He had gone over there. Numbly she stared out at the night and wondered why. Why hadn't he called the police? Any sensible person would have called the police....

And that was precisely what she was going to do right now. She saw the wall phone over by the kitchen table. Her hand barely touched it before she realized that her neighbor could get hurt if she called the police while he was over there. The cops wouldn't care who he was or why he was carrying that Ranger knife. They would be too hyped to care, too scared to take a chance.

Unable to do anything, she paced rapidly from one end of the large kitchen to the other, back and forth, until her nerves were stretched to breaking and she figured a primal scream wouldn't even begin to touch the tension.

God, what if he got hurt and she was responsible because she had asked him for help? But he shouldn't have gone over there alone. He should have called the police. That was all she'd wanted. That was all he'd needed to do.

Maybe she should call the cops now anyway. He'd been gone too long. Maybe he was hurt and needed help. Maybe—

"He got away."

The abrupt words, spoken in a voice as deep as the night and as richly textured as black velvet, brought her spinning around with a gasp. Her neighbor stood just beyond the screen door, a dark shadow in the darker night, standing back from his own kitchen as if he feared his very presence would terrify her.

Her hand flew to her throat, and she clutched at her scrubs. "There was someone there? I didn't just imagine it?"

"I didn't see anyone, but that doesn't mean anything."

Evidently he thought she was calm enough to handle him, because he pulled open the screen door and stepped into the kitchen. She hadn't been mistaken, she realized. He *was* a mountainous man, surely one of the biggest, tallest men she had ever met, and every ounce of him was well-defined, well-developed musculature. He wore nothing but a pair of snug jeans, hastily donned when she'd knocked, to judge by the way they were unsnapped. Zipped but unsnapped, and that unfastened snap seemed to catch her gaze the same way the breeze had snagged her hair.

"I'm calling the cops, Miss, uh, Miss—?"

"Honor Nightingale." Dragging in a deep breath, she managed to tear her gaze from the arrow of dark hair that seemed determined to point out his maleness to her. Darn it, Honor, you're a nurse. There's nothing there you haven't seen a million times.... "Please, just call me Honor. You shouldn't have gone over there. You might have been hurt...."

The word trailed off as he flipped on the overhead light. Now nothing was left to her imagination. Hurt? He might have been hurt the way the Incredible Hulk could be hurt, or Dirty Harry, or... Heck, any rapist in his right mind would flee like the wind at the sight of this man.

If faces could be likened to landscapes, then his was the north face of Everest, all angles, planes, sharp corners. A glacial, unforgiving face. It was a face that would never be comfortable with a smile, yet just now it smiled. Sort of. Just a quirk of one corner of his mouth, as if he found the thought of being hurt by anyone amusing. Almost as if he wished there were someone in the world who was capable of posing a threat to him.

"Nurse Nightingale, huh?" He turned toward the phone. "Or is it Doctor?"

"Nurse. Just nurse. And I've heard all the jokes."

"I just bet you have." He punched in the police emergency number and began to speak to the dispatcher. "My name's Ian McLaren. I live at 4130 South Davis, and my neighbor's house, 4132 South Davis, has just been broken into. No, the intruder is gone now. Yes. No. The back window is open, and the screen is torn. Yes, of course." He glanced at Honor over his shoulder and suddenly frowned. "You'd better sit down, lady. You're as white as a sheet."

That was when Honor realized she had completely run out of steam. The kitchen was tilting crazily, and her ears were buzzing as if she had stepped into a hornet's nest. And her field of vision was narrowing....

Some last vestige of sense caused her to slump onto a kitchen chair and drop her head between her knees. "I never faint," she muttered to her feet.

"Thank God for small favors," he replied, in a voice that sounded dryly amused. "Just keep your head down until I can hang up the phone. Then we'll find out if you've got any blood pressure left."

He might be gruff, he might be tough, his face might look as ravaged as a war zone, but he was essentially a nice man, she decided as she studied her white oxfords and noticed blood in the creases. There had been a lot of blood in the emergency room tonight. A three-car pileup, a woman who had been shot by her husband during a quarrel, a man who had removed half his hand with a table saw. No, she never fainted. She lifted her head.

The next thing she knew she was lying on her back on the floor, staring straight up at the overhead light.

"I told you not to raise your head," said a deep, dark voice. She knew that voice, didn't she? Oh, yes. Her neighbor.

"I don't faint."

"Nope, you sure don't. Just stay put, will you?"

That sounded like a good idea, she thought as her stomach did a curious flip-flop and beads of perspiration broke out on her forehead. Nausea caused sweating, and she was undoubtedly nauseated as a reaction to adrenaline. Pleased with her clinical observation of her own state, she closed her eyes and decided that she might faint, but she absolutely was *not* going to vomit. No way.

"Here," said that same deep voice a few moments later. Strong hands gripped her shoulders and eased her slowly into a sitting position. "Okay?"

"Yes." She gave an unsteady laugh, refusing to open her eyes, because she was afraid she would find herself face-to-face with that impressive expanse of hard, muscled chest. As a nurse, she must have seen a hundred thousand chests, but she'd never seen one under these circumstances. This was...different. "I think my blood pressure is back to normal."

He gave a grunt of some kind—maybe of agreement, maybe of approval—and then scooped her up with astonishing suddenness to set her once again on the chair. He had, she realized with shock, lifted her as if she weighed nothing at all. She wasn't sure she liked the feeling. It made her too aware of her defenselessness against such great strength.

Outside, the wind gusted, rattling the screen door in its frame and sending a wave of cooler air into the kitchen. Honor shivered.

"I'll make coffee," said her neighbor gruffly. "Or would you rather have tea?"

"Coffee would be great. Thanks." Arms wrapped around herself, she tried not to shiver again. "I really appreciate you helping me out." Her eyes followed him helplessly. Nurse or not, she finally had to admit she really hadn't seen a million chests like this one. Nor a million backs that rippled under sleek muscle. Nor shoulders so broad or hips so narrow or legs so powerful... Sternly she shook herself back to reality.

He scooped coffee into the basket of the coffeemaker on the counter and started it brewing. "Women are at risk in this country," he said after a moment. "The statistics are shocking."

"I know." She did. Too well.

"Men aren't doing their jobs."

"What?" The word was startled out of her, coming out as almost a shocked laugh.

He faced her, looking at her with cat-green eyes. "We're the warriors," he replied offhandedly. "Seems like we're doing a lousy job of making the world safe for our women and children."

"Oh." A philosophical perspective, not a practical one. At the moment, it was one she could live with. He had, after all, rescued her without question. "Well, I'm sure glad you feel that way. I don't know what I would have done otherwise. Just before I realized someone was in the house, the wind blew my car door shut. It's locked, and my keys are inside, so I couldn't even drive away." And then, helplessly, she shivered again. It really wasn't cold, but as the adrenaline subsided she was beginning to feel the fear, the reaction.

Without a word, on feet as silent as a cat's, Ian McLaren left the kitchen. Less than a minute later he was back, draping a soft blue thermal blanket around her shoulders.

"Thank you," she said.

He acknowledged her thanks with a nod, then placed the length of the kitchen between them again. He did so, she realized suddenly, so as not to frighten her. The funny thing was, she wasn't frightened of him. Not at all. Not even the merest quiver. Which, she thought as she looked up into his bleak, unforgiving face, might really be stupid. He didn't look like a safe man. He looked like danger on the hoof.

He swiveled his head suddenly toward the kitchen window. "The cops are here. That was fast."

She thought so, too. When there was no immediate

danger, cops generally took their own good time about showing up. Now, through the screen door, she could see the swirling lights of a patrol car. They would, she figured, check out her place first, and then come over here to ask questions she didn't have any answers for.

Her freshly brewed cup of coffee had cooled just about enough to drink when Ian McLaren ushered the two young police officers into the kitchen. He dwarfed them, she saw, and she didn't think either of the policemen liked the feeling. Their movements around him were defensive and uneasy. Poor guy, she found herself thinking. It must be awful to have people react to you as if you were a threat just because you're so big. In fact, thinking about it, she would almost bet that when he got in an elevator, women stepped off.

The first questions were the usual, boring ones. "My name is Honor Nightingale. I'm a registered nurse, and I work in the emergency room at Community Hospital. I was on the 3:30 to 11:30 shift this evening."

"Then you were probably on when Bill Cates brought in the little girl who was in the auto accident."

Honor nodded. There had been only one little girl involved, a four-year-old, mercifully unconscious.

"Bill was wondering if she was going to make it."

It wasn't exactly a question, Honor realized, but she answered it anyway. "It'll be touch and go for a while, I'm afraid. It all depends on whether they can keep down the swelling in her brain."

The young officer, Lambert, let it go. "So you got home a little after twelve?"

"A little. Maybe 12:20."

"When did you know someone was in the house?"

She explained about the wind slamming her car door closed with her keys and purse inside, and how she'd been thinking about the loose window latch and torn screen when she had the sudden feeling that someone was watching her from that very window. And then how she had heard the thump, as if something had fallen.

"Since I couldn't drive away, I came running over here to ask Mr. McLaren for help."

Lambert turned his attention to Ian, who stood leaning against the counter, one powerful arm crossed over his waist while he sipped coffee.

"You're Ian McLaren, the man who called us, right?"

"Right."

"Occupation?"

"U.S. Army, retired. I sometimes work on the air base as a consultant."

"What kind of consultant?"

Ian set his cup down and folded his arms. "I advise the Rangers and other special-operations groups on operational tactics and survival skills." The air base included a huge reservation of federal land set aside for training purposes. Not only did bombers practice actual bombing, but all the services practiced jungle-style combat tactics and survival skills back in there, as well. Among them were the army Rangers and the Special Forces, as well as certain elite marine units.

"So Ms. Nightingale came over here for help, and you called us?"

Ian shook his head, never taking his catlike eyes from the cop. "I went over there first. I found the window by the back door open and the screen torn. The back door was wide open, flapping in the wind. I imagine the intruder fled as soon as he realized Ms. Nightingale had become aware of him."

The young policeman nodded, satisfied. "You'll have

to come back over there with us now, Ms. Nightingale. We need you to tell us if anything is missing, and what damage was done, if any."

That was when Honor got the strangest feeling. She wasn't a fanciful person by nature, not at all given to odd feelings and psychic impressions. She was a woman of cheerful, optimistic outlook and a very simple faith in God that made her feel safe in the darkest of nights. But suddenly, unexpectedly, she shivered. Almost helplessly, she raised her eyes to Ian McLaren's.

"I'll go with you," he said abruptly. "I want to take a look at that window and see if I can't make the house safer for you."

She could have kissed him for that. Had he somehow understood her sudden uneasiness? Had it been that plain on her face?

She started to leave the blanket on the chair, but he picked it back up and wrapped it around her shoulders again. "You've had a shock," he said. "Better stay warm."

"Thank you."

First, much to her relief, one of the policemen retrieved a tool from his cruiser and unlocked her car for her so that she could recover her keys and purse. Then they climbed the creaky steps to the open back door.

"This house really needs a lot of work," Honor heard herself say. She wondered if anyone else could hear the nervous note in her voice. "I've been meaning to call all kinds of repairmen ever since I moved in, but I've been so busy…"

Ian gripped her elbow reassuringly, and she fell silent. There was, she reminded herself, no reason to be nervous. Not now. Not with two policemen and a former army Ranger beside her.

The policemen warned her not to touch anything and even went so far as to turn on the kitchen light with the tip of a key so that no fingerprints would be disturbed. A crime-scene unit would come out, one of them said, to see if they could find any fingerprints around the window or the door. She absolutely mustn't touch anything until the team had come through.

"How long might that be?" she asked politely, wondering wildly if she was expected to leave her house untouched for the next week or so.

"Oh, I'm sure they'll be here soon, ma'am," said the shorter of the two officers.

So she wasn't going to get any sleep, either. "Wonderful. I'd be willing to bet the man who broke in here is already tucked into his soft little bed for the night. How many hours or days does it take for this team to complete their work?"

"That'll depend on whether you find anything else missing or disturbed."

That could almost be taken as a threat, Honor thought tiredly. By chance her gaze met Ian's, and she saw a surprising amount of understanding in those cat-green eyes of his. She had the eerie feeling that he was reading her mind. Disturbed by the sensation, she turned quickly away.

Room by room she walked through the house, with the two officers hard on her heels. The survey tour served one purpose, she thought as she led the way upstairs. By the time she and the police had poked their noses into every closet, she could be sure there was no one else in the house. The intruder, whoever he had been, was definitely gone. Only as they returned to the kitchen did Honor realize how relieved she felt to know that for certain.

Ian McLaren, she noticed, had not intruded on her privacy. He had waited in the kitchen and was talking with the freshly arrived crime-scene team as they dusted for prints around the door and window.

"Nothing else has been disturbed," said one of the policemen to the new arrivals. He glanced at Honor. "That means they'll be out of here as soon as they finish what they're doing now, Ms. Nightingale. But if you happen to notice anything after we leave, don't touch it. Leave it alone and give us a call. Someone will come right out."

A short while later, having received some needless advice about better locks, Honor found herself alone with Ian. He had snapped his jeans, she noticed irrelevantly. Or maybe not so irrelevantly. The wind gusted sharply, making the whole house creak before its force, and thunder marched closer, a hollow drumbeat. The fresh smell of ozone spiced the air.

"Well," she said briskly, trying to sound like her usual fearless, capable self, all the while knowing that it was going to be some time before she felt fearless again. "I certainly can't thank you enough for all your help, Mr. McLaren." As she looked up at him, she wondered if she had ever before met anyone so expressionless. His face betrayed nothing, absolutely nothing. His walls, she realized, were all invisible, and utterly inviolable.

The man, she thought, was totally unique. Totally self-contained. Totally impervious to whatever the rest of humanity might think. He was a law unto himself, and he didn't care one whit whether she was grateful or not. He had done only what he believed to be right and necessary, and her feelings in the matter didn't come into consideration. He had acted purely out of principle.

He would be aware of her feelings, of anyone's feelings, she thought, but they wouldn't affect him. Not at all. Whatever decisions he made, he made to satisfy himself, and he judged them according to his own internal measuring stick.

Suddenly she sank onto one of her kitchen chairs and wondered if she was losing her mind. She couldn't possibly know these things about this man from a few words, a few actions, the lack of expression on his face. She couldn't know these things from a few glances of his cat-green eyes. No, she was overtired, overwrought and inexcusably fanciful.

"I'm sorry," she said, not knowing why she was apologizing. Maybe it was for dragging him out of his isolation and into her problems. "I need to sleep," she added suddenly. "And I don't think I'm going to be able to." Now why had she told him that? Why? "I'm sorry," she said again, pressing her palms to her eyes. She was losing it, she realized vaguely. She was going to sit here in front of this man with the expressionless eyes and the frozen feelings and go blubberingly, embarrassingly hysterical.

A heavy hand settled on her shoulder, and she jumped, startled. Looking up, she found him watching her.

"You go up to bed," he said quietly. "I'll be down here. Nobody's going to bother you tonight."

"But—"

"Look," he said, interrupting her, "there's no way you're going to feel safe tonight, and that's normal. And I don't see anyone else around here to watch out for you. Is there somebody you can call?"

Reluctantly she shook her head, unable to tear her gaze from his. "I just moved here."

"Exactly. And I'm not going to sleep over there, wondering if that creep might come back. So do me a favor and let me hang around over here so I don't have to worry." .

At that precise moment something thudded in the living room. Honor gasped and froze, but by the time the sound had died away, Ian was already moving toward the living room. Somehow the knife had once again materialized in his hand, even though Honor would have sworn he hadn't brought it with him.

She wasn't built to handle this, she thought wildly as she waited. Her heart was hammering as if she had just run a marathon, and she was breathing in huge gulps that never quite dragged in enough air. She couldn't handle this. She couldn't stand this. Her knuckles had turned white from the strength of her grip on the blanket, and she wished she could hide, just hide. Like a child, she felt that if only she pulled the blanket over her head and closed her eyes tightly enough, if only she didn't move and didn't breathe and didn't make a sound, whatever it was would go away.

In the emergency room, she knew what to do. Instinct and knowledge guided her surely in the worst situations. Her choices might not always work, but she wasn't helpless. And there was nothing quite like feeling helpless, she thought now. Nothing quite as undermining or terrifying. She had been fearless all along only because she hadn't come up against something she couldn't deal with. She couldn't even begin to imagine how she was supposed to deal with this. *What if that man came back?*

Ian returned to the kitchen a few minutes later, knife once again hidden wherever he hid it. "The wind must have blown something against the house," he said. "Everything's okay. There's no one here."

"Oh." Even that sound was a triumph of self-control. She was shaking now, shaking steadily, uncontrollably. "I think...I think I want to go to a motel," she said between chattering teeth.

"What good will that do?" he asked flatly. "Will you feel safe here tomorrow night?"

That was the crux of the matter, Honor realized. She wasn't going to feel safe again for a long time. Slowly she lifted her frightened, moist eyes and looked at him.

She was unaware of all that was written on her soft, young face and revealed by her damp blue eyes. The man who wore a mask of iron *was* aware, however. He read it all in a glance, and something in him shifted infinitesimally, like heavy stone dragging over stone.

Thunder boomed hollowly, and lightning flickered brightly enough to be noticeable. The wind whipped around a corner of the house and moaned gently. The live oaks whispered restlessly, and the cicadas were suddenly silent.

"You can stay at my place tonight," Ian said, his voice sounding as rusty as an unoiled hinge. "I've got a guest room that's all made up, and you're welcome."

He had a guest room? This isolated man had a guest room? "I couldn't impose—"

He shook his head. "Look, neither one of us is going to sleep tonight at this rate. Just come over to my place and try out the sheets on the guest bed. In the morning we'll see about making this place trespasserproof, okay?"

He somehow managed to make her feel as if she would be obliging him by accepting his offer, that she would be inconveniencing him if she didn't. "Thank you, Mr. McLaren."

Something in him shifted just a little more. "Call me Ian. Let's go up and get whatever you need for the night."

He stood in the hallway just outside her bedroom as she hastily stuffed the necessary items into an overnight bag. Her hands still trembled, but her terror was subsiding as she realized that tonight, at least, she didn't have to face this alone.

The man who waited outside for her was remarkable, she found herself thinking. He had only just met her, yet he was putting himself out in a way very few people would. Most people would have backed out of this situation just as soon as the police arrived.

If anyone had told her that a man's protectiveness could feel like a warm sable coat wrapped around her, she would have chuckled at the absurdity of it. Women, she had always believed, were perfectly capable of doing anything and everything men could do, if only they were willing to put forth the effort. She never would have imagined that she could want, could *need*, a man to stand between her and anything. Thank God nobody had told Ian McLaren he shouldn't!

"I'm ready." Stepping out into the hallway, she switched off the light behind her and let him lead the way down the stairs. That was protective, too, she realized. He was a very protective man. She wondered what he was like when he *cared*.

Wind whipped the leaves around, ghostly shadows in the night. The last of the moonlight had been swallowed by the storm clouds, and the lightning blinded more than it helped. Ian seemed to have preternaturally acute vision, however, and he guided her around the hedge toward his house as effortlessly as if it were broad daylight. For once in her life she didn't mind someone taking her elbow and guiding her. Somehow, this evening, she had lost a little of her newfound independence.

Once inside his kitchen, he locked the door behind

them, and the storm was silenced. "I'm going to turn on the air-conditioning tonight," he said, filling the sudden, obvious quiet. "That way all the windows and doors will be locked and you won't be uneasy."

"You don't have—"

"No, I don't," he said. His gaze scraped over her. "Maybe I should explain that I don't do anything I don't choose to. So save your breath. I'm doing what I feel is necessary."

She hadn't misread him, then. Well, she thought as she followed him down his hallway to the foyer, and from there up the stairs to the second story, it certainly made it easier on her not to have to worry about it. It appeared that Ian McLaren was a little like a force of nature. Like that storm outside. And it seemed she was now just along for the ride, like tumbleweed caught up in a cyclone. He would do things *his* way. If that meant sheltering her and turning on the air-conditioning, then that was what he would do. She wondered if he would consult her about anything at all.

His guest room was a bare-bones affair, not too different from a cell. There was a small four-drawer dresser, a metal cot, a straight-backed chair, and nothing else. That he had this room meant he sometimes had guests. That it was decorated this way made her wonder just what kind of guests they were.

"The bathroom is down the hall," he said abruptly. "Take a shower if you like—the towels are fresh. My room is straight across the hall. If you get nervous or need anything, holler, and don't worry about disturbing me. I seldom sleep at night."

With that enigmatic and totally intriguing statement, he exited the room and closed the door gently behind him.

Sighing, Honor dropped her overnight bag on the chair and looked around once again.

It really did look like a cell. And it occurred to her that she had just become a prisoner of fear.

Across the hall, Ian McLaren stood at the closed window of his bedroom and stared out at the wild, stormy night. As a rule, he needed very little sleep, and what little he needed usually eluded him at night. That didn't prevent him from attempting to be normal, though. Every night he came up here, stripped and climbed into that narrow bed. And every night he eventually rose, dressed and pursued other activities. He had been trying to sleep when Honor's pounding at the door summoned him, and he was glad now to have an excuse to quit trying, at least for tonight.

A natural inclination toward insomnia had hardened into something nearly pathological as a result of his military experience. He had been little more than a boy when he learned that the night hours were favored for surreptitious attacks, and that night was not a safe time to trust others to remain alert. For him it was easy to stay awake and alert, but it hadn't been for his comrades. When Ian had understood that, he had taken it upon himself to keep the night watches. Now, nearly a quarter century later, he was generally able to sleep only in the daylight.

Some people might have seen that as a problem, but since Ian had little regard for other people and preferred his solitude, it was no problem at all. When he needed to advise at the base, he usually did so at unconventional hours anyway, and when he needed to do a regular nine-to-five, a quick lunchtime nap was all he required to keep him going.

From his window he had an unobstructed view of Honor's house and garage. He had noticed her occasionally in the month since she moved in, had recognized at some point or other that she worked a rotating shift, and knew she didn't pursue a social life. He knew these things because survival depended on knowing your surroundings, and while he was no longer in that kind of danger, old habits didn't die.

So he knew a little about Honor Nightingale, more than she suspected. It was nothing she would object to him knowing, but she would probably feel uneasy if she knew that he'd paid that much attention to her. Once or twice he had considered picking up the phone to request a background investigation—a BI on her, then had dismissed the idea. He was retired, damn it. He no longer needed to know everything about everyone around him.

And now she needed him. Thinking about what she had come home to, he felt a familiar stirring of anger. Anger was about the only feeling he allowed himself, and then only when someone or something violated his sense of rightness. The crud might only have been planning to rob her, but Ian doubted it. No, the intruder had had more despicable things in mind. The question was whether he had happened on her by accident or whether he had planned this. Whether he wanted Honor in particular.

Disturbed, Ian turned from the window. It wouldn't be the first time a woman had attracted the obsessive attentions of a sicko. Well, only time would settle that issue.

Deciding he wanted a cup of coffee, he stepped out of his room and began to make his silent way toward the stairs. A gust of wind rattled the window at the top of the staircase, and a sharp clatter announced the first few raindrops. Lightning flared brightly, momentarily blinding him, and he gave up, turning on the hall light. The eye's adaptation to darkness vanished in an instant before flashes that bright.

He liked the night. He liked the quiet and the solitude. He liked being able to step out his door and take long, undisturbed walks. The whole world changed at night, and a whole different set of creatures came into the ascendant. Night was the time of the predators, and the time of those who hunted them.

Ian McLaren was a hunter. And this evening he had definitely scented a predator.

Chapter Two

Honor stood on the back porch of Ian's house and stared across the hedge toward her own home. The morning sun was bright and warm in Ian's treeless yard, but it failed to penetrate the shadows beneath the old oaks and Spanish moss that surrounded her house.

She had thought, when she first saw the house, only of its charm. It had the spaciousness of another age, large rooms and high ceilings, and it had solid oak floors. It had those little extras, like a built-in hutch in the dining room and huge walk-in closets, that were impossible to find in more recent construction. And the towering old live oaks and the shady curtains of Spanish moss had added romance to it all.

Now she looked at those same oaks and those same curtains of Spanish moss, and they looked ominous. The windows of her house seemed to be black and empty, holes leading into a pit. She wished suddenly that she had never set eyes on the place.

She had left her home in Seattle to escape the ghosts of sorrowful memories. Her father's long illness and death, her own failed marriage, a sense of grayness to her life, as if she were cut off behind a tinted wall of glass. The Florida sunshine had drawn her with the promise of burning away the gray fog that had swallowed her since her father became ill.

Now she looked at her home and felt as if not even the tropical sunlight were enough to banish the dark.

God!

Shivering, she turned to reenter the house and wait for Ian McLaren. He must have heard her stirring this morning, because he had had breakfast waiting for her when she came downstairs, eggs and ham and plenty of hot, fresh coffee. As soon as he had seen her served, though, he had vanished upstairs. When he came down, he'd said, he wanted to look over her house and decide what she needed to make it secure. Then they would go into town and get it, so she wouldn't have to worry tonight.

It was an awful lot of trouble for the man to go to, she thought, even if he *did* do only what he chose to. And maybe she was being too quick to trust him. But when she remembered how he had dashed out into the dark last night to look for the intruder, and how quick he had been to understand her terrors and take her under his protection, she felt guilty for even wondering about his motives. So what if his eyes were the strangest she had ever seen.

"Ready?"

She spun around at the sound of his deep voice and stared in astonishment. She hadn't expected him to appear all decked out in BDUs, the army camouflage uniform, combat boots and a red beret. Wasn't he retired? Dressed this way, he was even more overpowering than he had been last night. Bigger. Darker. More dangerous looking. And this morning those unusual cat-green eyes of his looked…eerie.

"I need to stop on the base on the way and check my schedule," he said, as if she had spoken her surprise about his uniform. "I believe I need to be in the field this weekend."

"Look," she said, hoping she sounded reasonable, not wanting to offend him, but suddenly wanting very much to be away from him, "you've obviously got important things to do, and shepherding me around is only going to get in your way. Why don't you just let me take care of this stuff?"

"No."

No. The word seemed to hang in the humid air between them, as uncompromising a sound as any she had ever heard. No qualifier eased it; no explanation expanded it. Just *no.*

Tilting her head back, she glared up at him, then had a sudden, unexpected sense of the foolhardiness of her action. This man could undoubtedly kill her with a single blow of his powerful arm. She, who had never feared a thing, suddenly wondered if a little fear might not be wise. What did she know about him, after all? A bubble of nervous laughter escaped her. The only change in his rocklike expression was the lifting of a single eyebrow.

"Okay," she said, swallowing another nervous laugh. "It's your time."

"That's right."

Turning, he exited his house and led the way around the hedge toward her back door. As she followed, she wondered what rank he had held before his retirement, then concluded that, whatever it had been, he was used to being followed and obeyed. It didn't seem to enter his head that anyone would do otherwise. It was an attitude she knew well; her father had been a high-ranking sergeant in the Rangers. The left hand of God, she had sometimes thought. His dicta had had the force of law.

It was still early, but the Florida sun was already burning-hot, promising a stifling September day. The normally humid climate was more so this morning, after the night's rain, and Honor wondered if she had been crazy to move here. Long ago, as a child, she had lived here, when her father had been stationed at the base. She had always remembered the Gulf Coast fondly, especially the white sand of the beaches and the aquamarine of the water. She had forgotten the heat and humidity.

Once around the hedge, they stepped into the cooler shadows beneath the trees, where the air seemed even thicker. The smell of rotting vegetation was strong here, almost overpowering, even though nothing grew in the shadows beneath the moss and the old trees. Honor shivered suddenly, despite the warmth of the air. Shadows that had seemed pleasantly cool only yesterday now seemed dank. Threatening. As if in stepping out of the light she had crossed some invisible barrier into an evil place.

Ian halted before they drew close to the house, and she halted beside him. He stood perfectly still, moving not a muscle, and she watched him curiously, wondering what he was doing.

Eventually she realized. He was allowing his eyes to adapt to the fainter illumination under the trees, but he was also taking in impressions with all his senses. His nostrils flared a little as he inhaled, and she wouldn't have been the least bit surprised to discover that he was separating out every scent and cataloging it individually. His eyes scanned everywhere, appearing to overlook nothing, and his head cocked at each sound, identifying it and locating it.

Like a hunter, she thought. Like a mountain lion. Like a jungle predator. Another shiver rippled through her, and she wondered again why she had trusted him so readily.

He stepped forward in a smooth gliding motion that made him look almost like one of the gently swaying shadows beneath the trees. "It's too dark under here," he remarked. "There are too many places to hide."

Honor looked around, wondering what it was he saw that she had missed. To her, except for the trunks of the trees, her yard looked positively barren. Grass couldn't grow in this shade, never mind bushes or shrubs that might hide someone.

"I can't do much about the shadows," she said, hesitantly. "I really don't want to cut down the trees." Although the idea was sounding more attractive by the minute. Why hadn't she noticed before just how tomblike it felt beneath all this moss? Damp, chilly, cut off.

"We might get rid of some of this moss."

Yesterday she would have been appalled at the very notion of disturbing that beautiful, graceful moss—which at this moment didn't look either beautiful or graceful. "Maybe," she said uncertainly. Lord, was she letting last night's events poison everything about her new home? But she couldn't seem to help it.

He glanced down at her. "Last resort," he said, plainly recognizing her reluctance. "Let's see to more practical things first."

She nodded and followed him around back. He didn't approach the house immediately, but instead circled the detached garage, checking out the windows and door.

"Don't park in the garage anymore," he said. "It's an

obvious place for somebody to lie in wait, even in the middle of the day."

"All right." She never would have thought of such a thing. Never.

"When you have to come home after dark, give me a call. I'll wait for you and make sure you get in okay."

"But—"

A look from his cat-green eyes silenced her. "There are things out there that masquerade as human," he said intensely. "They walk, talk and look like you and me. But they're not human. They're not human at all. They get their pleasure from inflicting pain. They feast on the suffering of others and make a banquet out of their victims' agony. The sweetest music to their ears is a tortured cry for mercy."

He faced her fully, impaling her on the glowing, gemlike hardness of his gaze. Honor instinctively took a step backward, feeling his intensity as if it were a vortex in the very air. As if he somehow gathered energy from the atmosphere and focused the power of it on her.

When he continued speaking, his voice was low, quiet, but forceful. "If one of them has set his sights on you, it will take more than ordinary caution to protect you. And sacrificing a little independence is a small price for avoiding capture by a demon."

The chill that had fallen over her in the shadows seemed now to reach to her very bones. "Demon?" she repeated hoarsely. No one talked in those terms anymore. She wanted to believe he was exaggerating, but the look in his strange eyes was deadly serious, disturbing. *Witch eyes*. "You mean like…possession?" She whispered the last word, hardly able to bring herself to say it.

"They're sure as hell not men." He looked past her,

seeing something elsewhere, elsewhen. "They're real, though. Too damn real."

He turned abruptly toward the house. "I can put locks on doors and windows to stymie them, lady, but I can't put locks on you. You have to exercise reasonable caution."

"Well, of course," she said weakly, following him. Maybe she was a fool to trust this man. He was talking about demons, after all, and if that wasn't, well, *weird,* then what was? "Uh…Mr. McLaren? I can just have someone come out here and install a security system—" She broke off suddenly, the full import of his words striking her. "Wait a minute." The words were little more than a croak.

He heard them and turned. Standing there in the deep shadows beneath the moss, he settled his hands on his hips and stared at her. He looked, she thought crazily, like a being from another world, not quite mortal. He was too big, too powerful.

"Demons," she repeated hoarsely. "You're not joking."

"No." Again, that single uncompromising syllable.

"But—look. Somebody broke into my house last night. And he fled as soon as he was discovered. There's really no good reason to think he'll ever come back. Making the house more secure is simply to make me feel better, right?"

He just stared at her with eyes that burned like green fire.

"This demon business… Well, I don't believe in that kind of stuff." She managed to say that firmly, with conviction. She even sounded normal. Inside, though, her conviction was losing force, and she was beginning to feel as if the firm ground on which she had so confidently stood were turning into quicksand beneath her feet. *Abomination.* The word whispered through her brain, so strange as to feel alien. She was too tense at the moment, though, to pay it any mind.

For a moment he continued to stare at her in silence. Finally he spoke, his voice a deep rumble, like thunder in the distance. "He may not come back. You're right. There's no reason to assume he will."

Honor nearly sighed with relief. At least he could be rational.

"However," he said, shattering her moment of relief, "you really can't afford to bank on that, can you?"

Suddenly angry with the way he was trying to frighten her, she glared at him. "Perhaps not. But I don't need to start imagining ghosts and goblins in every corner, either. With all due respect to you, Mr. McLaren, I don't believe in demons."

"'There are more things in heaven and earth, Horatio, than are dreamt of in your philosophy.'" He shrugged, his expression never changing. "I don't care what you believe, Ms. Nightingale. The question is whether you want to risk meeting one in your bedroom in the dead of night." The words hung starkly in the dark, heavy air.

Game, set and match, thought Honor grimly as she walked behind him to the house and tried to tell herself that it didn't matter what he called them. He would probably say Charles Manson was a demon.

Shivering internally against the chill that had settled over her the instant she stepped into the shadows, she glanced around her yard and wondered uneasily if perhaps there *were* more things out there than she'd dreamt of.

* * *

The house still held the night's coolness and seemed just as oppressive as the shadows outside. She tried to tell herself it was just an aftereffect of last night, but the fact was, if someone had offered at that moment to take over her mortgage, she would have been packed and gone before noon.

She'd been living here for almost a month, and only yesterday she'd found herself wondering why it was taking so long for this place to feel like home. As an army brat, she was accustomed to making a new home every year or so. Nothing about this move had seemed wrenching or unusual. The only difference was that she couldn't seem to settle in. Couldn't escape the really discomfiting feeling that when she stepped in here she was stepping into someone else's home. She kept telling herself that a fresh coat of interior paint would make all the difference, yet she kept putting off buying the paint.

Ian began his self-imposed task immediately. He pulled a small memo book out of one of his pockets and handed it to her, along with a pen. "Write down the measurements as I give them to you, will you?"

"We're not going to put bars on the windows or anything, are we?" She couldn't stand the thought. It would make the house feel like a prison.

He glanced at her and shook his head. "No, but I want to get some locking bars. They'll make it impossible to jimmy the windows, even if someone breaks out a pane of glass."

The windows were multipaned, and each pane was too small to climb through without breaking the wood frame, as well, and that would make a terrible racket. Honor nodded her understanding.

"I'm especially concerned about this window,

though," he said, indicating the one right beside the back door. "That's how he got in last night."

"That was how *I* was planning to get in when I got locked out of the car last night," Honor admitted. "It was the first thing that occurred to me, to break out a pane of glass and reach around to unlock the door."

"The only way to prevent that is to board up the window. Or shutter it. Could you live with a shutter?"

"On the inside?"

"Or outside. It doesn't really matter, as long as it can't be opened from the outside once it's closed."

She nodded reluctantly, unable to argue against the wisdom of it, and watched as he measured the window and its frame, inside and out. "This isn't right," she said a little later, as he worked his way through her house.

He looked at her, his eyes as hard as chips of jade. "No, it isn't. But this isn't a perfect world. Your only alternatives are to make yourself as safe as possible or leave the area."

She really didn't need him to tell her that. She might be only twenty-six compared to his—She glanced at him, wondering again. Retired from the army meant only that he had to be at least thirty-eight, but even knowing that much, she couldn't be sure. His hair was the dark color of teak, and the only gray in it was a startling, intriguing slash of white that looked as if it might have come from an old injury. Otherwise, the man was ageless. The lines in his face had come from the elements, from the sun and the wind, not from the years.

She followed him up the stairs, certain he was preceding her because it was safer, and found herself at eye level with his buns. Each time he flexed a leg, camouflage fabric tightened over his buttocks and revealed just how hard and muscled he was.

Oh, Lord, maybe she *was* losing her mind. How could she even be noticing his buns at a time like this? Last night someone had been waiting for her here, inside her very own house, and only because of some ancient survival instinct had she realized she was being watched. If she had walked up to the house and stuck her hand through the glass to unlock the door, if she had come into her own kitchen...

Something dark seemed to be hovering at the edges of her mind, something dark and threatening. It soaked the light from the room, the breath from her lungs. Suddenly she was standing in the middle of her own bedroom, with the hair on the back of her neck prickling as if some evil force still lingered in the house from last night.

Ian reached out suddenly. Cupping the back of her neck with one hard, callused palm, he forced her down until she sat on the edge of her bed with her head between her knees.

"Delayed reaction," he said, as calmly as if he were used to dealing with this kind of thing every day. "It'll pass in a little while. Just keep your head down for a minute."

God, was she turning into a wimp? she wondered miserably, remembering the darkness that had been closing in on her, not sure she had just been faint. But then, she told herself, she'd never had to deal with anything like this before. What did she know about delayed reactions and fainting except what she had seen as a nurse, as an observer on the outside looking in?

But now her safe little world had been invaded in the worst possible way, and instead of bucking up like the capable woman she had always believed herself to be, she was acting like a Victorian miss whose stays were too tight. Angry at herself, she sat up and waited for the brief bout of dizziness to pass.

"That's it," said the deep, dark voice of the man who seemed to be taking over her life with breathtaking speed. "Get mad. It's healthy."

He yanked the window open and leaned out to look around. Honor knew what he saw: the front porch roof, right under her window. She'd been thinking about building a small balcony there, thinking it would be a pleasant place to sit in the evenings, since a hole in the trees gave her the only real view she had, though it was only of the road leading up to the highway. Now she could think only of how easy that roof would make it for someone to get to her bedroom.

"We'll have to do something about this," Ian said, then turned in the window, leaning backward so that he could look upward. A moment later he pulled his head in. "This place is a defender's nightmare."

"I wasn't in the market for a fortress when I purchased it," she said glumly. A fortress was what she needed now, though, and the recognition of that fact rippled coldly through her. What if somebody really *did* want to get to her? Just her, Honor Nightingale. What if he came back and a few locks didn't stop him?

Ian ignored her irritation, somehow making her feel foolish. "I don't suppose you were," he said indifferently. "Let's see the other rooms. And there's an attic?"

She'd looked up there only briefly when the agent had shown her the place, and her thought had been that it could be transformed into a marvelous guest suite if she ever had the money to do anything about it. The stairs pulled down from the ceiling in the back bedroom, and she watched Ian climb them, knowing what he would see.

It was a spacious attic, and the roof was steeply pitched, giving it an almost cathedral-like quality. At both ends of the house, round windows allowed in just enough dim light to reveal beautiful lathwork and a solid plank floor. In another age it might have been servants' quarters. Now it was merely storage space, without air-conditioning or heat.

She remained below and listened to the sound of Ian's booted feet as he explored, especially around the two windows. Leaning against the wall, she looked out the window at the moss-shrouded branches of the tree just outside.

The moss took nothing from the trees, merely draping itself from the branches to expose more of itself to the air and humidity from which it took all its sustenance. But it slowly killed the trees anyway, because it smothered the leaves. So far her oaks had survived, growing upward ahead of the moss. Now all but the tips of the lower branches were leafless hangers for the brownish-green curtains, and only the topmost branches showed a healthy profusion of green. At some point the balance would shift and the tree would die.

Beautiful decay.

Suddenly cold again, she shivered and turned to watch Ian descend the stairs. It was always cold just here at the foot of the attic stairs, she thought. It seemed like such a waste of air-conditioning when she didn't even use this room. Glancing around, she looked for the duct, thinking that she might want to cover it with plastic. No vent was visible anywhere, though. Must be something about the way air flowed through the house.

"The attic won't be a problem," Ian told her. "I think we need to assume only a reasonable amount of determination if this guy comes back. He might lie in wait for you, he might even go so far as to try to get in through a window, but to attempt to protect against anything more would probably cost a fortune and wouldn't work anyway."

Rubbing her arms against the chill she couldn't shake, she looked up at him. "Why not?"

Nothing in his expression changed, and his gaze never wavered. He dropped his bomb emotionlessly. "If this guy is more than normally determined to get at you, there isn't a security measure in the world that would be totally foolproof. A man who is determined enough can get past anything. I know, because I've done it."

And then what? she wondered. What did he do when he circumvented all those security measures?

Somehow she thought she was better off not knowing. And that brought her back to the way he seemed to be taking over with breathtaking speed.

"You really shouldn't do this, Ian. You have a life of your own, concerns of more importance—"

"There's nothing more important than this."

"Why?" She faced him squarely, making it clear that she wasn't going to settle for a brush-off.

"I've devoted a lifetime to keeping innocents like you safe from the filth of the world," he said, in a hard, harsh voice, his strange eyes boring into her. "I didn't give up that duty just because I retired. If I don't look after you, who the hell will?"

Good Lord, she thought uneasily, the man sounded like a fanatic. Nobody talked like this. Nobody thought like this. It was creepy!

His tone had been angry, but his face revealed nothing. He took her elbow and motioned toward the stairs. "Let's go."

Honor yanked herself free of his grip, annoyed by his

tone and his manhandling, suddenly completely fed up with the way he was taking over her life. "You're weird, McLaren! You know that?"

"I know."

He said it flatly, as if it were an inarguable fact. The words fell harshly into the room, and the shock of their impact drove Honor's anger away, leaving her with a curious ache she couldn't have identified. And in that instant before either of them drew another breath, she saw a flicker deep in his eyes. It vanished quickly, hidden once again in the cold, hard depths, but she never doubted for an instant that she had seen the shadow of old hurts.

"Look," she said. "I didn't mean that. Not really. It's just that...that I don't know you. I was really grateful for your help last night, but you've just...taken over. And frankly, I don't know if I like having you take over without so much as a by-your-leave any more than I liked finding that creep waiting in the house for me. It's...not normal!"

He cocked his head to one side. "Normal," he said, with astonishing bitterness, "is walking away from a difficult situation just as fast as you can. Normal is avoiding involvement no matter what it costs someone else. Normal is turning your back when a woman screams for help. Normal is driving past an accident scene slowly enough to get a good idea of how bad it is, but neglecting to stop at the next telephone to call for help, because you don't have time."

Honor stared up at him, every other concern arrested as she faced the unlikely passion of this cold man. He cared, she realized. He really cared, for all that he looked and acted so hard. That caring defeated her in a way anger or hardness never could have.

"Okay," she said. "I get the picture. And you're right, of course." She had treated enough victims in the emergency room to know just how right. More times than she wanted to count, she had been appalled by the utter callousness of her fellow man.

"If you weren't alone, I wouldn't butt in," he said. "But you *are* alone. And I'll be damned if I want to live with myself if something happens to you while I'm being *normal*."

Honor almost winced at the sarcasm lacing the word. Truth to tell, she was appalled at her own behavior. Yes, it was reasonable for a woman to be cautious in this day and age, and certainly she should be cautious of strangers who acted in an unusual way, but still! To call the man weird and tell him to his face he wasn't normal, when he had done nothing at all except go out of his way to help her…well, she deserved to be slapped. "I'm sorry," she said sincerely.

"Don't be." He turned toward the stairs. "You're wise to be suspicious of me. Of any man. And just as soon as I get this place secured, I'll get the hell out of your life."

They were bombing on the range again tonight. Honor watched the eerie flashes of light as she drove home after her shift. Inside her car, with the breeze blowing through the window, she couldn't hear any sound accompanying the flashes. It was, she found herself thinking, like some kind of science-fiction film. Or like a dream. Unreal.

She hadn't called Ian McLaren before leaving work, either. The thought had crossed her mind, and he *had* insisted on it, but it had been easy, in the bright lights of the hospital, to tell herself that it would be ridiculous to call him. After all, she'd been coming home from work alone for years now, and she would be doing so for many years to come. Her reasoning had sounded good, too, until she realized she was in the nurses' locker room, changing out of her scrubs into the shorts she had worn to work, delaying her departure. Ordinarily she didn't bother.

Nor did her reasoning sound so good now that she was alone in her car. It was dark out here, moonless again, thanks to heavy cloud cover. She had left the back porch light on before leaving, so that would be some help...but not much. It would be one small light bulb in a world that suddenly seemed very dark and very threatening. And it certainly wouldn't tell her if somebody was inside the house. Not that anyone should be. Ian had done a thorough job this morning, installing deadbolts on her doors, locking bars on her windows, a steel shutter on the kitchen window by the back door. He had been mercilessly efficient, swift and silent.

She had insulted him. She knew it in her heart and felt guilty as sin. Whatever she thought of him or his methods or his manner, she had had absolutely no right to speak that way to him. He had only been trying to help, and whatever security she would be able to feel tonight in her own bed was because of him. And she had to give him his due—he hadn't let her attitude deter him from doing what he considered necessary.

But he had the strangest eyes. The mere memory of them made her feel shivery. Not too many generations ago, she thought, eyes like that probably would have gotten him burned at the stake. Something about them, about their color, didn't seem quite human.

God, it was dark! Her driveway looked like a tunnel into pitch blackness, and the back porch light must have burned out, because it was dark in her yard. Too dark. She switched off the ignition, careful this time to hold on to the keys, then sat listening to the night sounds.

Cicadas screeched ceaselessly; it was such a constant cacophony that she hardly heard it anymore. Tree frogs croaked their two hoarse notes, battling the cicadas for preeminence in the night. The offshore breeze was still strong, whispering of the night's emptiness, and the live oaks rustled uneasily.

She didn't want to get out of the car. A terrible feeling seemed to permeate the night, as if the air were a living, malevolent being. A shudder rippled down her spine, and she had to force herself not to drive away. This is ridiculous, she told herself. Her imagination was running riot, just as it had when she was four and believed there was a crocodile under her bed. Foolish imagination.

Finally she rolled up her window and climbed out of the car. Keys firmly in hand, she closed the car door and turned toward the house. There was, she reminded herself, absolutely no reason on earth to think the creep from last night had come back. None.

She had taken no more than two steps toward her door when the porch light suddenly came on. She froze, and terror trickled icily down her spine. Oh, God!

"Get in the car."

Whirling, she came face-to-face with Ian. He stood only a few feet away, Ranger knife in his hand. He wore black from head to toe and blended with the shadows. Her hand flew to her throat. "God, you scared me!"

"Get in the car and lock yourself in," he said quietly. "Give me your house keys. I'll check it out."

Her heart was hammering so loudly that she could

hear it, but adrenaline muffled her initial fear. "I'll go in with you." She didn't want to wait out here alone, and she didn't want him to go in there alone. Either would be intolerable, but if she went with him, at least she would know what was happening.

"I can fight better if you're not in the way. Give me the keys and get in the car."

Instead, she headed toward the back door, finding courage in the fact that he was right behind her. This is crazy, she thought wildly, but she wasn't going to back down. Her dad hadn't raised her to be a wimp, and life as an army brat had taught her to face things head-on. If this man was going to go in there, he wasn't going alone.

Bravado carried her to the door. It couldn't, however, keep her hand from trembling wildly as she tried to slip the key into the lock. How had he gotten inside? The question hammered at her, pulverizing any sense of security all those locks might have given her.

"Here." Ian stepped up right behind her, so close that his chest touched her back, and took the key from her hand. His touch was gentle, warm, not at all abrupt or impatient. He slipped the key in the lock, moved her to one side, then shoved the door open. "Stay behind me."

He ignored the light switch just inside the door and instead flicked on a powerful flashlight that he was carrying. Slowly, methodically, he passed the beam over every inch of the kitchen. Only then did he step inside.

"Close and lock the door," he whispered.

To prevent anyone from coming up on them from behind, she realized. Turning, she did as he asked, closing out the night sounds. But all the while some niggling feeling at the base of her skull told her the threat wasn't outside. No, it was inside. Locked in here with them.

Two doors led from the kitchen into the rest of the house. One opened on a hallway that led straight to the front door. Along one side were the doorways into the living and dining rooms. Climbing the other side was the stairway to the upstairs.

The other door opened directly into the dining room, and from an archway there it was possible to walk directly through double doors into the living room. It was therefore possible to make a complete circle of the ground floor without retracing one's steps, and Ian had evidently thought of that, because he closed the wooden door into the hallway and quietly braced a chair under the knob.

"Okay," he whispered, and opened the door that led into the dining room.

Honor stayed right on his heels, telling herself that no one could come up from behind because there was no way for anyone to get there, but feeling the back of her neck prickle anyway.

Someone was in the house. She was sure of it. She could feel it, almost as if their presence created some kind of pressure in the air, or as if some strange perfume were wafting through the rooms. Someone was here. *Abomination.* The word floated into her mind and then vanished.

The dining room was empty. Ian stepped through it and into the living room. Honor hesitated in the archway. She had never really felt comfortable in the living room. Time and again she had told herself that the feeling was simply some kind of subliminal response to the mustiness of the room, to the dingy paint and paper and the faintly moldy smell. Fresh paint and a good dose of white vinegar would clear it out, she had believed.

But now, standing there, it was almost as if a physical force held her back. She didn't want to go in there. Couldn't go in there. Ian swept the flashlight around, revealing nothing but an empty bookcase and a rocking chair. She had very little furniture, because she had planned to buy what she needed once she fixed the place up. Somehow what had seemed an innocent decision then took on ominous overtones now, as she stood there unable to cross the threshold.

Ian stepped back beside her. "Nothing. I'm going upstairs." His whisper was almost inaudible. "You go back into the kitchen and close the door until I get back."

For an instant, just an instant, her body refused to obey her brain. Then she turned and hurried back to the kitchen, her rubber soles silencing her footsteps. Her courage had vanished. She couldn't bring herself to walk through the living room or climb those stairs in Ian's wake, and somehow he had known it. He had known it even before she had faced it herself. That realization sent another uneasy shudder running down her spine.

In the kitchen, she wedged a chair under the knob of the second door and then felt around for the light switch. It was then that she realized the porch light had gone out again.

Fear locked her breath in her throat. The pounding of her heart was loud in her ears, loud enough to drown the sounds of the night outside. For endless seconds she stood frozen, her hand on the light switch, her back to the rest of the kitchen, acutely aware that someone might be right behind her. Terrifyingly aware of how exposed her back was.

She wished wildly that she could make her heart stop for just a few moments, so that she could listen and hear if someone was behind her. Then, having no choice, unable to stand the tension another minute, she spun around and pressed her back to the door, facing into the dark room.

Nothing. No one. Sobbing for breath, she felt around beside her for the switch. And then she froze again, wondering if she would regret turning on the light, afraid of what she might see. Terrified of not seeing.

Oh, God. Ian, hurry!

Then she was lanced with an ice-cold shaft of fear. Something in the kitchen had moved, making a scraping sound.

She wasn't alone.

Chapter Three

That did it. The breath left her lungs, and she pawed the light switch frantically, finally managing to flip it on.

The light nearly blinded her, but even so, she saw no one. Just at that moment there was a pounding on the dining room door.

"Honor! Honor, it's Ian! Open up!"

Drawing a huge, ragged breath of relief, she hurried over and pulled the chair from under the knob. As soon as Ian heard the chair come free, he threw the door open.

"Are you all right?" he demanded.

She flew into his arms. He might be crazy, he might be weird, he might be maddening, but he also represented safety, and right now she needed, absolutely needed, to feel strong arms around her.

Without hesitation, he caught her close and surrounded her with the shield of his strength. "I got this feeling," he said gruffly. "All of a sudden I knew you needed me...."

He trailed off, as if embarrassed to admit such a thing, but Honor didn't care how he had known. If he had said the wind had whispered to him, or that he had felt her fear on the currents of the air, she would have been grateful. It was enough that he was there.

Almost awkwardly, as if unaccustomed to such gestures, Ian stroked her hair and patted her shoulder with one of his huge hands. "There's no one in the house," he told her, his deep voice a reassuring rumble. "There must be an electrical problem with that porch light."

"It went out again," Honor said shakily, relief rushing through her. "And I heard something in here. It sounded...odd. Like a scraping noise. Or a scuttling."

He tightened his hold as she started to straighten, and, grateful that he wasn't in any hurry to let go, she allowed her arms to find their way around his waist.

"A mouse, maybe," he said. "Or a lizard. Or maybe just a bug. Want me to look?"

Drawing a deep breath, she tilted her head to say something about bugs and lizards and found herself staring right into his cat-green eyes. At this distance they were unusually mesmerizing, almost glowing, and they held her gaze as if by a witch's spell.

And something deep inside her stirred. She had noticed how attractive he was, had admired his flanks and his chest and his powerful build. But not until now had she felt that long-forgotten unfurling inside herself, that strange, edgy, hopeful, hungry feeling. Every thought in her head was arrested as her attention suddenly focused completely on the man who held her, on the womanly feelings deep inside her.

His eyes darkened, as if he felt it, too. His head bowed just a fraction, hesitated. And then, as if compelled, he bent and kissed her.

Honor hadn't kissed a man since her wedding day, eight years before. Jerry hadn't liked kissing, or so he'd claimed, and had kissed her just that once, passionlessly, because it was necessary. That was before she had learned there were a lot of things Jerry didn't like when it came to sex, every one of them having to do with the fact that she was a woman. He had hoped to hide his homosexuality by marrying, and instead had managed only to confirm it for himself—and nearly destroy his eighteen-year-old wife in the process.

Telling herself that Jerry's sexual orientation had nothing to do with her hadn't helped very much. She hadn't let a man kiss her or touch her since, because she couldn't quite escape the feeling that there was something intrinsically revolting about her. Something so repulsive that it had prevented Jerry from ever consummating their union. If she ever felt that revulsion from another man, she feared, she would dive off a bridge. She couldn't handle it again.

But now here she was, clinging to this man she hardly knew, this man who frightened her in some primitive way, but who made her feel paradoxically safe. Confusion swamped her as conflicting feelings warred inside her and drove away all thought of her earlier terror.

He wasn't gentle. He took the kiss with the same unswerving determination he had so far shown in everything. He didn't coax or tease or ask. He simply opened his mouth over hers and drove his tongue into her warm depths as if he had every right to do so.

Had he done anything else, she would have tried to back off. As it was, she never had a chance. An instant deluge of feelings washed her away, sweeping her toward passion in a breathless rush. All unaware, she dug her fingers into his muscled back, clutching him closer, frustrated by the layer of black cotton between her hands and his skin.

She wanted. Oh, God, she wanted as she had never wanted before. As she had never dreamed it was possible to want. She had once craved Jerry, craved him enough to marry him despite her father's objections, but what she felt right now surpassed craving by light-years. It reached into some primitive part of her, turning her into some cavewoman who was willing to lie down on the hard ground and spread her legs just so that she could feel this man's possession, just so that she could, for a few minutes, feel his strength and hunger answer her own.

God, was she losing her mind?

Suddenly Ian lifted his head, tearing his mouth from hers almost savagely. Before she could make a sound, he pressed her face into his shoulder, hard.

"Shh!" he hissed sharply.

On the edge of screaming from frustrated need, she froze. Then, with a suddenness that deprived her of breath, she understood that he had heard something.

His hand gentled a little on the back of her head when he realized she wasn't going to make noise. After an interminable span of nerve-stretching time, he whispered, "Did you hear anything?"

She shook her head, not certain she could find air to whisper back. She was scared again. Terrified. And the back of her neck was crawling with the feeling that somebody was watching her. Watching them.

He muttered an obscenity right into her ear. She was shockproof, having heard them all over the years, so she ignored it. It was harder to ignore her feelings when he set her aside. Reality had intruded, and she had only a deep-rooted ache to tell her that she hadn't fantasized that kiss or her reaction to it.

"Let's get your things," he said. "You'll use my guest

room again tonight. Tomorrow I'm going to find out what the hell is going on around here."

"But you said there's no one here."

"There isn't. I went through this place right up to the attic rafters. Lights going on and off might just be the wiring...which is dangerous enough, and I'll check it out as soon as I have light to see. Scuttling sounds are most likely mice or bugs...probably a damn roach or a cicada that came in with us. No big deal. But—"

By the way he broke off, she knew he had caught himself before he said something he didn't want her to know. And that angered her. "But what? What did you hear? What aren't you telling me?"

His eyes locked on hers, and a long moment passed before he answered. "It's a feeling," he said finally, with evident reluctance. "A feeling I don't like."

Hardly realizing she did so, she stepped closer to him. "I know," she said, her voice little more than a whisper. "I keep getting the feeling someone is watching."

For long, long moments, they stared at one another. Then Ian nodded, in acknowledgment of what she was saying. "Let's get your things."

Abomination. The word whispered into her sleepy mind, and Honor sat up abruptly, clutching the sheet to her breast as she peered into the dark. She was sleeping on the cot in Ian's guest room again, she remembered. Trying to sleep despite a nervous fluttering in her stomach, despite an edginess that warned her something terrible was about to happen.

Demon. Another whisper on the edge of her mind, almost as if someone were whispering in her ear. In her mind. The words felt alien; they were not words she would ever use.

Shivering against an internal chill, she lay down again and pulled the sheet to her chin. This was crazy, she told herself. A creep had broken into her house, and now she was becoming unhinged, looking for sinister purpose in an electrical problem and the vagaries of an overtired mind. Silly. Ian had planted these thoughts with his talk of demons, that was all.

Demons. Imagine it. A grown man who looked as if he didn't fear a thing—as if he didn't *need* to fear a thing—had spoken of demons. Remembering the look in his strange green eyes, she found it too easy to believe he knew what he was talking about. That he was himself personally acquainted with a few demons.

Her fingers tightened on the sheet and drew it closer. She was overreacting, she told herself. *He* was overreacting. Last night there had been some excuse for inviting her over here, but tonight?

After the horrible way she had treated him earlier— God, she still couldn't believe she had called him *weird* to his face—he had been waiting for her to come home. Waiting to be sure she got in safely. And they had both overreacted to a stupid electrical problem. A loose wire, no doubt, but they had still crept through the house looking for intruders, and afterward, hearing something, he had brought her home with him again.

They were *both* weird. He should just have said good-night and walked away. And when he didn't, she should have insisted on sleeping in her own bed and said good-night.

That was what they should have done. The fact that they hadn't was a mark of the depth of the threat she was feeling. Shivering again, she huddled beneath the sheet. It was more than a threat she felt, she admitted now.

It was something evil.

* * *

Sunshine bathed the world again in the morning. Honor, coming from Seattle, where people often joked that the sun was a UFO, still couldn't get over the sunniness of the days here.

When she came downstairs, she found coffee ready and poured herself a cup. Stepping onto the back porch, she looked across to her house and saw Ian busy with her back porch light. He hadn't been kidding, she realized. He meant to get to the bottom of this.

With a second mug of coffee for Ian, she rounded the holly hedge and approached him. He was standing on a cinder block, examining the light fixture. Snug, worn denim left little to her imagination, and she found herself recalling all the sensations of being in his arms last night. How hard he had felt against her. How solid and strong.

"Good morning," she said. *Witch.* The word whispered along the edges of her mind, a cold touch in the hot morning air. She ignored it.

"Morning." He glanced down at her. "Look at this." He touched the bulb and the light went on. Touched it again and it went off.

Relief was almost heady. "The wind," she said. Not a demon after all.

"Maybe." He didn't look nearly as certain as she would have liked. "The bulb's screwed in tight, though, so it must be something in the fixture or the wiring. Why don't you go throw the breaker so I can check it out?"

"Okay. Here's some coffee."

"Thanks." Bending, he took the cup from her.

The breaker box, installed at Honor's insistence as part of the deal on the house, had replaced the old fuse box in the corner beside the refrigerator. Maybe, she thought now, she should have insisted on having the wiring checked. All the breakers were labeled on little white tags in the electrician's handwriting. Kitchen 1. Kitchen 2. Upstairs. Dryer. Front.

Not certain which of a dozen breakers controlled the porch light, she threw the main and cut off all the incoming power. "Okay," she called out to Ian.

She was able to see him through the open door, and she stayed where she was, watching, waiting for him to tell her when to turn the power back on.

Hard to believe, she thought, how scared she had been in this very room only a few hours before. Hard to believe how real even the vaguest threats could seem in the dark, and how silly you could feel in the sunlight, remembering them. Remembering how scared you had been and how you had hurled yourself at a man who was practically a stranger because you were terrified of a rustling sound. Terrified of the feeling that someone was watching you.

He hadn't treated her as if she were crazy or skittish, though. And that kiss...

In spite of her intention to put all that firmly out of her mind, she found herself remembering the heat and the strength of Ian McLaren, the passion and hunger he had displayed in those all-too-brief moments. He had made her feel desired, and as one who knew too well what it was like *not* to be desired, she cherished the memory.

Yesterday she had been annoyed at the way he had barged into her life. Today she was grateful for his interference, grateful that he had been there last night when she arrived home, and grateful that he had insisted she stay with him. Because, broad daylight notwithstanding, she vividly remembered how terrified she had been last night.

But she didn't want to be sexually attracted to him. Down that road lay disaster, as she knew all too well. So while she might stand here and admire the way he looked in an olive-drab T-shirt and snug, worn jeans, she was not going to let herself fall into his arms again. Ever. Not even for another taste of his addicting passion. Because, in the end, she would be hurt. She didn't need anyone to warn her of that. A man his age who was unattached was unattached for a reason, and a woman who had been through all she had knew just how deeply and easily a man could wound her.

But, boy, she thought wryly, common sense couldn't keep her from dreaming.

And dream she had, last night. Endless dreams of lurking shadows and aching desire. Again and again Ian had come to her in her dreams, and again and again a shadow had slipped between them, driving them apart. More than once she had awakened in fright with an aching sense of desperation.

But nightmares didn't surprise her, given the events of the past two nights. It would be more surprising if she didn't have bad dreams.

"Okay," he called through the door. "Throw the power back on."

She turned and grabbed the breaker, throwing it back. There was a funny humming sound from behind her, and then she heard a sharp crack, followed by a hoarse shout. Swinging around, she was just in time to see Ian tumble backward to the ground.

Before she even barreled through the screen door, her mind was running through all the steps for dealing with severe electrical shock. Ian was lying flat on his back in the dust, and her heart nearly stopped at the sight. As she fell to her knees beside him, though, his eyes opened. He muttered a four-letter word.

"Are you all right? What happened? No, wait, don't move until you're sure you didn't hurt something."

He stared up at her, unable to see her face because her head was silhouetted against a brilliant patch of blue sky, probably the only patch visible in this part of her tree-filled yard.

Then, suddenly, the day turned dark. The sunlight faded from the sky, and the shadows moved in, surrounding her. Threatening her.

"God!" He sat up abruptly, and the vision vanished as if it had never been. The day was suddenly normal once more...except that he felt cold inside. Deep inside. In a place he had thought he had buried more than twenty years before.

"Ian?"

He knew better, he thought savagely. He ought to just get up and walk away right now. He knew better than to get involved, because when he got too close to someone, he eventually slipped. And when he slipped, they took off, acting as if he were some kind of monster. He'd already spent too much time with her, and already he was caring too much about what happened to her. Last night, for her sake, while moving through her house in the dark, he had pried the lid off the sarcophagus in which he had buried all those...abilities. All those feelings.

And now it seemed he could not put the lid back on. Using his abominable talent, he had reached out, seeking the source of the threat to her, and he had felt malevolence. Evil. Hatred. Now it was too late to abandon her. Even yesterday, he could have walked away, but now, having felt what he had felt, he could not leave her. Not that he could do a whole hell of a lot to help, he thought angrily. A vision that said she was threatened was about as illuminating as nothing, given what had already occurred.

"Ian? Ian, what happened? Are you all right?"

He turned and looked her straight in the eyes, seeing in those blue depths a genuine caring and compassion. Well, of course. She was a nurse. Naturally she would care. The other kind of caring…well, nobody felt that way about him. They never had, and they never would. *Demon spawn.*

"I'm fine," he said finally, hoping his face hadn't betrayed any of his unusually tangled feelings. He prided himself on being unreadable. "The damn fixture and wires seemed fine. There wasn't anything wrong that I could see. Then you threw the breaker, and the damn thing arced right across my hand." He looked up at the fixture. "It shouldn't have happened," he muttered to himself. "I'm no electrician, but that shouldn't have happened."

"Did you get burned?"

He turned his left hand over, studying it curiously. A vicious red mark seared two of his fingers. "Nothing to worry about."

"I've got some anesthetic cream," she told him. "And I'll get the electrician out here to look at that thing. Maybe I need all my wiring checked."

"Skip the cream." He looked up at the fixture. Even at this distance he could see that the arc had melted part of it. That was an awful lot of current. "Yeah, you'd better call an electrician. And then let's go to the beach."

"The beach?" Her mind was so preoccupied with what had almost happened that the suggestion didn't immediately register. "Why?"

"We could use some sun and relaxation," he told

her. What they really needed to do was talk. Away from here. And he had to figure out how much he was going to tell her.

Much to Honor's amazement, the electrician came right out, so the trip to the beach had to be postponed. She was at once relieved and disappointed. Being with Ian was incredibly intense—perhaps that wasn't entirely his fault, given the circumstances—but it was almost a relief to deal with someone else. Someone who whistled cheerfully and looked perfectly ordinary. Someone who didn't seem to move in an atmosphere of darkness and mystery and...and loneliness, she added. Ian McLaren was a terribly lonely man.

Standing on her back step while the electrician examined the destroyed light fixture, she stared into the shadows under the trees and felt the loneliness in her own soul. Part of the reason she had made the big move from Seattle was to escape all the things that had reminded her of that loneliness. For the past month or so she'd been so busy packing, moving and settling into her new job that she hadn't had time to feel lonely. Now she had the time again, and the move hadn't changed one damn thing.

"This fixture is all messed up, Miss Honor," Cal Ober told her. He, too, perched on the cinder block to examine the light. "No hope of saving it."

"I didn't really think there was, Mr. Ober. I'm worried about what caused the problem, though."

"Can't tell now if it was in the fixture. All the wires are fused."

"Is there some way you can test the rest of the wiring? To make sure there isn't another problem somewhere?"

He nodded. "Sure can. First let me put up a new fixture here, then we'll check out the rest."

She followed him through the house while he checked every outlet, removing the plates to verify that the wires were secure, and testing for voltage drops with a small meter that he plugged right into the sockets. He hummed and whistled while he worked, and occasionally fell into conversation.

"You know the Sidells up the road here?" he asked her.

"I met two of the brothers, Jeb and Orville," she replied. "At the hospital."

"When Orville got bit by that coral snake. Can't figure that boy. He's lived in these woods all his life and shoulda been looking out."

"Accidents happen."

"Reckon so." He glanced up with a smile, a smile that Honor thought didn't quite reach his eyes. Then he went back to whistling.

He next spoke when they were upstairs in her bedroom. "That fella next door?"

"My neighbor, you mean?"

"Him. McLaren. He grew up in these parts."

"Did he? He didn't mention that."

"Don't reckon he wants anyone to know."

Honor bit her lip, torn between wanting to ask why and hating to gossip about someone she knew. In the end she said nothing at all, even though she knew her curiosity was going to drive her wild. She had no business listening to idle gossip, she told herself sternly. No business at all.

"There was some trouble, long time ago," Cal said some time later. "There was some talk about witchcraft and satanism. Talk of animal sacrifices. Don't know if it's true. But he left and didn't come back until a year or so ago."

Honor's hand flew to her mouth, and she stood there,

trying to reconcile what she had just heard with the man who had so carefully protected her. "I can't...I can't imagine him doing such things," she said finally, feeling sick. Animal sacrifices?

"Don't know that he did." Cal plugged his meter into another outlet and watched the needle. "There was talk, I'm told, and the cops looked into it, but nothing ever happened, so maybe there's nothing to it." He glanced up then, his dark eyes strangely opaque. "I just thought a woman living alone ought to be on guard. In case. That's all."

The wiring had checked out okay. Around lunchtime, Honor stood in her bedroom, in front of the dresser mirror, and studied her reflection. Ian would be coming at any moment to take her to the beach, and the blue maillot that had seemed so modest last year didn't strike her as modest now. Turning swiftly away, she grabbed her white shorts and blue T-shirt and tugged them on.

Witchcraft and satanism.

God! Why hadn't she stayed in Seattle? At least there the threats had been known. During the past two days, she seemed to have stepped off the edge of reality into something really...weird. Strange. Spooky.

A rustling overhead drew her eyes upward. It sounded like something moving in the attic. Bugs, she told herself. Mice. Lizards. Maybe just a branch of one of the damn trees outside. *There was nothing else up there*.

She tugged her sneakers on and picked up her beach bag, checking to make sure she had included her sunscreen and keys.

A public beach in broad daylight. She couldn't possibly have anything to fear. And why should she fear him, anyway, just because of a piece of vicious gossip about things that might or might not have happened half a lifetime ago? Hadn't he taken care of her the last couple of days? If he was any threat at all, surely she would know by now. For heaven's sake, she had spent the last two nights under his roof! Safely. If he was going to harm her, he'd had ample opportunity to do so!

A rattle at the window snared her attention, and she looked out through the glass at the bright day beyond. She had chosen this room for her bedroom because a hole in the trees provided a view of the sky and road out front. Because it didn't feel so closed in.

The rattle came again, and she darted over to the window to look out. Down below, standing far enough back to be seen over the edge of the porch roof, was Ian. When he saw her, he pointed to his watch and then held up five fingers.

He had thrown pebbles at her window to get her attention, and the silly gesture eased some of the tension inside her. He could have phoned. He could have come right to the door. He could simply have shown up whenever he was ready. Instead, he had done something fun. Feeling somehow reassured, she waved and smiled back.

Above her, something in the attic made a soft scratching sound. Just a muffled, odd little sound. She glanced up and then dismissed it. Not forty minutes ago she had been up there with the electrician. A roach had gotten into the ceiling, she told herself. Or a mouse.

She rather liked the idea of a small gray mouse.

Ian took them away from the base, out across Choctawhatchee Bay to a strip of Gulf beach that was sparkling-white and virtually empty. A few vacation houses occupied the heights of the dunes, but they appeared to be deserted today. Here and there other couples were visible, but no one close by.

The pristine white sand of the beach disappeared in the amazing aquamarine water of the shallows. A short distance from shore, the deeper water was demarcated by an abrupt change of color to royal blue. Honor had never forgotten the colors or the beauty of this coastline. It was that memory that had brought her back.

She helped Ian secure the corners of the blanket with her beach bag and towel. Then he reached for his olive-drab T-shirt and tugged it over his head. She looked quickly away, feeling somehow that the act of stripping to a bathing suit was an intimate one. Which was silly, because she had never felt that way before.

She tossed her shorts and shirt aside without once looking at him, and trotted down to the water without daring a backward glance. She didn't want to know if he was watching her, didn't know what she would do if he was. The memory of last night's kiss was seared into her brain and made even the electrician's warning seem like a dim recollection from the distant past.

The swells were too big to allow any serious swimming, so she finally found a shallow spot and sat in the water, allowing the swells to lift and drop her gently, like a baby rocking in a cradle. The sun was hot and strong, and soon baked the tension from her muscles.

Feeling calm and utterly secure for the first time in what seemed like forever, she let herself think over the events of the past couple of days. What, she asked herself, had really happened? Not much. Somebody had apparently been in her house when she came home the night before last. Other than that, there had been nothing at all. Last night had been a case of nerves from a defective light. No one had been in the house.

And the feeling of being watched, of a presence... well, that was just imagination. She had been scared, and her mind had found no difficulty in embroidering things and turning imagined threats into reality. It was easy for the mind to play tricks like that in the dark. She'd learned that as a kid, sitting around campfires with her friends. More than once, ten shrieking girls had dived for cover over something as simple as a hooting owl. Fear of bears and Bigfoot had been half the fun of those campfires.

A gloomy sigh, swallowed by the restless sounds of the waves, escaped her. The wonder of it, she decided, was that Ian could take her seriously. In retrospect, she was surprised that he hadn't just left her in her own place last night. After all, he had checked the house and found no one there. At that point, any danger had been purely imaginary.

A tingling along her shoulders finally warned her that she was in danger of burning. Reluctantly leaving the water, she walked up the beach, only to find Ian stretched out and sound asleep.

For long moments she simply stared at him, filling her eyes with his powerful masculine beauty. Little was left to the imagination by his brief black trunks, and it didn't feel as if she were invading his privacy simply by standing there and gazing at what he was so blatantly displaying.

His chest was every bit as broad, hard and powerful as she remembered, and when he was lying down like this, his flat stomach turned into a hollow. His legs were long, perfectly shaped, powerful, and dusted with golden-brown hair that looked soft. Tempting. Her

palms itched with a desire to discover all those masculine textures. Ridiculous, she told herself, and plopped
on the blanket beside him. Ridiculous. Tugging her T-
shirt out of her bag, she pulled it on to protect her
shoulders.

Oh, God, she thought suddenly, she didn't want to
go home. She didn't want to go back to that house.
There was no escaping it. She could sit here in the sun
and pretend that all those bad feelings had been imagination, that she honestly believed she had nothing to
fear, but that was all it was: pretending. Something
about that house scared her the way the dark under her
bed had scared her as a child. It didn't matter whether
it was rational or not.

The sun still shone, but somehow the day had turned
suddenly dark. Shivering despite the heat, she looked
around her and wondered what had happened to the
colors. The water was now more gray than blue, and
choppy-looking, and the white sand, too, seemed to
have lost its brilliance.

Her gaze strayed inexorably toward Ian, and she
wished he would wake up. Suddenly the beach felt deserted, lonely, and the sun didn't feel quite so warm. She
wished, incredibly, stupidly, that he would wake up and
smile—she couldn't remember having seen him really
smile yet—and that he would reach for her and pull her
down into his arms. That he would give her another kiss
like the one last night.

Animal sacrifices. It couldn't be true. Could it?

Suddenly Ian's cat-green eyes opened, snaring hers
with their intensity. Honor had the terrible feeling that
he knew what she'd been thinking, that he had been
hearing every thought that crossed her mind. Crazy,
she thought, even as her insides fluttered nervously.

Crazy. But the feeling that he had looked inside her head wouldn't die.

Then his eyes were hooded by lowered lashes, and he sat up.

"Sorry," he said. "I didn't mean to fall asleep on you."

The innocuous, innocent comment almost startled her, when she had half expected him to mention the things that had been roiling in her thoughts. A couple of seconds passed while she gathered her scattered wits.

"I didn't mind," she said finally. "We're both a little short on rest after the last couple of nights." Now that he was staring at the water instead of her, she felt more comfortable. "Did you really mean it when you said you don't sleep at night?"

"Yeah." He drew one knee up and rested his forearm on it. "I've never needed much sleep. An hour or two here and there. I generally just nap when I need to. Like now."

"I don't think I could stand that. I love to sleep."

He turned his head and gave her a faint smile. "I do, too. I wouldn't mind doing it more often."

She smiled back at him and tried to ignore the niggling sense of unease the electrician had planted in her. No way was this man a satanist, she told herself. No way. He turned his attention back to the water, and she was free to run her gaze over his broad shoulders and powerfully muscled back. That was when she saw the scars. They were faint with age, almost invisible, but there were dozens of them, some looking like very old burns, some like knife slashes. She couldn't keep from gasping.

She couldn't imagine how he heard that small, soft sound over the pounding surf, but he did. He didn't turn his head to look at her, but he spoke.

"A demon caught me once," he said. "Years and years ago. Those are his marks."

She reached out instinctively, with a woman's natural need to offer some kind of comfort, but he had already risen from the blanket and was striding down to the water.

So alone, she thought, feeling tears prick at her eyes. He was so alone.

But then, so was she.

The light became flat, unnatural, as the sky grew hazy. There was nothing nearby to cast a shadow as brilliant colors turned leaden and the hot, humid air grew oppressive.

Honor felt a chill run down her spine, despite the stifling heat of the day. It was eerie, she thought, this sultry, flat light, the way the waves suddenly seemed to have grown quiet. Even the eternal seashore breeze had grown still. Turning, she looked up and down the beach and saw not one other soul.

Ian suddenly rose from the waves and walked up the sand toward her.

"Let's get out of here," he said as soon as he reached her.

She tilted her head back and looked up at him. The sky was so bright behind him that he was little more than a dark shadow. "What's wrong?"

He squatted, bringing his face nearly level with hers. Now she was no longer blinded by the brilliance of the sky behind him and could make out his face. His green eyes seemed to glow, and she suddenly understood how tales of witchcraft might have surrounded him.

"Tell me," he said with quiet intensity, "just what you *feel* has been going on for the last couple of days. Don't tell me the facts, don't tell me what you want to think happened. Just tell me what you *feel* is going on."

Her breath jammed in her throat. Say those things out loud? Things about feeling some kind of evil presence when she was all alone? Things about hating that living room, about the odor of decay that seemed to permeate the whole house, an odor she was sure hadn't been there when she bought it. Admit that the shadows beneath the old live oaks seemed to be *alive* somehow? Seemed to be occupied by things that, though unseen, she felt right at the base of her skull? Things she hadn't even admitted to herself? Things so fanciful and impossible that she hardly dared let the thought of them cross her mind?

The hazy light, so peculiar, cast no shadows across his face, and it made him look strange, like a painting with two real, glowing eyes looking out of it. "What do you feel?" he asked again.

She wanted to look away, but somehow she couldn't. His eyes were mesmerizing; they held her. She finally spoke, words springing to her lips before she was even conscious of them. "When I was little, I thought there was a crocodile in the dark under my bed."

He nodded. "I had a bear in my closet."

Somehow that made it easier. A long breath escaped her. "I feel that way about...about the house. About the dark in the corners and under the trees and in the attic—" She shook her head, denying what she said even as she said it. "There wasn't anything under my bed when I was a kid." She looked away, feeling an almost physical ripping as she tore her eyes from his. "I feel...I feel..." She could barely whisper the words.

"What do you feel? What?"

"As if...somebody's trying to get into my head." The words spilled out of her in a long, breathless rush, taking form on the sultry air before she was even conscious of having felt such a thing. Where had that come from?

She turned swiftly, expecting to see shock on Ian's face, but he looked as impassive as always. A protest spilled from her lips just as swiftly, trying to banish the words she had just spoken. Trying to deny the reality of the awareness they had unleashed. "I didn't mean that. God, I don't know why I said that!"

"Shh..." He touched a finger to her lips, then dropped it. "It's okay. I asked what you felt. I didn't ask for reasons. Some things don't have reasons."

He looked around at the strange, flat light, at the gray water and dull sand. "Something's going on. Something...unnatural. I feel it, too."

"It's crazy!" She knew the protest was useless even as she made it.

He shook his head, and suddenly his unearthly eyes were fixed on her again. "I'm a soldier. I feel it at the base of my skull when someone's watching me. I don't question the feeling. I act on it. It's saved my life more than once."

Icy tendrils wrapped slowly around her spine. "Someone's watching." She felt it, too. Had felt it all along.

He nodded. "I thought we'd get away from it by coming out here." He scanned the beach and dunes again, evidently seeking the watcher and seeing no one. "Let's get out of here. Let's just drive somewhere and see if we can't find some privacy to talk."

It wasn't until later that she wondered about his motives. For all that he appeared to be concerned for her safety, he spent an awful lot of time scaring her even more. Instead of reassuring her, he terrified her. Instead of promising that locks would protect her, he spoke of demons.

What if he was taking advantage of the situation to terrify her? What if he was engaging in some kind of psychological warfare to scare her out of her wits? To drive her away? Or drive her over the edge?

Abomination. Witch's spawn. The words whispered through her mind again, cold and deadly. Once again she tried to ignore them. They were *not* real. They came from some buried corridor of the subconscious, stirred up by her fright, and they were meaningless.

Or were they?

Chapter Four

Ian pointed his Jeep away from the base, taking them even farther from home. Honor knew a prickle of unease, wondering if she were utterly foolish to go so far—to go anywhere—with this man. Trusting him because he was a former Ranger, like her father, was like trusting someone because of his hair color—foolhardy.

Yet she would have bet, despite all her doubts about his motives and whether he was trying to scare her half to death, that he meant her no physical harm. She *was* betting precisely that, she realized with an unpleasant lurch of her stomach as they headed into one of the more sparsely populated parts of the Panhandle. Just by being here she was betting on her safety.

Half an hour later Ian wheeled off the road into the parking lot of one of those unexpected restaurants that sometimes appeared in the middle of nowhere in this part of the world. There were several cars in the lot, though at midafternoon it wasn't likely to be busy.

"They have great seafood here," Ian told her as he parked. "Local catch, fresh daily. Interested?"

She definitely was, especially with her nerves quieting at the prospect of a public place.

Inside, a couple of men sat at the bar, sipping beer. They looked up and nodded as Ian and Honor entered. Quiet country music played in the background.

"Seat yourselves, folks," the bartender said. "Wilma'll be right with you."

By the time they'd been served a pitcher of draft beer and a huge basket of deep-fried shrimp, Honor realized that for the first time in days she was actually beginning to relax. It felt somewhat like waking from a bad dream, or getting over the flu, to have the tension really gone. And only as it lifted did she realize just how tense and uneasy she had been.

Even Ian seemed to be relaxing in some subtle way, she realized. He was leaning back, legs loosely crossed, one arm slung casually over the back of his chair. From time to time he reached out and popped another shrimp into his mouth. The thing that struck her most, though, was the subtle change in his face. It no longer looked quite so hard or forbidding, so rocklike.

And he seemed every bit as reluctant as she to destroy the mood by discussing the very things they had come here to talk about.

Finally, though, when the shrimp were half-gone and the pitcher was half-empty, he uncrossed his legs and leaned toward her, resting his elbows on the table. His strange green eyes seemed to glow with a light of their own in the dimly lit restaurant.

"Since you don't believe in demons," he said gruffly, "I suppose you don't believe in ghosts or ESP, either."

Honor wanted to shake her head in a firm negative, but she couldn't. After a brief internal struggle, she answered. "Let's just say I'm beginning to develop an open mind."

One corner of his mouth turned up in a faint, crooked smile. "That'll do," he said.

Honor set her beer glass down, suddenly wishing she hadn't drunk anything. Her head didn't feel quite as clear as she liked it to, and now things were getting serious. Or would, if she allowed them to. "Let me guess. You're going to tell me my house is haunted." She shuddered inwardly as she spoke the words out loud. She felt crazy speaking of such things, but, after the last two days...well, she couldn't entirely dismiss them, either.

He reached for the pitcher and refilled both their glasses. "I grew up in the house I'm living in now," he told her. He glanced up, snaring her with his gaze, then let his eyes wander around the room. "So I know something about your place. There used to be an old woman living there, a Mrs. Gilhooley. She lived in that house better than fifty years, up until three years ago, when she died."

Watching his face as he spoke, Honor got the distinct feeling that this was a difficult subject for him. Since he didn't seem to have any trouble discussing demons, she wondered just what *would* give him difficulty.

Ian popped another shrimp in his mouth and washed it down with a sip of beer. "After she died, the house went to a cousin of hers, and he rented it out a few times while he tried to sell it. The last tenants moved out just about seven months ago."

She nodded. "The agent told me when he showed me the house. They left a lot of stuff behind that I made the owner clear out before I bought it."

Ian wrapped both his hands around his mug. The mug was large, but his huge hands nearly swallowed it. Honor stared at those hands, remembering suddenly how gently they had held her last night. How awkwardly they had patted her and stroked her. Those same hands, she had no doubt, could kill with swift, merciless efficiency. The dichotomy gave her a fractured sense of the man who sat across from her, a contradictory picture of Ian the soldier and Ian the man.

He spoke. "Did the agent also tell you that the last tenants left in the middle of the night? Only ten days after they moved in?"

Honor's heart thudded uncomfortably. "Uh...no, she didn't. Why did they do that? Do you know?"

He looked her right in the eye. "They heard things. The kids hated the place. But what happened that last night is anybody's guess. They were gone before dawn, leaving most of their stuff behind."

Honor was aware of the deep, slow thudding of her heart, an uneasy rhythm. "Some people scare easily," she said. "Some people attribute every sound to something unnatural. Once a person gets spooked..." She let her words trail off, wondering why she heard her father's voice speaking those same words in her head. As if he had once said such things to her. But it was irrelevant to the moment, so she tucked the question away for later.

Ian ignored her comments. "I understand they weren't the only tenants to leave abruptly in the middle of the night."

Her mouth felt as dry as straw. Sipping her beer, she wrestled with uneasiness and a growing sense of danger. A ghost! "Well," she said finally, "a ghost is nothing but a pain in the neck. I mean, sure, it can annoy you, I guess, if you let it, but what can it possibly *do* to you? If that's what's going on, I guess I'll just quit worrying about it."

She looked up at Ian then and realized he didn't agree with her. Something in his cat-green eyes and granite features told her that he didn't think a ghost was something to dismiss. That he wasn't thinking in terms of a jolly poltergeist or a veiled lady who didn't realize she had died. What he had in mind was very different.

He opened his mouth just a fraction, then closed it, evidently thinking better of whatever he had been about to say. Instead, he swallowed half a mug of beer, then ate another handful of shrimp.

Damn it, she thought. He kept scaring her half to death, and then, when she had the gall to argue with him, he clammed up and left her dangling, wondering what he had been driving at. Irritation pushed her past caution.

"What is it with you?" she demanded, keeping her voice low. "All this talk of ghosts and demons... Are you really a satanist?"

As soon as the words popped out of her mouth, she would have given almost anything to snatch them back. Ian froze, every muscle in his body going as rigid as stone. For the longest time he didn't even seem to breathe. Only his eyes appeared alive. Green, glowing, intense, they held hers almost by force, somehow forbidding her to look away. She glimpsed, in those moments, the hunter in him. With a deep sense of dread, she realized he would be implacable.

And then he let her go. All he did was shift his gaze from hers, and she felt as if she had been released.

"That's old gossip," he said. "What else have you been hearing?"

She felt at once horrified by what she had blurted out and defiant. She hardly knew the man, after all. Surely she had a right to wonder about him and question his trustworthiness? Even so, she couldn't bring herself to mention the other accusation. A moment later she was wondering if it had been written across her forehead and had the worst feeling that he had plucked the words right out of her mind.

"Animal sacrifices," he said, in a low voice. He turned his head to the side and swore softly.

An ache bloomed deep in Honor, and something in her heart shifted. Her mind kept telling her that she didn't know this man, not really, and that she would be wise to be cautious and careful. Her heart wasn't listening. Instinctively she reached out and covered his hand with hers, wanting to comfort him, sensing somehow that she had opened a very old wound.

Slowly he turned and looked straight at her. "You don't believe it," he said quietly.

Her hand on his acknowledged it. Honor tried to smile, and failed. "My mind keeps telling me I don't know you at all." She shrugged. "No, I don't believe it. Not where it counts."

He lowered his gaze to their hands, then slowly turned his over to clasp her fingers gently. "I was never a satanist," he said. "And I never sacrificed or tormented an animal. I never would." Slowly he looked up at her. "I'm no saint, not by a long sight. But I'd never do anything like that." One corner of his mouth lifted up a fraction, giving the impression of a sad smile. "To tell you the truth, I generally like animals a whole lot better than people."

Somehow that didn't surprise her. The ache in her deepened, and she had to draw a deep breath to ease it. This man, this hard, dangerous, isolated man, carried deep scars, she realized. And against every grain of common sense and every ounce of caution, she wanted to comfort him. Unconsciously she tightened her fingers around his.

Something leapt in his eyes at that, something scalding. Something sensuous. Her heart began to hammer a heavy rhythm in response. No, thought her battered and scarred heart. Not that. That was too dangerous. It would be too easy to get hurt.

Ian ran his thumb over the back of her hand in a gentle caress. Then he released her and reached for his mug. "About the house," he said, as if he hadn't just been looking as if he wanted to devour her.

Honor drew her hand back, wondering if he had sensed her sudden uneasiness. Maybe. She liked to think she had a poker face, but this man was beginning to make her feel as if she were an open book. "The house," she repeated.

He nodded, his green eyes scraping over her face as if trying to read an oracle. Suddenly he leaned over the table and touched her cheek with his warm fingers. "You're very pretty," he said, almost roughly. "Soft, warm, fresh. And so damn young. I don't know what the hell is happening at that place, but I'd hate it like the devil if anything hurt you."

"But what can a ghost do?" she asked, feeling somehow bereft when he drew his hand back.

"This may come as a shock," he said after a moment, sounding almost gentle, "but I really don't know. You probably think I'm into all sorts of occult stuff because of my remarks about demons." He shrugged a massive shoulder. "The truth is, I've never had any experience with ghosts or any interest in the subject. But there's something going on in that house. I can *feel* it."

An icy little shiver ran down her spine as she considered just what it would take to cause this man to make such an admission—unless, of course, he was deliberately trying to scare her. But no. Right here, and right now, she didn't think he was. Right now she felt that his concern was genuine, and that he had crossed a difficult barrier to tell her he *felt* something was wrong.

"You're saying there's a difference between a ghost and a demon?" Was she really talking about this?

"A demon is physical," he said baldly. "I told you. He walks and talks and looks just like a human being. But he isn't human. When you run into one, believe me, you know it. Cops talk about it, Honor. I've heard them. They talk about the *eyes*. There's something there that I—" He broke off abruptly and looked away. "Once you've seen it, you never forget it. And you can't mistake it, if you have any idea what you're looking for."

Again that ache settled into her chest, filling her with a yearning to reach out and somehow wipe away his anguished memories. But she couldn't. She didn't have the right, and she was sure she didn't have the ability. "You would know," she said finally.

He nodded briefly, and after a bit he looked back at her. "But I don't know ghosts. All I know is there's something wrong. And it worries me."

Honor spared a moment to wish she'd never even thought of leaving Seattle. Then she squared her shoulders and looked at the big man with the granite face who was waiting for her reaction. "Well, I'm stuck," she said. "My savings are tied up in the property, and my credit rating is riding on the mortgage. I'll just have to tough it out. Honestly, I just can't see what a ghost could do, other than scare me. The worst I've read about poltergeists sounds annoying but not terribly threatening. Anyway, I'm not even sure I have a ghost."

Something flickered in his unusual eyes, and then he nodded. "Okay. It's your call. But remember, I feel it, too. So don't you ever hesitate to call on me for help."

* * *

The sultry haze had turned into threatening storm clouds by the time they emerged from the restaurant. The leather seats in Ian's Jeep were hot and sticky, and he spread out a towel for Honor to sit on. She still squirmed uncomfortably, because her bathing suit wasn't quite dry beneath her clothes and there was sand in it. Suddenly she was eager to get home and into the shower.

And that thought, for some odd reason, had her turning her head to look at Ian.

She was torn between the sense that she ought not to trust him so quickly and the sense that she could trust him implicitly. Worse, all that confusion was tied up in a knot of sexual desire such as she had not felt since before her marriage. Nor could she tell herself it was just wishful thinking. Not after that kiss he had given her last night. This man had the power to set her ablaze.

Which was a good reason to avoid him, never mind anything else. But her mind kept straying that way, and she wondered why she couldn't have met him at a time when she might have felt freer to explore her feelings. But at another time, she acknowledged, he never would have noticed her. He was very self-contained and solitary, and the only reason he had spent this much time with her was because he felt she needed him. Last night's kiss had been an aberration, and she seriously doubted it had affected him at all…because if it had, surely he would have tried to kiss her again.

Just more proof, she thought glumly, of how utterly unattractive she was. Oh, Lord, listen to her! Drowning in self-pity again. Disgusted, she forced herself to look away from Ian. She was just tired from the stress of the last few days, she assured herself. Just tired.

Now, if only the house would let her take a nap.

It didn't strike her until much later just how odd that thought was.

Thunder cracked loudly just as they pulled into Ian's driveway. A gust of wind blew up the red dirt road, driving small dust devils ahead of it, and causing the long curtains of Spanish moss to sway slowly.

"Looks like it'll be a good one," Ian said as he pulled his keys from the ignition. "I'll walk you over."

She didn't argue. She didn't want to argue. Looking over at the dark, swaying shadows beneath those trees and the dark, fathomless windows of that house, she knew only that she didn't want to be alone in there.

"Why don't you join me for dinner tonight?" she heard herself say. "I've got the graveyard shift tonight, so it'll probably be around nine before it's ready."

He paused in the act of climbing out of the Jeep and faced her. She got the distinct impression that he was both shocked and pleased. And that was when she realized that this was the very first overtly friendly gesture she had made to this man. Shame burned her cheeks at the thought.

"I'd like that," he said. He didn't quite smile, but the feeling of it touched his face. "What can I bring?"

"Yourself." She smiled at him, wishing he would smile back. "Come in an hour or so, if you want. You can keep me company." Keep the shadows at bay, keep the loneliness away.

There was nothing quite like a slightly damp bathing suit full of sand, Honor thought as she peeled hers away with relief. She threw it into the tub and then climbed in with it beneath the hot spray. Oh, did that feel good after so many hours in the damp, chilly suit! It felt so good, in fact, that she stayed under the spray until she had used the last of the hot water.

Squealing at the change of temperature, she turned off the water and yanked the shower curtain open to grab a towel.

Her heart climbed into her throat.

The door to the hallway, which she had closed to prevent a draft, was standing wide open. Beyond it was only empty, echoing darkness.

A crack of thunder caused her to start and gasp. The hair on the back of her neck was standing up, and goose bumps broke out all over her. Reaching out with a shaking hand, never taking her eyes from the open door, she snatched a towel from the rack and wrapped it around herself.

Oh, God. Oh, God.

Maybe, she tried to tell herself, she hadn't closed the door all the way, even though she thought she had. Maybe a draft had just nudged it open. Maybe the door wasn't hung right and had just swung open. Maybe it was nothing at all. But her ears strained, listening intently to the silence, alert for any sound that might betray another presence.

A minute passed. Then another. She could hear nothing from the hallway beyond. Thunder cracked again, and the wind banged against something, but those sounds all came from without. Within the house there was no sound save her own ragged breathing and the hammering of her heart.

Finally, much as she had done when she was a child in the dark with a crocodile under her bed, she screwed up her courage and made a mad dash down the hall to her bedroom. There she slammed the door and leaned against it, gasping for air, wondering how she could be so foolish as to believe she had locked anything out.

But she did. Somehow she did. Somehow she felt safer here. Safe from what, she had no idea. Beyond her window, lightning flashed brilliantly, and thunder rolled in a hollow boom. The rain had not yet started.

And from overhead came the odd scratching she had heard earlier. Slowly she looked up at the ceiling. Please, she thought. Oh, please, let it be a mouse.

Ian, hurry! Please hurry!

Another flare of lightning drew her attention to the window. Ian wasn't due to come over for another half hour or so. She could get dressed, she thought, if she could pry her back away from the door and take the chance that something might come through it. She could get dressed and climb out the window onto the porch roof and shimmy down one of the columns. She could get out of here that fast. That easily. All she had to do was move away from the door and get dressed.

But she couldn't. Oh, God, she couldn't move. The sense of something on the other side of the door was growing past all reason, a sense of dark menace pressing inward, trying to slip past the door....

Oh, God, was she losing her mind?

And then, as if someone had flipped a switch, it was gone. Completely.

Shivering, Honor stood with her back pressed to the door, unable to believe that the horrifying presence had left, waiting for it to return. But it didn't. It was gone. With it had vanished the dark pressure in her mind and the fear at the base of her skull. In the blink of an eye, the world had returned to normal.

The suddenness of the change convinced her, as nothing else could have, that this was no figment of her imagination. What had been there had *really* been there. And now it was gone.

The afternoon grew darker and more threatening, but still the rain didn't fall. Honor dressed and stayed in her bedroom until she heard Ian knock at the back door. Then she flew down the stairs through the shadowy house and threw the back door open. At the last second she managed to avoid flinging herself into his arms.

"Hi," she said instead, summoning up a smile. Stepping back, she invited him in.

The back door had been locked, she realized, feeling a sudden compulsion to check the front door. What if somebody had actually been in the house? What if it hadn't been the "presence" at all, but a real person? The man who had been waiting for her the other night?

Suddenly her knees turned to water and her heart stopped dead. She hadn't even considered that possibility. Not once.

"Honor?" Ian frowned at her. "Honor, what's wrong?"

She blinked and managed to focus on him. "I, um…I need to check the front door."

Turning, she hurried down the hallway, not caring what he thought. She *had* to know if that door was still locked. She *had* to know the dimensions of whatever had been in this house with her.

The door was locked. She almost collapsed against it in sheer relief until she remembered the windows. Turning swiftly, she nearly bumped into Ian. He caught her gently by the shoulders.

"Honey, what's wrong?"

"I…just want to check the windows. Make sure everything is locked up." She couldn't bring herself to look up into his strange green eyes. The compulsion to check locks was almost irrational, and completely overwhelming. Then his choice of words struck her. Slowly she raised her gaze to his. *Abomination.* "I'm not your honey."

At once he stepped back, and something in his face grew tight.

Honor turned from him and headed into the living room to check all the windows. God, how she hated this room! *Witch boy.* The bars were all in place there and in the dining room. She wasn't worried about the upstairs, because only her bedroom was accessible from the ground without a ladder, and no one had been in her bedroom.

Back in the kitchen, she suddenly felt as if somebody had pulled her plug. She sank bonelessly onto a chair and put her head down on her arms. She heard Ian pull out the chair across from her and sit.

And suddenly, with a crawling sense of shame, she remembered her behavior of the past few minutes, the way she had spoken to him. Oh, God, what had come over her? How could she have been so rude? She had acted like a crazy person, not like herself at all.

Slowly, reluctantly, she lifted her head and looked at him. He was regarding her remotely, much as he had the first time they met, from across a chasm of emotional distance. That look, that chilly, distant look, made her realize just how close she had felt to him earlier that afternoon. And how rude she had just been.

Lightning flared brilliantly, so bright that for an instant Ian was nothing but a dark silhouette against the kitchen window. Thunder rumbled, long and low, vibrating the table beneath her arms.

"Something...something was in here," she said. "Before you came. I...was in the shower, and when I pulled back the curtain, the bathroom door was open."

His eyes never flickered. Not a muscle on his face moved. She forced herself to continue, needing him to understand.

"I...couldn't hear anyone. I ran down the hall and...hid in my bedroom. With the door closed. I...I don't think I've ever been so scared in my life!" The last words burst from her on a rising note.

Seconds ticked away in silence as he stared at her, unmoving. Finally he spoke. "What then?"

"It was gone," she said hoarsely. "Just like that, it was gone. As if it had never been."

Lightning flashed again, and thunder cracked deafeningly. The overhead light flickered and went out.

"Hell," said Ian. The room was dark, illuminated only by the flashes of lightning outside.

Moments later the light flared on again. Honor stared at Ian, feeling trapped in ways she couldn't have begun to explain, and wondering how she was going to get out of this. He couldn't help her. He had done so much already; what more could he possibly do? What could anybody do against something that even locks couldn't keep out?

She longed just to leave, but for financial reasons she couldn't do that. And even the thought of turning tail shamed her. She wasn't her father's daughter for nothing. *Face it head-on,* he'd always said. *Don't let anything get the best of you.*

But how could she face something she couldn't see? How could she stand up to something she couldn't touch? Earlier, she'd asked what a ghost could do except scare her. Now she knew that being scared was quite enough. She couldn't live in a state of terror, and she couldn't reason it away.

She returned her gaze to Ian's impassive face and wondered what he was thinking. *Witch eyes.* Why did she keep thinking these things about him? Witch eyes. Where had that come from? And the other stuff. Demon spawn. Abomination. Lord, she'd never used words like that in her life!

She shuddered, then nearly jumped when a deafening crack of thunder sounded overhead.

Suddenly Ian reached across the table and captured one of her tightly clenched hands. "Easy, lady," he said. "Nothing's going to happen to you while I'm here."

But what about later? she wondered miserably.

The storm continued to rumble angrily without raining throughout the evening. Ian seemed to have put her rudeness behind him, though there was a reserve in his actions that had nearly vanished earlier. There was distance between them again; they were not-quite-strangers thrown together by circumstance.

Since she had so little furniture, they were essentially confined to the kitchen. Ian had brought a bottle of white wine, but she decided not to have any, because she had to go to work later. He never opened the bottle.

He offered to help with the meal, but she insisted he just keep her company. She needed to be busy, and the work was a good excuse to keep going.

"You need a TV," he said. "Or a radio. Something to make noise in this place. And you should keep up with the weather, anyway, this time of year."

It would probably help, she thought. It would keep her from hearing things. Just as pulling the blanket over your eyes could keep you from seeing things. As if not seeing or hearing made things go away.

Dinner was simple: steak, salad and bread. She drank milk. Ian asked for coffee. For a few minutes, things seemed normal. Almost. She wondered if anything would ever truly seem normal again.

Looking at the hard, ravaged face of the man who sat across from her, she tried to imagine the roads he must have traveled in his life. Most men didn't stay with the Rangers throughout their careers. Most soldiers spent a few years there and then went on to join other units, where they were the seeds of a better, harder, tougher fighting force. Those who did stay were…special. Unique. The kind of men you would definitely want on your side in a fight. But not the kind of men any woman in her right mind would want to give her heart to.

They were too hard, she thought. Too toughened. Too devoted to honor and duty and country. Anything else took a decided second place. A man like that would turn his back on his own wife if ordered to. The way her father had turned his back on her mother.

Suddenly a door yawned open in the depths of her mind, and she felt herself tumbling backward into the past, like Alice falling down the rabbit hole.

Her father stood over her, a tall, intimidating presence in camouflage. He was big, so big, and she was small, so very small. And so very frightened.

"I told you to cut out that nonsense, Honor. You're a big girl now."

"Cleve, just let her be," said her mother from somewhere behind him. She sounded worried. Frightened. "She can't help these feelings."

"She sure as hell can," her father said sharply. "It's just her imagination, and I'm getting damn sick and

tired of her getting hysterical in the middle of the night because we have ghosts, for God's sake! As long as we keep pandering to this crap, she'll never quit it."

"Cleve, she's only five. She can't help being scared."

"But she can help talking about ghosts! She can learn to handle her fear the way the rest of us do."

"But she's so little!"

"And that's the whole damn problem, Sheila! You keep excusing her because she's so little. How the hell will she ever grow up?"

"Oh, my God," Honor whispered, forgetting where she was, wondering how she could ever have forgotten what had happened when she was five. Trapped in a terrifying corridor of memory, she closed her eyes and remembered being locked in the closet all night long so that she would learn to face her fears. Learn to control her wild talk of ghosts. Learn to deny what she heard, what she saw, what she felt.

Night after night after night...

Ian felt her slip away. He had resurrected his terrible talent for this woman's sake, and it was not something he could switch on and off now, like a light. He felt her slip into her memories, and he felt anguish grip her.

And around him he felt the gathering evil. Whatever had earlier scared her was strengthening again, growing, little by little filling the house with its dark presence. Gathering its power.

He instinctively looked up, toward the ceiling, but what he felt wasn't located there. It was everywhere, throughout this house. Thunder rolled deeply outside, and lightning continued to flicker, and even the force of the storm seemed like a small thing compared to the evil he felt growing here.

He looked over at Honor, and the expression on her face pierced him, pierced all the granite walls he had built for protection. He needed to help her. And because of his need, he reached over and touched her mind, forgetting that it was an invasion of privacy of the worst kind.

He went into the locked closet with her, and without a thought he tried to comfort the five-year-old girl who was trapped in the dark with no companion but terror.

"Oh, my God!" Honor gasped the words, and her eyes flew open. She had felt, unmistakably, a touch, an indescribable touch, in her mind. How could such a thing be? One moment she had been alone in a locked closet, reliving a horrible childhood memory, and the next she had not been alone. "Oh, my God," she whispered again, wondering if this was what it felt like to lose one's mind.

Ian watched her with those strange, cat-green eyes of his. He looked, she thought warily, as if he had felt something of her pain. She couldn't stand this anymore, she realized. She couldn't stand feeling these things and then keeping them all locked up, even if it was what her father had expected of her. Would expect of her. She needed desperately to know if someone else thought she was crazy, or sane. And Ian was the only person she could turn to.

"You won't believe this," she said, almost hoarsely.

He continued to regard her steadily. "Try me," he said quietly.

But just then she felt another pressure in her mind, a dark, sinister touch, like icy, wet fingers. She shivered and looked around, almost as if she thought she could find its source. And then she looked into Ian's eerie eyes. *Spawn of demons. Witch boy.* How could she trust him? she wondered wildly. What if he was the evil thing she felt?

Abomination.

"Let's get the hell out of here," Ian said suddenly, harshly. "I'll drive you to work."

She was startled, and the icy touch in her mind vanished. "But I don't have to leave for an hour yet."

"Good. We'll stop and get coffee someplace. We need to talk. There's...there's stuff I need to tell you."

A touch of stubbornness flared in her. "I thought we talked earlier."

"That wasn't everything. There's more. A lot more."

She opened her mouth to argue that they could talk right here, but before the words escaped, she felt it again. The presence. The dark thing that loomed in this house. It was strengthening. Growing.

She had to get out of here. Now.

She looked at Ian. "I'll get my stuff."

At the foot of the stairs, she froze, not wanting to go up there. Ian was suddenly beside her, touching her elbow. How did he know?

"I'll go up with you," he said. "You don't have to face it alone anymore, Honor."

Face what alone? she wondered. And wondered even more at the way his words dovetailed with the memory from her childhood. Her father had insisted she face it alone. Ian said she didn't have to.

It was all too weird. No one would ever believe...

At the top of the stairs, she looked back at the dark, hard man who followed her so protectively. *He* would believe her, she thought.

And she wondered why that thought didn't comfort her at all.

Chapter Five

Lightning flickered among the trees as they drove down the two-lane highway toward town. Pines and oaks crowded the shoulders of the road, dark shadows in the headlights. It was a relief, Honor thought, to be away from that house.

A half-hour later they reached the edge of town and Ian pulled into the parking lot of a brightly lit all-night hamburger place. Air Force uniforms were visible at a number of tables. A couple of guys in Ranger uniforms nodded to Ian as he guided Honor to a table in an out-of-the-way corner.

People. Normal, ordinary people. How wonderful they looked after a day like today.

"Coffee?" Ian asked. "I'll get it."

"Please. Black."

There was something so wonderfully normal about this place, the bright lights, the gleaming floors, the buzz of quiet conversation, that the past couple of days seemed like a movie nightmare. Almost.

When he returned with the coffee, Ian slid into the booth across from her.

"How are you going to manage to stay awake all

night?" he asked her, surprising her. "You've had one long day."

"I'll be okay. Adrenaline usually does the trick."

"I'll come to get you in the morning. Seven-thirty?"

Honor nodded. "I might be a few minutes late, though."

Ian shrugged. "No big deal."

A few more minutes passed while they sipped coffee in silence. Finally, looking about as happy as a man facing a firing squad, Ian came to the point.

"I don't want you being alone in that house anymore."

The first thing to hit her was a tidal wave of overwhelming relief. Then reality intruded.

"I can't afford to move out," she said flatly.

"I realize that. What we need to do is see if we can't get rid of this…whatever it is. There's got to be some way to fight it. Exterminate it."

She thought of the movies and spoke the word with difficulty, rebelling at the whole idea. "Exorcism?"

A strange thing happened then. It almost seemed to her that Ian's gaze slid away, as if he were uneasy with the subject. As if the word had struck him personally somehow. And that brought the rumors about him being a satanist racing to the forefront of her mind.

"No." He said it sharply, flatly, in a low voice, a commanding voice. "No. Don't even think that."

"What? Think what?"

"That I'm afraid of an exorcism."

"I wasn't—" She broke off, realizing that she had been on the verge of thinking exactly that, that a satanist would be terrified of such a thing. "What the hell do you do? Read minds?"

His mouth compressed into a tight line. "I'm not

afraid of it," he said, ignoring her question. "I've been through it."

Through it? He'd been *through it?* She sank back against the vinyl-padded bench and just stared at him. In all honesty, she wouldn't have guessed that anyone in this part of the world could even perform such a ceremony. And certainly not that someone she knew might actually have been through it.

"Why?" she said finally. "When?"

"When I was a kid," he said. The words came roughly, as if they were extremely difficult to force out, but his face never changed. "I was just six. Mrs. Gilhooley—the woman who lived in your house—had a goat. Damn animal was as old as Methuselah. Anyhow, I told her the goat was going to die. I don't even remember why I said it. Probably because it was so old. And damned if the goat didn't drop dead on the spot."

"Oh, my," Honor breathed, finding it not at all difficult to envision the progression of events. Just imagining it made her ache for the boy he must once have been.

"Mrs. Gilhooley accused me of witchcraft or being possessed or something," Ian continued. "I don't remember much of it very clearly. The preacher performed an exorcism on me. I mainly remember being locked up for days while people prayed and sang over me. I wasn't allowed to eat or drink, and sometimes they'd slap me silly, trying to drive the demon out."

He shrugged again, as if it no longer mattered, but Honor wasn't quite buying that. "How awful," she said softly. "Why would she ever accuse you of something like that? You were just a child!"

A child who saw things he shouldn't. Who heard the thoughts of others. Ian looked at her, but he didn't answer, because if he told her why Mrs. Gilhooley had hated him so much, she would be scared to death of him. And that wouldn't help at all right now. Instead, he lied by omission. "I don't remember much about the whole thing...except you'll never persuade me that exorcism is worth a whole lot."

She guessed she could understand that. For a moment she simply sat and looked at him, thinking that they both had childhood scars. It made her feel closer to him. "Did they think they had cured you?"

"For a while, at any rate." He picked up his cup and sipped. "Something like that sticks with you. Like the smell of skunk. When folks think you were possessed once, they're always on the lookout for it to happen again."

Honor nodded. "That must have given you a rough time for years." Even as she spoke, she realized that for him it had never been over. Just today the electrician had brought the subject up again, even though more than thirty years had passed. "Why did you come back here, Ian? Some of these people..." She hesitated. "Well, some of them evidently haven't forgotten."

His eyes bored into her. "It's my home," he said.

Honor shook her head slightly. "Being an army brat, I've never felt that way about any place. And I don't think I'll ever get to feel that way about *this* place. I like what you said about getting rid of this—this whatever-it-is—but how can we possibly do that?"

"I don't know yet, but I intend to find out. I'm going to check out the base library this morning. If they don't have anything, there's an occult bookstore downtown." One corner of his mouth lifted a little, just a faint suggestion of humor. "Maybe all we need is a garlic necklace."

A rusty laugh escaped Honor, and it struck her that

she hadn't laughed in two days now…and ordinarily she was quick to laugh. "Nothing in my life has ever been that easy."

"Or mine."

He went to get them some more coffee, and Honor watched him, noting how easily he moved, like a man in complete command of his body. He was used to being in command, that much was obvious. Faced with a ghost—or whatever awful thing was in that house—he considered himself quite capable of dealing with it. All he had to do was discover what needed doing. She liked his attitude and wished she could be so confident. All of *her* self-confidence was limited to nursing.

Turning her head, she stared past the reflections in the window glass and saw that the night was still storm-tossed, though it hadn't yet begun to rain. Odd weather, she thought.

She had very nearly forgotten being locked in the closet as a child. Her father had meant it to toughen her and to stop her from seeing things in the dark. It might have toughened her, but now she was seeing things in the dark again. And in broad daylight, for that matter.

Looking back at those endless nights of terror, when she had cried and shrieked and begged for hours to be let out of that small, dark closet, she wondered if they hadn't contributed to her mother's decision to divorce her father.

What struck her most now, though, was that this was not the first time in her life she had had a brush with…with the occult, for lack of a better word. Time had rendered her memory hazy, but she vaguely remembered lying awake in her bed, hearing sounds in the night. Footsteps, when no one was there. Voices, sounding distant and garbled, when no one was talking. Sights…

She caught her breath and stiffened. Oh, Lord, she had *seen* something as a child. A figure. Something. It had terrified her, and when her father had locked her in the closet, it had been there, too. There had been no escape.

"Honor?"

Ian slid into the booth beside her and wrapped a powerful arm around her shoulders. "Shh..." he said softly. "It's all right. It's all right."

Accepting without question that he somehow knew she was feeling scared and frightened, she turned toward him and buried her face in his strong shoulder. The terror was a memory, she reminded herself, an old memory. She was reacting to something that no longer threatened her.

But oh, how good it felt to be held. He even smelled good, like laundry soap and man, and the cotton of his olive T-shirt was soft against her skin. But she couldn't afford to notice things like that, she reminded herself. And this was certainly not the time or the place, anyway.

"I was remembering," she said. "I'd nearly forgotten...."

"Tell me."

"You'll think I'm crazy."

"Who, me?"

A weak chuckle escaped her then, and she eased back from his shoulder. He released her at once, and she wished he hadn't let go. Looking up almost shyly into his hard face, she found he was smiling faintly. Something about that smile made it possible to confide in him.

"When I was a kid, I saw and heard things in our house. My dad thought it was my imagination and locked me in the closet to break me of it."

Ian frowned. "He'd be arrested for that nowadays."

"Maybe. I don't think he meant to be cruel. He wasn't a cruel man. Just a hard one. What's important, though, is that...well, I've been through something like this before. If it's not my imagination—"

"It's not," he said, interrupting her. "I feel it, too. You're sensitive, that's all. I suspect some people wouldn't feel a thing in that house." He gave her another, very faint smile. "Some very *dense* people might not feel anything," he amended. "Whatever it is, it's strong."

"And getting stronger," Honor whispered, battling a sudden urge to look over her shoulder. The idea appalled her.

"Maybe not. I mean, if your father locked you in the closet to get you to suppress your sensitivity, it might just have taken a while for your awareness of this... thing to penetrate your barriers. It may have been this strong all along." He shrugged. "We're just speculating now, in any case. I suggest we wait until we find some useful information to base our theories on. In the meantime..."

Honor waited as he frowned thoughtfully, looking down at his coffee.

Here she was, sitting around talking of ghosts and other things that went bump in the night, and wishing that Ian McLaren would kiss her again, so that she could find out if the feelings she remembered from last night were real. Stupid. Incredible. But adrenaline had funny effects like that, she reminded herself. So maybe it wasn't stupid that she was thinking about sex when she ought to be thinking about how she was going to save her house from whatever was occupying it. Of course, maybe she was just overloaded.

Maybe she just needed a break, and thinking about her attraction to Ian was a great break from other things.

It might be a dangerous attraction, she found herself thinking. What did she really know about him...except that as a child people had thought he was possessed? Well, with those eyes...

Suddenly those eyes were fixed on her. "We've got a little time yet. Want to take a walk?"

Walking at night was something she had nearly given up doing, because it just wasn't safe for a woman alone, and she'd seen too much in the emergency room to remain ignorant of the hazards. Walking with Ian, all six-foot-five and two-hundred-plus pounds of him, made her feel completely safe. She was able to throw back her head, enjoy the stiff breeze and the smell of the sea. The storm had moved far enough away that she didn't think lightning was a real danger...though it still flickered off to the northwest.

They walked away from the bright lights and onto the athletic field of a nearby school. There they could see the silver-lined storm clouds when the moon occasionally peeked through.

"Some night," Ian remarked, "we'll have to take a walk on the beach. When the moon is full."

"I'd love that." Amazed that he was planning such things for them, she turned and peered up at him. He looked even more mysterious than usual in the uncertain light. Lightning flashed to the east, causing the shadow on his face to shift strangely. Even in this poor light, his eyes seemed to glow.

Surely, said a faint little voice in her head, she ought to be afraid of this huge man she hardly knew? But she wasn't. Not at all. Not at this moment. What she felt—*all* she felt—was an urgent desire to be kissed by him.

He read minds. She became almost convinced of it when his strong arms suddenly closed around her and drew her against him. Suddenly aware of the nerve-exciting textures of man, muscle and denim, she felt her knees turn soft.

"Me too," he said huskily. "Me too."

She wondered what he meant, but then she didn't care, because he lifted her right off her feet and brought her eager mouth to his. Strong. He was so strong. He made her feel small, delicate, fragile…and for once she didn't mind.

Caution was swept away on a riptide of long-buried passion. All the things she had denied herself, all the things she had thought she would never know, were suddenly within her grasp. Her arms wrapped around broad shoulders, and she reveled in the powerful flexing of his muscles as he held her effortlessly above the ground. Such a large, strong man. Every cell in her body responded to his potency.

And every wounded cell in her heart responded to the unmistakable evidence that he desired her.

He held her with one arm around her waist, as if she weighed nothing, and allowed his other hand to roam. Downward it swept, slowly, along the slender line of her back, the soft curve of her hip, to the silky skin of the back of her thigh. She gasped against his mouth at the exquisite sensation of his callused palm on her sensitive skin and tightened her arms unconsciously, trying to get closer still.

With steady, gentle pressure, he brought her leg up to his waist, and suddenly she was pressed with breath-stealing intimacy against his arousal, while his tongue pillaged her mouth in a blatant imitation of mating.

She had never...not in her wildest dreams... Her fingers dug into the corded muscles of his shoulders, and she tore her mouth from his, throwing her head back in surrender as she abandoned herself to sensations beyond imagining. An extraordinary tension filled her, a wild expectancy that made everything else seem insignificant in comparison.

She wanted. Blindly, heedlessly, instinctively, she wanted this man.

How did he do this to her?

The thought flashed in her brain like a warning beacon. This was too fast, too hot, too wild. Unnatural. *Abomination.*

A groan erupted from the chest of the man who held her, the man who had mesmerized her, bewitched her and turned her into flame. Suddenly she was on her feet, free of him, except for the hands that steadied her gently. Then, when he had made sure she wouldn't stumble, he turned his back to her.

Stunned by what had just passed between them, and by the abrupt change, Honor simply stood and stared at his back. She could feel it, she thought crazily. She could feel the control he exerted now as he stood with his hands on his hips and his head thrown back and waited for his own needs to subside. She could feel it as surely as she could feel her own body shriek its disappointment and its hunger.

She hurt. He hurt.

What had happened?

Abomination. The word twisted coldly through her mind, as repulsive and disturbing as a clammy touch. Alien. Not hers.

Troubled, frightened, she wrapped her arms around herself, feeling cold despite the muggy heat of the Florida night. Thunder rumbled distantly, an edgy reminder of a storm that had not yet broken.

"Ian?"

She said his name softly, in a voice that was barely more than a whisper, but he heard her and turned to face her.

"I...need to get to work."

After a moment, he nodded. "Let's go."

He dropped Honor off at the emergency room entrance and watched her cross the twenty feet of concrete, her cute rump an incitement in those white shorts she was wearing. His palm remembered in exquisite detail just how the smooth skin of her thigh had felt, and the rest of him remembered with excruciating accuracy just how she had wrapped herself around him.

He was spending too much time with her. Getting drawn in too far. He'd slipped badly tonight. Very badly. She'd almost caught him out twice.

He had felt her yearning for him as strongly as he had felt his own for her. He wanted her. She wanted him. It should have been enough—except that he was...an abomination. She had sensed it, too, tonight. He had felt her alarm. Felt her recognition that something was unnatural. She just hadn't realized that it was *him*.

He couldn't afford to get close to her like that. Couldn't afford to slip. Didn't think he could stand to see the revulsion and fear on her face if she discovered his secret.

He had plenty of experience in keeping a safe distance, and the few relationships with women he'd allowed himself over the years had been chosen because they would preserve that distance. And always, always, if he felt that distance begin to erode to even a small degree, he'd left before the woman could discover what he really was.

It would be a damn sight more difficult to recover lost distance with his next-door neighbor. If he had half a brain, he would leave her to deal with her ghost by herself, let her get driven out of the place like all the other tenants.

Evidently he didn't have half a brain. When she was safely inside, he turned his Jeep out of the lot and headed back down the highway toward home. He was going to check out that damn house. Tonight. While she wasn't there to add to the psychic confusion in the place.

The wind was picking up again by the time he pulled into his driveway. A new storm was moving in, this one more restless than the last. Lightning flickered in sheets, and thunder growled hollowly.

When he had put the deadbolts on Honor's doors, he had kept a key for himself—another in the long list of his transgressions in life. The problem with security, he had realized years ago, was that if you made it nearly impossible for someone to get in, you might pay a price for being unreachable. People burned to death in homes with barred windows. Medical help couldn't reach you quickly if no one could break in.

So he had kept a key. And now with it, he let himself into her house. He didn't bring a flashlight, because there was nothing he wanted to see. He stood inside her front door and closed his eyes.

And waited.

It was nearly dawn before he felt it. At first it was like a soft stirring of the psychic breeze, just a whisper of shifting shadows in the living room. Instinctively he turned toward it, though he would never see it with his eyes.

It strengthened slowly, as if waking from a long sleep. From a shifting in the shadows, from a whisper of movement, it grew. Dark. Roiling. Hateful. Evil.

Ah, God, so cold! It seemed to soak the last heat from the room, leaving a cold so intense it froze the soul. Oppressive. Suffocating. Like cold, oily smoke.

Aware. It was aware of him. It was gathering itself, gathering its strength and its hatred, and it knew him. Reaching out with icy tendrils of hate, it touched the edges of his mind and caused him to recoil helplessly.

Hunkering down and wrapping his arms around his knees for protection against a blast of cold that threatened frostbite, he waited it out. He needed knowledge of his enemy, and there was only one way to get it. Cautiously, he reached out with his mind.

And nearly died.

In an instant he was back in the pit that haunted his worst nightmares. Tied ankle and wrist with wire that cut to the bone. Helpless to protect himself. Helpless against the demon who tortured him. Naked to the eyes of his enemy. Knowing his every stifled scream of agony gave pleasure, because he could feel it with his abominable talent, could feel the pleasure of the men who tortured him. Wanting to die with a passion that beggared description, because it was his only way out.

No!

The word exploded in his head like a thunderclap as he grabbed for his self-control and refused to allow the vision power over him. Heedless of the cold that flayed his skin, he rose in the dark and faced his invisible tormentor.

No. By sheer effort of will, he forced his mind into

the present, forced it to bury again what had happened in the past. He had been there. He refused to allow a mere memory to wield that kind of power over him.

He was shivering violently now, from the cold that had swallowed all the heat, and he still hadn't found what he needed. Hate. It was full of hate. Rage. Bitterness. But nothing he could use against it.

Then, suddenly, something shifted. Something changed, a new scent on the wind. The cold withdrew a little; the direction of the hate turned a little.

A change of focus.

Seizing the opportunity, Ian reached out, seeking a clue, a weakness...anything.

What he found was another presence. Outside the house. Drawing closer. Bent on murder.

Turning, he dismissed the evil inside the house to concentrate on the threat outside. Cold breath brushed his neck, making his scalp prickle, but he ignored it, concentrating on the new threat, instead.

Fractured images filled his head, battlefield nightmares, the worst of the things he had ever seen in his life, as the hateful thing in the house assaulted his mind. Dismembered bodies, screaming friends, dead buddies. With a monumental effort of will, he ignored the visions that always haunted him, refusing to give a toehold to the thing that would use them against him.

He was still cold, but sweat broke out all over him, soaking him, as he wrestled for supremacy over his own mind. And the thing outside drew closer. It had been summoned.

Grabbing the doorknob, he twisted it and pulled the door open. The real threat was outside, and he had to face it.

But suddenly he froze, as the cold touched the edges

of his mind again. And buried deep in that cold and hate and rage, he thought he felt the touch of something…not exactly familiar, but something he had touched once before.

Before he could latch on to it, though, it vanished. Thunder cracked deafeningly, and the wind moaned around the corner of the house, reminding him where he was. When he was. The darkness in the living room shrank a little, pulling away from him.

And the thing outside was almost here. Swinging the door open the rest of the way, he stepped out into the wild darkness. The storm was right overhead now, and the old live oaks groaned before the buffeting of the wind.

A fork of lightning zigzagged downward, striking a tree farther up the road. The concussion made his eardrums hurt, almost distracting him from the awareness that something was watching. From out there. From across the road.

Keeping low, Ian hurried down off the porch and around to the side, so that he could circle around and come up behind whoever—or whatever—was over there.

Across the road, though a few scrubby pines grew tall, for some reason the vegetation was nearly tropical. Palmettos and ferns that had never been disturbed by man grew thickly. Running on silent feet, crouching to keep a low profile, Ian hurried fifty or sixty yards up the road and then crossed over. Behind him, he felt the presence in the house fade a little, weakening. As if it had used all the energy it could. Or as if its attention had turned elsewhere.

And then he discovered why he'd considered this threat worse than the one in the house.

Thunder cracked loudly, and lightning flared, illuminating the night. Then there was another sharp crack, an unnatural one.

Pain seared his side, and he went down. He'd been shot.

Thunder growled like a hungry beast at bay. Lightning slashed jaggedly toward the horizon from heavy clouds that hid the early-dawn light. On a clear day, the sky would be brightening by this time. Today it was a dark, leaden gray.

Ian didn't show up at 7:30. By eight, Honor was feeling impatient and irritated. This was why she hated to depend on someone else for transport.

By 8:30 she was beginning to worry about him. He didn't seem like an undependable sort of person, whatever else he might be. She called his house and received no answer.

By nine she was wondering if she could call the police. Something was wrong. She felt it in her bones.

Just as she was turning from the door to go back to the pay phone, she saw his Jeep pull into the hospital parking lot. Grabbing her purse, she trotted out to meet him.

"Sorry I'm so late," he said as she climbed in beside him. "I was unavoidably detained."

There was sarcasm in the statement, along with something else she couldn't quite define. She turned to look at him, really look at him, and gasped. "What happened to you?"

He looked pale under his tan, and his eyes appeared sunken. Running a professional eye over him, she realized for the first time that his olive-drab T-shirt had given way to a green hospital shirt. "Ian?"

"I thought we'd grab a quick breakfast and then hit the base library. That okay?"

She knew that tone of voice. Her father had often used it to indicate that a subject wasn't open for discussion. Instead of arguing, which was what she wanted to, she decided to bide her time. Things had a way of coming out if you were patient. "Okay," she said, and fixed her attention out the window.

He needed a shave, she thought as she stared out at the scenery. He looked like hell, he needed a shave, and something was very, very wrong. Once or twice she heard him mutter an oath as he took a corner.

They grabbed biscuits and sausage at a fast-food place, and large cups of hot, fresh coffee. They ate outdoors at a stone table, away from the other patrons, who were wisely avoiding the humid morning heat.

"Is it going to clear today at all?" Honor asked as she looked up at the leaden sky.

"I haven't heard the weather."

"I came down here for sunshine," she remarked. "I feel cheated when I don't get it."

It was a stupid, inane conversation, but it kept her from asking why he was moving so strangely. So stiffly. And why his mouth tightened at times, as if he were in pain. Not that she needed him to explain that he'd gotten hurt somehow. She did wonder, though, *how* he'd been hurt. And how bad it was. Instead, she talked of something else. Anything else.

"Do you really think we'll find anything useful at the library?"

He looked up from his third biscuit. "We're hardly the first people in the world to be faced with this problem."

"Well, no." Not likely. Not when she remembered an earlier encounter just in her own life. Tens of thousands of other people must have experienced such things.

One corner of his mouth lifted in that faint smile she

was beginning to find familiar. "The way things are, if two people have experienced something, one of them will have written a book about it."

She almost laughed then. He was right, of course.

"Even if we don't find something useful in terms of getting rid of the thing," he continued, "every bit of knowledge we can gather is potentially useful. And in the meantime, I want you to stay at my house."

She blinked, startled by both the suggestion and her own response, a swift upsurge of mingled relief and yearning. "I don't think—"

"Look," he said, "don't get all coy and prissy on me. You know damn well you're not comfortable in that house. Do you really think you'll be able to close your eyes and go to sleep there after what you tell me you felt yesterday? Are you just calmly going to ignore it and get into your shower again?"

Ice slid slowly down her spine. Inwardly she admitted he was right. She wasn't going to be able to ignore the presence in the house. No amount of arguing with herself would change the fact that she would always be on edge, listening, waiting.

"But it can't hurt me," she said, making one last protest.

His answer was uncompromising. "Oh, yes, it can," he said grimly. "It sure as hell can."

It was early afternoon by the time they returned home, bringing more than a dozen books with them. After the library, they'd gone to the occult bookstore, as well, and found a couple of additional volumes.

When Ian climbed out of the Jeep, he stood in his driveway and stared across at Honor's house. Silent, unblinking, motionless, he reminded her of a cat with its eye on a bird, its nose lifted to scent the breeze. He was a hunter.

"Let's get your stuff now," he said abruptly.

Honor was feeling as tired as she had ever felt, and her only desire at the moment was to curl up somewhere and sleep. Anywhere. Even in that damn house she had bought.

"Look," she said. "Why don't I just go home and catch some sleep? I can bring my stuff over later."

"No."

No? He'd spoken that single syllable in that uncompromising way of his, and it suddenly occurred to Honor that of all the things she disliked about this man, this was the one she disliked most.

"Damn it, McLaren, will you quit trying to run my life?"

Turning to face her, he yanked up the loose green surgical shirt and showed her ten inches of taped stiches in his side. "See that?" he said harshly. "It damn well *can* hurt you, and I'll be doubled damned if I'm going to let your stubbornness make you an easy target. We're getting your stuff. Now."

He started to tug the shirt down, but Honor stopped him by touching the skin below the wound with gentle fingertips. At her touch, a tremor passed through him. "Oh, Ian," she said shakily. "What happened?"

"I'll tell you later," he said. "For now, let's just get whatever you need for a couple of days. Now. While it's…sleeping."

"Sleeping?" A chill touched the back of her neck, and goose bumps rose on her arms, despite the day's heavy, suffocating heat. "What do you mean?"

He shook his head. "I meant while it's quiet. It's quiet now." God, he was slipping, slipping badly. He could see it in her eyes. It was almost as if some evil genius were driving him to betray himself.

"How do you know that?"

He looked down into her soft young face, into her concerned, frightened blue eyes, and wondered why he couldn't have been just a normal man. Wondered why he had been so savagely cursed all his days.

"Later," he said. "We're beat. We need to sleep. We can talk about everything later. Let's just get your things."

Something had flickered in his cat-green eyes, something that her heart recognized as anguish. Compassion rose in her and washed away her irritation. "Okay," she said. "Okay. But I don't want you carrying anything, not with those stitches."

He looked down at her, and then, for the first time in years, he laughed. It was a rusty sound, almost unrecognizable, but it lightened the shadows in his eyes. "Lady, you're a born dragon."

She would have bristled, except that she nearly lost her breath at a sudden glimpse of this man as he might have been, given a happier road in life. "I'm a nurse," she managed to say. "And from the look of it, they should have kept you in the hospital overnight."

He shook his head and turned toward her house. "The nice thing about being retired is that the base hospital can't call my commander anymore. They couldn't make me stay."

She could well believe that, Honor thought, following him. She could well believe that.

Chapter Six

Come home, Honor. It's all right. There's nothing in the house to hurt you. It's the man you need to watch out for. He's the one who's threatening you.

She awoke slowly in the early evening, stale air-conditioned air stirring in the room around her. Ian's guest room. The narrow iron cot.

She turned over and drifted, half in and half out of a dream. Her house was welcoming her, making her feel at home. The dark threat was gone, a figment of her imagination. She smiled and snuggled into her pillow, liking the sunny yellow of the kitchen.

She turned to smile at Ian, and her contentment shattered like exploding glass. He held a knife and was moving toward her, and there was murder in his strange green eyes.

Devil's spawn.

She sat up, suddenly cold and very much awake, and clutched the sheets to her.

God! What an awful dream!

Moments later, wrapped in her short cotton robe, she padded barefoot down the hall to take a shower. She needed to shake off the last of the strange dream, and this seemed the best way to do it.

It was certainly getting to her, she thought as she stood under the hot spray and let it beat the tension out of her muscles. She had stopped having nightmares years ago, but now she seemed to be having them almost incessantly.

And maybe, she found herself thinking uneasily, maybe there was something to the dream. Maybe her subconscious was trying to get through to her. Maybe she was looking at things from the wrong perspective.

Back in the cell-like room, she dressed swiftly in white shorts and a red tank top, then sat on the edge of the bed to buckle her sandals. What, she found herself wondering, had *actually* happened?

There had been someone waiting for her when she came home the other night. That much she was sure of. After all, she'd heard something fall. But other than that, what did she have? A feeling that someone was watching? A feeling that someone was in the house?

And what had Ian done, except encourage her in the belief that there was something in her house? He had added to her fear, hadn't he?

Sitting on the edge of the cot in the bare room, she rested her elbows on her knees and wondered what was going on. Was she really feeling something? Or was Ian taking advantage of her suggestibility? Why would he want to do that? What could he possibly hope to get out of this?

Or were they both caught up in some kind of folie à deux, feeding one another's delusions?

But no, she reminded herself. Yesterday, all alone in her house in the late afternoon, when she'd been thinking of nothing but cooking dinner and going to work, she had found her bathroom door open. Had felt the cold touch of something…something *other*.

If that was imagination, she never wanted to imagine anything again. She couldn't blame Ian for that, could she?

Or could she?

Witchcraft and satanism. Some people believed in those things. Believed it was possible to cast spells on other people. To make them see and hear things.

Abomination. Those eyes of his were…strange. Unnatural.

Suddenly shocked by the direction her thoughts were taking, Honor shook her head and stood up. No way. The man had done nothing but try to help her. He was a little strange, to be sure, but strangeness was not a hanging offense. Time to think of something else, she told herself. Time to think about something normal.

Twilight was just beginning to settle over the land when Honor remembered that she hadn't collected her mail. Feeling a little homesick, hoping one of her friends back in Seattle had written, she told Ian she was going out to the mailbox. Even with the fading of the day, the air was still too warm and muggy for comfort. In a little while, though, the breeze would start up, causing the trees to rustle and sway, and the tree frogs would begin their nightly chorus.

Stepping into the road so that she could reach the front of her mailbox, she saw the flattened carapace of an insect that had to be at least ten inches long. Were there really bugs that big around here? The largest she had seen so far were the tree roaches, and they were only a couple of inches at their biggest. Horrified, she stared at the bug and tried to tell herself it was something else.

"Miss Honor?"

Startled, she swung around toward the voice, then smiled as she recognized Orville Sidell, a ten-year-old boy who lived farther up the road, deeper in the woods. He had been one of her first patients, brought in by his older brother and sister after being bitten by a coral snake. She had seen him several times since, and as usual he was wearing only a dusty pair of shorts and a grimy T-shirt. "Hello, Orville. How's your leg?"

"Jes' fine." He held it out briefly for her inspection.

The tissue damage had been minimal, she saw with relief. Only a small pit marked the death of muscle. "That really looks good."

He nodded, then put his bare foot back down in the dust. "I brought you some squirrel."

"Squirrel?"

"Yeah." He brought his hand out from behind his back and held out two dead squirrels. "Shot 'em m'self."

"You did?" Honor had a feeling this wasn't the time for her to react as she would have in Seattle. "You must be a good shot."

Orville nodded. "Ma's got more'n she needs. Said you might like 'em."

Honor looked from him to the pathetic-looking squirrels he dangled by their tails. "For what?"

He grinned suddenly, amused by her stupidity. "Eat 'em, Miss Honor. They're good."

"Oh." She regarded the squirrels uncertainly. "What do they taste like?"

He shrugged. "Like squirrel."

"How do I cook them?"

"Any way you like."

She guessed she was going to have to do this. She certainly didn't want to offend Orville. "Tell you what, Orville. If you would be so kind as to clean them for me, I'll give it a try." She gave him an apologetic smile. "I've never had to skin a squirrel. I wouldn't know where to begin."

"Okay." He started to turn away, apparently satisfied, but then he paused and faced her again. "Miss Honor, my ma says you oughta be careful of that man."

"Which man?"

The boy's brown eyes slid past her. "Him," he said. "The army man."

Once again Honor felt a chill trickle of unease run down her back. "He seems like a perfectly nice man, Orville."

"Ma says he's got the evil eye."

At any other time, under any other circumstances, Honor would have been hard-pressed not to laugh. Right now, all she felt was a crawling sense of unease. "Well, he hasn't done anything to hurt me," she told Orville. "He's been very helpful. You can tell your mother I said that."

Orville simply stared at her, clearly nonplussed.

"Hey, Orville!"

Honor looked down the road and saw Orville's older brother, Jeb, wave the boy over. Jeb had been with Orville the night he came to the emergency room. He was an extremely big, slow-witted man who made a living at manual labor, and there wasn't a doubt in Honor's mind but that he loved his younger brother dearly.

"Comin'!" Orville shouted back. He started to leave, then glanced over his shoulder at Honor. "Ma says the old preacher used to shun him."

"Shun him? Who?"

"The army guy." Then he was off and running, the squirrels dangling from his hand.

Honor stared after them until they disappeared around a bend in the road and were hidden behind the dense foliage. *Shunned*. What on earth had he done to deserve that?

Damn it, now she was going to demand some explanations. He was still avoiding the question of his injuries, with his nose buried in all those books he'd gotten today. Surely she deserved some answers. Surely she deserved to know a little about the man whose roof she was sharing?

Clutching her mail, she turned toward the house and again noticed the huge squashed insect. Why hadn't she stayed in Seattle?

Ian was still seated at his kitchen table, with books spread all around him. Photos purporting to be pictures of apparitions stared up at Honor from several of the opened volumes.

"Find anything?" she asked.

"Plenty, but nothing that looks really useful yet." An hour's nap seemed to have nearly restored him. When he looked up at her, his eyes didn't appear nearly so sunken. "You must be getting hungry. I should make dinner."

"It can wait. How's your side?"

"Sore."

The sudden intensity of his gaze left her wondering if he had somehow sensed her determination to tolerate no further evasions. Feeling nervous, she pulled out a chair facing him and sat. "I've been waiting all day for an explanation," she said, refusing to chicken out, even though he had never looked more forbidding or more terrifying than he did at this moment. "How did you get hurt?"

For a moment, he didn't answer. He stared at her with those odd eyes of his, looking as if he could see past her surface to deeper things. Deeper feelings. "What," he asked, "makes you so sure you're entitled to any explanation at all?"

Honor gasped, as stunned as if she'd been struck. The man was incredible, she found herself thinking. She'd never met anyone like him for sheer, uncompromising, unapologetic rudeness—when he felt like it. Then she got mad. "What makes me think I deserve an explanation? How about you yanking up your shirt earlier to show me twenty or thirty stitches and then telling me that…that thing could hurt me? How's that for a reason?"

He gave an infinitesimal nod, but she was too wound up to register his agreement. "How about the fact that you're insisting I live under your roof? How about the fact that you keep telling me I need to be protected, but you won't tell me what from? How about—"

He laughed. Amazingly, incredibly, astonishingly, he laughed. The sound instantly halted Honor's diatribe, and she stared at him in utter amazement. He looked so…different when he laughed. So attractive. So nice. So warm. So…sexy. So damn irritating.

"What is so funny?" she demanded. "Why are you laughing at me?"

Still grinning, a wonderfully attractive expression on his face, he answered on a chuckle. "I'm not laughing *at* you. You just surprised me. I can't remember the last time anybody yelled at me."

"Well, of course not," she said sharply. "I imagine everyone is too terrified of you."

His smile broadened a shade. "Probably. But you aren't."

The casual statement struck her forcefully, reminding her afresh of how big he was, how powerfully built. A much smaller, weaker man with his Ranger training would be dangerous. A man like Ian McLaren would be lethal with very little effort.

His smile faded, almost as if he had sensed her renewed uneasiness. In the blink of an eye, he once again became the dark monolith she had first met, the extraordinarily powerful, solitary man who needed nothing and no one. The man who wore loneliness like a concealing cloak.

"I'd never hurt you," he said roughly, looking away. "But I can see you're not going to believe that."

"Ian..." She felt the need to say something, but what? From moment to moment, she was constantly unsure what she felt about this man, what she thought of him. Sometimes she longed to reach out and wrap her arms around him in hopes of easing the loneliness she sensed in him. Other times she was unsure she should trust him at all. What did she really know about him, after all?

"I was shot," he said abruptly.

"Shot?" All her other concerns scattered. "How? When? My God, how bad was it?"

"It was just a graze."

She had helped patch together a lot of gunshot wounds in her career; it was an inevitable experience in a city emergency room. She didn't lose her cool over such things.

Except that this time, the man who had been shot was someone she knew. Someone she...cared about. Her stomach twisted, and she pressed her fingers to her mouth, seeking self-control. "Oh, my God," she whispered, knowing too well what could have happened if that bullet had hit him dead-center. "Oh, my God."

"It wasn't that bad," he said, his deep, dark voice pitched soothingly. "Honey, it was just a graze. Not much worse than a cut. I put a pressure bandage on it and drove to the base hospital."

This time she didn't jump all over him for calling her *honey.* Instead she thought of him bandaging his own wound and then driving to the hospital. About what you would expect from a Ranger, she thought with amazing bitterness. An ordinary person would consider it a major achievement to have phoned for help. Not a Ranger. They weren't ordinary mortals. They were superhuman, or they were nothing.

If he'd had to, he probably would have sewed the wound himself. Look at him sitting there, treating it as if it were all in a day's work...which it was, for him, she reminded himself. So he wouldn't want any fussing or concern. He wouldn't want her to reach out....

But somehow she did anyway. Somehow she was bending over him, with her arms wrapped tightly around his broad shoulders and her face pressed to the warm, fragrant curve between his neck and his shoulder.

For an instant, he seemed frozen; then his arm lifted to curl around her waist to make her welcome. He tugged gently and pulled her down so that she was perched on his thigh.

"It's okay," he murmured.

"You could have been killed." She barely whispered the words, hardly daring to voice the possibility. Everything inside her felt as if it were twisted out of shape, as if she were trying to find some kind of equilibrium in a world gone mad.

"But I wasn't." She was wearing her hair down, and of its own accord his hand burrowed into the silky strands. He didn't want to think about how long it had been since he had risked letting a woman come this close. Right now he felt a very normal, very human, need to give in to some very normal human urges. He couldn't, of course, and he wouldn't. But, damn it, he could be forgiven for stealing just a few minutes of warmth.

After a few moments she gave a tremulous sigh and straightened. Looking at that slash of white in his dark hair that must have resulted from an injury, thinking about the scars on his back that spoke of great suffering, she ached for this man. Subjected to an exorcism as a child of six, slapped and shouted at for days. Shunned by his own church. He lived inside a concrete emotional bunker, she thought now. Letting no one come close. How sad. How lonely.

And wasn't she doing the same thing?

Lifting an unsteady hand, she pressed her palm to his cheek, felt the warmth of his skin, the prickle of his stubble. Masculine textures that made her ache deep inside for things lost, for a naïveté that had been stolen from her by deceit. Jerry had crippled her, but this man had come dangerously close to making her forget that.

Something cold seemed to touch the base of her skull, and she shivered. "I'm glad you're okay," she said, then rose from his knee. "Why don't I make supper while you tell me what happened, and why you think the ghost had something to do with you being shot? I mean, ghosts don't carry guns. Do they?"

"No, ghosts don't carry guns." He was perfectly capable of cooking their meal, but he sensed that she needed the activity, so he simply told her where everything was.

A short while later, as she shaped a hamburger patty, she faced him. "What happened last night, Ian?"

Something in his face shut down, and that was when she began to grow distinctly uneasy. Whatever he told her now, she realized, wasn't going to be everything. Not by a long shot. How could she trust him if he was withholding information? But how could she be positive that he was? The chilly touch at the base of her skull returned.

"I was checking out your house last night," Ian said finally. "I...get these feelings sometimes. I've mentioned them before."

He had, so she nodded. She knew about those intuitive feelings; she'd had them all her life, and she knew it didn't pay to ignore them. She just hoped the uneasiness she was feeling right now wasn't intuitive.

Turning, she set the patty down on a plate and started making another one. "What happened?" she repeated. His reluctance to talk wasn't making her feel any better. This man, after all, was the guy who could say no with all the finesse of a sledgehammer. The thought of him tiptoeing around something, anything, wasn't reassuring.

"I kept a key to the new lock I put on your front door," he said flatly.

Honor spun around and stared at him, aghast. "Why?"

"Because, damn it, when you lock everything out, you lock yourself in. If you needed help, how was anyone going to get in? The fire department. EMS. The cops. Think about it."

Slowly, reluctantly, she nodded, remembering a couple in Seattle who had arrived too late in the emergency room, killed by carbon monoxide in their home. The husband had called for help, realizing something was wrong with his wife, but the windows had been covered by iron bars, and the doors had been securely bolted.

By the time rescue personnel had managed to break in, it was too late. "You should have told me."

"You're right. I should have told you." But his expression never changed, and she remembered him telling her that he always did whatever he considered necessary, regardless of what others thought.

"I realize you don't give a damn what I think about anything," she said tautly, "but I would appreciate being informed when you take any action that affects me."

He gave a brief nod that told her nothing, his strange green eyes never wavering from her face.

"So you went into my house last night?" she asked. "Why?"

"To see if I could learn anything about what you've been feeling. What I've felt in there."

"And did you?"

"Yes," he said.

Honor looked down at the hamburger patty she had been making and realized she had squeezed it between her fingers. Did she really want to hear what he had learned last night? The icy touch at the base of her neck grew stronger, and she had the worst urge to flee, to just say to hell with it all, ditch the house and file for bankruptcy.

As soon as she thought it, she felt ashamed. Her dad had raised her to be tougher than that. You didn't run from these things; you faced them. The alternative was being locked in the dark closet of fear. Her father had been right about that, even if his methods had left something to be desired.

"What happened?" she asked finally.

"Just an hour or so before dawn, it came."

It came. The words were like ice water running down her back. "It? You felt it?" *It.* Oh, God, the word gave form to the thing. Made it more than a feeling. Turned it into an entity. A being. *It*.

"It's...pretty hard to describe," he said slowly. "But you felt it, so I guess I don't have to. It...seemed almost to gather itself. Like a storm. As if it's not there all the time and has to be triggered by something."

Honor sank slowly into a chair, the hamburger forgotten in her hand. "It has to be," she said quietly. "Otherwise I'd feel it all the time, and I don't."

He nodded briefly. "That's what happened this morning, anyway. It...gathered, for lack of a better word. The house grew really cold, as if it were sucking all the heat out of the air. All the energy."

Honor felt her scalp prickle as she thought of that cold spot at the foot of the attic stairs. "Oh, boy."

"Anyway, then I felt something from outside."

"Outside?" She stiffened. "You mean there's more than one?"

"No. It was...well, whoever was out there was human. It was no phantom that took a shot at me. But I think he might have been influenced by the thing in your house."

Honor closed her eyes. "Oh, no..." she breathed. "Didn't I tell you I felt like something was trying to get into my head? Didn't I tell you?" Her eyes opened in time to see Ian nod. "So you think this thing influenced somebody to shoot at you. Do you know how crazy that sounds? Why the hell do I believe it? But I do! I do!"

She jumped up and put the squashed hamburger down on the plate in front of her. "It was bad enough when I thought some spook was trying to scare me out of the house, but this is worse. This is incredible. Unbelievable. Guns!"

And if it could influence somebody to shoot at Ian, it could influence Ian.

The thought chilled her to the very bone. She would have given a great deal not to have even thought of the possibility, but now that she had, she couldn't ignore it. And it made the threat so much worse. So very much worse.

Outside, night had descended. Through the window she saw flickers that might be lightning or might be the bombing on the reservation. A hundred yards away was her house, in the possession of some...*thing*. Some evil thing that had tried to hurt Ian. That might well have been trying to kill him.

"What do I do?" The words escaped her as little more than a whisper.

"I'm going to keep reading," Ian answered. "Maybe I can find something. In the meantime, you're safe here with me. Absolutely no one and nothing is going to get to you without going through me first. That much I can guarantee."

She looked down at the raw hamburger meat and felt her stomach twist. But how, she wondered, would it get through him? By killing him?

Or by turning him to its purposes?

It wasn't until much later in the evening, with another thunderstorm breaking over their heads, that Honor recalled what Orville Sidell had told her.

Looking up from the book she was reading, she studied Ian's bowed head in the lamplight. They had moved into his living room, into worn but comfortable overstuffed chairs, and were reading the books he had gotten that day.

So far, all the books had done was give her a much more frightening idea of just what ghosts could do. Poltergeists, it seemed, had occasionally been known to set fires. She *did* have fire insurance, but she wasn't sure she wanted to be sleeping in a house when a ghost started a bonfire. And if it could do that, then it could do other things.

Ian looked up, the lamplight gleaming on his gray streak and glimmering oddly in his eyes. "Problem?" he asked.

"I was just having some unhappy thoughts about the fact that poltergeists have been known to start fires. And I haven't found one useful thing about dealing with them. Everything I've read so far just seems to indicate that these things eventually go away by themselves. The question is whether I can wait that long."

He pointed to the book he held. "This one suggests trying to tell the ghost it's dead."

Honor thought about what she had felt, about what Ian had earlier told her had happened to him. "Great. And hopefully it won't tell somebody to shoot us while we're arguing with it."

A smile cracked the frozen landscape of his face. "There *is* that problem. But a human agent can be locked out."

Instinctively she turned toward the window when a particularly loud crack of thunder startled her. "Yeah," she said after a moment. "And you think it's really going to listen?" Suddenly she wished she had to work tonight. She was off for the next three days, and while ordinarily she thoroughly enjoyed her breaks, this one loomed in front of her seemingly endless. Between ghosts and Ian McLaren, she would rather work the ER during a natural disaster.

"No."

Again that single uncompromising syllable. Honor looked at him. "It won't listen?"

"It didn't feel like a confused soul to 'me. It felt..." He hesitated, clearly reluctant to go on.

"Evil," Honor said. "I know. I felt it." She wrapped her arms around herself, feeling chilled. The wind rattled the rain against the windowpane. "I didn't always believe in evil," she remarked. "It's easy not to believe until you run into it, impossible not to believe once you've seen it."

She glanced at him and found him nodding in agreement. His eyes looked even eerier than usual in the lamplight. "Why were you shunned?" The words were out of her mouth before she was even aware that she was going to speak them. Shock at her own temerity trickled through her. She expected some kind of reaction from him—shock, surprise, anger. Anything. But like the Sphinx, he betrayed nothing.

"What else did Orville tell you?" he asked.

"How did you know it was Orville?"

"I saw you talking with him," he said dryly. "What else did he tell you?"

Honor hesitated only a moment before plunging ahead. They might as well clear the air, she thought. "He said his mother said I ought to avoid you. That's all."

"Annie Sidell." He nodded. "I went to school with her. She was a thorn in my side all along, but that was hardly surprising, considering old Mrs. Gilhooley was her mother. The woman had it in for me."

She studied him in silence, wondering why she had to feel so drawn to someone she wasn't sure she could trust. Wondering why she felt compelled to question him about things that she suspected had scarred him. She couldn't imagine anyone becoming as remote and removed as this man without a damn good reason. People were social animals, and instinct generally led them to reach out. This man must have powerful reasons for being so isolated. So unnatural.

Abomination.

Honor shrugged the cold whisper away as if it were nothing but an annoying insect. Whatever was working on her to drag such words out of her unconscious, she wasn't going to pay any attention to it. Not right now.

"There must," she said finally, "have been more to it than a goat as old as Methuselah."

The silence grew long. Heavy. Rain and wind rattled at the windows, a cold sound.

"There was."

She swung her head around to stare intently at him, having heard the tension in his brief statement. And the way he had spoken those words warned her it was not some minor, long-forgotten transgression. She waited.

With a suddenness that was jarring, he slammed closed the book he held. "I'm getting some coffee," he said roughly. "Want some?"

"Ian…" Surely he wasn't going to leave her dangling without an explanation?

"Look, lady." Suddenly he leaned over her. Loomed over her. She shrank back a little in her chair, unable to look away from his oddly glowing eyes. "You're asking questions about things that happened thirty-five years ago. Things I never talk about." His voice was a thunderous growl. "You're just going to have to let me do this in my own way. In my own time. It's the least you can do when you ask somebody to bare his soul."

"I didn't—"

"Oh, yes, you did," he said, almost savagely, spacing his words emphatically. "I've never told anyone what you're asking me to tell you. Never." Abruptly, he stepped back. "Now, do you want that coffee?"

Stiffly she nodded an affirmative. What, she wondered, had she unleashed? What had she asked? She had known it had to be more than a goat, but she hadn't envisioned anything so awful that he hadn't spoken about it in thirty-five years.

A strong gust of wind splattered rain against the window, and she looked toward it, thinking what a miserable night it had turned into. If she were working, she could have been sure of seeing a number of auto accidents. Right now she wondered if that wouldn't have been easier to face.

What a morbid thought! Dismayed because she ordinarily wasn't in the least morbid, she told herself that the lonely sound of the rain and wind was getting to her. She hadn't really been herself for a couple of days now. Not since the night she had come home to find someone—or something—waiting in her house.

"Here." Ian had come soundlessly into the room, and he was putting her coffee on the table at her elbow before she even heard him. Fresh coffee. Its aroma was homey, welcoming, a marked contrast to the man who had brought it. He returned to his seat in the chair across from her, then put his heels up on the scarred coffee table.

Looking around her now, it suddenly occurred to her that this was probably the same furniture he had grown up with. This room probably hadn't changed at all.

"So you want to know why Mrs. Gilhooley hated me," he said. His voice was low, rough. Reluctant.

"Well, she might have been crazy," Honor said, "but you have to admit, it's rather extreme for an adult to hate a child as much as she must have hated you to accuse you of being possessed."

Ian lifted his mug to his lips, then put it on the table

beside him. "First I was possessed. Later I was a witch. Finally I was—" He broke off. His jaw worked visibly. It was the first genuine sign of distress Honor had ever seen him show. The ache she felt for him deepened, and she wished there were a way to erase bad memories for people. To just take them away and make them vanish.

"What set her off," he said. It was not a question. "Her husband died. I remember it was August. Hot. Nobody had air-conditioning then, and we just endured the heat, the humidity, the bugs. I was just a kid, though, and it didn't bother me too much. When all the adults were indoors, staying as cool as they could, I was usually out playing.

"This one afternoon, I came around the rear of the Gilhooley house and saw old man Gilhooley flat on his back. He'd evidently been on a ladder, and the ladder fell over. I looked up and saw Mrs. Gilhooley standing in the open attic window, looking down. He was dead. I knew that right off. And I knew she had pushed the ladder over."

Honor shivered, seeing the scene so clearly in her mind's eye. "How did you know that? How *could* you know that?"

He ignored the question. "Being only six, I didn't have the sense to keep my mouth shut. I told my parents. I told the policemen who came to investigate. Nobody listened."

He reached for his coffee mug. "Except Mrs. Gilhooley. She listened. It wasn't long after that when she claimed I was possessed."

"But why would anyone listen to her? Why would anyone believe such a thing?"

Thunder rumbled, a deep, low sound. A gust of wind rattled the house.

"Given the beliefs of the church to which both my parents and the Gilhooleys belonged, it wasn't unheard-of. Or even difficult to accept."

"Did your parents believe it?" The ache she felt for him was growing stronger, as she considered how bewildering and frightening all this must have been for a six-year-old boy.

"Of course."

"So they performed an exorcism."

He nodded once, slowly, never taking his eyes from her.

"Didn't that put an end to it?"

"No. I told you, that kind of thing sticks like the odor of skunk. Nobody ever really trusted me after that. I shut up about the old woman killing her husband, but that didn't make her feel any more secure, I guess. She kept muttering about me being unnatural. Demon spawn, she called me." Now he did look away, as if he didn't want her to glimpse the pain in his eyes.

Demon spawn. She had heard that before, Honor thought, as a chill crept down her neck.

"Finally," he said, "her muttering got me shunned by the church members. My parents kept dragging me anyway, probably hoping some kind of sanctity would rub off on me. I don't know. They'd drag me, and then I'd have to sit in a special chair. No one would talk to me or look at me or even come near me. Made it kind of hard to forget what they thought of me."

"How awful," she murmured. She wanted to reach out to him, but she stopped herself. Nothing she could do now would ease the pain of what had happened to him so long ago. "How could your parents do that to you? How could they let you be treated that way? Why didn't they look for another church?"

Slowly he turned his head to look straight at her. "Because they believed it, too."

"My God." She breathed the words, hardly able to conceive of such a thing. "They believed you were— were demon spawn? A devil? Evil?"

He gave a slight nod.

Indignation swept through her, so hot and furious in its strength that she could no longer sit still. Leaping to her feet, she paced the lamplit living room. "That's awful. That's terrible! I can't imagine *any* parent feeling that way about a child. Oh, I know some parents are terrible, but—I can't believe it!"

"You were locked in a closet," he pointed out.

"Yes, but—" She broke off, realizing that his parents had probably justified themselves in exactly the same way her father had. "They did it for my own good."

"Exactly." Ian shook his head. "It didn't do me any good." One corner of his mouth lifted in a faint, wry smile. "About the time I was ten, I quit going to church at all. Nobody could make me. My dad whipped me half to death for it, but I refused to go anymore. I used to slip out of the house before everybody woke up and hide. And I was getting too big for him to force me. Finally he gave up and left me alone. And Mrs. Gilhooley married again and left me alone. For a while."

There was more. She knew there was more, because they still hadn't covered the events the electrician had referred to. So far he had said nothing to explain why he had been accused of witchcraft.

She stopped pacing near the window and looked out at the stormy night. It was so dark outside that she couldn't make out her house, or the trees and moss around it. They might have been alone in the universe, floating endlessly through empty space.

Then she caught sight of a glimmer, high up in the direction of her house, as if a distant light had been reflected on glass. Probably a headlight from the highway, she thought, that had somehow pierced the gloom and rain. As she watched, it flickered and was gone.

Then it appeared again, in the same place. And this time it looked...orange. More like...

Fire.

Chapter Seven

*F*ire.

Almost as soon as she spoke the word, Ian was at her side, looking out the window. He saw it, too, and swore. "Looks like it might be in the back bedroom." But with nothing visible in the darkness except the orange glow, it was impossible to be sure. "I'll check it out."

"I'm going with you."

"No."

She turned and grabbed his arm. "Ian—"

He shook free, glaring at her. "One, if I don't come out of there in ten minutes, I want you to call for help. If you're in there with me, you might get into the same trouble, and then we'd both be done for. Two, this might well be an attempt to get you back there."

Get her back there? "Why? Why would—?"

But he was already heading for the kitchen, so she followed him, trying to reframe her question. She stood back as he bent to the cabinet beneath the sink and pulled out a large fire extinguisher.

"Look," he said as he straightened, his strange eyes as opaque as jade. "Maybe it wants to hurt you. Maybe it just wants to scare you so bad you'll never come back. Maybe it wants to influence you somehow. Damn it, Honor, how would *I* know what it's up to? Just stay clear so it can't succeed!"

Once again she reached out and grabbed his arm, acutely aware of the strength of the muscles beneath her clutching fingers, well aware that he could fling her away with no more difficulty than if she were some troublesome gnat. But he held still beneath her touch, accepting the restraint...for a moment.

"I could say the same for you," she told him. "What if it wants to hurt *you?*"

He stared down at her, not a muscle in his face flickering, not the slightest movement of his eyes betraying his thoughts. "Then it's going to get its chance right now."

Then he was gone, leaving her in the silence of the kitchen. Through the open screen door, she heard the steady hammer of the rain, the low rumble of the thunder, saw the flicker of sheet lightning. The cicadas were quiet for once, and only a few hardy tree frogs kept up their nightly chorus.

Wasn't it only a few nights ago that she had stood in this same kitchen in the dead of night, scared out of her mind, while he went next door to check things out?

Ten minutes, he had said. Ten minutes. Lord, she didn't know if she would be able to stand it that long. Ten minutes was an awful lot of time. Long enough for that fire to get out of control. Long enough for terrible things to happen.

What if it wants to get you over there?

She shuddered and pushed open the screen door to stand on his back porch. Her ears strained for every sound, listening for any warning that Ian was in trouble. Through the rain and the heavy Spanish moss, she could still see the faint orange glow, but not clearly enough to tell if it had spread to any other window. By now Ian must be inside and climbing those stairs.

Ten minutes was too long, surely, for him simply to discover what was wrong. Of course, he meant to put it out if it was a small fire…but how long could that take?

She waited, holding herself so tightly that she was sure she would have bruises on her upper arms from her own fingers. Why would that thing want her back, if it was really trying to drive her away?

What if it was trying to get Ian *over there? Not to hurt him, but to influence him. To make him help get rid of her?*

The thought twisted into her mind as sinuously and smoothly as the serpent must have undulated into Eden. He had said he had gone into her house last night. Had kept a key without telling her—an action that hardly inspired trust, no matter how he explained it. He claimed he had been shot by someone who was influenced by that thing in the house, but how could he know that? He could have been shot by anyone, for any reason.

She glanced again at the luminous dial of her watch and shivered. Six minutes. Four left. She wondered if she could stand it.

What if—? She hated to let her thoughts stray in that direction, but she had been raised to ask tough questions and face unpleasant ideas. What if that thing in the house—she could no longer deny its reality, not after what she had felt yesterday—what if that thing *were* to use Ian against her?

She had wondered before at the way he seemed to be bent on scaring her even more. Now this idea of someone shooting at him because of that *thing*…well, it could have been anyone, for any reason, couldn't it?

Maybe it had only been an accident, someone like Orville out hunting birds or squirrels....

Oh, God, wasn't he ever going to come out of there? She glanced at her watch again and was appalled to realize that only one more minute had passed.

Maybe all this tension was getting to her, affecting her objectivity and ability to judge things. She didn't want to believe such horrible things about Ian. And on the face of it, he had only looked after her, hadn't he? Offered her a place to sleep when she was scared to stay in her own bed, kept her company... Hell, he'd taken her in. How could she even suspect such awful things?

It's foolish to trust unquestioningly.

Well, of course, she thought, as the back of her neck prickled from a cold touch. She wasn't trusting him unquestioningly. She just didn't want to leap to wild conclusions.

Abomination.

She shivered again and glanced at her watch. Eight minutes. A gust of wind blew rain under the porch roof, and she felt the cold spray against her cheek and bare leg. Damn it, where was he?

His own family had thought him unnatural. He had admitted as much. Maybe they'd had a reason. A good reason. And maybe she ought to be a lot more cautious of him.

Suddenly, over the hammering rain and rumble of thunder, she heard rapid footsteps. Moments later Ian trotted up onto the porch. He was soaked to the skin, and his T-shirt and jeans were plastered to him. To every muscular inch of him. Something in Honor responded to all that masculinity, even as she warned herself to be more cautious of him.

"Did you find it?"

He shook his head.

Instinctively she turned toward her house again and tried to pick out the orange glow. It was no longer there. "Then what was it?"

"I don't have any idea." He shook his head sharply and sent water flying. "I went in there expecting just about anything, to tell you the truth. There was nothing. No fire, no spook, nothing."

She faced him. "I didn't imagine it."

"Hell, no. I saw it, too." He reached for the screen door and pulled it open. The springs protested crankily. "Come on. I could use some more coffee. There's sure no point standing out here getting soaked."

But she stayed where she was. She heard the cupboard door slap shut as he put the fire extinguisher away. Then a clink as he set the coffee carafe back on the warming plate.

He was really going to go in, dry off and settle down with a cup of coffee as if nothing had happened!

Making an irritated sound, she turned sharply and stared toward her house again. Something had happened over there, and she couldn't stand not knowing what it was, couldn't stand the feeling that things were happening that were beyond her control. Couldn't stand not knowing how to deal with this threat, whatever it was.

Couldn't stand the idea that something had taken over her house. That some evil had moved in and forced her out.

Why had that light flickered up there? If it was some kind of ghostly manifestation, what had caused it, and why? She definitely had the feeling that it had wanted to draw attention. Hers? Or Ian's?

What had happened while Ian was over there? He'd

seemed awfully quick to deny having found anything, especially when he had been there for nearly ten minutes. It was hard to believe the ghost had manifested some kind of light and he had felt nothing. Not when he claimed to be sensitive to it.

The screen door squeaked, and she swung around, startled. Ian poked his head out. His hair had been toweled, and he had changed into dry jeans and a black T-shirt.

"Why don't you come in?" he asked. "If that thing wants to get our attention again, I'm sure it'll manage."

"You're probaby right about that." After glancing over her shoulder one last time, she moved toward the door.

And wondered if she was stepping inside with the very thing she was trying to evade.

Her malaise lingered all through the evening. Sitting in the living room with Ian, she found herself unable to concentrate on the book in her lap, gruesome and frightening though it was. Her gaze kept straying his way as questions taunted her.

He hadn't told her the entire story of how he had come to be accused of witchcraft. Why not? He knew she wanted to know, and since she was aware of the charge, shouldn't he want to put the record straight? What if there was no way to put it straight? The thought sent another shiver coursing along her spine.

Then there was this business of how he could know that his assailant had been influenced by the entity in her house. How could he claim that, then say he had no idea what the thing might be up to, as he had earlier? It didn't add up.

Nothing added up. Nervous, she rose from her chair and paced to the window again, looking out at the stormy night. From behind her came the sound of a page being turned. One thing she envied him was his evident ability to ignore all unanswered questions and concentrate on finding an answer to the real problem—how to get rid of a ghost. At least, she thought he was concentrating on it.

Maybe he was just sitting there pretending to read?

He spoke unexpectedly, causing her to jump and turn swiftly around. "I don't know how much help these books are going to be. So far, I've found ghosts who don't know they're dead, and ghosts who've left something undone and are hanging around worrying about it. Neither one seems right for your specter."

"Hey, it's not my ghost!"

He surprised her with a real smile, small though it was. "It's your house, and the ghost seems to be attached to it. That gives you proprietary rights."

"No thanks." Again that icy river ran down her spine. She didn't want to own a ghost, and she didn't want to make jokes about what she had sensed over there. She doubted any man could understand her sense of violation at finding her bathroom door open yesterday. At knowing some unseen watcher had invaded her privacy like that.

And then the feeling in her mind of something trying to get inside, of...what? There had been alien touches, of that she was sure. Those words that seemed to pop up out of nowhere sometimes felt as if they had come from outside. And sometimes she could almost have sworn someone else was inside her head, experiencing her thoughts.

She shuddered and kept quiet. Paranoia. Saying things like that out loud was enough to get you committed. But then she thought, no, it wouldn't get her committed. Not here. Not in the company of a man who had already announced that he thought that the thing was able to influence people.

"It keeps trying to get into my head," she said.

"I know. You told me yesterday, at the beach." His expression never changed as he stared at her and waited.

After a moment she decided to plunge ahead and watch his reaction. Certainly something ought to startle him. "Sometimes it feels as if it puts thoughts in my head. Oh, man, does that sound weird!" She was hugging herself again, feeling cold when she really wasn't. And feeling so, so alone. "Other times it feels like somebody's in there just listening. Just...reading my mind."

He looked away, and she figured he was embarrassed by her confession. She gave a little laugh. "Classic schizophrenic delusion."

That brought Ian instantly out of his chair. Before Honor even guessed what he was about to do, he had taken her into his arms and was holding her with surprising gentleness against his hard, broad chest. "No," he said quietly. "Don't even think it. These things that are happening are so far from normal that they seem crazy. But they aren't. I feel it, too."

"You feel like someone's trying to get into your head?"

He hesitated. Too long, she thought, but just as her distrust of him began to revive, he bent his head and kissed her, driving everything else out of her mind.

For a moment, just a brief instant, she resented him for being able to do that to her. Then she gave herself up to the reckless heat he stirred so easily in her, gave herself up to the escape he offered. She'd lived long enough to know that it was highly unlikely she would ever meet another man who could do this to her. Wary as she was of him, she needed his heat. Needed the feelings he stirred in her. Needed to taste the passion she had never before felt.

This time it wasn't quite so explosive, wasn't quite so fast. He held her with such care, as if he were afraid she might shatter. His tongue slipped past her guard easily, but without force, promising soft seduction rather than fury. It was as if he were saying, For this little while, forget. For this little while, don't be afraid.

She let her head sag backward under his gentle assault and let go of every worry, every concern. His tongue stroked hers as if he were thirsty for her, as thirsty for her as she was for him, she admitted. He had cast some kind of spell over her, because despite all her doubts and all her fears, she wanted him past reason. Past caution. Past thought.

His hand slipped slowly upward, finding its way beneath her blouse. At the first touch of his warm fingertips on her soft skin, she shivered in pure pleasure. And arched like a cat being stroked. Ribbons of fire plunged downward to her aching core, and instinctively she pressed closer. Wanting more. Needing more. Forgetting every painful lesson she had ever learned.

Gently, gently, his fingertips stroked across her midriff, as if they enjoyed the warm satiny feel of her. No higher did they climb, though she wanted it and began to will him to move his hand, began to will him to find her breast with those tantalizing, tempting touches. Raising her arms, she looped them around his neck in invitation.

A muffled sound escaped him, rising from deep within. She felt the vibration in his chest, and the sound thrilled her. Then he shifted his hold, turning her a little to the side and bending her over his arm.

Her eyes fluttered open when his mouth left hers, and

she found herself looking straight into his strange green eyes from a distance of only a couple of inches as he bent over her. They glittered almost like polished gems and held her gaze prisoner as his hand, slowly—oh, so slowly!—eased upward.

Honor caught her breath and kept perfectly still as anticipation filled her. No one had ever... Oh, she wanted his touch so badly! Suddenly unable to bear his stare any longer, she turned her face into his shoulder, buried her eyes and her nose in the soft warmth of his T-shirt and filled herself with the good scent of him.

He murmured something rough and sensual right into her ear, sending chills of pleasure racing along her nerves. Then his hand found her, at first with a gentle, almost comforting touch, as if he knew this was new and might scare her.

But it didn't scare her; it electrified her. It was better than her wildest imaginings, and unconsciously she dug her nails into his shoulders, encouraging him.

"Damn," he whispered unsteadily as he squeezed her breast. "Oh, damn."

A helpless moan escaped her. More. She wanted more. Much, much more.

Almost impatiently he found the clasp of her bra and uncovered her. Honor caught her breath, suddenly aware of him, of herself, of all her inadequacies, imagined or real.

But then he smiled at her, right into her eyes, with an expression of such warmth that she never would have imagined this man to be capable of it. "Beautiful," he said roughly. "Perfect."

She squeezed her eyes shut against an almost painful wave of emotion, then shivered with sheer pleasure as he closed his callused palm over her. Slowly, sending exquisite sparks to her core, he rubbed her hardening nipple with his thumb.

And then, utterly depriving her of breath, he bent and drew her nipple into his hot mouth. A low moan of pleasure escaped her, and he made a rough sound in answer as his lips and tongue taught her pleasure beyond her wildest imaginings.

He's seducing you.

The thought penetrated the pleasurable haze of desire like a cold whisper. A minor irritant. Another tug of his mouth on her nipple banished it. Helpless against her own long-denied hungers, she lifted a hand and tunneled her fingers into his soft hair, tugging him closer.

He's manipulating you.

The cold chill of that thought came to her just as his mouth moved to her other breast and spread the growing conflagration. A gasp escaped her, and she arched upward, begging for more. Not caring any longer whether he was using her or pleasing her, not caring about anything except finding the answer to the mystery of her womanhood.

Suddenly she was lying on her back on the couch. Ian knelt beside her, cherishing her with his mouth and hands in ways she had only dreamed of before. She clutched him closer, prepared to surrender everything to the relentless need he was building in her.

Remember Jerry.

In a flash her arousal vanished. Suddenly she was filled with the crawling sense of shame that had been Jerry's legacy to her. The feeling of inadequacy, of downright repulsiveness, he had given her. The fear. The paralyzing fear of a man turning away from her in disgust. Oh, no, what was she doing?

"It's all right, it's all right," Ian murmured thickly.

Lifting his head, he caught her face gently between his hands and looked down at her with eyes made heavy-lidded by passion. "Oh, baby, how could you think such a thing? You're not repulsive. He was the one who was wrong, not you."

Everything inside her stilled, and the chill that washed through her didn't spring from memories. Her heart seemed to stop beating, and the rush of blood in her ears became deafening. And as he stared down at her, his expression slowly changed, too. No longer did he look sleepy and aroused. He looked as he had when she first met him, remote and hard.

"Honor..." His voice trailed off, as if he had no words.

She didn't want words, anyway. It was too late for words. There was only one way to explain what had just happened, because she had never, ever told him about Jerry or the scars from her marriage. Never.

Slowly, afraid that if she moved too fast she might provoke him in some way, she sat up and pulled her blouse over her naked, aching breasts. "I...I think I'll go to bed," she said. She felt exposed, raw, invaded. Violated.

And scared.

How could you hide from a man who read minds?

If he could read her mind, then he could very definitely plant thoughts there, as well.

Huddled beneath the sheets on the narrow cot in Ian's guest room, she tried to organize her thoughts, tried to cope with her feelings, tried to figure out a rational course of action.

Not that anything about this incredible mess was rational. How could you react rationally to things that defied logic? How could you react rationally to things that were...paranormal? Supernatural?

What if there was no ghost in her house? What if all of that had been done by Ian? What if he was responsible for every feeling of being watched, every feeling that someone else was there?

If he was, he could have no innocent motive. He could only intend harm.

She had to get away. But how could she flee him when he could read minds? He must know every thought in her head.

She shuddered and pulled the blanket to her chin. No, she decided, he didn't read every thought in her head. If he did, he wouldn't have time for any thoughts of his own. It must happen sporadically, perhaps unpredictably.

And that gave her a chance to escape.

But first she had to sleep. To lull him. With a skill perfected by years of nursing, she set her internal alarm clock for four in the morning. It was the time when men were at their lowest ebb, least likely to be alert. By then he would consider her asleep for the night. He wouldn't be expecting her to slip away.

The storm had blown over. The night beyond the closed windows was quiet, still, in the predawn darkness. Even the offshore breeze had died.

With her shoes in her hand, her keys and wallet in her pocket, Honor crept down the stairs, taking care to set her foot down at the very edge of each riser so as not to cause a telltale creaking. She had tried, on her way upstairs, to note which steps were noisy, but she was damned now if she could remember which ones they were.

As soon as she got out of here, she was going to get in her car and drive far enough away that she could feel safe from mental eavesdropping and invasive thoughts. Until she felt that her mind was free of violation. Then she was going to try to figure out what in the name of heaven she could do about this mess.

Twice on the stairway she froze, her heart in her throat, thinking she had heard something. Both times the darkness mocked her with perfect silence.

Adrenaline increased her need for oxygen, and she fought to breathe silently when she desperately wanted to pant. Her own heartbeat grew nearly deafening in her ears. Step down. Again. Another step.

Finally she was at the foot of the stairs. A shaft of moonlight poked through the curtains covering the window on the front door and illuminated the hallway. Quietly she inched her way back to the kitchen, wanting to be as far as possible from the stairway, and thus as far as possible from Ian, when she opened that door. The lock was bound to make noise; the screen door certainly did.

Once in the kitchen, she paused, listening, and heard nothing. Finally some deep fear of the evil that had touched her caused her to take a butcher knife from the block on the counter. In case, she told herself. Just in case.

That's right. Protect yourself.

The kind of person who could try to make her believe in ghosts, who could wantonly invade the sanctity of her mind, probably wouldn't hesitate to hurt her.

Don't let him stop you. He intends you harm.

Yes, she thought, opening the door slowly. Obviously he intended her harm. That was very clear now.

Outside, the night held its breath. Only the irritating background chatter of insects disturbed the dark, motionless air. In the pale, watery moonlight, the Spanish moss turned into shadowy giants, looming figures made of living darkness.

Keep moving. You don't want him to find you. He'll hurt you.

She hesitated on the porch step, and something in her squeezed with a tight, dry grief as she thought of what she was losing. All unaware, in the last few days she had given part of her heart to the cold, lonely man she had sensed in him. Even while she had been uneasy about him and his motives, some part of her had yearned toward him. Some part of her had become his.

Now all that was hopeless. Just another source of pain. But maybe she was wrong about him....

No! He violated your mind. Invaded the most private place you have. Exposed your secrets.

Her hand tightened on the knife handle, and she stepped off the porch. She had to get away. Had to.

By the time she reached the end of the holly hedge that separated their yards, she was sure she was going to make it. Relief eased the rapid pace of her heart. Now all she had to do was get into her car and drive into town. She would be free, and she would be able to think, able to come up with some kind of plan.

"Going somewhere?"

Gasping, she whirled around and came face-to-face with Ian. The moonlight caught him from the side and made his face look like a carved mask, made his eyes glitter.

"Damn it, Honor," he said, "you could get hurt out here! I just got shot last night!"

He reached out toward her. She panicked.

Protect yourself! Stop him!

Instinctively, without conscious thought, she raised

the ten-inch butcher knife in self-defense. "Stay away!" she gasped. "Stay back!"

But he shook his head and continued to reach for her. With an agonized cry, she lunged at him with the knife.

What came next happened in a blur, so fast that the next thing she knew she was being held hard against him, her hands firmly captured behind her back. The knife was gone. For a long moment she strained against his hold, trying to break away, panting almost wildly. He held her effortlessly, painlessly, moving with her struggles and preventing her escape.

And then realization washed through her in a tide so cold she felt chilled to the bone. She had tried to hurt him. Had tried to stab him. Oh, God, she was losing her mind!

"Shh..." he said, shifting his hold to a gentler one as he felt her sag in shock. "Easy, honey. Shh... It's okay."

"Oh, God," she whispered into the soft cotton of his T-shirt. "What was I doing?" His heart was racing as hard as hers, she realized. Adrenaline filled them both, unsatisfied by the abortive fight. She tipped her head back and looked up at him, tangled feelings pulling her in a dozen directions.

Passion, never far from fear, surged suddenly. She felt it as an almost physical change in the atmosphere, and then his mouth was on hers, his tongue plundering her hot depths as if treasure were hidden there. As hungry as he, wild with the need for something human and warm, she tugged her hands free of his grip and dug her fingers into the hard muscles of his upper arms. Heat. She needed his heat, needed his hunger, needed to find reality in his strength and his passion.

Suddenly he tore his mouth from hers. Another gasp escaped her as he effortlessly lifted her into his arms, reminding her of his vast strength, reminding her that he could probably snap her in two with his bare hands. But his hands, though hard as steel, didn't hurt her. They touched her flesh with exquisite care.

He carried her back to the house with long, impatient strides. His breathing never even deepened as he mounted the stairs with her in his arms. There wasn't a doubt in her mind as to what was coming now. The fires they had ignited between them had never been doused, and fear and anger had fueled the blaze with adrenaline.

Nor could the primitive cavewoman he had first awakened in her protest. Only a couple of days ago she had wanted to lie on the hard ground and take him into her without thought, without caring, without affection. Now, however much she distrusted him, she cared, and caring made the need so much more intense. So much more undeniable.

He set her down on his bed, an iron cot hardly wide enough for two. It didn't matter. Lying over her, his leg pinning hers, his arms holding her tight, he plundered her mouth with a kiss so hungry, so needful, that it forced everything else from her mind. She became woman at her most basic.

There was little tenderness, a lot of eagerness and some roughness. He stripped her clothes and his own away with equal impatience and molded her flesh with touches that just missed being painful. She didn't care. How could she care when this man made her feel so *wanted*? Oh, how she needed to be wanted!

His mouth closed on her nipple, sending spears of longing straight to her womb. His hand stroked the smooth skin of her hip, and then dived impatiently between her thighs, seeking her heat, her moisture, her life-giving core. Wildly she arched, an inarticulate cry escaping her. She was caught in a storm, with no desire to escape. Whatever he took was rightfully his.

Raising his head, he muttered guttural words of encouragement as his touch lifted her higher and higher. Too fast, too fast, she thought dizzily, and then stopped worrying as he took her closer and closer to the brink she dimly sensed was waiting.

"So sweet," he growled in her ear, sending another river of excitement pouring through her. "Come on, honey. That's the way."

When her hands clawed for purchase, tearing at the sheets and him, he guided them up to the headboard and wrapped them around the iron spindles. "Hang on," he said roughly, and settled between her legs.

Gasping for air, she clung to the headboard and looked up at him from eyes that were dark with arousal. He loomed over her in the dark, so huge, so powerful, so strong. She'd never thought, never dreamed, never imagined, that anything could be so overwhelming. Every cell in her body was begging for him, for completion, for the answer to the screaming ache he had awakened in her.

He touched her. Gently, finding that delicate knot of nerves, he lifted her higher and higher until she hung suspended in exquisite agony and nearly screamed his name.

"Now!" he said hoarsely. Slipping an arm beneath her hips, he lifted her to him and took her in one swift, deep thrust.

If there was any pain, she was past noticing it. The precipice was close, so close, and his every movement drove her nearer the edge. Letting go of the headboard, she grabbed his shoulders, digging her fingers into smooth, muscled flesh, drawing him down, needing his weight as she had never needed anything. Needing him.

"Let it happen," he growled in her ear. "Damn it, Honor, let go!" and then, with a single long, deep, twisting thrust of his hips, he pushed her over the edge.

And moments later, his face contorting, he arched into her and followed her over.

It occurred to her that she could curl up into a tight little ball and pretend to be catatonic. She could deny all knowledge of the woman who had just lain beneath this man and acted like a wild thing. She could fake a multiple personality and blame the last fifteen minutes on someone else.

It had been hot, swift, and very, very basic. Nothing romantic about it. Sighing, she turned onto her side and buried her face in his warm shoulder and decided not to deny anything. Her mind could never have conceived of such a thing, but now that it had happened, she admitted she wouldn't have missed it for anything.

He drew her closer, squeezing her. "You okay?" He sounded gruff.

"I'm fine."

"Good. I don't usually come on like gangbusters, but…"

She covered his mouth with her hand. "If you apologize, I'll get embarrassed. If you don't mind, I'd prefer to skip that part."

A low rumble of laughter rose in him, and then he astonished her by rolling to his feet and sweeping her up into his arms. The first time he had picked her up with such ease, she had been uncomfortably aware of how dangerous his strength could be. This time she felt confident that he wouldn't use it against her.

At least not right now.

In the bathroom, he set her on her feet and bent over

to turn on the shower. Taking the opportunity to look at him in the light, she trailed her gaze from his broad shoulders to his narrow waist and hips...and saw blood. As a nurse, she knew about these things, knew that she certainly shouldn't be embarrassed by anything so perfectly normal and natural—but she was anyway. Somehow it was different when it was her blood. She closed her eyes.

"You should have told me," he murmured huskily. "I could have hurt you."

"I thought you could read my mind," she said weakly, grabbing his shoulders as he lifted her into the shower.

"Only when you broadcast at top volume. Never purposely. We'll talk about that later, I promise."

Slowly she opened her eyes and looked right up into his. At this moment they looked almost...tender. His hands moved over her carefully, soaping her with exquisite care. Her heartbeat grew heavy, and she drew a deep breath.

"Is that why you ran?" he asked. His hand slipped between her legs, washing her oh-so-carefully.

"Is this an interrogation technique?" She gasped and dug her fingers into his powerful shoulders. "When you knew how I felt—" She broke off abruptly, unable to continue. "I don't know exactly what happened. When you knew that, I thought...well, I thought you might be responsible for that feeling I get sometimes. Like someone is in my mind."

His eyes darkened, and he turned her suddenly so that the shower spray rinsed her.

"Come with me," he said harshly. "Let's get out of here. Let's go somewhere away from that...thing."

She hesitated, remembering her fear of him and the fact that he had looked into her mind.

"I promise I'll tell you everything," he said. "I swear. Let's just get out of here. Come with me."

Turning her head, she looked up at him, and some part of her realized that she was committed to riding this train to the end of the line, wherever that might be.

"All right," she said. And acknowledged that if Ian McLaren was the villain, she was going to curl up and die.

Chapter Eight

They drove past Fort Walton Beach and nearly to Pensacola before Ian pulled over at a motel and took a room. One room.

The sun was up, and the curtain was open. Ian stood in a puddle of golden light as Honor looked around and finally sank onto the edge of one of the double beds.

"I'll go rustle up some breakfast for us," he said. "And then we'll talk."

She nodded. "How far do you have to go to escape a ghost?"

"Damned if I know." He came over and squatted before her, taking one of her hands. "If you get any urges to run, or anything like that, fight them."

She stared at him, absorbing the meaning of his words. "You...you think that when I...that I..."

He squeezed her hand. "You don't strike me as the kind of person who reaches for a knife too readily. And you definitely don't strike me as the kind who would lunge at me with one. It would be more like you to try to evade me."

She nodded slowly. "I know. I can't believe I did that.

I can't believe that was *me*. It was like being caught in a dream of some kind. A bad dream."

And maybe that was exactly what it had been. Alone again while Ian went out to find some food for them, she curled up tiredly on the bed and thought about what had happened. She still didn't entirely trust him, but she no longer felt as endangered as she had last night.

And that was the creepy thing, she thought. That *thing* had affected her mind. Had made her feel emotions that perhaps hadn't been entirely her own. In retrospect, now that she was free of the dark feelings that had haunted her last night, she found herself far more disturbed by the thought that the ghost might have planted thoughts in her head than by the idea that Ian had read her mind. It was far, far less distressing to have someone know what she was thinking than to have someone—or some*thing*—make her think things.

A sudden shiver passed through her, and she curled up into a tight ball. There was no doubt that she had been manipulated. No doubt. And the thought was horrifying. The question now was who, or what, had done it?

"Are you reading my mind right now?" Honor asked him while they ate eggs and biscuits and drank hot coffee at the small table by the window.

"No." Ian put down his plastic fork and leaned back in his chair, looking at her. "I never did it purposely. Never. But sometimes…it's as if you broadcast. Or shout. It's impossible not to hear."

"*Could* you do it on purpose?"

"Yes."

"Damn," she said, putting down her coffee. "I hate the way you do that."

"Do what?"

"Those single unvarnished syllables. No. Yes. Either way, it drives me crazy. Elaborate, why don't you?"

He almost smiled. She caught the glimmer of it in his eyes. "Yes, I can sometimes read minds on purpose. It's something I avoid doing, for obvious reasons."

She shook her head. "Not so obvious to me. And what do you mean, *sometimes* you can do it on purpose?"

He really didn't want to discuss this. It was apparent in the way he turned his head to one side and fiddled with a plastic spoon.

"It's a wild talent," he said finally, his voice rusty with suppressed feelings. "When I was little, it just happened sometimes. It wasn't something I did consciously, or that I was actually aware of doing. I think the first time I knew there was something different about me was when Mrs. Gilhooley killed her husband."

He tilted his head back and closed his eyes, and there was something about the way he did it that told Honor how difficult it was for him to remember these things.

"I *saw* it," he said after a moment. "I saw it in her mind, just as she saw it standing at the attic window. I saw it from inside her, saw her push the ladder away from the wall. She pushed hard. Really hard. It was no accident."

Her scalp prickled, but then, almost before she thought about how creepy that was, she thought how terrifying it must have been for a six-year-old boy to witness. Worse, to witness it from inside the head of the murderess.

"I remember…I remember how scared I was when no one believed me, because I knew Mrs. Gilhooley was furious with me and was planning to get even. I had nightmares about it for weeks."

Imagine, she thought, how terrifying it must have been for a six-year-old boy to know such things. To know that someone capable of murder wanted to get even with him.

"How," she asked, "did you ever stand it?"

He shrugged slightly. "You get through things because there's no alternative."

It was as if he had spread out his life before her and let her see the gray, bleak world in which he had lived. You get through things because there's no alternative. She had felt like that at times. Occasionally there was no other way to feel. But she had the sense that this man had lived his *entire* life that way, and sadness tightened her throat.

"Was this, um, before or after the goat?" she asked, hoping he didn't notice how her voice had thickened.

"Before. The goat was the last straw, I guess. My memory of events isn't too clear, because I was so young, and because I wasn't part of a lot of it. I don't know what she did, what she said or why she was believed. All I know is, not too long after the goat, they tried exorcism on me."

Again she felt the impulse to reach out, but she stifled it. He kept evading her gaze, as if he were afraid she might read emotion in his eyes. He would hardly appreciate her touch, or her overt sympathy.

"Anyway," he continued after a moment, "after three or four days, the preacher decided the exorcism was a success. After that I screwed up a few more times. I just...sometimes I just knew what people were thinking. And I was young enough not to know how to conceal the knowledge. I slipped. Again and again. After a while, I was shunning other people as much as they were shunning me."

He rose from his chair and went to stand at the window, looking out at the sun-drenched day, as if the light could drive away the darkness inside him. He shoved his hands into the back pockets of his jeans, and for a long time he didn't speak.

"It was…like it was with you," he said eventually. "I slipped. I don't know if you can understand, but for me it's the same as hearing you say something. I react to it in the same way, and even if I'm on guard, sooner or later I say something or do something that reveals the fact that I know something the other person doesn't think I should. It's just about impossible in retrospect for me to distinguish knowledge gained one way from knowledge gained the other. So I slip. Or I get involved so deeply in what's happening that I slip. And nobody on earth likes to be around a telepath."

He was silent for so long that Honor felt he was waiting for some kind of response from her. She wasn't sure what she felt about what he was telling her. He was a telepath. An exceptional one, to judge by what he was telling her. And, yes, it was unnerving to have someone read your mind. She wasn't sure she liked the idea at all.

But something else had also gotten into her mind. Something evil. And that was worse by far. Shuddering inwardly, she shook away the memory of last night and tried to focus on Ian. He needed something from her right now, and she wasn't sure what it was. Or even if she could give it.

Finally he spoke again, his voice low, tense. "The business about the witchcraft, well—" He broke off abruptly and shook his head. Honor couldn't see his face, but she didn't need to. The difficulty of this for him was apparent in his tension, in his voice.

"I was seventeen," he said flatly. "Mrs. Gilhooley had two daughters. Annie—Orville's mother—and Maggie. Maggie was fifteen. She...got herself pregnant by... um...by her stepfather, Bill Gilhooley."

"Mrs. Gilhooley remarried?"

"Yes. I guess I forgot to tell you that. She married Bill Gilhooley about eight months after she buried her first husband. Anyhow, Maggie claimed I was the kid's father. Said I'd, uh, witched her and had my way with her."

"Oh, my God!" Honor scarcely breathed the words, horrified and aching for him. Such terrible, terrible things to have lived through. "Nobody believed that, surely!"

He gave a snort, but he didn't look at her. "Oh, yeah, lots of people believed it, even when it was proved that I was somewhere else the night she claimed all this happened. The cops investigated, but they didn't bring any charges, because there wasn't any evidence. Some folks believe that was witchcraft, too. Then...then one night Maggie called the cops and said she'd taken poison, and that she didn't want to die with a guilty conscience. Said I hadn't touched her. She died and...everybody believed I'd done that, too.

"So I left. Joined the army and left."

And left the human race, too, Honor thought, staring at his unyielding back. How awful. How unspeakable. No longer restraining the impulse, she rose and went to him, touching him gently on the arm, aware that he might reject her touch.

But he turned suddenly and faced her, and there were no secrets left. There, in the anguish stamped on his face, in the redness of eyes that could not weep, she saw just what it had cost him to tell her. Just how deep his scars were.

"Oh, Ian," she whispered on a broken breath. Stepping toward him, she wrapped her arms around his waist and held him close.

At first he remained rigid and unyielding, as if he were resisting her concern with all his might. As if he had forgotten how to open himself in even this small way. But then, with jerky reluctance, he wound his arms around her and squeezed her closer.

For a long time neither of them spoke or moved. Honor absorbed all that he had told her and suspected that he was reconstructing the inner walls behind which he had probably entombed all those memories. How awful, she thought. It was a miracle he had survived such a childhood.

"Come on," he said after a while, his voice calm and expressionless once more. "You haven't finished your breakfast, and you need to get some sleep before we go back."

She tilted her head and looked up at him. "What are we going to do?" As soon as she spoke the question, she wished she hadn't because there didn't seem to be any answer.

He didn't answer, just shook his head. "Eat," he said. "Then sleep. When we've had some rest, we'll brainstorm."

Honor had fallen asleep almost as soon as her head touched the pillow. Ian, cursed with insomnia, lay wide awake in the next bed, his hands clasped behind his head.

Years ago he had done his best to bury his abominable talent, and until a few days ago he had succeeded, relatively speaking. It was possible for any skill to atrophy through lack of use. His telepathy might have been born of genetics, but it was also a skill that could atrophy.

And it had. But not nearly as much as he had thought, and he was recovering it more quickly than he would have dreamed possible. He hadn't tried to read Honor's mind—he'd been telling the absolute truth about that—but it was getting so he was receiving flashes from her all the time. Never before in his life had that happened with anyone to this extent. It made him uneasy.

Even now, the flashes of her dreams were dancing around the edges of his mind. Just random snatches that told him she was having a mild nightmare about some inchoate threat. If she started to get really frightened, he would wake her…or would that be an invasion of her privacy?

The thought had troubled him ever since he'd grown old enough to be concerned with such things. If he couldn't help doing it, how could it be an invasion? But perhaps he should leave the illusion of privacy intact, for the sake of the person he was eavesdropping on?

He didn't know, and he wasn't sure he even cared anymore. In his adult life, he'd had a couple of intimate relationships. Each time he had carefully chosen a woman in uniform, one who would understand the demands of his job, the fact that he might leave without warning and offer no explanations when he returned. Someone with whom the army provided enough impersonal topics of conversation that he could avoid getting too intimate, too involved.

And each time, eventually, he had slipped in a way they could not ignore. Each time he had seen horror in their eyes. Uneasiness. Condemnation. He was an abomination.

Mrs. Gilhooley had first called him that, and the word had been echoed by many in his childhood. Away from the atmosphere of his parents' church, the epithet had changed, but not its meaning. *Weird* was the word he'd heard most often. *Creepy* was another one.

Lifting his head a little, he looked over at Honor. She was still dreaming, and a little more anxious now. He wondered how long it would be before she turned from him in horror again. She had last night. He'd known the instant when she realized that he had looked into her mind. He'd felt her horror and fear.

That seemed to have faded considerably since their lovemaking, but he never for an instant doubted it would return. He'd grown up hearing that he was some kind of unnatural genetic accident. A mutation. An abomination.

And nothing in his life since had convinced him that he wasn't.

Honor woke slowly, feeling more comfortable than she had in a long time. It was as if she had reached some kind of resolution in her sleep, as if some internal equilibrium had finally been established. Or maybe, she thought drowsily, it was just a protective reaction to all the stress of the past few days. At the moment, she didn't care. It was enough that, for right now, the tension had let go.

For now the looming black shadow was gone.

She opened her eyes and looked straight into Ian's cat-green ones. He was on the next bed, just three feet away, but suddenly Honor felt he wasn't close enough. She wanted him here, beside her. Touching her. Exploring some of the incredible possibilities he had opened up for her last night, in those all-too-brief moments when they had lost control together. It was as if some fire in her had been ignited last night and only slightly damped down by fulfillment. As if a craving had been planted in her, a craving that could never quite be satisfied.

He saw it. Read it. Perceived the yearning, however it was that he did such things. And this time she didn't mind. There was only a momentary uneasiness that quickly fled.

"Yeah," he said, and sat up. Crossing his arms before him, he tugged his olive T-shirt over his head and bared his chest. "I hear you," he said roughly. "I feel you. I've never been so in tune with anybody in my life. I don't know if this is good or bad, but I'm through pretending it isn't happening. This is the way I am, lady. If you can't handle it, let's find out now."

He stood and unbuttoned his jeans, never turning away, just watching her steadily, waiting for some objection. She didn't object. Instead, she held her breath as expectancy grew heavy at her core. He shoved his jeans and briefs down together and kicked them aside. Then he stood there and looked down at her, waiting. He was completely exposed to her, completely vulnerable to whatever she might say or do to him. He was making himself as vulnerable to her as she felt to him. As vulnerable as he could make himself. Her throat tightened at the understanding.

Whatever her mind might be broadcasting to him, she realized, he was going to wait for her to say yes or no. He understood that her desire for him might not be something she wanted to acknowledge or give in to. He was granting her the right to decide, regardless of what she was thinking and feeling. And that eased her discomfort a little more.

And, oh, he was magnificent! Honed to a peak of physical perfection in every respect. And so perfectly male. Slowly she lifted her arms and reached for him.

He sank down beside her on the bed and wrapped her in his arms, drawing her flush against him. The layers of her clothing were only a small impediment as she felt the strength of sinew and muscle against her.

"I can hear you," he murmured roughly, touching her tousled hair. "I can feel what you want. Do you want me to pay attention? Or do you want me to try to ignore it?"

Her breath caught a little, and she gave a moment's serious thought to the degree of intimacy he was talking about. Making up her mind proved surprisingly easy. "Listen," she said. "You're right. If I can't handle it, let's find out now."

He nodded and closed his eyes. For a moment her heart stopped beating as she realized he was listening to what was going on inside her, to her scattered thoughts and powerful yearnings. To every barely formed desire.

And then he caught her chin gently in his hand and took her mouth in a breath-stealing, soul-searing kiss. His tongue plunged deeply, roughly, coaxing hers into erotic play. And, as always, just his kiss was enough to ignite her smoldering hunger.

He broke away from her mouth long enough to tug away her shirt and shorts, just long enough to pull away her bra and panties. Then he rolled half over her, pinning her to the bed with a thigh between her legs, and his chest against her aching breasts.

And then he caught her face between his hands and stole her breath by the simple act of whispering her name as if it were torn from the depths of his being.

"Honor..."

Her eyes fluttered open, and she gazed into the depths of his. And saw into his soul. Saw loneliness. Terrible, terrible loneliness. And a yearning. White heat. Hunger.

"Touch me," he whispered. "I need…"

She understood, though she didn't know how. Even as her own hungers made her restless, she felt his needs in her heart. Touch him. He hadn't been touched in so long, hadn't allowed himself even that very human contact. He had held himself aloof, and now he was asking her to shatter his isolation. She spared one last hope that this wouldn't prove to be the biggest mistake of both their lives.

Then she gave herself up to the blossoming heat and touched him. Her hands stroked down his shoulders to the small of his back, enjoying the incredible smoothness of his warm skin, thrilling to the way he shuddered at her touch. Then her hands traveled lower, finding his muscular buttocks and instinctively digging her fingers in.

Finally, driven by a restless hunger and a need to possess this man in whatever way he would permit, she shoved gently, urging him onto his back. Without a murmur, he rolled over, offering himself to her eyes and hands.

There was something incredibly seductive about holding a man like this captive to her hands, her whims. Something even more seductive about the feel of steely muscles bunching beneath her palms as she swept them over him. Something thrilling about the restless, helpless movements he made in response to her touch and his rising heat.

Slipping her hand downward, she skipped over his silky length to tender, delicate, private places. When she cupped him, he shuddered and went perfectly still, drawn taut as a bowstring. The man who seldom suffered another to touch him now permitted her to trespass. Needing her touch more than he needed safety. Trusting her to do no harm.

The weight of him filled her palm, a promise of life, strength and virility. His submission to her touches was the most erotic experience of her life, and her own body responded with a flash of heat and dampness. Licking her lips, breathing raggedly, she ran her fingers teasingly up his length.

He groaned and was suddenly galvanized. Reaching for her, he turned her onto her back, lying over her and driving his tongue into her mouth again. He found her breast with his hand, kneading fire into her every cell. Rivers of burning lava poured through her, causing her to arch upward against him and clamp her thighs around his. She heard herself moan his name, heard him groan in response. She needed more. More. Much more.

And he knew it. Dimly she was aware that his hands and mouth moved to answer her every wish, her every ache, her every desire, no matter how fleeting or un-formed. From her mind he took the least of her impulses and wove them into an erotic fantasy around her, at once satisfying her and deepening her need.

And somehow, as he answered her every whim, she felt the longing in him, the need to be cherished in return. His life had been so lonely, so empty, and for so long he had been on the outside, held at a distance by hatred and fear.

Tears prickled in her eyes even as her body arched upward in passion and begged him to finish it. Even as she reached for the sunburst within, she reached out to wrap him in the first human warmth he had known since childhood. With arms and legs she surrounded him and tried to shelter him, with heart and soul she yearned to give him ease.

And he felt it. A great shudder tore through him, and he opened his eyes, hiding nothing from her, not the shimmer of unshed tears, not the agonizing need for acceptance. He kept them open as he settled between her legs and slowly drove his flesh into her, claiming her body with his.

And when he was buried deeply in her warmth, he cradled her face gently in his hands and gave her a tender, almost reverent kiss. Then, with slow, deep, satisfying thrusts of his hips, he carried them both up and over.

Afterward she wondered how she could ever have been so naive as to think anything would change. Ian stayed beside her, holding her while the cool air dried their damp skin, but he had withdrawn in another way. He had let her see his vulnerability, had let her glimpse the lonely man who yearned to belong to someone, and then he had pulled back inside himself, as if he really didn't care at all.

Unconsciously sighing, she tunneled her fingers through the soft, dark hair on his chest and savored the warm skin beneath. Maybe, she thought, he was feeling uncertain because he had revealed so much and wasn't sure how she would react. Whether she might use it in some way. He had said, after all, that he couldn't read every thought in her head. Maybe he had no idea what she was thinking right now.

And maybe she owed him some of the same honesty he had given her. He had revealed his past at her insistence, had exposed painful wounds to her. Didn't she owe him the same trust in return? A secret for a secret, so that no one felt at a disadvantage?

"Ian?"

"Mmm?" The sound was a deep rumble in his chest. She loved the way his low voice vibrated inside him. It was one of the many very masculine things about him, things that affected her in ways that were hard to explain, but that drew her to him.

"Are you reading my thoughts right now?"

"No."

No. That damn word again. "Not at all?"

"Not a thing. It's not constant, not infallible, and it sure as hell isn't reliable. You're a closed book right now. Completely private."

And maybe that was part of his problem, she thought. She was closed to him, and he couldn't tell what she thought and felt about what had just happened. About him.

Tilting her head back, she looked up at him. "We're going to need to discuss that thing in my house before we go back."

He nodded, looking watchful. That wariness hurt her a little, after all that had just happened between them, but she understood it now that she knew about his past. And the best way to deal with that was to tell him something equally private about herself and her past. To offer him her emotional vulnerability.

"Do—do you remember last night?" she asked, her mouth going dry and her voice growing a little unsteady. God, this was hard! "When...I was afraid I was repulsive, and you said I wasn't?"

"Yes."

She couldn't force herself to look at him. "Do you know why I felt that way? Or did you just pick up on the feeling?"

"Just the feeling." He shifted his hold on her, and then astonished her by tucking her closer and stroking her back soothingly. "Who made you feel that way? Tell me what happened."

"I got married when I was eighteen." Her heart was

beating a nervous, rapid tattoo, and she was sure he must be able to hear it. "My...Jerry was a really nice guy, and I think he was just seriously confused. I honestly don't think he meant to hurt me. It's just that... well, he was homosexual. And...he couldn't have sex with me. So I—" Her voice broke, and she couldn't continue.

"Got to feeling inadequate and repulsive," he finished for her. "Got to feeling maybe you were responsible for his problem."

Slowly she lifted her gaze to his face, and she was astonished by the incredible amount of understanding there.

"It's okay," he said. "You're not repulsive. You've been driving me out of my mind since I first laid eyes on you. And now that I've got you right where I want you, I think I'll take advantage of you one more time."

The look in his eyes right then seemed to reach deep inside her and untie some old, aching knot. Free of its constriction, she felt as if she could draw her first unfettered breath in years.

They showered, dressed and went looking for a restaurant for dinner. They'd spent the entire afternoon making love, talking little, but as evening approached, they both knew they were going to have to face the horror lurking at home. The interlude was over.

And with the return of reality came the return of Honor's uneasiness. What did she really know about this man, except that he had had an unfortunate childhood, and that he had taken her to the moon, proving that all those romantic old songs weren't lies?

But he had distanced himself again, almost as if his earlier exposure of himself and his feelings had left him raw and unable to bear any closeness. What if he had only used her? What if she had just been convenient?

The restaurant he selected served everything from steak to seafood casserole. When they had ordered, he turned his strange green eyes on her. "We have to talk about what we're going to do. If it could manipulate someone into shooting at me, and you into trying to stab me, there's no telling what else it can do."

Just like that, the last lingering glow from the afternoon was gone. Honor leaned forward, resting her forearms on the table, and absently drew a pattern on the Formica with her fingertip. "I don't see what we *can* do, to tell you the truth. You didn't find anything useful in those books, did you?"

"Actually, I think I did, indirectly. After reading about all those lost ladies and murder victims and all the rest of it, it occurred to me that most of them had one thing in common—unfinished business. If we can figure out what your ghost—"

"It's not my ghost," Honor told him, suppressing an unhappy shudder. "God, I wish you wouldn't keep saying that. It makes me feel…cold. Like someone walked on my grave."

"Okay." He gave a little shrug. "*The* ghost. We need to figure out what's holding the ghost here."

"Of course!" Honor couldn't keep the sarcasm out of her voice. "Just walk up and ask it, right? I'm sure it'll sit down with us and explain…" Her voice trailed off as understanding struck. "No," she said hoarsely. "You can't. I won't let you. That thing could hurt you. It could get into your mind and do terrible things. Ian, no!"

He reached across the table and captured one of her hands with his. "What's the alternative?" he demanded quietly. "You can't live in that house. You can't afford to live anywhere else, and even if you stay with me, you're obviously at risk, to judge by what happened last night."

She wanted to look away from his eerie, haunting gaze, but she couldn't. A small shiver passed through her, and she felt her fingers return his clasp. As if she trusted him, even though right now, to be truthful, she wasn't sure she did.

"Honor, we've got to get rid of that thing."

She nodded. "I know." There didn't seem to be any alternative. "But, Ian, that…that thing has twice caused someone to try to hurt you. What makes you think you can just open your mind to it and come away unscathed? What if it provokes *you* into hurting someone? What if it turns *you* into a criminal? People could get hurt, and you could wind up in prison for the rest of your life!"

Something in his gaze grew chilly and remote. He had gone away to some place so deep inside himself that she was almost sure he had forgotten where they were. Had forgotten he was not alone. And then, after a long moment, his green eyes focused on her, and he spoke, his voice low, intense.

"No one can control me," he said levelly. "It's been tried by the masters. I don't break, and I don't kneel."

Hell looked out of his eyes then, just a glimpse of the anguish of the damned, before he turned away and leaned back to allow the waiter to serve them.

When the waiter left, Ian faced her again and held her gaze unwaveringly. "Trust me," he said quietly. "In this, just trust me."

Famous last words, she thought grimly, and looked down at her plate of steamed oysters. "I don't know if I can," she said finally. "I honestly don't know if I can."

* * *

Another storm was gathering as they drove east toward home. Honor didn't remember this much rain from her years here as a child, and she commented on it.

"Late afternoon thunderstorms frequently blow up over the Gulf and move inland at this time of year," he answered. "It'll get better."

Leaning her cheek against the headrest, she watched him drive and thought about all that had occurred between them in the past twenty-four hours. Part of her desperately wished she could savor the change in her, practice her wiles and give herself up to the wonder of having Ian McLaren for a lover. Another part of her, though, whispered warnings and cautions, reminding her that she certainly ought to know by now that very little was what it appeared to be.

"When do you go back to work?" he asked.

"Thursday morning." Two days.

"That'll give us time to move whatever else you might need over to my place. In addition to what you brought yesterday."

She stiffened a little, not sure what he meant and how she should react. He turned and looked at her from those incredible eyes of his, and a faint smile curved one corner of his mouth. She realized with a twinge of discomfort that he was hearing her thoughts again.

"It's okay," he said. "As much or as little as you want, Honor. I swear. I just don't want you trying to live in that house until we take care of this thing."

"And what if we can't? Take care of it, I mean."

"Then we'll think of something else." His jaw squared as he stared down the long, winding ribbon of wet pavement that stretched before them. "We'll think of something else."

Five more wet miles passed before he spoke again, startling her. "I knew your father."

She twisted on the seat and looked at him. "I wondered." Both men had been Rangers, after all.

"I was First Battalion, out of Fort Stewart." Georgia.

"He was Second Battalion." Fort Lewis, Washington.

"I know. But years ago...years ago he saved my life. He led a team in to rescue me and a couple of my men after we were...captured. Maybe he wasn't a perfect dad to you, but he sure was one hell of a soldier."

"It was his whole life," she said. "His *whole* life."

"No room for you?"

"He made some after Mom died. I'll give him that. He ran me like one of his troops, though. Why did you bring this up?"

"Because I owe your old man. I want you to know that, if you start to get scared of me again. I owe him. And if the only way I can pay him back is to look after you, I will."

"Why didn't you tell me this before? Didn't you think I needed to know?" She didn't know whether to be annoyed or frustrated with him.

"I wanted..." He hesitated, then forced the words out with evident effort. "I just wanted you to accept me for what I am. Since that's out of the question..." He shrugged and let the words trail away, appearing not to care one way or the other.

Honor knew better. *Out of the question?* Suddenly she wasn't wondering what she should feel. She knew; she was mad. "Who said it's out of the question? And if you think I'm going to trust you just because you say you owe my father—" She broke off sharply, spluttering.

And suddenly, catching her utterly by surprise, sorrow pierced her with a sharp ache. He had just wanted her to accept him for what he was. Without trading on old relationships or old obligations. Just him, Ian McLaren, what she knew of him. Was that so awful? Was that too much?

"I don't want your pity," he said harshly.

He had picked up on her feelings again, but he had read them wrong. "Believe me, I'm not feeling any pity. You're not in the least pitiable. And if you're going to read my mind, at least do it right."

His head jerked a little, as if she had caught him by surprise. Then he asked, "It doesn't bother you?"

"It's bothering me a lot less than I thought it would," she admitted. "Maybe because I don't have any real secrets. Certainly none after..." She felt herself coloring and let her words trail away.

He laughed softly and reached out, snagging her hand and holding it on his thigh. "I loved it," he said. "Believe me, I loved it."

"But you must have—" Embarrassment smothered the words. She couldn't really be asking this, could she?

"Never," he said gruffly. "Never before. I never let myself. I never dared to."

"I wish...I wish I could read your mind."

"I wish you could, too. And sometimes I think you almost do."

She thought back over the day and realized that sometimes she felt she could tell what he was thinking, what he was feeling.

"There have been a couple of times," he continued, "when I've been almost positive you're a latent telepath. When we first met. And today. Most definitely today. You read me like an open book."

"Not an open book. You'll never be that." Another mile passed, then another, and she realized they were almost home. And then she remembered something he had said, something she had wanted to ask him about.

"Ian?"

"Hmm?"

"What did you mean, you were captured by a demon?"

Suddenly he slammed on the brakes, turning off the two-lane highway onto a muddy dirt road so sharply that the wheels skidded briefly. He brought them to an abrupt, rattling halt. For a long moment there was no sound save the quiet rumble of the engine, the whoosh of the air conditioner and the patter of rain on the hood.

"God, Honor," he said finally. Just that.

She wondered if she should apologize for bringing up the subject, but that didn't seem right, since he had told her about it when they'd been nearly strangers. Maybe, she thought, maybe she had just caught him unawares by dredging up deeply buried memories. Painful memories.

Spurred by her concern, she released her seat belt and slid closer to him, ignoring the stick shift. He let go of the steering wheel immediately and wrapped her in his powerful arms. A shudder ripped through him as he released a long, ragged breath.

"Sorry," he said gruffly.

"No, I'm sorry. I shouldn't have brought it up."

She felt him shake his head, and his arms tightened. "I just...don't like to think about it. If it catches me off guard, like just now, I...react kind of strongly."

Pressed against his shoulder, she inhaled his rich, musky scent and wondered why she had never before realized how good another person could smell. How comforting that aroma could be. But there were more important things to think about now. She tipped her head back and tried to see him clearly. "You've buried a lot of things, haven't you?"

"A few."

Well, she understood that, she guessed. Imagine her having forgotten being locked in that closet when she was so little. Imagine having forgotten that kind of terror. Imagine terror so great that you *had* to forget it.

Ian unleashed another sigh, cupped the back of her head in his hand and gave her a soft, quick kiss. "It was that time I mentioned before, the time your father led the rescue team. I took a patrol on a reconnaissance into...never mind. We were taken prisoner and...tortured. Only three of us were still alive when your father arrived."

Honor held him as close as she could and waited, willing him to feel how much she cared.

"The worst...the worst of it," he said raggedly, "the worst was knowing what that guy was thinking. Knowing how much...pleasure he got out of the screams. He was—he was getting off on it."

Something inside Honor grew silent and still, grew cold and empty as shock filled her. As a helpless anger was planted in the soil of her caring. As she wondered how anybody could survive such a thing. Turning into him, she held him as fiercely as she could, trying to tell him what words never could.

"I didn't scream," he said, in an oddly calm voice. "Not once."

It had been his victory. His only victory in that hell. Honor stifled a sob and blinked back tears as she came to understand. He didn't break. He didn't kneel. He endured.

And now, for her sake, he was going to face the evil and hatred in her house.

Chapter Nine

Her house seemed to brood in the shadows beneath the trees. Honor watched it draw closer as they drove slowly down the road. And when they pulled into Ian's driveway, an overpowering sense of impending doom seemed to fall over her.

"Let's get out of here."

He turned to look at her as he switched off the ignition. "I feel it, too," he said. He looked over at her house.

"It's...worse." Far worse, if she was feeling it over here. It hadn't rained here yet, she noted vaguely. The ground looked dry.

"I'll take you to a motel," Ian said decisively, reaching for the ignition key. "It's...angry. I don't want you around here."

Honor reached out and stopped him. She felt his muscles tense beneath her fingers, felt how he was still reluctant to be touched. Even by her. It hurt. "Are you coming with me? Or are you coming back to face it alone?"

He didn't answer, which was an answer in itself. "Forget it." She shoved open the door of his Jeep and climbed out.

Ian jumped out his side and came after her. "What the hell are you doing?" he demanded.

"I'm not leaving you to face this alone." She turned, setting her hands on her hips and glaring up at him. "I'm not sure I trust you, sometimes I don't even think I like you, but I'll be *damned* if I'll let you face this alone!"

He scowled at her. It was a look that had terrified dangerous men. She never flinched. "Damn it, Honor! There's not a damn thing you can do that I can't do just as well. Or better."

"Yes, there is! I can make sure you're not alone!" She started to turn away, then paused and looked up at him again. When she spoke, her voice wobbled, betraying things she hadn't said. Things she wouldn't say, because she didn't yet trust him enough. "You've been alone long enough."

He swore. Violently, viciously, savagely, he swore. Then he snatched her up in his arms, lifting her feet right off the ground and holding her as close as he could without hurting her.

She hated it when he did that, hated the way it made her feel small and helpless against his larger size, but before she could say something nasty, his hold on her gentled, grew tender and cherishing. And instead of yelling at him, she ached in response, her chest growing heavy with feeling, her eyes prickling with unshed tears. She wrapped her legs around his hips, pressed her face to his warm neck and hugged him back.

"Okay," he said. "Okay."

Thunder growled threateningly overhead, and rain started to fall warningly. Holding her close, he carried her into the house with him.

In the kitchen, he set her on the counter, but stayed

where he was between her legs, bringing her mouth to his for a kiss filled with tender savagery.

"God, what you do to me, woman," he said huskily. "You've got my head as scrambled as my hormones. Honor, honey, I couldn't…handle it if something happened to you."

"I couldn't handle it if something happened to you," she answered back. "Looks like you're stuck with me, McLaren."

He was pressed snugly to her womanhood, and she felt his answering hardness against her. All around them shadows were gathering in the air, looming with threat, making it impossible to truly forget what they were facing. That thing was angry. Furious. And neither of them could guess what it might be capable of.

Which just added desperation to the explosive passion between them. Ian rocked his hips against her, slowly, deeply. Groaning, Honor closed her eyes and threw her head back in an ancient surrender, in a timeless invitation. Wrapping her legs around his thighs, she held him to her and pulled him closer.

He lifted his head and looked down at her, just as lightning flashed outside. "You sounded an awful lot like your father just now." His voice was rough, like grating gravel, and his hips ground into hers once more.

She gasped, never opening her eyes, and dug her nails into his powerful shoulders. She had to force the words out. "He did most of my raising." He'd called her his little soldier and demanded she behave like one. Bravely. Honorably.

"It shows." His hands were at her waist, holding her to him, but now they slid slowly upward, taking her T-shirt with them. All of a sudden she felt the touch of cool air on her nipples. They puckered eagerly, just in time to receive the heated caress of his callused hands. Lightning zapped through her, rivaling the storm outside.

His next words came out roughly, brokenly. "I haven't told you...how pretty...pretty breasts..."

She hardly heard him. She was tugging his T-shirt up, needing his skin beneath her hands as desperately as she had ever needed anything. She clawed the shirt up to his shoulders, and then his hands came to her aid, yanking the cotton over his head. Then he bent, arching his lower body away from her so that he could suck her tender, yearning nipples to ecstasy.

She left marks on his back; she was sure of it. Never had she felt so desperate, so needy, so violently hungry. Her nails raked him as she writhed, trying to bring his hips back to hers to answer the throbbing ache he was feeding with his mouth at her breast.

She felt the button on her shorts pop, heard the rip of the zipper. Then his hand was inside, gripping her buttocks as he lifted her and yanked away the shorts and her panties. Then he was back, pressed to her, denim rough against her tenderest skin. She loved it.

"Here," he muttered. "Here." He drew her mouth to his own nipple, and she took the invitation with wild delight, tonguing him, nipping him, sucking him, listening to his deep groans, then groaning herself as his fingers found her. Unerringly he found the delicate nub where she was most sensitive. She was so slick and so wet already that his fingers filled her easily, and she groaned again as he worked his magic. It was almost enough. Almost.

But not quite. Blindly she reached for the button of his jeans. And suddenly everything grew still.

Something in her quieted. Something in him quieted. They both looked down. He withdrew his hand from her and stepped back, just a little. Slowly she released the button. Slowly she drew the zipper down.

And released him.

He was hard, thick, ready. When she curled her hand around him, he groaned and shook from head to toe, as if barely able to restrain himself. "Yes," he whispered. "Yes…"

Guided by the same primitive instincts that always drew her to this man, she lifted her heels to the counter, opening herself as never before, opening herself as she had never imagined doing. Then, slowly, watching every incredible moment, she drew him to her and watched him take her. When he was buried deeply, she lifted her blue eyes to his face and found that he was watching her. Watching them. And the look in his eyes…

He whispered something awed. Something reverent. And she knew she would never be the same again.

"Now," he whispered, and kissed her. His tongue plunged into her mouth in a rhythm that matched the lunging of his hips, making her feel totally and completely possessed. Totally and completely wanted. The ache grew, the power between them thrumming almost audibly.

And then everything inside her exploded in a cataclysm of pleasure so intense that it hurled her beyond thought.

He held her close for a long time, while their breathing slowed, and their bodies cooled and dried. Little by little she became aware that her T-shirt was bunched up under her arms. That his jeans were tangled around his legs. The realization brought a silly smile to her lips, and as she rubbed her cheek against his chest, she wondered if it would always be this way between them—quick, hot, hard.

"God, I hope so," Ian murmured roughly.

Not minding at all that he was reading her thoughts again, she tilted her head back and smiled. "Yeah," she whispered. "Yeah."

And then they both felt it, something chilling, like a soundless howl of rage. Ian's head jerked, and he seemed to be listening intently.

"What is it?" Honor asked after a moment. "Ian?"

He shook his head. "If we don't do something, *it's* going to. We'd better get in gear, honey."

Honor nodded. She suddenly felt cold. So cold, as if an icy wind had blown out of eternity.

"Did you bring some jeans over? I'd feel better if you wore something that would give you some protection against...scrapes and things. And better shoes. Sandals aren't very stable if you have to run."

If she had to run? What was he expecting to happen? Upstairs, she changed quickly, feeling more nervous than she had in a long time. Her hands shook, fumbling with the buttons on her long-sleeved shirt, having trouble tying her jogging shoes.

Downstairs, she found Ian waiting, dressed in camouflage and combat boots. On his hip he wore his sheathed survival knife. He looked ready for anything.

But how did you prepare for a ghost?

"All I'm going to try to do," he said, "is figure out what it's up to. What it wants. I want you to stand back and keep watch for...anyone else, I guess. If the entity calls the person who shot at me, we could be in big trouble. So you keep watch and yell if you see anyone. *Anyone.*"

She hadn't thought of that. Her heart slammed in her

chest, and she bit her lip. "Okay." And he had been planning to do this alone, while she huddled safely in a motel? She suddenly scowled up at him and poked him in the chest with her finger. "Damn you, Ian! You need a reality check! You're not indestructible! How could you ever have suggested doing this without help? You would be completely exposed! Vulnerable!"

He shook his head. "No."

No. She wanted to scream in frustration. He must have picked up on it, because he suddenly bent and kissed her lightly on the mouth.

"If you weren't with me, I'd just keep part of my attention focused outward. I would have stayed alert. With you there, I'll be able to concentrate harder on finding out what's going on."

"Thank you," she said with dignity.

"For what?"

"For explaining."

He amazed her then with a crooked smile that was astonishing under the circumstances, a smile that forced itself past the tension that gripped them both. "I could feel you were ready to pop your cork."

A soft, rueful laugh escaped her. "Yeah. My temper tends to get short when I'm scared."

"Everyone's does." He turned toward the door, but stopped when she touched his arm.

"Ian?"

He faced her fully, looking down at her worried face.

"What if—what if it influences *me?*" The thought had occurred to her while she was changing, and it kept piercing her, like a stiletto.

"It might try," he said after a moment. "But I don't think you'll let it."

She nearly gasped in her amazement. "But it did last

night! And look what I tried to do to you! How can you be so sure?"

He simply looked down at her, as impassive as the damn Sphinx. "I trust you," he said.

Oh, great! she thought as she followed him out the door. Oh, great. He trusts me.

She sure as hell didn't trust herself anymore.

The rain had stopped, but thunder still growled like an angry beast at bay. The shadows beneath the Spanish moss were nearly as dark as night.

And alive, Honor thought as they approached. They were alive. Crazy as it sounded, she was convinced there was something in those dark places, something formless that was created out of shadow. Something evil.

Perhaps Ian felt it, too. He certainly picked up on her uneasiness. Pausing, he wrapped an arm around her shoulders. "I can take you out of here," he said quietly. "I'd be glad to do it, babe."

"I'm not leaving you alone." No amount of terror could make her do that. She would never be able to forgive herself for such cowardice.

He dropped his arm and took her hand. "All right."

The butcher knife that he had knocked out of her hand the night before still lay in the dirt, already showing signs of rust. Honor shivered when she saw it. Last night, when she had picked it up, it had looked barely adequate as a defensive weapon. This evening it looked wickedly dangerous. She hated to think how badly she might have hurt Ian if she had succeeded in stabbing him just once.

It crossed her mind to pick up the knife in case she needed to protect herself, but she immediately squelched the notion. It was horrifying to realize how little she could trust herself, but it would be foolhardy to forget what had happened last night. A weapon in her hands could be dangerous to Ian.

And he trusted her. Unconsciously she shook her head.

Beneath the trees, the leaden gray light of evening became a near-dark gloom. If, Honor promised herself, *if* they managed to get rid of this ghost so that she could live unmolested in this house, that moss was definitely going to go. The romance of it was gone forever.

The air beneath the trees was dank and carried the cloyingly sweet scent of rotting flesh. As soon as she smelled it, Honor halted.

"It's just a dead rat or a mouse," Ian said.

They entered the house through the front door. Inside, the air was stale, and stench of rotting flesh was even stronger. Something must have died in the crawl space beneath the house, she thought, hoping desperately that that was all it was.

Ian had stepped inside first, blocking her view with the breadth of his shoulders, but suddenly he stepped aside. Lying in the middle of the hallway, in a line leading back to the kitchen, were open packages of meat. Chicken, beef, fish, everything that had been in her freezer.

"Well, that explains the smell," Ian remarked.

"Do you...think the ghost did it?"

"Or the ghost's accomplice."

Honor started forward instinctively to clean up the mess, but Ian stopped her. "Leave it for now," he said. "Just keep your eyes and ears open while I see if I can sense it."

"But why would it do something like that? What's the point?"

Ian shrugged one shoulder, looking grimmer than

usual. "Maybe that's just its way of saying we're going to be dead meat."

Honor's heart skipped a couple of beats. Oh, God, what a thought!

Ian turned and threw the deadbolt on the door, locking them in securely. "You stay right here," he said. "Keep an eye on the road in case anyone approaches."

"Where will you be?"

"Right here. This is where I felt it last time. It seems to be attracted to the living room, for some reason."

At least she would be able to keep an eye on him. She wouldn't have settled for anything else.

There were no fancy preparations, nothing that the movies had led her to expect from a séance. And this *was* a séance, wasn't it? What else could you call trying to talk to a ghost? But all Ian did was stand in the living room archway with his legs splayed and his hands clenched into loose fists. He didn't even close his eyes.

Turning her attention to the window at the foot of the stairs, forcing herself to ignore the way the back of her neck kept prickling, she kept watch and waited.

It was almost like being locked in the closet when she was a child. Honor's tension grew as the last of the day's light faded away, leaving the interior of the house black, leaving the night beyond the window fathomless. She couldn't see a darn thing. How was she supposed to keep watch?

Ian hadn't moved a muscle since he'd turned his back to her. The tempo of his breathing remained steady and relaxed, and he was so silent and still that she would have thought he had fallen asleep, if he weren't standing.

Either whatever she had felt when they first returned

from Pensacola had evaporated, or she had become inured to it. The house seemed empty. Echoingly empty.

It seemed, she found herself thinking with sudden uneasiness, like a huge emptiness. A vast, immense emptiness. An emptiness too big for the house.

Shivering suddenly, she turned and looked into the impenetrable darkness inside the house. Something was happening.

Suddenly Ian disturbed the absolute silence by drawing a long, deep breath. "Stay back," he whispered. "Whatever happens, stay back there."

Oh, God! She could feel it. The emptiness was growing larger, growing colder, until the air felt like ice. Beyond Ian, she could almost see something. Something darker than the dark. Something that swallowed even the last little bit of starlight that had gotten through the clouds and into the house.

A curse escaped Ian, little more than a hiss. The darkness beyond him was swirling like thick, oily smoke, growing darker but more visible, as if it were some kind of black light.

Honor's scalp crawled as fear filled her. As terror turned her blood to ice in her veins. Suddenly she was that little girl locked in the closet again, and she started to slip to the floor, to curl up into herself, to hide within her own arms from the forming horror.

But she caught herself. Gasping for air as if there were none left in the universe, with the hammering of her own heart a deafening drumbeat in her ears, she resisted the overwhelming urge to hide. Because Ian might need her. Bracing her back against the wall, she forced herself to stand straight and watch.

"Stay back," Ian whispered again.

The column of swirling smoke grew until it reached

from floor to ceiling. Sudden, loud raps came from the walls and ceiling of the living room, a staccato burst that seemed somehow angry. Honor suddenly glanced upward, remembering the scratching she had heard from the attic. And now she heard it again from the floor directly above, as if...as if that thing were following her thoughts.

Shuddering with a fresh chill, she dragged her eyes down and forced herself to watch Ian. He might need her, she reminded her terrified mind and heart. He might need her. But, oh, how she wished she could run, or scream.

Ian still hadn't moved a muscle. A faint murmuring seemed to fill the air, a sense of voices that were not quite audible. The column of oily smoke began to expand, as if it meant to fill the entire room, and it seemed impossible that it made no sound save the faint murmurings and now the occasional rap on the wall. It ought to howl and roar with the fury of the storm, Honor thought. The thing she had seen as a child hadn't been like this. It hadn't carried with it this sense of...evil. Truly consuming evil.

It was moving toward Ian. Oh, God! Stiffening, she moved away from the wall and clenched her hands. Then a loud bang sounded behind her, and she whirled, expecting to see someone. But there was nothing. Not a thing.

Quickly she turned back to Ian and found him swallowed up. Oh, dear God, that smoke had surrounded him, nearly obscuring him, winding and twisting like a million snakes that wanted to devour him. And still he never moved a muscle. He might have been carved from stone.

Oh, God. She had to *do* something! But what? If she

plunged her hand into that smoke and tried to yank him out, she might infuriate that thing. It might hurt him. Or her. From what she could see now, it wasn't actually doing anything except...surrounding him.

Stay back.

There wasn't a shadow of a doubt in her that Ian had just touched her mind. It felt like him, the warmth, the concern, the distance he couldn't quite keep. The way he felt when they made love. Sobbing for air, she clung to the last shred of her control and waited. Outside, the wind picked up as it did every night, moaning forlornly around the corner of the house.

All of a sudden Ian gave a hoarse shout and threw himself backward, out of the coiling smoke. He stumbled once, then swung around toward Honor.

"Get out of here! Now!"

"But you—"

He grabbed the knob of the deadbolt and twisted it before flinging the door wide. Outside, the night was normal—windy, warm and damp. It seemed like another world as he hustled her through the door. Behind them, something slammed violently against something else.

"Let's go," he muttered, and when she stumbled on something, he simply swept her up and carried her. He didn't walk, he trotted. His hurry worried her as much as anything he might have said.

"Ian, what happened?"

"Just wait a minute." He trotted up the steps to his back door, fumbled with the combination lock.

"Put me down and make it easy on yourself."

But he kept his hold on her. When he got the door open, he stepped swiftly inside and then locked it again before he set her down. "Stay right here. I'm going to check out the house."

"Wait." She grabbed his arm, half expecting him to throw off her touch. But he didn't. Impatient though he was, he waited, looking down at her with enigmatic eyes. "Ian, what's going on? No one could get in here past the locks."

"Maybe, maybe not. Just wait a minute while I check it out."

She stood in his kitchen, shivering with a chill that wouldn't seem to abate, and waited impatiently while he prowled through the house. Lord, he was silent, even in those big, ugly combat boots he favored. She didn't hear him, not once, not climbing the stairs or moving through the hall and bedroom above her head.

Finally he returned to the kitchen. "All clear," he said as he went for the coffeemaker and started it brewing. Then, and only then, did he turn and pull her into a warm embrace. "You're ready to burst with questions," he remarked.

She tilted back her head and pretended to glare at him, even though she was really feeling extraordinary relief that they were out of that house, that he was safe. "Wouldn't you be? It doesn't take a mind reader to know that!"

He gave a short, soft laugh. "No," he agreed. "I'm sorry I was so rough about getting you out of there, but when it realized that I'd figured out it was protecting something, it got pretty pi—You know."

"Yeah. I know." She was distracted suddenly by the stubble on his strong chin, chocolate-dark prickles that she had an instant, urgent desire to feel against her skin. She drew a sharp breath, embarrassed by the turn her thoughts had taken.

"It's okay," he said, his voice turning totally husky. "It's okay. Adrenaline makes you...hungry. It does for most people." Bending, he pressed his cheek to hers and let her feel that prickly stubble against her cheek.

Such an erotic, masculine texture, she thought. Then she sighed as she corralled her thoughts. "I was so scared," she admitted. "But I'm okay now. Tell me what you learned."

"It sounds weirder than hell," he said, straightening. "That thing—that ghost—is evidently whatever is left of Mrs. Gilhooley."

"Mrs. Gilhooley?" Honor repeated. "You mean the woman who used to live there? The one who was so mean to you?"

He nodded. Honor reached for a kitchen chair and pulled it out from the table. Sitting, she put her elbows on her knees and wondered if she had gone stark, raving mad. And then she knew with grim certainty that she had not. Who better to be a haunt than that nasty, evil old woman?

"I almost couldn't figure it out," Ian said. "It wasn't like touching a human mind. Something is very…different. As if only *parts* of her personality are here."

"The hateful parts," Honor said, lifting her head quickly. The room immediately began swimming, and she waited a moment for the blood to reach her head again. "The vile, nasty, murdering parts of her, right?"

"Looks that way."

"Well, what the hell is she doing in my house? Why doesn't she just go away and burn in hell?" She was getting mad. Putting a name to the ghost had an incredible effect on her, banishing her fear and making her furious. "How *dare* any part of her get stuck here!"

Ian studied her for an endless moment, and then he broke into a huge, tension-breaking laugh, a laugh so unexpected that it startled her right out of her anger. It didn't last long, but while it did, it made him look years younger, erasing all the cold distance he usually kept between himself and the rest of the world.

He should laugh more often, Honor thought. And it did her heart so much good to see it that she couldn't even get mad at him.

"I'm sorry," he said a few seconds later. "I wasn't laughing at you. It was just the absurdity of the whole thing." Leaning down, he kissed her; it was a hard and quick salute that promised more later. "It sounds crazier than a loon, doesn't it? I felt stupid even saying it out loud."

He poured two cups of coffee and joined Honor at the table with them. Crossing his legs loosely, he settled back in his chair and sipped coffee.

"It was her," he said again. "Worse, it's not what I would call rational. It's more like distilled feeling with a blind purpose."

"What purpose? What is she trying to do?"

He shrugged. "Protect something. I'm not sure what, but she doesn't want something to be found. Which means, if we want to get rid of her, we're going to have to find it."

"How can you find something if you don't know what it is?"

"I have a feeling we'll know when we see it, Honor. Something tells me there'll be no mistaking it."

Sometime during the night Honor found herself standing at the window of Ian's bedroom, looking out at the windy night. The rain had stopped, and the moon sailed on a sea of stars. The trees in her yard tossed restlessly before the wind, and the moss swayed eerily in a shadowy dance.

Abomination.

She knew now where those strange, alien words came from, and she shuddered a little as she felt the touch of that thing. Mrs. Gilhooley. She shivered again.

Demon spawn.

Honor wondered if Ian had heard those epithets from that mean old woman while he was growing up. Probably. She sounded like a broken record, the same few words, over and over again. Now, dead and buried for three years, she was still up to her despicable tricks.

Personalizing the evil over there hadn't made it any less terrifying. She could feel the threat even here, with Ian sleeping behind her. A smile almost dispelled her uneasiness as she thought about him. Evidently good sex was an antidote for insomnia. He'd been asleep for more than an hour now.

But almost as soon as it strayed, her mind returned to the threat over there. In her house. Damn! It made her mad and sad and frustrated, all at once. Why the hell hadn't she sensed the thing when she'd first seen the house? Useless question, considering there couldn't be any possible answer.

And now this. Something hidden in the house. And what was keeping her awake long past fatigue was the simple terror of knowing that it was Mrs. Gilhooley in her house, and that Mrs. Gilhooley had always hated Ian, had tried just the other night to get him killed.

What if she still wanted to kill him? What if the old woman wanted Ian's death as much as she wanted to keep her secret? What if there was no secret at all, and Ian was her real target?

"Can't sleep?" A husky voice filled her ears as strong arms closed around her waist from behind.

Honor sighed and leaned back against Ian, enjoying

the warm texture of his skin and hair from her shoulders to her hips. She rested her hands over his. "You were sure sawing wood."

He blew a soft laugh right into her ear. "*La petite mort.* Such sweet death." His arms tightened just a little. "And you're over here worrying loud enough to wake the dead."

"Sorry."

"Don't be. Come back to bed and let's talk about it."

The words were like a warm wind blowing into the cold places of her heart and soul. In the six brief months of her misbegotten marriage, nothing had been discussed in bed. Bed had become a place to avoid, an instrument of torture and disappointment. Now, hearing those beautiful words out of the mouth of a man she had come to care for, she realized just how badly she had needed to have someone feel that way about her.

There was, she thought, a world of difference between a man you could go to bed with to make love with, a friend you could lie on a bed with to talk to, and a man with whom you could do both. A man who wanted to hold you while you talked.

Because the cots were so narrow, they had made a pallet on the floor with the mattresses from both their beds. They snuggled up there now, him propped against the pillows, her curled on his chest.

"When this thing materialized, did you see it?" Honor asked.

"The black smoke, you mean? Yeah."

"I was terrified when it wrapped around you. It reminded me of snakes."

"I wasn't exactly comfortable with it myself. It was like being touched by cold worms."

"Yuck!" She shuddered and tightened her hold on his

waist. "I was so scared. I wanted to snatch you right away from it, but I was afraid if I did anything, it might get madder and hurt one of us."

He stroked her arm soothingly and pressed a kiss to the top of her hair.

"What made you jump back the way you did?" she asked. "What happened? You were in such a hurry to get out of there."

"She was calling somebody," he said flatly. "She was trying to get someone to come. I could feel it, and I figured it was the guy who shot me, so I wanted us both out of there fast."

"Oh, no." Her hold on him tightened even more, and unconsciously she dug her nails into him. The crease in his side was healing beautifully, but she hated to think how close it had come.

"I think," he said quietly, "that it might be wise for you to get out of here while I try to deal with this. I know it'll play hell with your sense of honor, but if something were to happen to you…"

He didn't finish, and this time she didn't really need him to. Slowly she lifted her head and looked right into his strange green eyes. Dark though the room was, they seemed to glow. "Don't you know I feel the same way? Can't you tell?"

He muttered something almost prayerful and touched her cheek with his fingers. "But you don't trust me, babe. Not yet. I can feel that, too."

Unable to deny it, she lowered her head again to rest on his chest. It was true, she thought. Partly because she had learned painfully that things were not always what they seemed, and partly because she didn't know him that well yet. And partly because of that thing in her house. It had influenced someone to shoot Ian. It had influenced her to try to kill him. How could she be sure it wasn't influencing him to do some horrible thing, possibly to her?

Because she couldn't discuss what lay between them, she turned to the problem at hand. "What are we going to do?"

He stroked her hair gently, with a tenderness that seemed odd in such a hard, harsh man.

"We're going to go over there and look for whatever it is. Short of burning down the house, there doesn't seem to be an alternative."

She huddled closer to him, wondering what the ghost would try to do when it realized they were searching for the very thing it was trying to conceal. She had an unhappy feeling that the thing hadn't yet fully displayed its powers.

"We'll go in daylight," Ian said quietly. "It seems to gather strength in the darkness. We'll go when the sun is bright and high, and we'll search the damn place from bottom to top."

She shivered again as a cold wind touched her. "Maybe I should just give up the house. I mean, it's only money, right? I can just tell the bank I'm leaving and it's theirs. So what if my credit rating is ruined. It's only a credit rating—"

He squeezed her so tight that she gasped and covered her mouth in a devouring, demanding kiss. "No," he said when he lifted his head.

"No?" That damned word again. Frustrated and scared past bearing, she hammered her fist once against his chest. In an instant she was spread-eagled beneath him, pinned so that she couldn't move, exposed so that she couldn't defend herself.

"Nobody," he said softly, "*nobody* hits me."

Sudden fear turned her veins to ice. Looking up into those strange, glowing eyes, she looked into the eyes of a hunter. She'd done it, she realized. She'd aroused the sleeping tiger.

Chapter Ten

Honor had never felt so defenseless or so exposed in her life. She had been aware before of his vast strength, of his skill in using it. All along she had known he could kill her with no more effort than it would take to swat a fly. But never before had she been acutely aware that he might well do it.

Staring up into his eerie green eyes, completely helpless beneath him, she wondered if she had trusted him too much. Wondered if, once again, she had completely misjudged a man.

But she knew, too, that she should never have hit him. Gasping, trying not to struggle against his hold for fear of angering him even more, she waited, wondering what he would do. Terrified, a mouse trapped by a lion, she forced herself to go limp so as not to arouse his hunting instincts further.

For long seconds neither of them moved a muscle. Then, suddenly, with a savage oath, he levered himself off her and the bed. She heard him this time, heard him pad barefoot and naked down the stairs, heard him slam a cupboard shut. Heard him open the back door.

Oh, God, surely he wasn't going over there?

Scared in a new way, she grabbed up the first wearable piece of clothing her hand found and pulled it on. It was his olive T-shirt, big enough to make anything else unnecessary. Hurrying, she padded down the hall and stairs after him.

He had turned none of the lights on, which was why she saw him through the screen door. The moonlight brightened the night enough that she saw him standing on the porch, hands on hips, legs splayed, head thrown back.

She thought she had been silent, but he stiffened when she reached the screen door. One way or another, he knew she was there. Uncertain whether she should do anything, she simply waited.

And in the waiting she realized that she trusted him more than she had trusted anyone since her marriage. Whatever resistance she had felt toward trusting Ian had sprung from self-doubt, not from anything he had done.

And now, even in rage, he had not hurt her, not even when she had hit him.

He turned. "I'm sorry I scared you," he said levelly.

"I'm sorry I hit you," she answered, her voice quavering just a little. "Truly sorry. I've never done that before, and I despise women who think they can hit a man, knowing he won't hit back."

"We agree on that." He turned away again, looking out into the night. "I shouldn't have scared you, though. I know my size is intimidating, and to hold you down like that…" He shook his head.

Honor pushed the screen door open and stepped out. The night was alive with cicadas and tree frogs, and she tried not to think about that huge bug she'd seen mashed on the road. She crossed the porch to stand beside him.

"I imagine," she said after a moment, "that you've suffered a lot for your size. And your unusual eyes."

He stirred a little. "I don't pay attention."

"Of course you do. You're not deaf, dumb and blind."

The wind gusted, rustling the trees in her yard and whispering sorrowfully through the darkness. It sounded as if the night were sighing. Tentatively, aware she might well be rejected, she touched Ian's forearm with her fingertips.

He turned toward her instantly and gathered her close. "I'm sorry," he said gruffly. "Damn it, I'm sorry. I never wanted to scare you...."

Whether he admitted it or not, he had been hurt by the way people reacted to him, Honor thought. Between that and his telepathy, it was no wonder he lived behind impenetrable walls.

It felt so good to have his arms around her again, so good to lean against his strength and feel welcome there. She clung to him for a long while, soaking up his warmth, and the scent that was uniquely his.

"You didn't hurt me," she said. "And that's all that matters."

One of his big hands found her hair and tunneled into it, combing gently. "I've never met anybody like you," he said roughly. "Anybody else would have run from me ten times over."

"I guess you haven't been looking in the right places. I'm nothing special."

Bending, he kissed the top of her head again. "That's what *you* think. Come on, let's go inside. I don't want anyone to see you out here with me like this."

At this hour of the morning? Honor wondered. Who could possibly be watching? And then she remembered the person who had shot Ian, the person the ghost had been calling. He might be out and about. The thought was like a chill breath on the back of her neck.

"Sorry," he said, hustling her through the door. "I'm great at destroying a mood, too."

When they were inside and he was locking the door, Honor turned on him. "Damn it, Ian, quit apologizing for everything. There's not one thing you need to apologize for! I'm the one who hit you, and I deserved to be swatted back. If I were a man, you'd probably have nailed me to the floor."

Satisified with the deadbolt, he faced her. "Maybe."

"There's no maybe about it. All you did was scare me a little. Quit worrying. Quit worrying about everything." She hated this. Hated knowing just how abnormal he felt he was. Only years of experience could have made him feel that everything about him was wrong, from his size to his eyes.

Reaching out, she touched his arm. "There's nothing wrong with you," she said softly. "Not one damn thing. You're different, but different is *not* the same thing as wrong."

"There are a lot of people who wouldn't agree with you." He spoke stiffly, as if for some reason he was afraid to relax.

"Maybe so, but they're not here right now." And suddenly it was all very clear to her. Maybe she didn't trust this man with her heart, maybe she still wondered if he could be influenced by the ghost the way she had been, but it was eminently clear now that he would never purposely hurt her.

But he expected her to be afraid of him, as so many others had been. He never entirely relaxed, always maintained a rigid control, for fear he might do something to scare her—as he had when he pinned her to the mattress. Yes, she had been scared. Terrified, even. But the important point was that he had not hurt her.

He stood now in the kitchen, unselfconsciously naked, a magnificent man who had been shunned all his life because he was a telepath and because he was a deadly fighting machine. He said he didn't care; she didn't believe it.

She took his hand gently. Raising it to her lips, she kissed the backs of his fingers and then his palm. "Everything else aside, Ian, I am *not* afraid of you."

She heard him catch his breath. Then, with the swiftness of a striking hawk, he scooped her up into his arms and headed for the stairs.

Honor knew exactly what was coming, and arousal trickled through her to her center, tingling and warm. Life had turned him into a closed-up, locked-up man, and he had only one means of expression still left to him. What he couldn't say with words, he could say with his body.

And, oh, was she ready to listen!

He was gentle at first, taking exquisite care, treating her as if she were priceless crystal. But then, at some point, he dared to let go, dared to test her declaration that she wasn't afraid of him. Dared to be himself without inhibition.

It was like catching a ride on a cyclone, Honor thought dimly and much later, when she lay trembling beneath his sweaty, exhausted body. Like riding a rocket, or driving a car without brakes. The whirlwind had swept her up and carried her to a world of sensations so intense they surpassed thought.

And there she had found a long-lost piece of herself. Smiling, she held Ian close and slipped away into a deep restful sleep.

* * *

Ian didn't sleep. He had made the ghost aware of him, and he felt the threat strengthening. Directed at him now, he thought, and not Honor at all. While she slept deeply, he went to stand at the window and watch her house through the trees. Lights flickered in the windows, in a restless movement that bounced here and there in seeming frustration. He felt it commanding him to come, but he would choose his own time.

It seemed, he found himself thinking, that he and Mrs. Gilhooley were fated to have it out. He was reluctant to think in terms of destiny and eternity, and his faith had been all but destroyed in childhood, but he stood in the dark and looked over at Mrs. Gilhooley's house and wondered why he and that nasty old woman had been locked in mortal combat since his childhood, and why the conflict seemed to have extended beyond the grave.

Given a different life, he might have been a mystic, but he wasn't a mystic, and he felt uneasy with the ideas that were rolling around in his mind now. It was, he told himself, simple happenstance. If he hadn't felt compelled to return to this house to prove to himself that the terrors of his childhood no longer had the power to hurt him, he never would have run into this mess.

He had meant his return here to be a kind of excision, a cutting-away of old scar tissue. He had told himself he was setting himself free of the last of his emotional baggage, that when he had dealt with the memories this place represented, he would be beyond the reach of anything and anyone.

Instead he found himself faced with his old nemesis and collecting fresh baggage. Wherever he went now, Honor Nightingale would haunt him. The first woman, the only woman, not to be afraid of his strange talent. The first person to become aware of his talent without thinking of him as an abomination.

This bedroom he stood in now had been his as a child. The one in which Honor had slept had belonged to his older brother, long dead. His parents' room was empty of everything, cleared out by him to remove the last traces of an abusive father and a mother who had refused to touch him ever again from the day the church had shunned him.

Nothing his father had done to him had cut him as deeply as what his mother had refused to do. He had locked those memories in the deepest, darkest vault of his mind, then had come home specifically to dig them up, face them and toss them away. It seemed amazing now, and even a little ironic, that Honor had accomplished with a few words what he hadn't managed to do in nearly a full year. She had set him free of his past.

Except for Mrs. Gilhooley, of course. There was one last raveled end to deal with, and he would deal with it first thing in the morning. The old woman had met her match. Ian McLaren was going to uncover her secret— or die trying.

"How are we going to do this?" Honor asked.

They were standing in front of her house, looking at the black, empty windows. The day had turned sunny and hot, though it was still early, and humid. She wiped her brow with the back of her arm and wished a breeze would stir.

"It seems quiet this morning," Ian said. "She was restless all night, but now…it's as if she's asleep."

Honor felt a chill despite the heat. It was disturbing to hear Ian refer to that thing as *she*.

"I guess it'll be safe if we split up," Ian said. "If she starts to get active, I should sense it. I'll start on the second floor, and you start in the front down here. I'll work my way up to the attic, while you go through everything on the ground floor." He turned and looked down at her. "I know it's a bigger task downstairs, but you're better equipped to tell what's yours and what isn't. And I'll leave your bedroom for last, so we can do that together."

"Fair enough."

"Unless you'd rather we do it together. We can start in the attic."

For some reason she remembered the chill she often felt at the foot of the attic ladder and shook her head. "No, this is fine." Bad enough that she would have to go into the living room. Her mind had retained an indelible image of the swirling darkness that had surrounded Ian last night.

"If we start to come close to what we're looking for," he continued, "we may stir her up. I should sense that, too."

"That would be a dead giveaway, if the ghost starts getting nervous."

One corner of his mouth hitched upward. "We can always hope."

It was really too hot for jeans, but Ian had insisted on protective clothing again. Inside the house it was cooler, from the air-conditioning, but the carrion smell had become almost asphyxiating. Gagging, Honor had to back right out the door, but Ian forged forward with a trash bag and picked up all the rotting meat.

"At least she didn't smear it all over the walls," he remarked as he passed Honor on his way out with the bag. They opened all the doors and windows and turned on the house fan to blow the smell away, and Honor mopped the hallway with vinegar. When she had finished, the smell seemed nearly gone—or maybe her nose had just turned off, she thought sourly. Damn the old woman, anyway!

She didn't feel nearly so defiant, though, when Ian had at last gone upstairs and she was left alone in the hallway, facing the living room. There was no longer any doubt in her mind as to why she had hesitated to paint and furnish the room. If evil had a smell, that room reeked of it.

"Miss Honor?"

Startled, she whirled around and then sighed with relief when she recognized Jeb Sidell. He was plainly agitated, shifting from one foot to the other and twisting a porkpie hat in his hands. "What's wrong?"

"Orville. He fell, and his leg busted like bad wood, and he's bleeding bad. My ma's calling for help, but—"

She ran upstairs to grab some clean pillowcases to use to make a pressure bandage. Pausing by the foot of the attic ladder, she ignored the clammy chill that clung there and called up to Ian.

"I'm going out with Jeb! Orville broke his leg and needs help!"

She didn't wait to hear if he answered. Splints. She needed something to use for splints. Forget that. It would take too long. The bleeding had to be stopped before anything else could be dealt with.

Downstairs, she hurried out the door, Jeb on her heels. "Where is he?"

"I'll drive," Jeb said, pointing at a beat-up old truck. "We'll get there faster."

She climbed up into the cab, hoping against hope that it wasn't too late for the little boy.

A surprising number of the attic floorboards were loose, as if no one had ever bothered to drive the nails back in as they worked free over time. In many places, the nails were entirely gone. And beneath each loose board was an easy hiding place between the joists that supported the flooring. A careful inspection of the lath showed that it, too, was loose in places and concealed fair-sized spaces between itself and the wood.

It would take a couple of hours, at least, to explore all the possible hiding places in the attic, Ian estimated. Mentally he blocked the entire area off in sections, intending to search section by section from one end to the other.

As he worked, he whistled softly, a habit from childhood that he'd nearly forgotten. Back then he'd whistled most of the time to avoid hearing what people were thinking. It made a kind of screen, concentrating on something like a melody. He did it now without even thinking about it. Not initially.

At some point he felt the day beginning to darken. Sitting back on his heels, he dropped a board back into place and looked toward one of the round attic windows. Beyond the filmy, dusty glass, the sky looked as blue as ever, but the sense of darkening was still there.

Glancing around, he saw that the warm-toned wood looked oddly gray, and that the light coming through the windows seemed to have lost its brightness. A glance at his watch told him it was just past noon. Too early for the light to change so drastically.

Getting to his feet, he walked over to the west window and looked down from the same place where Mrs.

Gilhooley had stood when she shoved her first husband to his death. Nothing looked different out there, he thought.

Turning, he stared across the length of the attic to the other round window. There, near the middle of the attic, he thought he saw a shimmering in the air, a distortion like heat waves over pavement. The attic might almost be that hot, he thought, but something wasn't quite right. Something about the way the air moved, the way the room beyond it was not only distorted, but subtly darkened, as well.

He smiled then, a private, rare expression of satisfaction. "We're getting close, aren't we, you old bitch?"

If he had hoped to provoke some kind of response, he was disappointed. The shimmering remained unaffected, the light staying oddly darkened. He waited a few minutes, wondering if something else would happen, or if the disturbance would disappear.

When nothing at all changed, he shrugged and reached for another board to lift. That was when it occurred to him to wonder if Honor was experiencing anything strange. If she wasn't then he would be willing to bet the item they sought was somewhere in the attic. If she was...well, they wouldn't be any worse off than they had been to start with.

He had to pass through the shimmering area to reach the ladder. The sensation was faintly unpleasant, cold and damp, like a cave, or a tomb, but after last night's encounter he hardly noticed it.

Until he reached the other side. In an instant he realized he had been duped, and fury rose hot in his blood. Turning, he looked back at the shimmering, and saw that it was a wall, ceiling to floor. And just beyond it he saw the faint gray smoke that he knew was Mrs. Gilhooley.

Sounds filled his ears now, the normal sounds of a house, of the breeze outside. Once again his mind picked up impressions, mostly vague thoughts cast adrift in the psychic either by people he would never know. All the background cacophony of life.

Sounds neither his ear nor his mind had heard for…hours? It had been so subtle that he didn't even know when it had been. He had been cut off. Deliberately.

But why?

And he thought of Honor.

He hadn't heard a sound from downstairs since the old woman had cut him off. Anything could have happened.

He dashed down the attic stairs, hoping against hope—yet he already knew. Free of the old woman's deception, he could feel Honor's absence as surely as he would have felt it if his heart had been ripped out.

The door of the linen closet in the hall stood partway open. It had been closed when he had gone up to the attic, so she had been up here since. He opened it wide, peered in and saw nothing amiss. He could feel her there, though, could sense in some subtle way that she had touched these things just recently. But why? He scanned neat stacks of towels and sheets and could see no answer.

Her room was undisturbed, as far as he could tell. There was no sign of a struggle, at any rate, and no sign of a hurried departure. He wondered if Mrs. Gilhooley had managed to scare her away again. Maybe Honor was running from him again, as she had just the other night.

Downstairs, he walked through the undisturbed rooms and found nothing. Only the front door, unlocked, told him anything at all. Outside, he found tire tracks in the driveway behind her car, which hadn't been moved since well before the last heavy rain. Someone had been here this morning.

Someone had been here, and now Honor was gone. And the only clue he had was tire tracks that headed out toward the highway. Standing beside the dirt road, he followed them with his eyes. And then he noticed that they had initially come from the other direction. From up the road, toward the Sidells' place.

Moments later he was backing out of his driveway and heading up the road to question a woman who had spoken to him only once in thirty-five years, and then to call him a murderer and wish him an eternity in hell.

She was sitting on the porch of a run-down house, looking as run-down as a woman of forty could manage. Too thin, too worn, she had plainly had a hard life. She didn't move when Ian climbed out of his Jeep, and no one came out of the house to join her. It was just the two of them and the stifling Florida day.

"Annie." He nodded, staying well back, not wanting to frighten her by approaching.

"Ian." She didn't nod, but she didn't look away or get up and leave. "Heard you were back."

A year ago, he thought. He'd come back a year ago, and she acted as if she'd just heard it. But the old bitterness was nothing beside his current worry. "Yeah. You got your wish, Annie."

She cocked her head a little. "I never got a wish in my life. What're you talking about?"

"You wished me to hell. I went."

For a long moment, she stared unwaveringly at him, her lips compressed. Then she nodded. "Me too, Ian. Me too. My boys are good, but—" She cut herself off sharply and shook her head.

Ian didn't need to hear the rest of the sentence to

know Jack Sidell had the temper of an ornery rattler. At least she was talking to him. "I'm looking for my neighbor lady, Honor Nightingale."

"The nurse lady. She ain't been here, for sure."

"Well, we were at her place. I was doing something in the attic for her. When I came down, she was gone. Never said a word. Didn't leave a note or anything, but her car's there. And I saw some tire tracks in her drive-way. They came from up here, pulled in the drive, then headed out to the highway. Anybody been up this way this morning?"

Annie shook her head and lifted a chapped hand to brush sweat from her brow. "Sure been hot."

"Mmm…"

"Jeb headed out to town 'bout an hour ago. Said he didn't know when he'd be back. Still looking for work. They don't hire him too quick, 'cause he's slow, but he's a hard worker. Ain't never been fired from a job."

Ian nodded, restraining his impatience. "I've heard good about the boy."

"Nobody's got a bad word for any of my boys. I raised 'em right."

This time he just nodded. A couple of minutes ticked by while she stared at something he couldn't see. Just as he was about to decide there was nothing to be gained here, she focused on him again and spoke.

"I'm sorry for what I said all them years ago, Ian. You didn't kill her. Maybe you knocked her up, I don't know, but you didn't kill her."

And for the first time in all the years since, he said what no one had believed at the time. "I never touched her, Annie. Never."

Annie shrugged. "Don't matter anymore. But Jeb…"

When she hesitated, Ian had to restrain himself from saying more than "Yes?"

"Something's wrong with that boy lately," Annie said. "He's not right. He's acting funny. Orville won't even go hunting with him no more. Worries me." She leaned forward a little bit. "I don't know where he went. But if he's got that nurse lady, there's no good in it. No good at all. I don't know what's been driving him lately, but he kicked his coon dog last night, and I ain't never seen Jeb kick a thing in his life..."

Ian never heard the rest. He was in the car and moving.

A hundred yards down the road, though, he pulled over and set the brake. Here, where he had nothing else to concentrate on, he closed his eyes and reached out, trying to find some hint, some flicker, of Honor's mind. Or even Jeb's. Some hint of where they might have gone. Never in his life had he tried so hard to reach out with his mind. It felt like straining a long-unused muscle, and the effort left him with a blinding headache.

But he had a general idea as to which way they had gone.

Dusk was closing in, and along with it a sense of hopelessness to add to her other miseries. Honor sat tied to the base of a tree by ropes that crisscrossed her chest and stomach. Her ankles were tightly bound, and her wrists were raw from the rope that held them together in her lap. Her face was swollen from numerous mosquito and fly bites, so swollen that her eyes opened only to slits, and the itching was driving her crazy. The only bright spot was that Ian's insistence that morning had left her wearing jeans and long sleeves, preventing further discomfort.

She was the prisoner of Mrs. Gilhooley, and the longer she sat here and listened to Jeb Sidell rustling in the undergrowth and talking to the ghost of his dead grandmother, the easier Honor found it to believe.

And, worse, as night closed in, she was beginning to feel the old woman's presence herself. It was a chill in the air that trapped the brutal heat of the day in the thick vegetation, a chill that had nothing to do with temperature.

Suddenly Jeb appeared out of the shadows and hunkered down near her. "Water," he said, holding out a rusty tin cup.

Honor drank eagerly, having too much common sense to turn down a necessity to make a point. When he offered her pieces of a candy bar, she wolfed those down, too.

"I didn't want to do this, Miss Honor," he said as he fed her.

"Then why did you?"

"Gram said she'll hurt me if I don't do what she says."

Honor peered at him, wishing the dusk weren't concealing his expression so effectively. "Hurt you how?" Lord, was it only a couple of days ago that she'd told Ian she couldn't imagine how a ghost could hurt anyone? She was beginning to get a good idea.

"She makes things inside my head hurt."

"Oh." She accepted another bite of candy. Things inside his head. She could almost imagine it.

"She said she'd send another snake to bite Orville, too."

"Do you think she can make snakes do what she wants?" Honor shuddered, thinking of the coral snakes and water moccasins that inhabited this place. After the rain, water moccasins could be almost anywhere, too, not just in the rivers and creeks.

"Sure," said Jeb. "Easy." He gave her more candy bar.

The darkness was thickening, and with it the chilling sense of the old woman's presence. Honor looked around, wishing for light. Any light. Some source of illumination to tell her what other threats might be emerging from the dark. Mrs. Gilhooley was bad enough by herself, but the thought of snakes and bobcats and all the other things that inhabited the dark made her just as uneasy. Just as scared.

"Jeb." She looked at the young man. "What you're doing is wrong."

"I know." Even in the dark, his anguish was palpable. "I know."

"Then don't do it!"

"I have to! She'll hurt me! She'll hurt Orville!"

"Why would any grandmother want to hurt her grandchildren?"

"I don't know." It sounded as if he were crying. "I don't know. She scares me, Miss Honor. And I can't let her hurt Orville. But she's not going to hurt you. She promised she won't hurt you. I made her promise, because you saved Orville before."

For hours Honor had been dragged through the thick, junglelike growth of the forest. She'd been terrified, she'd fallen so many times that her entire body was sore and bruised, and now she was sitting in the dark with the man who had kidnapped her and dragged her for miles, and she was supposed to believe she wasn't going to get hurt because she had helped Orville. The same Orville who was being threatened by another snakebite.

Somehow she didn't feel very reassured. And she still didn't know what they were doing out here.

"Why did you drag me out here, then?" she asked

Jeb. "If you're not going to hurt me, why am I tied up like this?"

"She made me." He whispered the words, as if he, too, felt the encroachment of the evil thing that was his grandmother. "She made me."

"But why? Why does she want me here in the woods like this?"

He cocked his head to one side. Though he was just a shadow in the deepening gloom, the movement was still visible. "We're gonna catch him," Jeb whispered.

Something deep inside her froze to ice. "Catch who?" she asked, her own voice dropping to a whisper. But she knew. Oh, God, she *knew*.

"Catch the demon spawn," Jeb whispered. "Catch the witch man." Then he rose and disappeared into the night.

There were more than a half-million acres of land on the air base, nearly a thousand square miles, most of it virgin forest and subtropical jungle. A man could get lost in there and never be found, and he could die from dozens of causes, everything from poisonous snakes to bobcats, from drowning to falling.

Ian knew the reservation as well as he knew the back of his hand. He'd guided troops through it for years, in daylight and pitch-darkness. He sometimes thought he could tell where he was by the smell of the vegetation and the lingering odors of explosives and jet fuel that never quite blew away.

He drove until his sixth sense warned him to stop, and there, with eyes trained by years of practice, he saw the hastily concealed signs of the recent passage of a vehicle. He didn't have to walk far into the woods to find Jeb Sidell's old truck. From there they would have walked, and anywhere a man could walk, Ian could track.

He took time, though, to check out the truck's cab. He saw two of Honor's pillowcases, crumpled on the floor boards. There was no doubt they were hers, because they smelled of her laundry soap, and faintly of her. They were dirty from muddy footprints, and spoke to him of a struggle. If Jeb had hurt her, he was going to be one sorry kid, Ian thought grimly as he slammed the cab door. One damn sorry kid.

Closing his eyes, he reached out again. Strained to feel Honor somewhere out there in the hot, muggy evening. It had taken him too long to get here, he thought. Soon it would be dark, and tracking would be harder.

And then he felt her, a whisper of her fear, of her fatigue. Just a touch, a light, almost fragile touch. Two minutes later he was on his way into the woods with night-vision goggles and his knife. He didn't need a gun. He had *never* needed a gun.

She hadn't gotten much sleep the night before, and after being dragged through the jungle and running on adrenaline for hours, Honor was exhausted. She dozed against the tree, despite the bugs, the possibility of snakes and her fears for Ian. Periodically she awoke and listened to the whispers of the breeze, but not even Jeb disturbed the nighttime silence.

Jeb was out there somewhere, waiting, his trap laid and ready to spring. Honor doubted that it could be much of a trap, given the young man's reluctance, and his slow-wittedness, but that didn't keep her from trying to "beam" a warning to Ian, wherever he was. Somehow she had never considered the possibility that he wouldn't find them. She never once worried that he might not have figured out where she had gone, never once imagined that he might not look for her.

She guessed she trusted him after all.

And that was a terrible thing to realize now, when she couldn't do anything about it and they might well both be dead before she got a chance to tell him. And if ever anybody in the world had needed to be trusted by someone, it was Ian. He needed it the way a sturdy tree needs rain, and it was the one thing no one had ever given him. Except his army superiors, of course, but that was a different thing altogether.

Well, she trusted him, and if they lived long enough, she was damn well going to tell him.

She drifted off again, but sleep came in fits and starts, a little here, a little there, punctuated by crushing anxiety and fear.

Sometime during the endless hours of dark, Jeb finally returned. He woke her by shaking her shoulder.

"He's coming."

"Who?" She refused to let this boy know that she knew who he had meant when he referred to the "demon spawn."

"McLaren."

"Him? What do you want to hurt him for? He's never done anything wrong."

"He's a witch. He has to die."

"He is *not* a witch!" Honor was tired, hungry and fed up, and her temper was fraying. "When have you ever seen him call up a demon? Come off it, Jeb. You know damn well he's never done anything wrong!"

"Mama says the old preacher used to shun him."

"So? Have *you* seen Ian do anything wrong? With your own eyes?"

"Gram says he's evil. Evil!"

"Your gram's the evil one!"

"No! Don't you say that! She's not! She's not!"

Honor heard him hurry away, trampling vegetation as he went, trying to escape her words. If she hadn't been so scared for herself and Ian, she might even have felt pity for the young man.

And then she heard the most spine-chilling sound in the world—an abruptly cut-off shriek of terror.

"Jeb? Jeb? Jeb, answer me!"

But he never did. Apart from the whisper of the wind in the treetops, the night remained deadly silent.

Chapter Eleven

The night had been terrifying before, but now, knowing something had happened to Jeb, Honor found the dark intolerable. Tipping her head back, heedless of the way the ropes cut her as she twisted, she tried to see the stars, but the thick pine needles hid even that much from her.

Anything, anything at all, could come crawling out of that darkness now, and she couldn't even run or try to protect herself. Thoughts of foot-long bugs and giant spiders seemed a lot worse than Mrs. Gilhooley.

Who was still hovering around like a bad odor, Honor thought, shivering. Oh, God, how long till morning? How long until night would give way to dawn, until the chill would succumb to the warmth?

And Ian, even with Jeb out of commission, was walking into some kind of trap, and there was no way to warn him. Short of sending him frantic messages, which wasn't an easy thing to do when she couldn't be sure he was getting them.

Her skin prickled suddenly, as if it had been brushed by something. But nothing was there. She thought immediately of insects. Snakes. Ghosts.

And then she heard the low rumble. At first she wondered if it was a distant storm. But gradually she realized it was approaching, growing louder. Aircraft engines. Lots and lots of aircraft engines.

A bombing mission, she thought, and wondered how close it would be. It couldn't be here, of course, or there wouldn't be any trees. All the trees would long since have been knocked down or blown to smithereens.

As soon as she had the thought, the night burst with the brilliant white light of explosion. Almost before she understood what was happening, there was another... and another...and another. Coming closer. Oh, God, coming this way!

Why were they bombing the trees?

Dirt showered her, and her shoulder stung as something hit her. The shock waves kept rolling over her, leaving her breathless, and she couldn't even cover her ears with her hands. She felt as if she were caught inside the thunder.

She was going to die. There wasn't any doubt in her mind that she was going to die.

Another series of explosions began to approach from the same direction as the first. Carpet bombing. Saturation bombing. Oh, God, whatever you called it, they weren't going to leave a tree standing or an inch of ground untouched. An explosion. Another one. More dirt showered her.

Suddenly something fell on her, covering her. She opened her mouth to scream, to release the intolerable terror in the only way she could, when she realized it was a body. A body had fallen on her. Jeb?

"Honor! Honor, it's me!"

Ian! Oh, God, it was Ian! His mouth against her ear. His hands gripping her shoulders.

"We've got to get out of here," he shouted, even as he slashed at her bonds with his knife. They gave way quickly. He didn't bother with her hands. Another run of bombs was making its way toward them. He hauled her to her feet, but her legs gave way, numb from endless hours of immobility. In an instant he tossed her onto his back and held her by her wrists as he ran through the night.

She couldn't imagine how he could see anything at all. Nature had never made a night as dark as this, as dark as a cave's interior, the darkness punctuated only by the hellish explosions of the bombs. The light kept blinding her, and she couldn't see a thing. How could he?

They were both going to die, she thought as dirt struck them again, this time with enough force to sting. Ian shouted something to her, but another explosion drowned out his words.

Turning her head, she buried her face against his neck and tried to close her mind to the danger and the fear. How could he run like this with her on his back? Tirelessly, it seemed. Effortlessly.

Another bomb exploded, so close this time that her cheek stung from the heat from the blast. Then another. God, they were coming closer! She pressed her face to Ian's neck and prayed harder than she'd ever prayed in her life.

And on into the night he ran.

"Here." Slowly Ian squatted and eased her from his back to the ground.

"The bombs..."

"It's okay now," he said. "It's okay. They're heading the other way now." He reached for her wrists and began to saw away the rope.

She couldn't see a thing until another bomb exploded and the light fell across them. He was wearing some kind of goggles, she realized. That must be how he managed to see when she felt utterly blinded.

Another explosion, and she realized he was right. The sounds were retreating now. Dirt was no longer showering them.

"Somebody's going to get hell come morning," Ian remarked, as calmly as if they were sitting on the porch sipping tea.

"Why?"

"They missed the bombing range by a quarter mile, that's why."

"They weren't supposed to blow up the trees?"

He finished cutting the rope that held her wrists, then raised his head and looked straight at her. She couldn't read his expression, because his eyes were hidden behind those strange goggles. "No," he said slowly. "They weren't supposed to blow up the trees. Or you."

Suddenly he grabbed her, and she found herself crushed to his hard, broad chest, held as if she might slip away if he didn't hold her tightly enough. And suddenly, very suddenly, she felt safer than she'd ever felt in her life. And closer to tears than at any time in her memory.

"Is it…is it okay if I get hysterical?" she asked shakily.

"Sure, baby. Sure. But…maybe you can hold off just a little longer? Until we get to the car?"

He helped her to stand again, and this time her legs were able to support her. He led the way through the thick growth at a brisk pace that kept her breathing heavily. From time to time he paused and let her catch her breath, and then they were off again. In silence. With a sense that something was following. Pursuing them.

Not until they were in Ian's Jeep did the feeling of pursuit quit. When she drew a long, sobbing breath of relief, he reached out and squeezed her thigh gently. "Just a little longer, honey. Hang on just a little longer, babe."

So she did. But it wasn't easy. As the realization of safety, however temporary, sank in, the control that had kept her going all day began to evaporate.

They were driving down the dark road at breakneck speed, and she had no idea where they were going. Some corner of her mind kept trying to tell her that she at least ought to ask, but it somehow didn't seem to matter. All that mattered was that he had found her and saved her at the risk of his own neck. After this night, there was nothing she wouldn't trust him with.

She was astonished when she realized they were on the air base proper, and even more astonished when he pulled up to what appeared to be a motel beneath towering oaks.

"What's this?" she asked.

"Base TLQ. Temporary Lodging Quarters. Be right back."

Before she could enquire further, he was out of the Jeep and headed for a brightly lit doorway. *Temporary Lodging Quarters,* she thought inanely. Count on Uncle Sam to come up with a name like that. What were they doing here?

Ian was back in just a couple of minutes. Without a word, he drove down to the end of the long, low building and then parked. "You're staying here tonight," he said.

She was? Moments later they were inside and the night was locked out. Ian stood with his back to the door like a guard and looked at her. "Now you can get hysterical."

She shook her head slowly. She didn't feel like it anymore. She felt exhausted, miserable, filthy and scared, but not hysterical. "I just want to shower. Why did you bring me here?"

"I want you someplace safe while I go take care of that old woman once and for all."

"What—?" No. She cut herself off. Not right now. Right now she was going to get in the shower. Maybe then she would be up to questioning him about his plans. But now, right now...

His arms were suddenly there; his hands were suddenly helping. Some kind of dissociative state, she thought. She was numb, and she only thought she was coping.

Gently he stripped her filthy, sweaty clothes away, then his own. Gently he helped her into the shower, and gently he washed her from head to foot, using bar soap on her hair, but that was all they had, and anyway...anyway...

She never knew when she started crying.

Afterward, she remembered Ian lifting her from the tub, wrapping her in towels, drying her as tenderly as if she were a baby, and finally tucking them both beneath the warm covers of the double bed. There he cuddled her close and let her cry her eyes out.

"I thought I was dead." Her voice was rusty, cracked, and her eyes ached from weeping.

"Me too. Oh, God, baby, me too." His voice was a husky sound in the dark. Rough. "I didn't think I'd get there in time. You kept falling asleep, and I couldn't feel you...."

"That's how you found me?"

"After dark. Before dark I tracked you. It was easy. But when it got dark...you remember that game where you're blindfolded and trying to find something, and somebody directs you by saying you're getting hotter or colder as you move? And then you'd fall asleep and there wouldn't be any 'hotter' or 'colder' to guide me."

"Something happened to Jeb. I heard him scream."

"He's dead."

There was a finality to his tone that said he was sure of it. She didn't question him further. "It was a trap. You were supposed to get killed."

"I know. And you were the bait. I know."

"But...the planes weren't supposed to bomb there."

"Yeah." He paused and then squeezed her close. "It sure makes you think, doesn't it? If she could do something about that, affect instrument readings or whatever..." He let the words trail away.

"What do we do now? Give up?"

"Screw that," he said, steel running through his voice. "No. I'm going to put that bitch to rest for good, if I have to take that house apart board by board to do it."

He touched her damp hair and patted her shoulder with the awkwardness she found somehow endearing. "Now, try to get some sleep," he said. "I'll be right here. Nobody's going to hurt you, Honor. Ever again."

That promise warmed her deeply and eased the last of the tension from her. In a little while she was asleep, surrounded by his strength, his heat, his promise.

* * *

Pink light edged around the corners of the generic white curtains on the windows and cast a rosy glow through the room. Honor sighed, trying not to think about the problems still facing them, and turned onto her back.

And looked in cat-green eyes. Ian was propped on his elbow, watching her, and he made no secret of what he was thinking. It was plain in his eyes, in the flush on his cheekbones, on his parted lips. He wanted her.

"Like hell on fire," he said, in answer to her thoughts. "Like nothing I've ever wanted before."

She turned toward him with no thought except that the man she loved wanted her and there was no greater joy on earth. All the horror of the day before faded away beneath the brush of his hands, the heat of his mouth and, finally, the weight of his body.

"I want you to stay here while I go back and get to the bottom of this." He was lying on her, still joined to her, as the sweat on their bodies slowly dried. She was running her hands along his sides, but she stopped suddenly when he spoke.

"Why?"

"I don't want to put you at risk again. Look what happened yesterday." He lifted his head so that he could look down into her eyes. "She knows we've figured out that she's hiding something. She tried to kill you. Tried to kill us both. You don't think she's going to leave it alone now, do you?"

"So you expect me to let you go back there and face it—*her*—alone?" Her voice was calm, but she saw at once that he wasn't deceived. That was the tough part about dealing with a telepath.

Suddenly he grinned, and his incredibly boyish expression at once amazed her and warmed her to her very toes. "Don't even try," he said, his voice a deep rumble. "The better I get to know you, the easier you are to read. You're not coming with me, and that's that."

Two hours later she was beside him in his Jeep. She'd just had to be stubborn, that was all. And had to promise to stick to his side as if she were attached by glue. Not that he would have hog-tied her in the room or anything. Ian wasn't like that. He would never force her to do anything against her will.

But he could exact a lot of promises, and he had.

It wasn't that she wanted to face that ghost again. At this point she was all but ready to abandon the house and spend the rest of her life paying off the mortgage. But she couldn't let Ian face that thing alone. No way. If she had stayed behind, she would have chewed her fingers and climbed walls and finally called a cab to take her there anyway.

As they neared their neighborhood, Honor could have sworn she *felt* Mrs. Gilhooley, as if the old woman's ghost were poisoning the air with evil. And for an instant, one long instant, she allowed herself to wish she was driving away from here, never to return.

She glanced at Ian from the corner of her eye and wondered what he was thinking. Wondered if he were reading her mind. Damn it, there ought to be some kind of flag he put up, so that she would know when her privacy wasn't absolute.

But even as she had the thought, she cast it away as

petty. She didn't have a thing to hide, except possibly her anxiety that he would lose interest in her the moment the ghost was gone. And to tell the truth, she honestly couldn't imagine him staying interested in her for long. Why should he? She certainly didn't have anything a billion other women didn't have.

"What are we going to do about Jeb?" she asked him as they jolted down the dirt road toward their houses.

"I already notified some people that he had been out there. They'll look for him."

"I wish I knew what happened to him. I was arguing with him, and he ran away into the woods, and then I heard him scream." And the memory of that scream was going to stay with her for a long, long time. Ian's hand settled comfortingly on her shoulder and squeezed. She gave him a grateful look.

"He probably tripped on something and broke his neck," Ian said quietly. "But all I know for sure is that he was dead before I found you. I can't explain how, but I just know when someone dies."

Honor waved her hand dismissively. "Don't even try. I probably couldn't understand in a million years what it's like for you."

If it was possible, the shadows beneath the live oaks around her house looked even darker this morning, as if the Florida sun couldn't penetrate them at all. As if they were doorways into another world.

"Listen," Ian said. "You just wait at my place while I search."

"No."

He turned his head and looked straight at her with those odd green eyes. "No?"

"You taught me how to use that word," Honor remarked as she shoved her door open. "No."

Ian filled an insulated jug with water and ice, while Honor changed into clean clothes. Then they headed next door with the jug, a couple of crowbars and two flashlights.

He really meant it, Honor thought. He was going to take the place apart board by board if necessary. And she was darn well going to help him. Enough was enough. There couldn't possibly be anything hidden in that house worth Jeb's death. Worth the attempt to kill the two of them.

The shadows sucked the heat from the day, and there was no mistaking the chill beneath the trees. It wasn't natural, Honor thought now. No way should shade be this dank and cold.

The house was worse. Never in a million years would she have bought this place if she had felt then what she felt now. Mrs. Gilhooley's presence was an evil miasma, haunting the entire house, her rage an almost palpable thing.

Honor instinctively glanced at Ian, thinking that if *she* could feel it, it must be much worse for him. His face revealed nothing, probably the best indicator that he was exercising a great deal of self-control.

"Let's start in the attic," Ian said. "Something about her antics yesterday made me think I was getting close."

"Six of one…" Honor shrugged, leaving the sentence incomplete.

At the foot of the attic stair, the chill had grown almost arctic.

"Maybe you'd better go wait at my place," Ian said as she recoiled from the cold spot. "Honor, really, all

I'm going to do is wreck your attic. I can do that all by myself."

She tried to smile, but couldn't quite manage it. "I'm not leaving you alone. Quit suggesting it."

"This doesn't have anything to do with the way your dad raised you, does it?" he asked as he started climbing the stairs.

"Probably. All that stuff about not deserting your buddies got to me."

He gave a small chuckle that was probably supposed to be humorous but didn't quite make it.

Almost the instant they were both standing in the attic, the wind outside kicked up savagely. The roof creaked threateningly overhead, and branches tapped like bony fingers at the round windows.

"Probably building up to another afternoon thundershower," Ian remarked as he set down the jug and the flashlights. "Okay. I started at that end yesterday and got as far as that one raised floorboard over there. That's where we'll start. The only question I have is, do you want me to nail everything back in place as we go?"

Honor looked around and shook her head quickly. "No, damn it. Let's just get this done. I'll worry about fixing things if we managed to get rid of her."

"We might save some damage if you try to peer behind the lath with the flashlight. Chances are any place she used for hiding something would have been easy for her to get to, so it's likely to be easy for us, too."

"We wish." She jumped a little as the tree limbs tapped on the glass again and realized they had lost the sunshine. Well, so what? Picking up a flashlight and a crowbar, she started where Ian indicated.

For a long time, the only sounds were the creaking

of nails being pried up, and the clatter of boards being moved, along with the protesting groans of the roof as it was battered by the growing wind. Ian stopped once to take a drink and peer out the huge round window.

"Storm's brewing," he said.

"So what's new?" She had her nose tucked into a small crack and was wishing there was some way to bend light so that she could get illumination in behind one of the thin boards.

"It's a coastal climate," Ian remarked. "We get more sun than Seattle, but we get our share of rain, too."

"There's been an awful lot lately." At last she succeeded in figuring out that there was nothing in the small crevice. "It would sure help if we knew what we were looking for. A ring could be hidden almost anywhere. A diary, on the other hand—" A loud rumble of thunder made her look up. "More of that, too, I guess."

"Yep." There was a creak as he yanked up another board and a clatter as it fell aside. Wind gusted again, and for an instant it sounded as if hail were rattling against the windowpanes.

All of a sudden, lightning flared and thunder cracked deafeningly, the strike so close that the house shook and Honor felt her hair stand on end. At just that moment the attic stairs snapped up and closed with a slam nearly as deafening as the thunder.

Honor and Ian looked at each other across a space turned gloomy by the falling light. Neither of them wanted to comment on the stairs' closing without human assistance. After a moment Ian turned his attention back to the hole he had just opened in the floor. A hollow drumbeat of thunder sounded again.

"Honor?"

She turned to look at him. "Yeah?"

"I found it."

It was a diary, the cardboard cover mildewed, many of the pages stuck together from humidity and age. Neither of them even thought of going downstairs and getting comfortable with a beer. They sat cross-legged on the floor and used both flashlights for illumination.

"I'm almost scared to see what's inside it," Honor said as Ian used the tip of a penknife to pry pages apart. "I mean, if she could murder her husband, I hate to think what else she might have done. And there must be something she really wants to hide."

A loud clap of thunder shook the house with its force as Ian lifted the flyleaf and gently folded it back.

"At least the atmosphere's right," Honor remarked, trying not to notice the way the shadows were deepening. "If we had candles, they'd blow out right about now."

He answered with a soft chuckle, but kept his attention glued to the diary. These were the answers they needed, and everything else would have to wait. "Reading this could take a while. But at least it looks as if she didn't write a whole lot on most pages."

Nor was it a very thick or large book. It was, in fact, a fifty-page marbled black composition book of the kind that Honor had used throughout elementary school. The first page was given over to the rather childish inscription My Diary, Mary Jo Schmidt.

Inside, the pages were dated, and it was soon apparent that Mrs. Gilhooley had started this diary while she was still a little girl. And it was soon equally apparent that the horrors had started early.

There were tales of mutilated frogs put in other children's lunches. Later she wrote how she had drowned a little boy's new puppy. And on each page there was more.

Honor shuddered inwardly. "It looks as if she only wrote down the terrible things she did. There isn't anything else in here."

Ian nodded. "A listing of her crimes, as if they were triumphs. And look how she gloats that no one ever suspected her."

That was just as chilling as anything else, the way the child understood that her actions were wrong, hideously cruel. They weren't simply acts of petty, childish vengeance, but instead were carried out only for the pleasure they gave her.

More than once Honor looked up and met Ian's eyes, sharing their recognition that Mrs. Gilhooley had been twisted all her life.

The storm was drawing closer, growing worse. Rain rattled like machine-gun bullets at the two windows, and each gust of wind made the house groan. Neither of them noticed. As they turned the pages, one by one, they journeyed deeper into the darkness of an evil mind. Whatever had been wrong with Mary Jo Schmidt as a child had grown into something far deadlier as an adult. The incidents became rarer, but grew worse, until at last they found her description of killing her first husband.

I fixed it up so I could have Bill Gilhooley. Old Ted sure did look funny when he figured out I was pushing that ladder over. All the way down he just looked at me like he couldn't believe it. Man always was such a fool. But now I can have Bill. Just have to wait a little while so nobody wonders.

And that devil spawn brat next door, I'll fix him, see if I don't. I'll fix him good. He musta seen me push that ladder. It was funny, but nobody believed him. But I'll fix him.

Honor edged closer to Ian, instinctively wanting to offer comfort, even though the scars were a lifetime old. He already knew all of this, and there couldn't be any unpleasant shocks for him here, but still she wished she could make him feel better.

He didn't seem to notice the gesture, though. He just kept turning pages and scanning them while the storm raged and the light faded to almost nothing.

"There," he said suddenly. "I knew there was something else to that. I wondered if the old woman ever knew the truth of that, or if Maggie lied about me on her own."

Honor peered over his shoulder, squinting to read the faded ink by the yellow beam of the flashlight.

Maggie says it was Bill what got her pregnant. Swears he come to her room damn near every night.

"Bill?" Honor asked. "Her stepfather?"

Ian nodded. "Bill Gilhooley. Damn, that explains a whole lot, her knowing about that."

I ain't believing it. Gotta be someone else. Someone she's protecting. Maybe that demon next door with his witch eyes.

There was more, a lot more, about finally forcing Maggie to swear it was Ian who had gotten her pregnant. Forcing the girl to swear that Ian had "witched" her and made her do things against her will. Bill Gilhooley himself helped with the "persuasion" that forced the girl to lie. It was hardly to be wondered that she killed herself. Or that Mrs. Gilhooley, her very own mother, had given her the rat poison to do the deed.

Ian closed the composition book. "I guess there's no question what she's been trying to keep hidden."

"I guess not. It kind of makes you wonder, though, what kind of mind would do such things and then become so obsessed with hiding them, even after death."

Ian just shook his head. He'd seen plenty of the worst people could do, things that made Mrs. Gilhooley's activities seem like minor peccadilloes, but he didn't claim to understand such people.

"Well," he said, "it seems all we need to do is get this diary out of here and turn it over to the police. Then she won't have anything to hide anymore, and maybe you can live here in peace."

Instead of feeling relieved, Honor felt a piercing sense of impending loss. She could live in peace, and he could go back to his undisturbed solitude once he no longer felt honor-bound to protect her. The prospect was grim. And another thought occurred to her. "Won't she get mad now that her secret is out?"

"Probably. But only for so long as it takes us to expose it." In one smooth, easy movement, he rose to his feet and extended a hand to help her up.

"Want to celebrate?" he asked, a sudden, unexpected sparkle in his eyes.

The expression made her breath catch, and she ignored a deafening explosion of thunder. "Celebrate how?" Her mind threw up a whole series of exotic, erotic images.

"Exactly like that," he said. "Each and every one." Catching her to him, he initiated a deep, hungry kiss that promised a night filled with sensual delights. "Oh, baby," he whispered roughly, "just you wait. Now, let's get out of here so we can have fun."

Releasing her, he walked over to the attic ladder and stepped on it. The ladder, which was sprung like a fire escape, should have swung down beneath his weight. It didn't. He jumped on it a couple of times, then looked at Honor. "Has this ever gotten stuck before?"

She shook her head. "There's no way it *can* get stuck. If the springs were broken, it would just fall open. And it only locks in the open position."

He jumped again, harder, with no success. "Well, hell," he said disgustedly.

That was when Honor smelled the smoke. Ian smelled it, too, at almost the same instant. Bending, he touched the stairs with the palm of his hand. As soon as he looked up, Honor knew the worst.

They were trapped in a burning house.

Whenever it had started, the fire was seriously out of hand by the time they discovered it. A look around the shadowy attic revealed wisps of smoke that had been gathering in the air, seeping up from the floors below. Even as they looked around the attic, flames burst up between a pair of joists that Ian had left uncovered as the ceiling material below went up in smoke.

Oh my God, Honor thought numbly. Of all the ways to die, she would have picked anything else in the world. Smoke stung her eyes, and she coughed, watching with disbelief as Ian put the floorboards back over the exposed areas.

"To slow it down," he said. Reading her mind again. Then he grabbed a crowbar and went to knock out the beautiful round window at the back end of the attic. When only jagged pieces remained in the frame, he yanked off his T-shirt and used it to protect his hands as he pulled the last of the glass away.

Honor found herself standing right beside him, watching the play of his muscles as he let in the fresh, stormy wind and prepared a hope of escape for them.

"People jump," she said. "When the heat gets to be too bad, they jump rather than burn."

His strange green eyes met hers. "I know, honey. I know. If it comes to that, we'll jump together. We're only on the third floor. We'd have a shot."

Suddenly she was more scared of losing him than of dying in a fire. Much more scared.

"Ian…Ian, I never said…I never told you—oh, God, I'm so glad I met you!"

He caught her in a brief, bone-crushing embrace and muttered something in her ear that sounded like, "You're the only person on earth who's ever felt that way." Then he released her and went back to clearing the window frame of glass.

It seemed to take forever, though it probably took only a few moments. Finally he hoisted himself up and leaned over the edge, taking stock of the situation. A muffled explosion below was followed by a tinkle of glass, telling him the fire downstairs had reached flashover. It would be a raging inferno now, and the only way out would be through this window.

But the branches of the oak that had been rapping against the window were slender, bony fingers without the strength to bear even Honor's weight, and any sturdier branches were beyond their reach. Trying to jump would offer only a slim chance of success.

All of a sudden, he reached for the snap of his jeans. "Give me your jeans, too."

Confused, she didn't move immediately. She was still trying to cope with the idea that they might burn alive.

"Honor, your jeans. I'm going to make a rope."

Understanding at last, she quickly stripped them off, then watched as he slashed both pairs in half with his ever-present hunting knife. Then he tied the strips together into a rope that, while not quite long enough, would make it possible for them to get down to the first story before jumping.

"Okay, grab the other end and pull as hard as you can," he said. "See if the knots hold."

The smoke was getting thicker in the attic, and her eyes burned like fire from it. Doing as he said, she leaned back with all her might and weight to test the knots.

Suddenly the attic stairs fell open, and flames fountained straight up, almost instantly igniting the lath above it.

"That does it, babe," Ian said roughly. "Options all used up. You go out that window first. I'll hold the rope."

He was tugging her to the open window, but she resisted briefly. "How will you get down?"

"I'll nail the rope to the wall. Don't worry. I've been in tighter spots."

She didn't doubt it for an instant. But she very definitely wanted him out of this one *now*.

It was like being in gym class again, she thought wildly as she watched him wrap denim around his forearm so that it wouldn't slip. Then he was helping her over the window ledge and she was perched dizzyingly, her feet against the siding, her hands hanging on to the denim rope for dear life.

"Come on, sweetheart. You can do it. Just back down slowly. Go on."

Reaching back for skills she hadn't used in years, she inched her way down, ignoring the shrieking of her muscles, ignoring her fear, ignoring everything except the fact that the sooner she got down, the sooner Ian could come down, too.

And then she reached the end of their makeshift rope.

"Jump, Honor. Go on. It's not eight feet to the ground. The worse that'll happen..."

Is a bruise, she thought, and let go.

As soon as she hit, she knew she was going to have a football-sized bruise on her hip. But that didn't matter. Scrambling to her feet, she backed away from the burning house and looked up at Ian.

Only he wasn't there. The denim rope hung down the side of the house, but there was no Ian to be seen. And where he should have been, there was nothing but flames.

Chapter Twelve

"Ian!" She shrieked his name, wondering how the fire could have gotten to him so fast. And surely, if it had, he would have jumped…

Smoke. Maybe smoke had overcome him while he'd been lowering her. But no, he'd shouted to her to jump. He hadn't sounded strangled or woozy.

"Ian! Ian, damn you, answer me!"

Smoke was pouring out the window now, great black clouds of it. She made a dozen promises to God as she shifted from one foot to the other and tried to figure out what she could do. Every window in her house was belching smoke and flame. There was no way she could go in there, no way to get to him. Even a call to the fire department would take too long. "Ian!"

And then, suddenly, filling her with a relief that nearly left her weak, she saw him. Blackened by smoke, he swung over the windowsill and climbed down the denim rope. And sticking out of the back of his black briefs was the damn diary. At any other time the sight would have been funny. Right now it just made her want to cry and scream. He'd risked his neck to bring that damn book out with him. She could have killed him.

He jumped the last ten feet, rolling with all the practiced aplomb of a paratrooper and ending up on his feet, facing her.

"What happened?" she shouted at him, furious in her relief. "Damn it, I thought—I thought—"

He knew what she had thought. He crushed her to him, holding her so that she could barely breathe. She didn't care. She held him back every bit as hard. "The diary isn't worth this," she sobbed. "Ian, you should have left it. You could have been hurt. You could have been *hurt*."

"I had trouble getting the damn rope nailed to the wall," he said. "That's all. It wasn't the damn diary."

Her whole life was going up in flames, she thought dismally. Everything she had ever worked for was going up in that house. Even the last few mementos from her parents were burning in the vile old woman's rage. But none of that seemed to matter beside Ian's safety.

With a sudden, deafening whoosh, one of the curtains of moss burst into flame. Ian grabbed her hand and dragged her toward his house, wanting them out of there before any more moss ignited.

"Maybe we shouldn't go to your house," Honor gasped as Ian dragged her around the hedge. "What if she sets your house on fire, too?"

At the hedge, Ian halted and looked back at her house. "Do you have fire insurance?"

"Yes, of course. The bank insisted."

He nodded. "Good. Wait here a minute." Then he left her standing there while he trotted back toward her burning house. Flames were shooting out the windows now, and the front door burst open with a loud bang. Overhead, the storm raged, seeming almost paltry in comparison to the fire. A steady drizzle soaked her, chilling her.

Ten feet back from her front porch, Ian halted. He yanked the notebook out of the back of his briefs where he had tucked it; then, after only an instant's hesitation, he threw it onto the porch.

"Ian, no!" That was his proof he had done no wrong! What was he doing? She took a step forward, but it was already too late. A geyser of flame erupted through the open door and fell on the notebook, setting it on fire instantly. As if the old woman had reached out for it.

For a long time they both stood where they were, watching the book burn, watching as the house was devoured from within. An ominous groan from inside finally seemed to shake Ian as he turned and walked back to Honor, an incredible figure in nothing but soot and black briefs, his strange green eyes glowing like unearthly fire. Witch fire.

"Let's call the fire department," he said. Behind him, the roof caved in with a shower of sparks that ignited more of the moss.

Thunder rumbled in response, and the rain continued to fall.

The trees stood like ghastly black skeletons, denuded of moss and leaves. Dead. The house, too, was little more than a blackened heap of rubble, with the occasional charred finger reaching to the gray sky.

Standing on the road near her mailbox, Honor watched as the charred lump of the notebook stirred on the blackened remains of the porch and sheets of ash riffled and blew away. The last of it. The absolute last of it. Thunder rumbled, retreating.

A footstep alerted her, and she looked around to see

Annie Sidell and her son Orville. Annie's eyes were red. She was weeping yet for Jeb, who had been found at the bottom of a ravine. Neither Honor nor Ian had told her the real story, leaving it to the authorities to speculate about why Jeb had been on the range, where no civilian should have been.

"I'm glad it's gone," Annie said after a moment.

"You grew up in that house." Honor hadn't expected that reaction at all.

"I lived there till I was eighteen and got out quick as I could. It's a terrible thing, Miss Honor, but I never did like my mama. She was a mean woman, mean through and through. I was…I was so scared Jeb was getting to be like her, these last few days."

Honor turned and looked at the older woman, and felt genuine compassion for her. "I'm so sorry about Jeb."

Annie merely nodded. "You'll be leaving now, I reckon."

"I…guess so." There was evidently no reason to stay. She'd slept alone on the cot in Ian's guest room last night, when he hadn't returned from the range. He had said he might be gone a few days, depending on how much the Rangers needed him to do this time. He'd told her to make herself at home, but he hadn't suggested she stay. She wondered if she should just pack her few remaining clothes and go.

The hospital had given her a week off to take care of her homeless state, and she guessed she'd better get on it. Either she had to find another place to live, or she had to think about looking for a job elsewhere. Nurses were always in demand, so she wasn't concerned about that. She could go anywhere she chose. The question was what she chose…and whether Ian wanted her to hang around.

And what she might be hanging around for. Lord, she

didn't want to lose him. The very thought made her ache and brought tears to her eyes. But what could they have together if he only wanted sex from her? If he never shared himself in any other way? She knew now that a man could want her. Knowing that, she wanted so much more. If Ian couldn't give it to her...well, it would be better for them both if she moved on.

Annie headed back up the road with Orville, leaving Honor with the distinct impression that she had seen what she wanted to see, that seeing the house gone for good had satisfied her somehow. Maybe Annie, too, had felt her mother's evil presence there over the years. Maybe she, too, was feeling free at last.

Free herself, Honor went indoors and started cooking dinner for Ian and herself. He might not show up, but if he did, dinner would be ready. And maybe now he would talk to her. She had asked him twice why he'd thrown the diary into the fire, and he still hadn't answered. There were a lot of questions that needed answering before she left.

"You're not leaving."

Whirling, she saw Ian standing in the kitchen door. Dressed in camouflage and his red beret, knife and sidearm strapped to his hips, he was the archetypal soldier. Just now, for some reason, he looked bigger to her than he ever had, tall, imposing. His face was still as harsh as granite, and she didn't doubt he could kill a man with a single blow. But she also knew how infinitely gentle he could be, and the memory of his touch brought her to the edge of tears again.

"You're not leaving," he said again.

"There's no reason to stay."

"No?" He crossed the floor between them like a springing leopard and caught her right up off her feet.

"Seems like we've got a few things to settle," he said, heading for the stairs.

"Dinner—"

"Can damn well burn!"

She guessed it was probably going to. "You've got to stop grabbing me like this, Ian! I don't like it! I'm not a piece of baggage for you to haul around any time you feel like it!"

"Sorry," he said unrepentantly as he set her down beside their makeshift pallet. "We'll argue about it later. Later you can tell me how I'm supposed to treat a lady. I've never had a lady to treat right before. I've never had anyone…anyone…."

He didn't seem to be able to continue, and she no longer cared. There was something about the way he was pulling at her clothes, as if he couldn't wait another minute, yet was terrified she would shove him away, terrified he might hurt her. Such infinite gentleness and complete impatience that she nearly burst into tears on the spot. Oh, God, how she loved him.

He'd never had anyone.

He could have found no better words to reach her heart. He had someone now. He had *her*, and she wanted him to know it. She wanted him never to doubt it, and she had stopped counting the cost to herself. She was his, body, heart and soul.

He set her gently down on the mattress and stood over her, stripping away his clothes with rough, impatient hands. And when he was naked, he stood there looking down at her with such hope and longing in his eyes. Waiting. Waiting for her to invite him. Sensing, finally, that some things could not be bulldozed.

Instead of reaching for him, she rose on her knees. His jutting arousal was right before her eyes, and she heard him catch his breath as she leaned forward and pressed her face to his groin. How good he smelled, she thought as she nuzzled him. Coarse hair, satiny skin, the very essence of him. And when he trembled, she knew the first real sense of power she'd felt in her entire life.

"Tell me," she whispered. "Tell me how to please you."

She took him into her mouth and learned his textures and tastes with a hunger to reach him in ways for which there were no words. If this was the only way she could show him, tell him, let him see...

He was shaking like a leaf in a hurricane when he fell down beside her on the bed and pulled her into his arms. With his hands and mouth he painted fire over her from head to toe until she was begging him, begging him, begging him....

And then he was in her, over her, part of her, giving her the essence of himself, giving her his seed as he had given her himself. Claiming her as his very own.

She saw it in his eyes in those final moments, and she exulted fiercely.

He went downstairs and turned off the oven, the steaming rice and everything else. When he came back up, they bundled together in blankets and looked at one another in the shaft of sunlight that had somehow found its way in through the window.

"I love you," she said. But a whole bunch of doubts had risen in her. Weakening her earlier determination to stay no matter what. She couldn't force herself on him. He had to love her, too. But he hadn't said he did.

He nodded; he had read her mind after all.

"That's why I can't stay."

He shook his head. "That makes no sense."

"But it does, Ian. Don't you see? Loving you day

after day when you don't love me, waiting for you to find someone else—"

He covered her mouth with his hand. He had a lot to learn about handling women. "Who said I don't love you?"

She gasped, her blue eyes widening. After a moment she yanked his hand away. "You never said you did!"

He closed his eyes briefly. "I've...never said that to anyone. I've never had anyone to... Honor, I'm lousy at this. Ask me how to blow up a bridge, jump out of an airplane, field-strip an AK-47 blindfolded. That's stuff I know how to do. This stuff is..." He shook his head. "I don't want you to go. Ever."

She caught her breath, and a warm glow began at her center, spreading everywhere, driving away the chill left by the years. "Ever?"

He shifted uneasily. "I could understand if you don't want to stay. I know I'm unnerving to be around. Plenty of people have refused to have anything to do with me once they found out what I am."

She ached for him. Oh, how she ached for him, understanding that, however alone she had felt, he had been utterly isolated.

"I'm...unnatural," he said, his voice husky. "I know that. I understand that. And it's human instinct to avoid people who are...mutants."

"Oh, my God." Honor barely breathed the words, as she understood fully, for the first time, the scars that this man bore.

"So I can understand why you wouldn't want to stay indefinitely."

"But you want to keep me around for...a little while?" Anger was beginning to stir in her, but not anger at him. No, it was anger against all the people who had made him feel that he wasn't good enough.

"As long as you can stand me."

Considering that he considered himself totally undesirable, that admission had taken guts. Guts of the kind she seemed to be a little short of herself. She was asking him to take a blind leap she wasn't prepared to take herself, and the understanding shamed her.

Tilting her face up, she kissed him with every ounce of passion and love she felt for him. "Then you'd better plan on marrying me."

He went instantly still. Not stiff, not rigid, just utterly, perfectly still, as if everything in him were arrested in a moment of utter amazement. When he spoke, his voice was thick. "Marriage?"

"Kids, too, I think. We haven't exactly been behaving like responsible adults in that department, but that's okay, because I want several. Well, maybe a half dozen."

"Kids?"

He looked stunned, and she was scared half out of her mind, because there really wasn't any reason on earth why he should want her. Why he should love her. Jerry hadn't—

"Stop it," Ian said fiercely. "Stop thinking about that creep. He was wrong about you. Wrong about everything. I want you. I need you. I love you, damn it! And if you're crazy enough to love me, then I'm not crazy enough to let you get away!"

"Even if I want kids and marriage?"

"Especially if you want kids and marriage. I never hoped—Oh, God, baby, I never dared even dream it!"

For a long, long time she held him as close as she could and considered how odd it was that they had both lost their dreams and then rediscovered them because of that wicked old woman who was probably even now gracing the halls of hell.

A long time later, Honor asked the question again. "Ian, why did you burn the diary? It was proof you hadn't done anything wrong. You could have cleared your name."

He sighed and stared into the deepening twilight for a few minutes before he answered. "All that mattered," he said finally, "was that I was free. I was free of all of it, but I don't know how to explain it. It was as if reading it in that diary was a vindication for me. Nobody else mattered."

"But Annie thinks—"

"I don't know what Annie really thinks," he said, interrupting her. "Nor does it matter. She's the only person who might have been interested in the truth anymore, and I just couldn't do it to her. She's had to live with enough. She didn't need to know that her mother was a murderer, or that her stepfather raped her sister. What possible good could it do anyone now to have all that filth come out?"

"But people still think you did terrible things."

He shrugged a shoulder. "But *I* know I didn't. That's all that matters. I came back here with some crazy notion of laying old ghosts to rest, and that damned diary did it for me. I don't know how or why, but it did it. I'm free of my past, Honor. Finally."

He rolled onto his side and smiled at her, really smiled, and it transformed his entire face. "Now I have a future for the first time in my life. I want to build it with you, with our babies. I want to build it with sunshine and happiness. Away from here. Away from old ghosts and old memories. I want us both to have a fresh start, even if it's just a couple of miles up the road.

"I want us to build our own house and fill it with ghosts of our own making. Fill it with laughter and joy and all the things life should be blessed with. There's no room in tomorrow for the bitterness of yesterday."

He sighed, his smile fading just a little bit. "I set her free, too, Honor. She's gone. Can you feel it?"

Honor nodded and kissed his chin. "You set us all free. I love you."

He cupped her chin and smiled down into her misty blue eyes. "So...will you marry me?"

"I thought that was obvious!"

He chuckled. "Honey, I may be a telepath, but I'm also a very ordinary man. I need the words as much as the next guy."

So she leaned up to his ear and whispered all the words he wanted to hear. And in her ear he whispered all the words she needed to hear.

The only thunder that night was in their hearts and minds, in their souls and bodies.

And it was just the beginning.

* * * * *

THUNDER MOUNTAIN

For Margaret Cheney,
my dear Aussie friend,
whose letters bring joy to many a day.

And for Cris,
[(Always)]

AUTHOR'S NOTE

While some Lakota words are used herein for flavor, the
ceremonies practiced here, and the viewpoints expressed by
Gray Cloud, are purely fictional. They are not intended in
any way to reflect accurately the beliefs or practices of
any particular Native American group or nation.

Chapter One

Gray Cloud watched the woman toil up the rocky side of the mountain. She was foolhardy, coming here all alone, he thought. But *wasicu* women prided themselves on such courage these days, and this one displayed both courage and determination as she struggled up a steep slope over loose scree. Again and again she slipped and came down hard beneath the weight of her heavy pack. Time and again Gray Cloud held himself back. He would not aid her if she might be a threat. Nor would she appreciate his assistance.

The *wasicu* didn't trust him. They called him the Renegade of Thunder Mountain and thought he was dangerous. He didn't care about that, but he didn't wish to frighten this woman, who had come to do a task for her people. He, too, was here to perform a task, and that task did not include terrifying this woman—yet.

Standing back in the trees, he watched her painful progress and stood ready to intervene should she come to harm. But she did not. Scrambling upward on hands and knees over loose talus, she pushed on with dogged determination. At places she slipped back a foot for every two she advanced, but she never paused.

Gray Cloud felt a glimmer of admiration. Some people were strong of spirit, strong of heart, and it appeared this woman was one of them. She thought she was alone and unobserved, and yet she forged steadily ahead, refusing to give in or even slow down. Stubborn, Gray Cloud thought. Stubborn was good. Stubborn stuck when everything else fell away. That could be a problem for him. For the mountain.

He could have told her an easier way to go, but the woman and the mountain were settling things between them, so he simply watched it unfold. The mountain challenged her, and she accepted. The Stone People teased her with the sharp talus but didn't try to seriously harm her with a rock slide. Thunder Spirits grumbled and flickered in the dark clouds that always seemed to surround the very peak, but they didn't threaten her.

Gray Cloud and the mountain watched her progress.

The Indians called the mountain Thunder Mountain. It towered in rocky splendor and grim isolation over the surrounding peaks, a forbidding upthrust of granite and soil. It was a place of strong medicine, and it got its name from the thunder that often rolled down its stark sides into the valleys and plain below.

Wasicu scientists claimed to have explained the rock slides that rolled down the slopes with a roar of falling boulders that could be heard for miles.

Gray Cloud knew the white man's theory and dismissed it. The *wasicu* collected bits of information the way magpies collected little bits of straw and glass for their nests. They gathered all those small nuggets together, formed them into pretty patterns and called it knowledge.

Gray Cloud knew better. The mountain rumbled when the Stone People spoke. And *Wakinyan*, Thunder, dwelt in the air over the peak to bring enlightenment to those brave enough to seek visions on the mountain's shoulders. As a child he had come up here and had his first vision. All alone, in the dead of night, whipped by the wind as a storm raged around him, barely nine years old, he had stood on this very mountainside and spoken with the Thunder Beings. They had told him who he was and what he must do with his life, and ever since he had been different from other men.

They who spoke with the Thunder were set apart forever, charged with a task that might last a lifetime.

For Gray Cloud, it had *become* his life. There was, up above, a bowl-like depression in the mountain, a place called a cirque by white men. In that huge depression were multitudes of sticks bearing colored strips of cloth that the Lakota called *shina,* or robes. These robes marked the presence of all the people who had climbed Thunder Mountain to pray or cry for a vision. It was a holy site, and Gray Cloud's life was dedicated to protecting it from encroachment by miners and loggers, and by the curious. He was here to prevent the religious practice of his fellows from being turned into a spectacle, even thwarted entirely. And he would do whatever was necessary.

There were few enough holy places left to the red man. Gone were *Paho Sapa*, the Black Hills and heart of the world. Gone was Bear Butte, now crowded with tourists so that a man couldn't find silence in which to pray. A person needed solitude to pray or cry for a vision. Some ceremonies were meant to be publicly witnessed, but others were meant to be private, and prayer was meant to be a private conversation between the Earth People and the Creator.

Gray Cloud was dedicated to preserving the sanctity of Thunder Mountain.

But the woman climbing so steadily was not a threat to the sacred ground. At least, so he believed. She had come to study wolves, the first to come this far south in many years. The wolves dwelt in the caves on the western slope, away from the sacred ground of the cirque. The woman would study the wolves, and Gray Cloud would leave her in peace so long as she did nothing else. The wolves were strong spirits, after all, and could well take care of themselves when it came to a solitary woman. She would be no trouble.

As long as she didn't trespass.

When he saw that she had safely passed the most dangerous part of the climb, he drew back even farther into the concealment of the forest. Among the *wasicu* who had charged him with the murder of his sister's husband, he was believed to be a dangerous renegade. The woman would not be happy to know he was watching.

What was her name? he wondered idly. The spirits who had told him of her coming had not spoken of her name.

Tomorrow Woman.

The words whispered into his mind, carried by the wind. She was Tomorrow Woman. But she would not answer to the name. She would not know it. She would have a white man's name of some kind. But the spirits would not tell him that.

Tomorrow Woman. He wondered what it meant.

The mountain stirred, rousing a bit from its ancient dreams, aware of a trespasser on its slopes. Those who came to pray hardly caused a ripple in the mountain's awareness, hardly disturbed dreams that were almost as old as the planet. This trespasser didn't come to pray, and the mountain felt a dissonance.

The woman climbed steadily, never giving in. Her determination could be a problem. From everywhere, the mountain watched her and took her measure, and knew that she could not be ignored.

And then, elsewhere, the mountain felt a greater dissonance. A disruptive sense of invasion. There was another trespasser, one bent on destruction. One who would certainly cause harm.

The mountain shuddered a little, wakening further, and forgot the woman for now. There was danger on its slopes. A threat that could not be ignored.

Mercy Kendrick felt someone or something watching her as she struggled up the talus slope. The sensation was a prickle at the back of her neck, which she forced herself to ignore. It had to be a bird, or perhaps some small forest creature. Even a bear. Whatever it was, it was unlikely to bother her, so she refused to give in to the need to pause and look around.

It never entered her head that it might be the Renegade of Thunder Mountain who watched her. She quite simply didn't believe he existed, except as the product of overactive imaginations. Many Indians came up here to pray, and none of them was ever troubled. No doubt a combination of events and sights over the years had yielded the story of the Renegade, that desperate murderer who had never killed anybody on this mountain.

Oh, people died on this mountain. There was no question of that. The geological instability of the rocks made many places dangerous, and from time to time someone would be caught in a rock slide. Or struck by the fierce lightning that often played along the slopes.

The mountain seemed to create its own weather, and its very peak was usually shrouded in clouds. There was a place in Alaska like that, she seemed to remember, though she couldn't remember its name. Panting in the thinning atmosphere, struggling to climb on hands and knees, she didn't particularly care *what* mountain in Alaska made its own weather. Mountains everywhere impacted the weather, and when they were as big as this one...

She slipped and lost her footing, landing with a grunt on her stomach. Loose rocks tumbled away below her, the clatter loud in the natural silence. Then, from above, came the hollow boom of thunder, reminding her that at any moment the clouds could unleash a deluge, and then this slope would become slippery as ice. Gritting her teeth, she reached out with a leather-gloved hand and grabbed at a small bulge in the rock face. Tugging mightily, she pulled herself upward.

Rock climbing was easier than this, she thought. At least she wouldn't be struggling under a sixty-pound pack and sleeping bag. Nor had she expected this part of the climb to be so difficult. She had, in fact, expected it to be relatively easy, and she'd certainly climbed more difficult terrain in her time. But this mountain felt as if it were fighting her. Even El Capitan hadn't felt that way. El Capitan had been tolerant of her climb. Thunder Mountain didn't feel tolerant at all.

Exhaling, she blew her breath upward and shoved a strand of hair back. People would think she was crazy if they ever discovered that she believed mountains had personalities. That some were benevolent, some impatient, some evil. Well, maybe not evil. Thunder Mountain didn't feel evil, exactly. But it sure wasn't indifferent.

Oh, yeah! They would think she was crazy.

At last she reached the top of the rocky incline and was able to stand on a more level piece of ground. Turning, she looked back the way she had come and wondered if she were, in fact, losing her mind. The rock face she had just traversed looked a hell of a lot more dangerous from this perspective than it had from below. From below she hadn't even been tempted to give thought to finding another way. From here, she wondered how she had managed to climb it at all: smooth, without toeholds or handholds in its unmarked face, it was too steep. Steeper than she had originally imagined. Steep enough that she would certainly know better than to come back this way.

Now she could see, over the tops of the trees below, a breathtaking panoramic view of the ranches of Conard County, Wyoming. So much wide-open space, cut by the winding veins of draws and gullies, and all of it green with spring splendor right now.

Closer by, at the edges of the forest, colorful wildflowers bobbed their heads. Mercy gave herself a few moments to soak up the beauty, but she had promised herself that she absolutely would not stop until the light began to fail or the weather closed in. The sooner she reached the caves, the sooner she could verify the presence or absence of the wolf pack.

Turning, she shifted her backpack a little to resettle the load, then began to climb again. The terrain here was somewhat easier, and she was able to stay on her feet.

It would be a matter of considerable interest if there really were wolves on Thunder Mountain. In the first place, wolves hadn't been seen in this part of Wyoming for a couple of generations, at least. And it would be rare anywhere, even in wolf country, to find a pack at this altitude. Of course, it might be an adaptive feature of this particular pack. Certainly the higher country would be safer for them during breeding season.

But she was taking a serious career risk in coming up here on what might well be a wild-goose chase. The sightings of the wolves of Thunder Mountain were few: a hunter here and there who had wandered up the slopes after an elk; talk among the Indians who came up here to pray; sightings in the foothills among ranchers...who might well have mistaken a large coyote for a wolf at a distance. It wasn't as if wolves were an everyday sight, easily identifiable.

But the sightings and reports, scarce though they were, were enough to bring Mercy up the side of this treacherous mountain in the early spring. If there *were* indeed wolves up here, this would be the best time to locate them. During gestation and the first three weeks after the birth of a new litter, the pack tended to remain in one place. Thereafter they would move with increasing frequency. Long before that happened, if there were any wolves up here, she hoped to put electronic collars on at least a few of them so she could track their migrations.

But, of course, she might find nothing. That possibility weighed on her. Wolves had lately been reported in Yellowstone National Park, far to the north, but it wasn't yet certain if there were just a couple of strays or an actual pack, whether the wolves had really returned to the area, or some animal had ventured out on its own. Wolves were known to do that, too.

A lone wolf might be interesting to observe, but it would hardly have the impact on the field that she hoped to achieve. But a lone wolf would be infinitely better than none, because if she returned with word that there were no wolves at all on Thunder Mountain, the department chairman was going to have a field day at her expense. Dr. Lewis Clark Thomas wanted nothing more than to see Mercy Kendrick fall flat on her face. In his opinion, if she wanted to study anything, it ought to be apes. She was wasting her time on predators such as the vanishing wolf. No future in it, he said, and he would undoubtedly use a failure to find wolves here as another excuse to deny her tenure.

Future or not, she was inclined to think he was on her case because she was too independent to suit him. Instead of bowing to his authority and knowledge and just generally kissing up to him, she was prone to argue when she didn't agree. Oh, yes, he would love it if this proved to be a fool's errand. She would spend the next year hearing a daily "I told you so" from him. Smiling wryly now, she wondered if she would be able to endure it.

But wolves had all but vanished from the lower forty-eight states. There were some in Minnesota still, and reports of Canis rufus, the red wolf, in East Texas and Louisiana—although there was a great deal of disagreement about whether they were wolves or coyotes, or a mix of the two.

But none had been seen in this part of Wyoming for a long, long time. No, she couldn't pass up this opportunity. If the wolves were here, it would be a marvelous sign of resurgence, a banner marking the return of a species to its native habitat. It would be a small victory on the ecological battlefield.

Again she felt the prickling at the base of her skull. This time she halted and looked around, no longer quite so blithely certain that whatever was watching her was harmless. If it had followed her...

Shivering inwardly, she adjusted the straps of her pack and tried not to think about *what* might be following her up the slope of this mountain. A wildcat of some kind? A black bear? The thought of a sow with cubs made her scalp prickle. This far out, wild animals should still be wild animals, wary of humans. But with the Indians coming up here regularly to pray, perhaps the mountain's inhabitants were not entirely wild any longer. Perhaps they had lost their fear of men.

And that was when they became truly dangerous.

The slope steepened sharply, and for a little while the sense of being watched vanished. She was too busy trying to breathe, anyway. As she approached ten thousand feet in elevation, the air was thin enough to make heavy exertion uncomfortable. Reminding herself of the dangers to one who came from a lower altitude, she deliberately slowed her pace. Pulmonary edema could be deadly.

A little farther on, the mountain eased up on its challenge, giving her a fairly level run that allowed her to catch her breath and gave the backs of her legs a much-needed respite.

Heavy exertion always threw her deep into the well of reflection, so that minutes stretched into hours almost unnoticed. She really had little idea of how much time had passed or how much farther she had walked when she realized that the light had changed from an ordinary, almost colorless gray to an eerie, ghostly green.

Halting, she looked upward at the clouds and felt a sudden awareness of danger. These were no longer the familiar, leaden cumulonimbus of a thunderstorm. Instead they had become a writhing, seething mass of gray-green swirls that seemed to defy the very air currents on which they were borne.

A gust of wind suddenly swept down the side of the mountain and hit her hard, causing her to stagger sideways. Overhead, thunder cracked with deafening intensity, a warning she couldn't ignore. The air was chilly, and if she got drenched she would quickly become hypothermic. Her day's hike was over.

Gray Cloud watched the woman dig a trench so water would run around her, then climb into a sleeping bag between two layers of waterproof tarp. No tent. The wind would likely have blown down any nylon tent.

Another challenge to her, this time from the Cloud People and the wind. A small challenge, a minor testing of her mettle. She was handling it well, with no evidence of frustration or annoyance. Most *wasicu* perceived the weather as a nuisance unless it was sunny and mild. This woman betrayed none of that in her actions.

Nodding to himself, Gray Cloud settled down to await whatever might happen next.

During the night, the mountain and the elements ceased their teasing and challenged the woman in earnest. The wind snatched the tarp, scooping it up and away, exposing her to the deluge of the heavy thunderstorm. The rain lubricated the rocks above, and the thunder of a landslide added its roar to the thunder from the sky.

Mercy sat up, trapped in the wet sleeping bag, and tried to see through a night as dark as pitch, where not even a glimmer of starlight pierced the clouds. Beneath her, she felt the trembling of the ground that announced the rock slide, felt it like giant footsteps. She couldn't tell, though, whether she was in danger—and if she was, there was no way she could move when she couldn't see an inch before her nose.

The sensation of impenetrable dark induced a panicky feeling of claustrophobia in her. The sense of being trapped was almost overwhelming, and she began to struggle against the confines of her soaked sleeping bag, needing desperately to feel as if she could flee, even if she might break her neck doing so.

Suddenly, stunning her with its unexpectedness, a heavy weight hurled itself out of the dark and flattened her to the ground, pinning her.

Oh, my God! Terror swamped her panic, and she

began to struggle in earnest, convinced a bear was attacking her. And closer came the heavy, pounding footsteps of the rock slide. Some corner of her mind realized that death was imminent, that her life was now measured in mere seconds. The realization battered down the terror enough to let a rational thought through.

Don't move.

Almost as if echoing the thought in her mind, a voice growled in her ear, "Don't move!"

It wasn't a bear that was pinning her to the ground! It was a man!

For an instant relief swamped her. And then she remembered that a man could be as deadly as a bear. Remembered the tales she had dismissed about the Renegade of Thunder Mountain. Instinctively, she shoved at the weight crushing her.

"Don't move," he growled again. "The slide is coming this way!"

He was sheltering her with his body! "We should get out of the way," she heard herself argue with more presence of mind than she would have believed she had at that moment.

The man on top of her grunted sharply. It was here, she realized. The slide was here. The storm sounds were drowned in the deafening roar and clatter of the falling rocks. The world had gone insane, and there wasn't anything to be done except endure it.

The body sheltering hers jerked sharply, then they were free of the slide, the thunderous roar now below them on the slope. Moments passed as they lay there, still, waiting to be sure it was over.

A soft word escaped the man as he rolled off her. It

sounded like an oath, but it wasn't English. After a moment Mercy dared to move, sitting up, still trapped inside her sleeping bag.

"Are you—" Her voice broke as she tried to peer through the dark at her rescuer. "Are you all right?"

"Mm." It was a short, affirmative grunt.

Her pack had been on the slope just above her head, and she reached for it now to get out her flashlight. As her hands touched the nylon, she realized just how much this man's body had sheltered hers. Her pack was covered with small stones, sharp pieces of splintered rock and one stone large enough to have killed if it had hit either of them. Shoving it aside, she pulled the pack toward her and felt around for the flashlight.

"We could have been killed," she said. A stupid, useless thing to say, but it was suddenly necessary to speak. Necessary to move. Necessary to do anything at all to hold at bay the realization that she might have been crushed to death under tons of rock. Or that she might have been buried alive.

Light. Oh, Lord, she needed light now. Light to shove the walls of darkness back and assure her that she wasn't buried. Despite the raw wind that whipped her cheeks and blew her hair wildly about, despite the smell of forest growth and the feel of rain pouring onto her head, she still felt closed in by the night. Trapped.

At last her hand closed on the flashlight, and she fumbled with the switch. Suddenly the night jumped back, and the rain became a yellowish haze as it refracted the beam of the light. And the man sitting across from her looked like a vision carved from stone.

Gray Cloud. The Renegade of Thunder Mountain.

There was no doubt in her mind that she was facing the man around whom the myths had grown. A man like this would draw uneasy attention wherever he appeared.

His Sioux ancestry was apparent in every plane of his dark face, in the dark eyes that stared unblinkingly at her, in the long jet hair that whipped wildly in the wind. He was dressed in ordinary enough fashion—jeans, boots and a zipped-up jacket—but otherwise there wasn't an ordinary thing about him.

He was large—even when he was sitting cross-legged, that was apparent—and in the uncertain light the shadows added to an aura of danger and hardness that was almost terrifying. His hands were resting casually on his knees, and there was nothing at all threatening in his posture, but her mouth went dry, anyway. Dimly she heard herself make a small sound, something like a sighing moan.

"I am Gray Cloud," he said.

She swallowed hard. "I kind of...thought you might be. I'm, um, Mercy Kendrick."

"Mercy." He repeated her name as if accustoming his tongue and lips to the shape of the sound. "A name that sounds like the sigh of a sad heart." He turned his head, looking over his shoulder into the rainy night. "Come with me. There's a cave not far from here. I can build a fire there, to warm you."

Had she been in any major city in the country, or even any small town, she never would have gone anywhere with a stranger...and certainly not one with this man's reputation. But this was not any town or village; it was the isolated side of a mountain in the wilderness, and if Gray Cloud intended her any harm, he could do it here as easily as anywhere else. She was effectively his prisoner, caged by her isolation and the pitch-darkness of the cold, stormy night.

Sensing her agreement, he shouldered her pack and then waited while she struggled out of the sodden sleeping bag. When she was free, he scooped up the heavy bag as if it weighed nothing.

"Walk behind me," he said. "Hang on to my jacket or the backpack."

She handed him the flashlight, but he flicked it off as soon as she had a good grip on the waist of his jacket.

"How can you see?" she asked as they started off into the blackness. It was so dark that with each step she felt as if she were in danger of falling over a cliff edge. "You can't possibly see anything!"

"I can see." The flat statement was no answer at all, but as they moved forward through the darkness, she could not doubt that somehow he *was* able to see. Clearly. As clearly as if it were daylight. He moved forward surefootedly, and because she was right behind him, she encountered no obstacles that he didn't see first and warn her about.

The sound of the rain falling through the trees and striking the ground was a steady roar that drowned all other noises. It was, Mercy thought, like walking through a solid wall of sound, all her senses dead save hearing...and touch. The touch of her feet on the ground, the grip of her hand on his jacket.

Thunder boomed hollowly, echoing against the sides of the mountain, but no lightning was visible. Twice she was sure she felt something brush against her shoulders, something...batlike.

Then, ahead, she saw blue sparks, little dancing sparkles that seemed to appear out of nowhere and then vanish.

"What's that?" she asked, tugging on Gray Cloud's jacket. "That blue light. Do you see it?"

"Spirits," Gray Cloud said.

Spirits? Mercy felt her jaw dropping open, and only the slap of wind-borne rain reminded her to close it. Spirits. Every college-educated bone in her body rebelled at that unscientific answer, and she had to bite her tongue. This man came from a different culture, she reminded herself. Moreover, he was reputed to be some kind of crazy medicine man. Witch doctor. Whatever it was. So, naturally he would speak in terms of spirits.

And regardless of what they were, the blue lights continued to flicker here and there, in a Tinkerbell-like dance, the only things visible in the rain-darkened night.

Some kind of static discharge, she told herself. An electrical phenomenon, like the lightning. And when one brushed near her cheek as if it were a cobweb, she became convinced. The night was charged with electricity—any thunderstorm was—and they were practically in the clouds. This was just some strange kind of lightning.

But it was odd how it seemed to dance before them, as if lighting their way. Her natural curiosity surged, distracting her from her discomfort and the chill of the sodden night. Surely this was something never before studied?

But suddenly all the dancing blue sparkles were gone, and the rain was no longer pouring on them.

The cave. Here the wind was shut out, as was the

downpour, the only detectable changes as they escaped the night's savagery.

"Here," Gray Cloud said. "Just settle down right here until I get the fire going."

Reluctantly, she let go of his jacket and settled cross-legged on the floor of the cave. The undisturbed darkness was disorienting, as was the echo of the rain off the cave walls. Only the solidity of rock beneath her assured her that she wasn't tumbling wildly through space.

Nor could she hear any sounds as Gray Cloud moved around in the cave. For all she could tell, he might have abandoned her. Well, if he had, he'd at least left her someplace dry and out of the wind. Turning her head slowly, she tried to penetrate the dark and wondered why there were no more blue sparkles.

Orange light flared suddenly, and gradually, from a small flame, a camp fire grew in the darkness. It was not enough light to reach the cave walls, so it still felt as if they were sitting on the edge of the world, but she could see Gray Cloud in the flickering light, along with the curtain of rain beyond the huge cave mouth.

"Come closer," he said. "You're wet, and you don't want to get a chill."

Almost as if his words had made her aware that she was soaked to the bone and that the night was cold, she began to shiver. Scooting quickly across the cave floor, she got as close to the blazing heat of the fire as she could and held out her hands in gratitude.

Gray Cloud settled on the far side of the fire, a choice that made it clear he offered no threat at the moment. The cave opening was behind her; she could run without obstruction. Or try to. She shivered again, realizing that even if she tried, she wouldn't get very far. He didn't have to guard her; there was no way she could escape him if he was determined to keep her.

After he sat down, he chanted something quietly. Some kind of prayer, Mercy thought, maintaining a cautious silence until he finished. When his black eyes opened and met hers unblinkingly across the fire, she found her voice.

"I heard about you before I came up here," she blurted. "I didn't think you were real."

His eyes never wavered, and his expression never changed. Nor did he answer. Well, of course not, she thought. What could anyone say to something like that, except to state the obvious? And this man didn't look like the kind who would often state the obvious about anything.

"You came to study the wolves," he said.

Mercy started. "How did you know that? I only told the sheriff!" And Sheriff Nate Tate was famous for not being a gossip.

Seconds ticked by, marked by the drip of water from outside. "I just know," Gray Cloud said finally. "You're *wasicu*. You wouldn't understand."

Wasicu. White. Mercy squelched a flare of irritation, thinking that it couldn't possibly be wise to annoy this man who was reputed to be a murderer...although Deputy Huskins, who had filled her in on all the wild rumors, had admitted that Gray Cloud had been acquitted of the crime. Not that that meant much; criminals were acquitted all the time, thanks to smart legal maneuvers.

"Well, why don't you try telling me, anyway," she said, unable to keep all her irritation out of her voice.

"I don't want anyone to know what I'm doing up here." To protect the wolves, if they existed. Ranchers from the valleys below wouldn't hesitate to hunt down any wolves in the vicinity, whether the animals were a threat or not. Nor would they regard the fact that wolves were an endangered species. So were bald eagles, yet they were being killed all the time.

Another long silence. Gray Cloud, it appeared, could not be hurried into speech. That would make him a maddening companion, Mercy thought. Finally he spoke.

"*Tate* told me." He pronounced it *tah-day*.

"*Tate?*"

"You call it the wind. The wind spoke to me of you. *Wakinyan,* the Thunder Spirit, said you would come. The mountain has awaited you."

The wind spoke to me of you. The Thunder Spirit said you would come. The words caused a chill to trickle down her spine, an instinctive, primitive reaction of fear. Reminders that this man was of a different culture, with a different set of beliefs, didn't comfort her at all. In this dark cave, with no light save the camp fire, with Gray Cloud's intense dark eyes boring into her and the wild storm raging outside, reality seemed to have suspended its normal rules.

"I told you that you wouldn't understand," Gray Cloud said. He spoke as if it didn't matter to him one way or the other. "You're *wasicu*. You don't understand these things."

In fact, Mercy realized with another burst of irritation, he was speaking to her the way parents spoke to children who lacked knowledge...or had drawn erroneous conclusions from their observations. It was a gentle tone, almost kindly. Indulgent.

All her life long, because of her diminutive size and pretty face, she had had to fight to be taken seriously. She had been indulged, patronized and frankly dismissed simply because men tended to dismiss pretty women as fluff. Her instinct, as always, was to fight back. To argue. To prove she was *not* a bit of fluff.

But this man, the Renegade of Thunder Mountain, wasn't dismissing her because she was female or pretty. He wasn't even exactly dismissing her. He was stating in a kindly manner that cultural differences prevented understanding between them on this subject. It took her a minute to battle down her instinctive response to the tone, but when she had, she realized she was curious.

"Tell me what I don't understand," she heard herself say to him. "Please."

He continued to study her in silence, a moderately unnerving experience. She had to fight an urge to shift uneasily and look away. More than a minute passed, then he rose and disappeared into the shadows. When he returned, he carried a blanket. In silence he shook it open and draped it around her shoulders. Then he returned to his side of the fire.

"What you don't understand," he said finally, "would require years to explain."

She drew an exasperated breath, ready to argue, but he continued as if he were unaware of her reaction.

"You were raised in a world that separates man from his environment," Gray Cloud said quietly. "You don't understand that spirit is in everything. That *Skan,* the

force that animates everything, is in every stone and
rock, in every tree, in the breath of the wind. We speak
of the Stone People, the Cloud People, the Four-
leggeds…. It is as ordinary to me that I should hear a
secret on the wind as it is to you to hear one from a
friend."

"Animism," Mercy said. "I've heard of that."

"Animism." Gray Cloud repeated the word and
shook his head. "You will label and define and separate
and isolate…and all understanding is lost by so doing.
There is a word your people have—*gestalt*. The whole
that is greater than the sum of its parts. You are a gestalt, Mercy Kendrick. And if your scientists cut you
into a million tiny pieces and label them all, they will
still not define Mercy Kendrick."

He was right about that, she thought. Looking away,
she watched how the rain just beyond the cave mouth
glimmered in the firelight.

"So," she said presently, not looking at him, "did,
um, the wind say it was okay for me to study the
wolves?" If this man was going to obstruct her, she
wanted to know it up front.

"The wolves will make that decision." Gray Cloud
shifted, and the fire flared suddenly. Mercy turned her
head swiftly, in time to see flames leap high, then fall
back to a comforting glow.

"I mean them no harm," she said.

His black eyes bored into her. "No, you probably
don't," he agreed. "Sleep here by the fire. I'll get you
another blanket."

A few minutes later, with her back to the dancing
flames, she watched the endless fall of rain, little flick-

ers of orange and yellow, and felt sleep begin to steal over her.

And then she saw the dancing blue sparks again, just at the edge of her vision, as her eyes grew heavier and heavier.

Spirits, Gray Cloud had said. *Spirits*.

And as she drifted into sleep, Mercy realized that she had left the normal world behind and stepped into a place where the familiar rules no longer applied.

Chapter Two

The first gray tendrils of light touched the mountain's shoulders lightly, signaling a change of ascendancy among its inhabitants. Mice slipped into burrows; owls settled onto safe perches; bats returned to their caves. Birds welcomed the new day with chirps of song, and does led their fawns to streams to drink.

And the mountain awakened ever more, stretching and flexing powers long unused. The storm during the night had been a mere testing, the rock slide an exercise of atrophied muscles.

And neither had accomplished very much of purpose. The invaders were still on the mountain's slopes, unhindered, undeterred.

Deep inside, the mountain frowned. This was not good.

Mercy opened her eyes to a pale gray light and the sound of steadily falling rain. The wool blankets wrapped around her had kept her warm despite her wet clothes, but it was definitely a morning when she longed for a hot shower.

Sitting up, she discovered that she was alone in the cave. Seizing the opportunity, she struggled out of the blankets and pulled fresh clothes from her backpack. They were clammy, too, but not as sodden as the ones she had on. A minute later, dressed in fresh jeans, a wool sweater and relatively dry socks, she was willing to forego the shower. A granola bar made an easy breakfast.

The fire still burned in a pit hollowed out of the cave floor, and nearby was a stack of wood. Settling as close beside the flames as she could get, Mercy watched the steady rainfall and considered the likelihood that people had been seeking shelter in this cave for ten or twenty thousand years. The fire pit might have been hollowed out by hands that had been dead for centuries. Had there been more light, it would have been interesting to explore for drawings on the cave walls.

Shivering in the cold, damp air, she inched closer to the fire and wondered if Gray Cloud intended to return. She told herself she didn't really need to fear him; had he been a threat, surely she would have discovered it last night. But offering herself such reassurances didn't really help. Not at all.

He had saved her from the rock slide and brought her to a dry cave for the night, but that didn't mean he was a safe man. He was, after all, an accused murderer. He might have killed once. If so, he could surely be capable of killing again. She would have to be very cautious, very careful not to arouse his ire in any way.

But she couldn't run. In the first place, she no longer had any idea where on the mountain she was. Their long walk through the rainy dark had left her utterly disoriented. If she tried to find her way either up or down, she would probably get lost. It wasn't as if Thunder Mountain was a smooth pyramid where up was always up and down was always down. No, the shoulders of this mountain were ridged and rilled, and up and down could be utterly deceptive when it came to direction.

But there was also no point in running. Gray Cloud lived on this mountain, and she was going to have to accept that fact if she wanted to study the wolves. She couldn't drive him off, and, renegade or not, he was no longer a wanted man, so she couldn't ask for help from the Conard County sheriff or the Forest Service. No, he had every right to be here, and she was just going to have to get used to the fact that her nearest neighbor for fifty miles might be a murderer.

The shiver that poured through her didn't come entirely from the chilly, damp air. Common sense kept arguing that she would be a fool not to leave this cave right now and head out of here. But common sense had also warned her not to go rock climbing, because it was dangerous. Mercy Kendrick never gave in to fear, and too often common sense was nothing but fear.

Gray Cloud might have killed someone, it was true. But no one had suggested that he had ever killed anyone else. The Conard County Sheriff's Department hadn't warned her that she shouldn't come up here because a mad killer was on the loose. When she had filed her plans with the Park Service, they hadn't advised her to stay clear because a murderer stalked the park. The slopes of Thunder Mountain weren't littered with the corpses of murder victims. Nowhere was there any evidence to imply that the man was a vicious repeat murderer or a serial killer. As long as she kept out of his way, she probably had nothing to fear.

And nothing was going to keep her from looking for these wolves. It was too important in too many ways.

The hypnotic sound of the falling rain mesmerized her, and she let it. There wasn't enough light to read or write by, so for once she was able to do absolutely nothing and not feel guilty for wasting time. Drawing her knees up, she wrapped her arms around her legs and stared dreamily out into the rain, watching how the water seemed to leach the color from the world, turning everything a misty gray.

Much as she enjoyed hot showers and the comforts of civilization, she had always been happiest when out in the wild like this, particularly in the mountains. Something about the outdoors soothed her soul in a way nothing else could. And when she listened to the rain and turned her thoughts inward, she could almost feel the power of the mountain beneath her, could almost hear voices in the steady patter of rain.

Inevitably her thoughts wandered back to the night before, to the strange man who had rescued her and spoken of Thunder Spirits and Cloud People. Well, Gray Cloud wouldn't laugh at the notion that mountains had personalities. Not the way Merle had.

Thinking about Merle Stockton soured her mood immediately. Ten years ago he'd been her climbing partner, a fellow graduate student and her best friend. Then he had wanted to be her lover. She still didn't understand what had dragged her back from the precipice at the last instant, but something had, and a good thing, too, because Merle had been engaged to another woman—a fact he had neglected to mention to her.

Just as he had neglected to mention that his father was primary shareholder in Stockton-Wells, Inc., one of the largest mining and lumbering concerns in the West. Not that Merle was responsible for the logging of the last of the primordial forest. In fact, Merle had, on a couple of occasions, been quite vociferous about the need to protect the old-growth forests. Still, when she had learned who his father was, she had felt deceived.

In retrospect, she wondered how she had ever believed he was a true friend. His deceits had been bad enough, but he had mocked some of the tenderest parts of her, such as her shyly confided feeling that mountains had personalities.

Unconsciously, she sighed and drew her knees closer to her chin. She had always been a little strange, feeling like an outsider looking in, but she had grown up strong and independent as a result. And being considered fey had led her to become fiercely intellectual... except for lowering her guard with Merle that one ill-fated time.

But last night Gray Cloud had spoken of things every bit as fey as any she had ever felt. Instinctively she had resisted what he was saying...but internally, part of her had heard him and understood him. What had he said? The force of life was in everything? Cloud People. Stone People...

Sighing again, she inched a little closer to the fire and wondered if he would return. Surely he must realize she had become lost during last night's trek. He couldn't just have abandoned her, could he?

Turning, she tried to scan the dark interior of the cave, hoping to see some sign that he would return. She could see nothing, however, except her own belongings, the fire and the woodpile. If he normally sheltered here, he had no extraneous possessions. Giving up, she returned her chin to her knees and stared out into the rain.

All of a sudden, as if it had happened while she blinked, a black wolf appeared at the mouth of the cave. Dark, almost blending with the rainy shadows behind him, he materialized as if from nowhere and stood utterly still, watching her with steady yellow eyes that reflected the firelight.

Mercy felt the hair on the back of her neck rise in a primitive reaction. The eyes that studied her were intelligent. Knowing. Eerie.

Then he was gone. As if she had imagined the entire thing. She'd heard that about wolves, that they could come and go like dark wraiths and move so fast you weren't sure you'd seen them. But that didn't prevent her neck from prickling with the uneasy feeling that she had just seen something supernatural.

Suddenly Gray Cloud filled the cave entrance, almost as if he had sprung right out of the ground or been formed from the wolf that had just vanished.

Mercy blinked quickly several times, wondering if she had been so hypnotized by the rain that she had fallen into some kind of trance...or dozed off. For a while he just stood there, silhouetted against the gray world behind him, an imposing figure in jeans, boots and jacket. A perfect male archetype.

Then he moved, shattering the almost dreamlike feeling of the past few moments, and came to squat beside the fire. He held out his hands to the heat, while water dripped from his long black hair.

"I saw a wolf," she said.

He turned his head and looked at her, his face revealing nothing. "Here?"

She nodded. "At the mouth of the cave. One minute he was there, and the next he was gone. It was incredible!"

"My people tell of how the wolves are so silent and stealthy that they can creep among a herd of horses in the dead of night and never disturb them."

Mercy felt herself nodding. "After what I just saw, I can believe it. But you were as silent yourself. Maybe the rain..." Her voice trailed off as he shook his head.

"We call the wolf *sunkmanitu tank,* which means essentially *spirit that looks like a dog.* Warriors have long tried to emulate his silence and stealth. You haven't been around wolves before?"

"In the wild? Not a lot." Actually, not since childhood, when a park ranger in Minnesota had introduced her to the wolves there and the wraithlike animals had stolen her heart, but she wasn't going to admit that. She'd already heard all she wanted to from her department chair about harebrained schemes. His obsidian eyes regarded her piercingly, as if he could see past her words to the truth in her mind, but he let her assertion pass.

"In the wild," he said after a moment, "wolves aren't at all the way your myths make them out to be. My father told me that, as a boy—when wolves were still plentiful—he and the others boys used to go out and dig up their dens and play with the pups."

Mercy drew a sharp breath. "Didn't the bitch object?"

He shook his head. "Wolves rarely attack humans. The female and her mate would watch from a distance but never threaten the boys. And when they were done, the boys put the pups back. In the wild, wolves are wary of humans. Wary and respectful. They could be a nuisance, of course, stealing food and killing the foals, but as a rule, the wolves had more to fear from man than man had to fear from them."

He shifted, settling cross-legged on the cave floor so that he faced her, with the fire beside him. "The wolves here are still wild. They won't give you any trouble, but they'll be shy of you. Observing them won't be easy."

"I really didn't expect it to be. But at this time of year they tend to stay close to their dens and not migrate as much. Mainly I want to ascertain whether there's a viable pack here."

His dark eyes bored into her. "Why?"

Mercy shifted, feeling suddenly uneasy, though she couldn't have said why exactly. "Because it's wonderful if the wolves are returning. And if they're here, we can protect them, make sure that no one hurts them."

His gaze never wavered. "The ecology of this continent was safe in the hands of the native peoples before the *wasicu* ever crossed the oceans. The wolves and the eagles abounded. The buffalo were like a black sea moving across the plains. We never cut down a tree without asking its forgiveness first. We lived in harmony and believed in balance.

"Now, less than two centuries after the white man first came to this part of the continent, it has become a matter of scientific interest that wolves have been sighted on the slopes of Thunder Mountain."

Mercy nodded, accepting the implied rebuke. There was no way to deny that the buffalo, the eagles and the wolves had been carelessly and needlessly slaughtered into near extinction.

"When you go down from here," he said after a moment, "you'll tell your people that there are wolves here. And the ranchers below will start to see wolves behind everything that happens to their cattle and sheep."

"Word is already getting around that there are wolves up here. That's how I heard about it."

"But no one was sure. You'll make them sure. And when that happens, traps will be set."

"Only on private property."

"You think the wolf knows the difference between private property and public domain? Do you think he cares? If he crosses a corner of the Bar C and gets his foot caught in a trap that Jeff Cumberland puts out because a calf has disappeared, do you think the wolf will know he has trespassed?"

"But if Mr. Cumberland's calves disappear, he's going to put out traps regardless. It could be bobcats, or coyotes or bears or…"

"Or stray dogs. Pet German shepherds have always been a greater danger to livestock than wolves. It wasn't so long ago a meat-packing company in Minnesota put a bounty on German shepherds because they were decimating the livestock in the area. The local farmers still went out and slaughtered wolves."

Mercy nodded, surprised that this isolated man had evidently studied the issue. She hadn't expected a renegade medicine man to be familiar with such things. In fact, she thought with an uncomfortable flushing of her cheeks, she hadn't even expected him to be literate, much less articulate and apparently educated.

"If a calf disappears," he continued, "the local ranchers are immediately going to assume the wolves are at fault. How are you going to protect them against being hunted?"

She looked down at her hands and considered the question, knowing full well that protected status for the species was no real protection at all. It certainly hadn't been for the bald eagle. "If they know the wolves aren't really a threat…"

"The information is available. They don't want to hear it. The assumptions are something they were raised with, and when men believe things to be a certain way, they become blind to other truths."

Well, she certainly had personal experience with the truth of that, Mercy found herself thinking. She had been blind to a few truths herself.

"What are you saying?" she asked finally. "That I shouldn't study the wolves?"

During the seconds that followed, she had the eeriest feeling of something brushing against the back of her neck, a chill, clammy touch that sent a shiver running down her spine. Instinctively she looked behind her, but there was nothing there. Just the wind, she told herself. *Tate,* Gray Cloud had called it.

Turning back, she found him staring at her with a steadiness that was unnerving. "No," he said when she met his gaze. "I'm just asking you to be careful what you do with the knowledge you gain."

But, she found herself thinking, if he felt she was endangering the wolves, he would probably do his level best to get her off this mountain. It didn't help to remember that he had been accused of murder. That even though he had been acquitted, his own people had cast him out. Whether or not it was murder, someone had died at this man's hands. Another chill trickled down her neck, but this one was purely psychological.

Just then a gust of wind swept a curtain of cold rain through the cave entrance and slapped it right against Mercy. Startled, she jumped and blinked.

"When the rain stops," Gray Cloud said, "I'll take you up the mountainside to where the den is."

"You know where it is?" She hadn't expected a boon like this, but had, in fact, expected to have to hunt for the den.

He nodded.

"Then you know how many there are? How long they've been here?"

Eyes like shards of obsidian stared back at her impassively. "I didn't count them, but there are more this year than last."

"Last year? How long have they been here?"

"Almost five years."

"And I never heard about it!" Mercy shook her head. "I'm surprised this place hasn't been crawling with wildlife biologists and conservation people."

"This place, as you call it, is sacred to my people. It had better not crawl with biologists and conservationists. Just leave it to the Indians, Ms. Kendrick. We'll take care of everything on Thunder Mountain, simply by letting it be."

Mercy returned his stare steadily for several seconds, then shook her head. "You know better than that, Gray Cloud. You know it won't be left alone. If I don't study the wolves, someone else will."

It was eerie, she thought, how he never moved a muscle, never blinked. Motionless, as if he had been carved from stone, he studied her. Just the way the wolf had earlier, she found herself remembering. With the same intent, focused regard.

At last he spoke, but on an entirely different subject. "The rain will stop shortly."

Mercy instinctively looked out of the cave, but she could see no sign that the steady downpour was abating, or that the day was lightening. "How do you know that?"

"I just know."

Slowly, she turned her head and looked at him again. Her impulse was to ask how he knew, but he would undoubtedly reply with something about the Cloud People or the wind, and she would be no wiser than she was right now.

"There's a cave that will make a good base camp for you," he said. "I'll show you where it is."

At least he hadn't changed his mind about taking her up there, she thought as she settled down to watch the rain. For a minute, when he had started talking about leaving the mountain to the Indians, she had begun to wonder.

By midmorning the rain had stopped, though the sky remained overcast and low clouds touched the peak of Thunder Mountain. The air was chilly, almost cold, but the wind had stopped, and the stillness took the bite out of it.

Every gorge and gully was filled with tumbling, rushing water, which made the journey difficult and sometimes dangerous. It wasn't long at all before Mercy was grateful for Gray Cloud's company. He knew the slopes of this mountain as intimately as most people knew their backyards, and he unquestionably saved her countless hours of retracing her steps to look for a passable route.

He had recovered her tarp from wherever it had blown to during the night, and he carried it for her now, along with her sodden sleeping bag. She wondered if that would ever dry out, then shrugged away the concern. She had her survival blankets, and Gray Cloud had insisted she take his wool ones, also, assuring her that he had more.

"Wolves don't usually venture this high," she remarked to him after one particularly rough climb up a steep, rocky slope.

Turning, he offered a hand and helped her over some loose rocks. "It's not safe for them to venture many other places anymore."

She glanced up at him, struck anew by the absolute midnight of his gaze. "You think they came here to be safe?"

"Perhaps." Releasing her hand, he turned and looked up the slope. "See the ravens?" He pointed to dark specks circling in the sky over some trees higher up. "That's where you'll find the wolves now. The birds are waiting for their turn at the kill."

Mercy nodded, wondering how he could tell that

those specks were ravens. Must be the way they were flying, she decided. She had heard, of course, of the symbiotic relationship between the birds and wolves. The ravens were known to locate weak prey for the wolves, and then would feed on the kill when the wolves were done. Some researchers claimed the relationship was a close, social one. She would reserve judgment until she saw it with her own two eyes. She had more than once seen how easy it was to humanize behavior that had other adaptive explanations.

"This way." He headed them away from the circling birds, toward the more forbidding terrain to the north. "There is a harmony in nature," he told her. "What the wolves kill will feed many besides themselves. Nothing will be wasted."

And what about what he had killed? she wondered. Caution kept her from voicing a question that surely would have angered him, but she couldn't help wondering about the contrast between the man she had heard about and the man who was guiding her to the wolf den. "Do you...? Do you stay up here year-round?"

He glanced at her, then indicated the path with a jerk of his chin. "I live on this mountain."

"Why?" The question came automatically, out of her mouth before she could prevent it. When he halted and turned to face her, she wished the ground would open up and swallow her. Nosiness was inexcusable at any time, but when someone had secrets like this man's, it became more than inexcusable—it became dangerous.

"This mountain is sacred to my people," he said flatly. "Someone has to protect it for them."

That certainly wasn't the answer she had expected to hear. "Protect it from what?"

"From development. From timbering. These are public lands, Ms. Kendrick. That means a lot of people have a lot of ideas for using them. And most of those ideas are incompatible with the needs of my people."

"But surely you could come to some kind of compromise?"

For a moment he didn't move, not even the slightest little bit. When he spoke, his voice was dry. "Of course we can reach a compromise. When the *wasicu* allow us to use their churches and cathedrals for our secular needs. Maybe we can hold a powwow in the nave on Sunday morning."

Under other circumstances, Mercy would have found the image amusing, but this man didn't intend it to be funny. And he was right, she admitted. Holy places should be treated with respect, and she seriously doubted that hordes of tourists and developers would treat the mountain that way.

He resumed their upward trek, leading the way across another rushing torrent with a familiarity that said he knew this mountain and its moods intimately. Mercy longed to ask him how long he'd been up here and what he thought he could possibly do to prevent timbering or development if the weight of the Forest Service and corporate America ever got behind it.

The ideas that occurred to her—sabotage and murder—were so unsavory that she left the question unspoken. If this man was as dangerous as his reputation led one to believe, she didn't want to know it. She much preferred to think the tales were exaggerated. Besides, he had taken care of her in more than one way since last night's rock slide. He had placed his own body between her and danger. For now she would give him the benefit of the doubt—and hope that she wasn't making a disastrous mistake.

A finger of cold air snaked down inside her sweater, and she shivered. The clouds appeared to be thickening again, and the air was heavy with moisture. A low rumble of thunder sounded in the distance, and she wondered if they would reach their destination before another storm was unleashed on them.

Ahead of her, Gray Cloud suddenly halted and squatted. From where she stood, Mercy was treated without warning to the sight of powerful thighs and hard buttocks stretching old denim tight. Uncomfortable with her response and with the fact that she was all alone in the middle of nowhere with an incredibly virile man, she dragged her gaze upward and tried to focus on his hawkish profile.

"Something wrong?" she asked.

"Footprints."

She edged closer and peered over his shoulder. There, in mud left by the rain, were the unmistakable prints of heavy hiking boots. "Don't a lot of people come up here?"

"No." He lifted his head and looked ahead. "We get a few hunters in the fall, but not many. And hikers usually keep to the lower slopes." He pointed to the boot prints that were visible all the way across the shallow depression ahead of them before vanishing into a stand of pine trees. "I didn't know anyone at all was up here except you."

Mercy opened her mouth to ask him how he could possibly know that about a mountain this big, then caught herself. He would probably say the wind told him. "Well, it's public land," she said after a moment.

But he remained squatting, studying the prints. "Someone walked through here in the last couple of hours. As heavy as the rain was, it would have washed out these prints pretty fast." After a couple of moments, he straightened and looked down at her. "I don't think you should stay alone out here until we find out about this guy."

The absurdity of the idea struck her, but she managed to turn her head swiftly and bite her lip before she could remind him that she was already out here alone with a strange man, and, what was more, a man who had been accused of murder.

"Just what do you expect me to do?" she was able to ask finally. "I'm here to study the wolves, not hide out. And there's no reason to think anyone would want to harm me, anyway. Or that we'd even run into each other on a mountain this size."

She half expected him to argue with her, if only because he seemed like the type of alpha male who wouldn't care to have his dominance questioned. He said nothing, though. Whatever he thought, he kept it to himself.

But she couldn't fail to notice his increased alertness, the way he intently scanned the ground ahead of them, the way he frequently cocked his head as he tried to identify sounds. Not even a birdsong escaped scrutiny.

And gradually it began to dawn on her that this man, renegade or not, was a far better judge of what was worrisome on this mountain. If he thought the presence of someone else in this location at this time of year was worth worrying about, she might well be wise to listen.

"Not much farther now," he told her when they paused for a break during the early afternoon. "The cave I'm thinking of isn't too far from the den, but not so close that your presence would disturb the wolves."

"I really appreciate this, you know. Last night. You taking me up here."

He looked straight at her for the first time in hours. "You mean well. I have no quarrel with you."

As if to say that he would, if her intentions changed. As if to say he might, with someone else. It sounded suspiciously like a threat, and Mercy felt the back of her neck prickle. The silence between them suddenly seemed strained, uneasy, and she needed desperately to fill it.

"Do you stay up here all the time?" she asked him, since the question had never truly been answered before.

He nodded once, briefly.

"But—" She caught herself again, before impulsively asking if he didn't miss other people, didn't miss the comforts of civilization. Stupid questions, she scolded herself. Why should he miss other people? And maybe he couldn't afford any of those comforts, anyway.

Almost as if he read her thoughts, something in his face shifted, easing the harshness there just a little. "Some people are complete in themselves, Ms. Kendrick. Needing others is a weakness."

"Or a strength," she said impulsively. "What kind of world would we live in if no one needed anyone else?"

She fully expected him to retort, but he stiffened just then, and stared into the space beyond her.

"What's wrong?" she asked.

"Shh."

Looking around behind her, she could see nothing, so she strained her ears to hear. Beyond the omni-present sound of rushing water, she couldn't hear a thing.

"Let's get going," Gray Cloud said abruptly.

She turned to him. "What happened? Did you hear something? See something?"

"I heard a couple of gunshots."

"Somebody signaling for help?"

"Maybe. Come on. Let's check it out."

She wasn't at all keen on checking out gunshots, but she couldn't in good conscience object. If there was any possibility at all that someone was hurt, they *had* to go to his aid. She didn't approve of guns, though, and generally didn't much care for the uses to which people put them.

Gray Cloud quickened their pace considerably now, out of concern that someone might be in serious trouble. Mercy couldn't imagine how he had heard the shots over the roar of running water that seemed to fill the entire forest, but there was no doubting that he'd heard something, and that he was making a beeline in the direction he thought it had come from.

Maybe he hadn't heard anything at all. The thought twisted sinuously into her mind as if whispered into her ear. Why would he pretend to hear something? But how *could* he hear anything over the rushing water? Why hadn't she heard it, too?

Because he was better attuned to the forest sounds from living here all the time. Because an unusual sound, however faint, would probably catch his attention faster than it would hers.

Struggling upward behind him, breathing heavily from exertion and the thin air, she tried to argue with her growing uneasiness. From the moment he had shielded her with his body last night, he had taken good care of her. There was absolutely no reason to think he had a hidden agenda of any kind.

After all, she told herself, if he wanted her off this mountain, there was no reason to drag her all over it. Instead he could have scared her away with very little effort at all. She wasn't so dedicated to studying these wolves that she would have withstood a serious threat.

Panting, she neared the top of a steep climb and gladly accepted Gray Cloud's hand when he turned and leaned down to offer it to her. In that instant, as she watched her small pale hand disappear into his huge dark one, she became aware of him as a man.

Awareness caught her between one breath and the next, hitting her like a blow to the solar plexus. Gasping again, this time with the shock of it, she felt him lift her with one hand, pulling her up the slope as if she weighed no more than a feather.

No, she thought as her feet settled firmly on the ground once again. No. Of all things, not that. She didn't need or want sexual attraction in her life ever again. It was too painful, too distracting. She was here to work. Period.

"Stay behind me now," he said in a low voice. "It can't be much farther."

"How can you be sure of that?" she asked, keeping her own voice at a level barely audible over the rushing water. "How can you even be sure we're headed in the right direction?"

"There were two shots. The second gave me the chance to locate the direction it came from. As for the distance…" He gave a little shake of his head. "Sound can't travel very far under these conditions and still be distinct."

He was right, she guessed, as she followed close behind him into the shadowy depths of a thick stand of pines. Just as she was drawing a breath to ask him how he had learned such things, he stopped abruptly and held out an arm, silencing her.

His nostrils flared as he lifted his head and tested the air. "Blood," he whispered. "Stay here while I check it out."

She didn't feel the least urge to argue with him. He moved as silently as a wraith, she thought as she watched him slip away farther into the shadows beneath the trees.

Under the sheltering boughs of the trees, the shadows were deep, almost nightlike. As she waited, the wind kicked up a new waterfall of sound as it whispered through the treetops. Cold air trickled down the neck of her jacket, and she tugged at the collar, trying to close the gap opened by the pack on her back.

Blood. That could mean so many things. Someone seriously hurt. An animal killed by a poacher. An animal killed by another animal. Maybe a predator had brought down prey of some kind, and someone had shot at it. A lynx, maybe.

Or a cougar? Suddenly she couldn't remember if there were still any cougars in these parts. Uneasy, she looked around at the shadows, which seemed to be darkening and deepening visibly as she stood there, and thought of all the animals that *could* present a danger. Bears. Grizzlies. Not every predator was as harmless to humans as wolves. Some, like grizzlies, wouldn't hesitate to attack.

Shivering a little, she hugged herself and shifted from one foot to the other.

It was dark in here, under these trees. Darker than just a few minutes ago. Thunder rumbled hollowly, and some of the taller trees groaned as the wind caught their tops and made them sway. What was taking Gray Cloud so long?

Shivering again, she turned around slowly, trying to shake the crawling sense that the day was turning sinister, that the entire mood of the mountain was growing threatening. Silly, she told herself. It was just that the clouds were thickening and dimming the light. Mountains might have moods, but that was just her interpretation of the difficulty of their slopes, not a real manifestation of feelings. Not something that could change and alter as a person's moods could.

Certainly not.

But the feeling was inescapable, and as her uneasiness grew, so did her impatience. What could possibly be taking Gray Cloud so long? If someone were seriously hurt...

If someone were seriously hurt, he would have to do what he could for them before coming back for her. Simple as that. And it might take an appreciable amount of time. The weight of the backpack on her shoulders seemed to be growing more onerous with each passing second, and finally she shrugged it off and leaned it against the trunk of a tree.

Overhead, the quickening wind sighed through the tops of the pines like a soul in torment. A drop of rain found its way through the maze of branches and needles and struck her icily on the cheek. Slowly, she tipped her head back and looked up at a patch of dark sky. The gray of the clouds had taken on a darker, greenish cast, and the clouds themselves, from what little she could see, seemed to be moving with terrible swiftness.

Thunder rumbled suddenly, loud enough to make the ground beneath her feet tremble like a drum skin. It seemed to go on forever, strengthening, fading a little, then reaching a deafening crescendo. Instinctively she squatted, making a smaller target of herself, hoping that none of the trees would become a lightning rod.

The mountain was angry. Something had happened to anger the mountain, and, crazy as the thought was, she believed it. At this moment, with the ground trembling beneath her and the thunder rolling over her head in an endless, stunning wave of sound, she could only believe that Thunder Mountain was crying out in rage.

Clapping her hands over her ears, she pressed her face to her knees and tried to tell herself it was just an ordinary storm, just ordinary thunder, no more threatening than any other natural fury she had endured in her life. But she couldn't quite believe it.

"Mercy."

Gray Cloud's deep voice pierced the comparative silence when the thunder's growl died away. Lifting her head, she saw him crossing the pine-needle carpet with long, fluid strides. At once she straightened, feeling foolish at being found huddled like a child in a dark closet.

"Did you find someone?" she asked.

He shook his head, a brief negative. "A poacher shot a doe and fawn."

"Oh, no!"

Bending, he lifted her pack and indicated she should turn so he could help her into it. "I want to get you up to the cave," he said. "Away from here. Then I'll come back and look for the killer."

"Why don't you look for him now? He might get away if you wait." The straps of the backpack settled onto her weary shoulders, and she nearly winced from the bruised feeling.

"I can hunt better alone."

The thought of the murdered deer caused her lips to part, her lungs to draw air, her mind to frame an argument. But then thunder roared furiously overhead, and the green light filtering through the trees darkened even more.

He was right, she thought. The deer were already dead, and the mountain was enraged.

Besides, she realized with another chill trickling down her spine, she didn't know what Gray Cloud meant when he said *hunt*. And she wasn't at all sure she wanted to know.

Chapter Three

Thunder Mountain felt the death of the doe and fawn all the way to its root in the heart of the Earth. Needless death. Needless destruction. Violation of the sanctity of life. The doe and her fawn had not been killed for food, but for pleasure. For the sake of killing.

The mountain knew humans. For more than ten thousand years men had climbed its slopes, seeking the powers of the universe, seeking answers to questions and visions to guide them. And then had come the invaders from the east. Only a short time ago, as the mountain felt. Only a little while ago had come the hordes from the east, men who killed for sport and enjoyment. Men who had nearly exterminated the buffalo and the wolves and the eagles. Men who respected nothing and never dreamed that they were trespassing on old and ancient powers, that they were breaking covenants that had existed since the dawn of time.

Puny little mortals, yet so destructive.

The mountain shrugged, and its shoulders trembled. The invaders must be driven out. The threat must be re-

moved. Thunder Mountain had to protect its denizens, from the smallest lichen to the oldest owl.

Wanton killing could not be tolerated.

The mountain reached out for Gray Cloud, the mortal who was the servant of Thunder. Gray Cloud could be counted on to help.

The cave where Gray Cloud left Mercy was little more than a chamber scooped out of the side of the mountain. It provided shelter from the rain and wind, and had only one tunnel leading deeper into the mountain. After a few moments' study, she decided that the mouth of the tunnel and the passageway behind it were too small to allow casual human exploration. Satisfied that she needn't fear poachers or bears coming from that direction, she dismissed it.

And there was wood. Though he'd said nothing about it, the presence of the woodpile meant either that he sheltered here himself often, or that he had prepared for her arrival. She would have thanked him for it, and for guiding her here, except that he never gave her the chance.

He'd stared at her long and hard, a look that cleaved her tongue to the roof of her mouth, and said, "I'll be back by morning to take you to the wolves." And then he was gone, as if he had never been. Slipping away into the rainy forest as swiftly and silently as the wolf had done earlier.

It was, Mercy found herself thinking as she shivered in the chilly air, a good thing his eyes were dark and not tawny. If he had looked at her with a wolf's golden gaze, she would have begun to believe in werewolves right there and then.

But his gaze was as dark as obsidian, and just as hard. It chilled her and challenged her all at once, just as his masculinity kept frightening her and challenging her with an awareness she didn't want. He was a killer, she reminded herself. Maybe not a murderer, but there seemed little doubt he had killed someone. Maybe the killing had been justified. Maybe that was why he had been acquitted.

And maybe she should have paid more attention and learned more about the situation before she had come up here. It was a little late now to be worrying about what Gray Cloud was capable of.

The first thing she did was build a fire in the pit hollowed out in the rock floor of the cave. Again she wondered how many generations had built fires here, wondered if mammoth hunters from long ago had camped in this very cave and sat on the floor right here as the fire caught and began to burn.

She could almost imagine their weather-wizened faces gathered around the flames as she spread out her soaked sleeping bag in the hope that it might dry sometime in the next month or so.

Thunder rumbled again, but the cave walls deadened the sound a little, making it less threatening. The day had darkened until it was almost nightlike. Flickers of lightning could be seen now through the cave opening. Thunder Mountain was certainly aptly named, she told herself when at last she settled close to the fire and tried to warm her nearly numb hands.

All of a sudden another deafening crack shook the ground with earthquakelike ferocity. On and on it rolled, causing the ground to tremble as if heavy trucks were rolling by. Wrapping her arms around her knees, she stared out through the cave mouth and watched as pitchforks of lightning sizzled through the air, blinding in their intensity.

The mountain is angry. This time she didn't even argue with the thought. It was as good an explanation as any for this terrifying display of the power of the elements. Safe and dry in her little niche, she thought of Gray Cloud tracking the poacher. Surely he couldn't even be attempting it in the midst of this violence?

It was easy, as she huddled by the fire, to understand why this mountain was believed to be sacred. Short of a tornado she had survived as a child, short of a force-five hurricane, she had never seen nature unleash such ferocity. Thunder had begun to rumble almost continuously, and lightning flashed and flared over and over, bringing a brighter-than-daylight brilliance to the waning afternoon. Nothing would be afoot in this. Any creature with sense would have hunkered down to wait out this wrath.

And unbidden came the memory of the blue sparkles she had seen last night, the dancing blue lights that Gray Cloud had called spirits. Some kind of electrical activity, certainly. It had to be. No other explanation was acceptable in a rational world.

But this was not a rational world, whispered a voice in the back of her mind. Not on this mountain. Somewhere during her climb up the rugged lower slopes she had left behind the world she knew. This was the world of sentient nature, of shamans and spirits and powers beyond imagining.

Shivering again as that strange chill trickled down her

neck, she inched closer to the fire until the skin of her cheeks tightened from the heat, and still she felt cold and her back felt exposed. For the first time since she had conceived of this trip, it occurred to her that it might not be a simple matter of camping out and watching wolves. Other things might be involved. Other forces.

What had Gray Cloud called the wolves? *Shunk*-something. Spirit that looks like a dog. She shivered again, remembering the eerie golden eyes of the wolf she had seen earlier. Eyes that had seemed too intelligent. Too knowing. Too human. Not the big, sad brown eyes of a dog at all. It was easy to understand why wolves had received so much bad press over the years, but even knowledge of the true nature of the beast didn't prevent the atavistic response to an animal with eyes that were too knowing.

Suddenly her breath locked in her throat, and every thought flew from her head. Standing in the mouth of the cave was a black wolf. The same one she had seen this morning at the other cave. And he was looking at her with those incredible glowing eyes, looking at her with recognition, as if he, too, remembered their earlier meeting.

Those golden eyes transfixed her, preventing her from looking away, preventing her, it seemed, from even thinking. They seemed to absorb her, drawing her into the heart of the fire that lay between them, drawing her into whirling mysteries of blue lights and golden eyes.

And then, just as she sucked a ragged breath of air into her lungs, the wolf released her by the simple expedient of closing his eyes slowly. Lazily. Almost drowsily. Then, turning, he sat on his haunches with his back to her and stared out at the wildness of the storm.

As if he were standing guard.

The sound of her tattered breaths was smothered by the fury of the storm without. Even the crackle of the fire was almost inaudible. Reaching out, never taking her eyes from the wolf, she felt around for her pack. From it she pulled a pen and pad, then, by the light of the fire, she wrote down all her impressions of the creature who sat in calm and complete disdain of her presence. It was as if, she found herself thinking, the wolf had measured her and judged her to be no threat to him.

Thunder hammered at the sky again, and lightning danced from cloud to cloud and then zig-zagged to the ground. The wolf's ears pricked, turning a little this way and that, but otherwise he was undisturbed by nature's violence.

When she had written down everything she could think of, Mercy dropped her chin to her knees and just watched the wolf across the top of the fire, the heat giving the scene a wavery, dreamlike effect. Such a beautiful creature, with a nobility and edge that few dogs had. And such big feet...

Suddenly the wolf rose onto all fours, crouched, hackles rising. A low growl filled the cave, along with the sound of the coming storm's fury.

It could be anything, Mercy told herself as her heart started to hammer. A rabbit. A squirrel. Just some strange smell borne on the wind.

And then, with shocking suddenness, the downpour began as the heavens unloaded a heavy, concealing curtain of rain. The wolf stayed tense for a short while, then slowly settled back on its haunches in a pose of alert relaxation. Mercy released the breath she had been holding and relaxed, too, albeit more slowly.

Inevitably she wondered if the wolf had somehow sensed the coming rain and decided to shelter here from it. Well, of course the wolf hadn't *decided*, she amended silently. Not in the way a human being would make such a decision. The animal had simply learned through experience that he could keep dry here.

Almost as if he'd read her mind, the wolf turned his shaggy head and looked at her over his shoulder with those uncanny, intelligent eyes. Looking into that unblinking gaze, Mercy found it dangerously easy to believe this animal could have made a decision, could indeed have reasoned, in the human sense of the word.

Oh, Lord, all this talk of spirits and Cloud People was getting to her. What did it matter what had brought the wolf to this cave? Regardless, she had an incredible opportunity to observe one closely and the even more incredible experience of feeling protected by him. For surely, if anything threatened the wolf, the animal would protect her as a consequence of protecting himself.

Suddenly aware of how close to the fire she was sitting and that her cheeks were beginning to feel like singed paper, she scooted back a little. Once again the wolf looked at her over his shoulder, then resumed his watch over the rain-soaked mountainside.

And suddenly, in the oddest way, she became acutely aware of just how isolated she was, of just how high up this mountainside in the middle of nowhere she was sitting. She could scream her lungs out, and no one would hear but that wolf and a few other forest creatures. If she died, they might not find her bones for years.

It was as if she rose above herself and with an eagle's eye saw the little speck that was herself surrounded by the vast untamed wilderness of the mountain. Had she been insane to come up here alone?

Once again the wolf looked at her with eyes that were too knowing. Too intelligent for any beast. The last time she'd had the feeling she was looking into an eye as intelligent as her own had been with a humpback whale she had been studying off Australia. She had believed then that whales could think. She was beginning to believe that this wolf could, too.

And the feeling didn't make her comfortable at all.

The wolf was still with her when night fell, but shortly after total dark blanketed the world he rose suddenly, raised his nose to the wind and let out a long, long howl that made the hair on Mercy's neck stand on end. He was answered from out of the night by other howls, and for the first time in her life Mercy heard the famous harmony of a wolf pack, each animal picking a different run of notes, with the result that three or four wolves could sound like a dozen or more.

Then her companion gave her one last, long look and disappeared from the cave into the rainy, windy night. Shivering, Mercy reached for her notebook and bent to the fire to scribble her impressions of what had just happened.

All of a sudden she was aware of not being alone. Her scalp prickled as she slowly, reluctantly raised her head.

Breath left her in a rush as she recognized Gray Cloud. "Lord, you scared me!"

"Sorry." He stayed where he was, just inside the cave

mouth, regarding her with eyes that, despite the difference in color, reminded her of the wolf's.

"You didn't catch the poacher?"

"There was a slight wrinkle."

She tipped her head back a little farther to better see him. "What kind of wrinkle?"

"There are more than one of them. And two of them, at least, were headed up this way when it started to rain."

"Headed this way? You mean to *here?*"

He gave a brief nod.

Pushing herself to her feet, she crossed to the cave mouth and stood beside him, looking out at the pitch-dark, rainy night. "They can't move in this."

"I did."

She glanced at him, noting that once again he was soaked, but apparently oblivious of it. *You're not an ordinary man.* The words rose to her lips, but she bit them back. And then she remembered.

"There was a wolf here earlier."

"Again?" For an instant, an instant so brief she wasn't sure she saw it, one corner of his mouth quirked upward. "They like you."

She shook her head, not prepared to consider any such possibility. "I could have sworn it was the same one that turned up this morning. But that's not the point."

"It isn't?" He turned so that he faced her. "Wolves approach you twice in one day, and you don't consider it significant?"

"I didn't say that! But I'm trying to make a point here, if you'll just let me finish!"

He made an inviting gesture with one hand.

"The point is, the wolf came and sat here at the cave mouth for several hours, and once he acted as if something disturbed him. Growled, raised his hackles. Maybe somebody was out there."

"Could be." He moved another quarter turn so that he, too, looked out into the rain-soaked night. "Well, you're not alone now. As for the wolves—lady, you need a change in your perspective."

She felt her hands clench into fists but managed to speak evenly. "What does that mean?"

"Wild animals have approached you twice in one day. Think about it. The wolf honors you. Appreciate it."

Adopting a different perspective was something like running head-on into a brick wall, Mercy thought. She had been aware that seeing the wolf twice was exciting, unique, but she hadn't thought of it as being honored. And yet...

Staring out into the night, she considered what he had said. Considered what it might indicate. "You think he sought me out deliberately?"

"Once might be chance. Twice is something more."

Something in her was inclined to agree. Something purely unscientific, of course. Something that...could see spirits. "That implies that wolves think," she argued, instinctively reaching for her ivory tower of objectivity.

"Are you so sure they can't?" The question was asked mildly enough. Almost casually. "Open your mind."

That stung her. "My mind *is* open." The very nature of scientific inquiry required it.

But Gray Cloud shook his head ever so slightly. "Within your preconceived limits, your mind is open. You equate the wolf with the domestic dog. Your ability to perceive the intelligence of other species is limited by your notion that man's intelligence is at the top of a pyramid in lonely splendor. That no other species approaches it."

Before she could marshal a response, he held out one hand, cupping his palm as if to receive something. Instantly a light appeared there, a sparkle of electric blue. "You see it," he said. "What do you call it? The *wasicu* have no name for it. No definition. Most of them couldn't even see it, because it doesn't exist within their accepted framework. *You* see it. You perceive many things beyond the fringe of your knowledge, but you try to hide them even from yourself, because they don't fit."

He held his palm out a little more, as if offering it to her. She folded her arms tightly across her breasts, refusing the invitation, barely managing to keep herself from stepping back.

"Call it magic, if you will," he said after a moment. Slowly he closed his palm, and the light vanished. "But it's as real as you are. As I am."

"What do *you* call it?" she asked.

He shook his head. "It doesn't matter what I call it. You're merely looking for a reason to dismiss it."

The realization that he was right was discomfiting. If he called it anything—anything at all—she would have a starting point from which to dismiss it. And that wasn't very scientific, was it?

But it was, she realized with a queasy sinking sensation in her stomach. It was exactly the scientific frame of mind. If you couldn't label it and put it in a laboratory, it didn't exist. There was a certain perverted security in dismissing anything that couldn't be precisely quantified. Or in dismissing anything that could be reproduced through quackery. Like that group of scientists who insisted on dismissing paranormal phenomena because the effects could be reproduced by a magician...never realizing that being able to produce those effects didn't necessarily mean they had found the *only* means by which they could be produced. That was like saying a full-spectrum light bulb produced light the same way the sun did simply because both produced the entire spectrum.

When had science become so perverted? she found herself wondering. When had it stopped recognizing that it was a search for the real causes behind observable effects, that it was not in the business of dismissing effects because the cause was not apparent?

Well, she thought uneasily, that wasn't true of everyone, of course. Or of all fields. But it seemed to be rife in some, and she had evidently fallen prey to that way of thinking. She ought to be excitedly questioning the man beside her, trying to learn about that blue light. She ought to accept the evidence of her own eyes and set about finding out all she could. Instead...instead she was standing here trying to dismiss it as a magician's trick of some kind.

And that was dishonest. Horribly, frighteningly dishonest.

Slowly she lifted her gaze to his and saw a kind of patient understanding. "What...what is it?" she asked.

He cupped his palm again, and the blue light reappeared. "The life force," he said. "It's in everything. All around us. Hold out your hand."

Slowly, shaking internally, she held her hand out almost reluctantly, palm cupped upward in imitation of his. She half expected him to place the blue light into her hand, but he didn't. Instead, he reached out with his other hand and touched her palm gently with his forefinger.

"Here," he said. "Don't you feel it?"

What she felt was a sudden, shocking, totally unexpected surge of sexual awareness that zinged like lightning along her nerve endings straight to her core. Instinctively, she leapt back as if she'd been burned and immediately turned away, afraid he might see her reaction on her face.

He should have questioned her, but he didn't. Finally, surprised that he said nothing at all, she dared to dart a look in his direction. He was staring out into the night as if nothing at all had happened.

What a strange, strange man, she thought, wrapping her arms around herself, wishing away the ache he had awakened. What a very strange man.

Thunder continued to grumble into the night. Gray Cloud settled himself before the mouth of the cave, leaning back against the wall with his long legs stretched out before him.

A completely self-sufficient man, Mercy thought as she curled up in blankets and watched him across the fire. He needed no one, nothing. And that meant he was utterly free, didn't it?

Sighing, she let her eyelids droop. And slowly, slowly, she felt sleep stealing over her. As her mind began to drift into dreams, she saw Gray Cloud rise and come to her side, felt him reach down and touch her cheek with gentle fingertips. Dreamily, she watched as he lay down beside her, felt herself sink happily into his embrace as he drew her against him, as his lips began to scorch a path across her cheek, toward her mouth.

It was as if some long-held tension inside her let go. With a long sigh of blessed relief, she arched her neck, begging for the warmth of his mouth on the sensitive skin there. A gasp escaped her when he obliged, covering the hollow of her throat with his hot mouth. Little by little his tongue and lips trailed upward and to the side, closer and closer to her ear....

Sharp pleasure speared through her as his mouth found the sensitive spot behind her ear. Warm waves of aching arousal surged through her, causing her to press against him, silently begging him to come closer.

Closer...

His tongue in her ear, warm, wet, provocative. A shimmery shiver of delight ran down her neck from her ear...soft caress of fingertips along her throat...quicksilver thrills dancing down her side...clothes slipping easily away...

She turned her head to watch his hand trail toward her breast, and saw blood on his fingers....

A frisson of shock brought her jolting awake. Sitting up abruptly, she unleashed a ragged breath as she realized the cave was nearly dark, the fire merely embers. A dream. It had been a dream. Gray Cloud was still on the other side of the cave.

He watched her with eyes that seemed to guess what she had been dreaming. But there was no way he could know, she told herself a little hysterically. No way he could realize her body was still aching with a desire that had been born in the fog of a dream. That her flesh remembered touches that had never happened.

"Shh," he said softly. "Be silent. Someone is out there."

Fear trickled through her veins, banishing the last of the passionate glow left by the dream. Quickly she tossed the blankets aside, ignoring the cold night air, and reached for her hiking boots. Her breath made little clouds of ice crystals as she struggled to pull the boots on and lace them with fingers that were quickly growing numb. Lord, it was cold! The dying fire provided almost no heat and very little illumination.

At last, boots on, she crawled quietly to Gray Cloud's side. Beyond the entrance the night was still, silent except for the whisper of the wind in the pines. Clouds scudded across a gibbous moon, and the cold, eerie light seemed only to heighten the darkness of the shadows beneath the trees.

"How do you know?" she whispered finally. "Did you see something?"

He shook his head and laid a finger to her lips in a gentle remonstrance. He barely glanced at her before he resumed his study of the world outside.

He wasn't crouched as if he expected trouble, Mercy realized. But he was watchful, alert to any sound or movement from the woods. How could he be sure that it wasn't just some animal moving about in the dark? There were many creatures who stirred only in the shadows. But he seemed convinced that whatever was out there was some kind of threat, and if he believed it was an animal—a grizzly, say—he would want them to make as much noise as they could to scare it away.

Therefore he believed the threat was human.

Shivering, this time more from fear than the late hour or the frigid air, she instinctively inched closer to Gray Cloud. He offered the only safety and protection on this dark, cold night. The strength of sinew and bone was little enough against some terrors, but it was all there was right now.

"Look." He whispered the word, a mere breath of sound instantly lost in the forlorn sighing of the wind. A jerk of his chin indicated the woods to the right, where the deepest shadows lurked.

Mercy stared until she thought her eyes were going to come out of her head, until the shadows themselves seemed to become twisting, sinister shapes. Exhaling a soft, frustrated breath, she closed her eyes and rested them for a moment, then opened them again.

She gasped as she saw what Gray Cloud was talking about. There beneath the trees she could see fox fire, the soft bioluminescence of decaying wood. And against it she could see something dark moving, an incomplete silhouette mostly swallowed by the shadows.

She wanted to believe that it was an animal, but Gray Cloud had said someone was out there, and after a moment she realized the shadow had two legs. Only two legs. Who would be out there in the dark moving around?

And why?

Whoever it was could unquestionably see the glow of the fire in the cave, too, for the dying embers in the pit were at least as bright as the fox fire, and maybe more so. Had she gone behind the fire to reach Gray Cloud, her shadow would have been as visible to the man below as he was to them.

Shivering again, she leaned closer to her companion and drew a quick breath when he astonished her by draping his arm around her shoulders and holding her to his side. The embrace was in no way intimate; it was the kind of casual action any friend would take under the circumstances, but Mercy's reaction to the touch was not at all casual.

Her breath tangled in her throat, as if uncertain whether she meant to inhale or exhale, and her heart skipped a beat. And just as swiftly, her mind rebelled at her reaction, reminding her that she didn't need this attraction, nor did she want it. Nor was it appropriate, she told herself sternly. Someone was out in the woods below the cave, possibly intending harm, and this most definitely wasn't the time to get distracted.

But no argument could keep her insides from turning into molasses when the arm around her shoulders tightened a little, bringing her closer still to his warm, hard side. She ought to be running as if all the hounds of hell were at her very heels, but she knew with distressing clarity that even if she tried, her body wouldn't obey her command.

What it wanted—*all* it wanted—was to sink deeper into this man's embrace. In defiance of common sense, in defiance of the threat in the dark woods, her body cast aside every instinct for self-preservation.

Tilting her head a little, she looked at the shadowy profile of the man who held her and wondered wildly if he hadn't somehow managed to cast a spell over her.

Just then a sharp crack of sound pierced the murmuring of the wind. The next thing Mercy knew, she was lying flat beneath Gray Cloud.

"Gunshot!" he whispered sharply in her ear. "Don't move."

A moment passed before understanding penetrated her shock, but when it did, she froze. A few seconds later, Gray Cloud eased off her and inched back toward the cave entrance.

The uneasiness she had felt just moments ago didn't hold a candle to the fear she felt right now.

Easing around a little, she was able to see his shadow as he stood in the mouth of the cave. Silhouetted against the slightly lighter gray of the clouds, he appeared huge, threatening. She hoped whoever had fired the shot couldn't see him from out there.

Who could possibly be shooting in the dead of night? she wondered. Shooting in the dark showed appalling carelessness. A person who would do that didn't much care what he hit.

The night grew hushed as the wind suddenly stilled. Then a blue pinprick of light appeared in the air beside Gray Cloud. Mercy caught her breath in amazement and watched as the blue light slowly expanded until it was the size of a golf ball. It made no sound that she could detect, and its light barely illuminated the side of Gray Cloud's face.

In an instant it winked out. There was a moment of absolute silence and stillness, as if the night, too, held its breath; then the wind unleashed a tree-rustling sigh, and the world returned to normal. In the distance, a low, irritable growl of thunder could be heard.

Gray Cloud turned, a looming monolithic shadow in the darkness. "He's gone."

Mercy sat up immediately. "Gone? You mean the person who shot at us? How can you know that?"

As soon as she asked, she wished the words unsaid. She was in no mood to hear that the wind had told him, or the spirits had whispered secrets to him. But he didn't say anything at all. Maybe he considered it pointless to answer her because she wouldn't understand.

And that made her feel stupid. She didn't like to feel stupid. She was a biologist, not an ethnologist, and she had no background from which to understand this man's beliefs, his perspective. That was not stupidity!

But perhaps it was mulishness, she found herself thinking. Since yesterday she had been feeling that there was something beyond normal ken on this mountain. That the usual rules of reality were different here. Just take that cold, cobwebby brush she had felt on her neck several times. No breeze, however chilly, had ever felt like that. And what about the blue lights? Was she going to deny seeing them?

Tilting her head back, she looked up at Gray Cloud. He was a man; he had two arms and two legs. But he was more, she realized. He spoke to the wind and heard the voice of the Thunder Spirits, and he lived in a world populated by Stone People and Cloud People. In the palm of his hand, blue light danced.

If she acknowledged these things, then she acknowledged that he might know that the person with the gun was gone. The question was, was she going to believe it?

A shiver ripped through her, born of something other than the chilly night air. If the usual rules of reality didn't apply, then what rules did? Rules that allowed spirits to communicate with mortals might also allow invisible things to do harm.

She shivered again, and suddenly Gray Cloud was squatting beside her, touching her cheek with gentle fingertips. "You're cold," he said, and moments later he had her cocooned in the warmth of wool blankets.

An unusual man, she found herself thinking as she shivered again and yet again. He had given her his blankets last night to replace her sodden sleeping bag, and now he wrapped her in them because she shivered. He had cared for her every single moment since he had placed his body between her and the rock slide.

A cold-blooded murderer? No way. He might have killed, but it seemed impossible that he could have done so in cold blood. Not a man as protective as he was.

She turned her head and tried to see him, but the darkness, hardly lightened by the faintest red glow from the fire pit, kept its secrets. He remained nothing but a powerful shadow. "Do you think that person was shooting at us?"

A moment passed, then another. When he spoke, his voice was low, intense. "The wind whispers of fear, not death."

"Which means?"

"That someone was trying to scare one or both of us off this mountain."

She shivered again, contemplating the possibility while her heart began to beat in an uncomfortable rhythm. Scaring someone could get nasty. Very nasty. "But why?" she asked after a moment. "Why would anybody want to do that?"

He had been squatting beside her, but now he lowered himself to the ground and sat cross-legged beside her, facing out toward the restless night.

"You'd better get some sleep," he said.

She could have spluttered in frustration, even though she knew there was no answer to her question. He could have speculated, but what good would it have done?

"Just one more thing," she said. "Could you tell what he was shooting at?"

In the dark she saw him turn his head slowly and look straight at her. Stray starlight caught his eyes and made them gleam eerily. "He was shooting at me."

Chapter Four

Again an act of abomination. One of the man-things had attempted to harm Gray Cloud, he who was keeper of sacred trusts, he who was guardian of the holy places.

The mountain stirred, deeply troubled.

Slumbers as old as time had been disturbed, sacred trusts had been broken, and now the sanctified peace of the mountain's slopes was threatened.

Some things could not be tolerated.

After the gunshot, Mercy gave up all attempts to sleep. However she looked at it, there was a very real and very human threat on the slopes of this mountain. Shooting into the dark like that went far beyond an act of incaution. Whoever had done that really didn't give a damn who got hurt. He was willing to hurt anyone and anything to achieve his purpose.

She shivered inwardly, horrified that anyone could be so uncaring. So callous.

Yet someone evidently was, and that someone was stalking these woods with a gun.

She shivered again and wrapped the blanket tighter

around her shoulders, wishing morning would hurry up and get there. Not being able to see made everything so much worse.

"Gray Cloud?"

In the darkness she could dimly see his shadow move as he turned toward her. "Yes?"

"Why would anyone be trying to kill you?"

"Who can fathom the mind of a *wasicu* killer?"

Exasperated, Mercy sat up and glared at him in the dark. "Damn it, don't go all inscrutable Indian on me!"

"Why not?" He sounded faintly amused. "That's what I *am*."

"Oh, stuff it! You must have *some* idea why someone would want to kill you! Even crazed *wasicu* killers generally have some kind of motive!"

A low, quiet sound filled the cavern. It was a moment before Mercy realized that Gray Cloud was chuckling. *Chuckling!* "I'm glad you find this so amusing!"

In an instant his laughter died, and when he spoke, there was no hint of it in his voice. "I don't find it amusing at all."

"Well, good! Now suppose you tell me why you *think* somebody might want to kill you."

For a long time, it seemed, there was no sound but the forlorn moaning of the wind through the trees and the lonely sound of an owl.

"This mountain," Gray Cloud said finally, "could make many people very wealthy. There's a fortune in timber alone, and the mineral wealth has been estimated in the billions. Apart from that, the resort potential is phenomenal."

"None of that explains why anyone would want to shoot you."

Despite the dark, she felt his gaze on her, no less intense for being invisible. It was as palpable as a touch in the dark.

"All of that explains why someone would wish me dead," he said levelly. "I'm dedicated to preventing the rape of Thunder Mountain."

"But how would anyone *know* that?"

"I've made no secret of it. I've warned developers away before."

Slowly Mercy lay back against the rolled-up blanket she was using as a pillow. "Warned them away how?"

He didn't answer.

She didn't like that. What could he be hiding? she wondered. Maybe there was more to fear on this mountain than one fool with a gun. Maybe Gray Cloud was as dangerous as rumor had painted him. Maybe she was a fool to trust him at all.

Yet, she reminded herself, he hadn't hurt her. Not one little bit, and he'd had ample opportunity to kill her or terrorize her, if he wanted to. None of which answered the question of how he had warned developers away.

Shivering again, she burrowed deeper into the blankets and thought longingly of her warm, soft water bed at home, of the calm predictability of academic life. Why had she ever thought she wanted to climb the side of a mountain to study wolves?

"So you think the gunman has something to do with developers?" she asked.

"Very likely."

"But why should they go to such extremes? Why

should one man be so important that they think it's necessary to kill him?"

Again he was silent for a long while before he answered. "I have dedicated my life to preserving the sanctity of Thunder Mountain. I will die to protect this
place for my people. A man who will die for his belief
is dangerous."

"There are other ways to remove you."

"None that would silence me. And your wolves are
a threat, too, Mercy Kendrick. A very big threat. Every
bit as big a threat as I am, if word of their presence on
this mountain becomes widespread. Any development
effort would be tied up for years by environmentalists
determined to protect the wolves."

"Any development effort would be tied up for years
by environmentalists anyway. Removing the wolves
would hardly change that."

"Removing them would make it easier."

Mercy sat up again, disturbed and deeply chilled.
"They couldn't possibly—"

"Why not? If the wolves are wiped out right now, and
if I'm removed, who's to ever say that the wolves were
here? Preservation of an endangered species will become moot. And ordinary environmental considera-
tions are not enough to prevent timbering and mining."

Mercy drew her knees up to her chin and wrapped
her arms tightly around them, hugging herself. She
didn't like the sound of this at all. If someone really were
after the wolves, they would be after her, too, just as
soon as she verified the existence of the pack. Never had
she imagined that being a wildlife biologist could set her
up for murder.

Another shiver passed through her. "I don't like the sound of this."

He gave a grunt of agreement.

"Why—why have you dedicated your life to protecting the mountain. Isn't that unusual?"

"*Wakinyan* spoke to me, and I was given this vision for my life. A vision must be fulfilled."

A vision must be fulfilled. Mercy's scalp prickled a little with the realization that what drove this man was far beyond her understanding. Forces she had heard mentioned, but never really believed existed, drove him. Imagine a lifelong dedication to fulfilling a vision. Imagine feeling bound to expend your last breath in defense of a place.

"What is the extent of your vision?"

"To have Thunder Mountain protected by white law as a holy place of my people. To have your people acknowledge the right of mine to this place."

"How can you possibly hope to accomplish that?"

"The opportunity will come." He spoke with absolute conviction, and Mercy could only nod her head; there was no way one could argue with conviction.

All of a sudden she felt the ground beneath her tremble slightly, a faint vibration as if a heavy truck were rolling by—only there were no trucks on this mountain.

Thunder, she thought. It had to be thunder, a growl so deep and low that it was beneath the threshold of hearing. But then the tremor came again, a slow shaking of the ground beneath her.

And the mountain groaned.

Earth sounds. The moan came from deep within the

heart of Thunder Mountain, an eerie, inhuman groan that rose from the bowels of the earth.

"What's that?"

Gray Cloud's answer was casual. "The mountain."

"The mountain? Mountains don't make noise!"

"They do when they move. Thunder Mountain is angry."

Because it was dark, she couldn't see anything but his shadow against the slightly lighter night beyond the cavern mouth. Right then, though, she wished desperately that she could see him. Even though there would be nothing on his face to read, it would have helped her to be able to see him. "Why?"

"Because the doe and fawn were murdered. Because there are people on the mountain who respect nothing at all. Because they intend harm to all that the mountain protects."

She had always believed that mountains had personalities, and she could even believe they had moods—certainly she'd felt those moods when she'd been caught on the side of a mountain in a sudden storm or had seen the changing faces of the peaks as sunlight dappled them. But the concept of a mountain actually reacting to events on its slopes...

Well, why not? she asked herself. Hadn't she felt that El Capitan welcomed her climb? Another rumble, barely felt, passed through the ground beneath her, accompanied by a low moan that made the hair on her neck stand up. A thinking, reacting mountain. A living mountain. An entity of rock and earth rising nearly fourteen thousand feet.

Suddenly realizing that she was holding her breath,

she expelled it on a long sigh. She was surrounded by the mountain. Here in this cave she was surrounded by rock and earth, held in the loose embrace of Thunder Mountain.

Sitting in the dark with nothing to distract her, it was easy to imagine she could feel vast power surrounding her, easy to think of all the ways a mountain might exercise that power. Rock slides, earthquakes...

Another shudder passed through her, this time her own, as she considered just what powers a sentient mountain might have. Man believed himself to be in control of his environment, but the truth was that the elements were more powerful than man, as they proved time and again with floods and tornadoes. But the earth... Unless one lived at the foot of a volcano, the powers of the earth itself weren't usually apparent. But sitting here in the dark, surrounded by the rocky arms of the mountain, Mercy had no illusions about its power. She could feel it thrumming in some subtle way, could sense it somehow, almost the same way she could feel a static charge when the hair on her arms stood up.

"Why?" she heard herself ask Gray Cloud. "Why should the mountain care?"

"Why does a mother care about her babies?"

"Oh, come on! A mountain that thinks is already difficult to accept, but one that cares about a deer? One that cares about what some puny man is doing? If a mountain can think and feel, it has to have a very different perspective from ours. A human lifespan would have to be a mere blink of an eye to it. How could it possibly care about what mortals are doing?"

"It cares," he said presently. "It cares. And if I were

you, Mercy Kendrick, I'd be hoping that Thunder Mountain doesn't decide I'm a threat."

She shivered again and told herself it was from the chilly night air. In fact, it was from the uneasy awareness that she and Gray Cloud were *not* alone in this cave—that the rock arms that sheltered them belonged to a being that might well be listening.

Like sitting in the stomach of a whale, Mercy thought uncomfortably. Devoured by stone.

And the mountain could, she realized unhappily, do just that in an instant. It would take no longer than that for a rock slide to seal this cave off and trap her forever in the maw of the mountain.

I mean you no harm. She caught herself thinking the words, trying to communicate that simple reassurance to the mountain. *I mean you no harm.*

And she just had to hope that the mountain perceived it that way. That the mountain believed her.

Because it could surely destroy her.

Morning slunk into the cave with watery gray light and a distant growl of thunder. More of the same, Mercy thought as her eyes fluttered open and her body shifted stiffly on the hard cave floor. Another rainy, stormy day on Thunder Mountain. Did the sun ever shine up here?

Turning her head, she sought Gray Cloud with her eyes and saw that he was gone. Instead the black wolf sat at the cave entrance, watching her with his strange golden eyes, unblinking golden eyes. Eyes that were far too intelligent.

And she was feeling just disconnected enough, just

crazy enough, this morning to think that that wolf had to be Gray Cloud's alter ego. It only came when Gray Cloud was gone and always vanished just before he returned.

Shapeshifter.

In an instant she remembered old tales of the powers of shamans, tales that spoke of men who turned into beasts to hunt and kill their enemies. Tales of men who could become any animal to accomplish their purpose. Were Native American shamans capable of shape-shifting?

She had no idea, and not for the first time she cursed her lack of knowledge of the subject. She had come up this mountain expecting to observe wolves, not to deal with a totally alien culture or a sentient mountain.

Or a wolf that might really be an Indian medicine man.

God, was she losing her mind? These thoughts were insane! She shouldn't even be wondering about such things. In reality, no one shape-shifted, werewolves were merely the inventions of fiction and...

And wolves didn't come in from a rain-soaked day to keep company with a human in a cave.

Although, why not? she wondered. All over the world there were tales of wolves nursing human infants. Romulus and Remus were merely legendary members of a small but widespread fraternity of children who had been raised by wolves. If wolves would nurse human children, why wouldn't they come into a cave with a human? And hadn't her readings told her that wolves accepted the dominance of humans?

But that didn't really explain why this wolf kept showing up to watch her as if *she* were the subject of a scientific study. Or why he would then turn and assume a position very like that of a guardian.

Why should a wolf want to protect her?

Why should a mountain moan in anger?

Had she somehow slipped into another reality during her climb up the side of Thunder Mountain?

The wolf blinked slowly, offering no answers to her questions. Those strange golden eyes that seemed to see through and beyond her, that seemed to see into the dustiest corners of her soul, offered no solutions.

Where had Gray Cloud gone? He was supposed to take her to the den this morning. But perhaps he was scouting for information about the man who had shot at him last night. The man who had killed the doe and fawn.

The thought made her shudder again.

The wolf edged farther into the cavern, almost as if he wanted to approach her. Mercy found herself holding her breath in hopeful anticipation. It never even entered her head that perhaps she should fear the animal. Not once. All she felt was a sense of awe that the wolf didn't seem to fear her.

Releasing her pent-up breath silently, she waited. The wolf eased closer, moving in a slightly crouched position, almost as if stalking, yet without the appearance of threat. More of a cautious approach. And his eyes never once left her.

So beautiful, she thought. So beautiful and perfect with his big feet, his eyes more widely separated than a dog's, his long, slender legs. Wolves were beautiful creatures.

Just then the ground trembled again, and a deep, hollow groan, just barely audible, rose from the rocks beneath. The mountain was angry. Mercy was suddenly as sure of it as Gray Cloud had been last night. And today the thought terrified her.

Thunder cracked, a deafening gunshot of sound that reverberated within the cavern and caused Mercy to cover her ears. The wolf's hackles rose, and he turned swiftly to stare out into the gray morning. Wind tossed the treetops, causing a rush of sound like a huge waterfall. Thunder rumbled again, a deep-throated grumbling that seemed to shake the ground.

The earth shook again, and some instinct impelled Mercy to scramble to her feet and dart toward the cave entrance. Just as she reached it, a rain of rocks broke loose from the ceiling of the cavern—mostly sharp, jagged little pieces that might have cut her but would not have seriously harmed her.

A sudden, ominous silence blanketed the world, as if the universe was holding its breath. Then, with a shocking crack of sound, a large piece of rock broke loose from above and crashed to the floor of the cave.

Right where Mercy had been sitting.

The wolf tilted back his head and howled, an eerie, lonely sound. From the distance came an answering howl, and the animal took off, moving so swiftly he was but a blur as he slipped past Mercy into the rainy morning.

Mercy hardly noticed. Horror made her skin crawl as she stared at the piece of rock that could have killed her. *Would* have killed her if some instinct hadn't driven her to move.

The mountain was angry, and it seemed it was angry at her.

* * *

"What happened?"

Whirling around, Mercy came face-to-face with Gray Cloud. He was wet again, soaked from the rain and appearing not to notice...or care. He was one with the elements as surely as were the trees towering around them. He knew what had happened, Mercy found herself thinking. He *had* to know. The conviction made her skin crawl even more.

"The mountain tried to kill me." The bald statement hung shockingly in the stormy air. Part of her mind rebelled, refusing to believe such a thing, refusing to accept that a mountain could be sentient, let alone that it could try to kill. But in her heart, in her chilled blood and stunned mind, she knew it was the truth. The mountain had tried to kill her.

Gray Cloud didn't speak. He stepped past her and peered into the cave, which was little more than a dark maw in the side of the mountain. The day was darkly gray, and the cave seemed to swallow what little light there was.

But Gray Cloud saw. She knew it in the way his back stiffened as he stared at the boulder lying right where she would have been. The boulder that would have crushed her as easily as a man would have crushed a fly.

He backed up a step before he turned his head and looked at her. "You'd better leave."

Leave? "Why? Why the hell should I!" Fright was replaced in a violent rush by anger. She hadn't succeeded as a rock climber because she was afraid of a moody mountain.

And as anger cleared away the last of the fear, she

looked at the fallen boulder and told herself that it had been a random occurrence. The rock had probably been loose for centuries, and the vibration caused by the deafening peals of thunder had simply caused it to fall at last. It was merely coincidence that it had fallen where she had been sitting moments before. There was nothing more sinister in it than that. Nothing.

It was all that talk Gray Cloud had spouted about the mountain, as if it were a fully aware being, that had made a natural occurrence appear to be so menacing. The truth of the matter was that nothing unnatural was occurring here at all, and that it was simply suggestion that was making it all so ominous. Just a little thunderstorm and a tremor, and she was turning it into a Hollywood horror concoction!

"No," she said to Gray Cloud. "I'm not leaving." She half expected him to argue with her, to warn her away, but he didn't.

And that was perhaps the most ominous thing of all, the way he simply looked at her as if her decision to remain mattered not at all, as if she were too insignificant to worry about.

She looked from him to the boulder in the shadowy cavern and wondered if she were being utterly foolhardy. Yes, she thought uneasily, she probably was. But she hadn't let the forbidding faces of Devil's Tower and El Capitan deter her from climbing them, and she wasn't going to let a fallen rock prevent her from studying the wolves. Wolves that she knew beyond a shadow of a doubt were here, reestablishing themselves in the country they had once roamed freely. No, a rockfall wasn't going to drive her away.

Nor was she going to allow herself to become un-nerved by Gray Cloud's mystical attitude toward this mountain. Yes, Thunder Mountain had personality and moods—all mountains did—but it wasn't capable of striking out against individuals on its slopes. No way. Let Gray Cloud view it however he chose, but she was *not* going to allow herself to be drawn into some insane belief that this mountain was as much an actor on this stage as she was.

Absolutely not.

She faced Gray Cloud squarely. "You said you would show me the dens."

He nodded his head once, regarding her impassively from obsidian eyes. Water dripped from the ends of his long black hair, and a drop clung to the tip of his hawk-ish nose.

"We'll have to climb another five hundred feet, and it's difficult terrain. Bring whatever you'll need, be-cause you won't want to come back here until the end of the day."

He was right, she thought a little while later. The climb was really rough. It would have been easier to go straight up a rock face than it was to climb up and down the ravines he led her across while traveling ever higher into thinner air.

Worse, because conversation was out of the ques-tion; she had ample time to think about all that he had told her, all that he hadn't said. Time to think about what was really going on on this mountain, and why anyone should want to kill someone else over it. After all, she had only Gray Cloud's word that a doe and her fawn had been killed, or that the gunshot last night had been directed at him. Only his word that anyone was actually trying to hurt anything at all on this mountain.

He'd lived up here for a long time. All by himself, devoted to a mystical purpose in what might actually be a form of insanity. Even as the thought slithered across her mind, she felt guilty for having it. It was wrong to judge the manifestation of a different culture as some kind of insanity; even a wildlife biologist knew that. But she couldn't help wondering if his preoccupation with protecting this mountain wasn't a little extreme, even in his own cultural terms.

A fanatic. Yes, he probably was a fanatic. And who could say exactly what a fanatic might do in attempting to achieve his goal? He certainly might attempt to terrify a lone wildlife biologist into vacating the mountain. He might be willing to out-and-out lie about things like the doe being shot. He would surely be capable of fabricating things he told her in an attempt to scare her.

Well, she wasn't that easily scared. But she *was* uneasy about being alone on this mountain with a fanatic who might be capable of anything at all in pursuit of his ends.

Sliding down the side of a ravine, struggling to keep her balance on loose dirt and gravel, she wondered if she was insane to be following this man higher up the mountain. True, he had done nothing overtly threatening, had in fact protected her, but...

But he really didn't need to lead her farther up the mountain if he wanted to get rid of her. They'd been completely isolated since their first encounter. He could have killed her at any time and left her body for the scavengers. A search party would have found only bones, and probably not for months or even years. This mountain was so vast and dangerous that if she disappeared up here, no one would even suspect foul play.

So he didn't have to lead her higher if getting rid of her was his goal. Which meant that he didn't want to hurt her. Didn't it?

Logically, it made sense to her that he was trying to be helpful, not obstructive, but emotionally she wasn't quite so ready to believe it. Not when he kept trying to frighten her with tales of sentient mountains and gunmen. Pausing at the foot of the ravine, she drew a deep breath and then embarked on an upward climb with Gray Cloud just ahead of her and to one side.

Thunder, which had been growling steadily like an angry beast at bay, suddenly shattered the air with a deafening crack. At the same instant a rock on the slope above her broke free and began to roll straight at her. She saw it coming toward her in a horrifying freeze-frame of instant awareness that she was about to die.

Gray Cloud saw it, too. Turning swiftly, he braced his feet and bent, grabbing her forearm in an iron grip. With one powerful yank he tugged her out of harm's way. The momentum of his movement threw them both in the same direction, causing them to fall and slip downward on the slope as the boulder rolled by.

Mercy came to an abrupt halt wedged against a rock, and Gray Cloud half slid over her before he could stay his motion. Stunned, she lay gasping, unable even to open her eyes. But finally she did look up at him, and the world spun away.

Gazing into his dark eyes was like staring up into the night sky. The darkness seemed to swallow everything, seemed to be a bottomless pool into which she was falling. So black, so deep. Endless night.

Mesmerizing.

His eyes seemed to contain entire worlds, she thought hazily. If she could only manage to see far enough into them, she was sure she would find the answers to ancient questions.

And the answers to newer ones, such as why was her heart beating so hard and so loudly? Why did everything within her feel as if it were turning to warm molasses? Why did her eyelids feel so heavy and droopy, and why, oh why, was she breathing so deeply, like a sprinter at the end of a race?

And why was she wishing, hoping against hope, that Gray Cloud would come closer, that his firm lips would part a little and that he would lean down and would…

Kiss her.

His pupils dilated suddenly, as if he'd had the same thought at the same instant, and then his mouth was on hers, answering all her questions with the warmth of his touch and the weight of the powerful body that half covered hers. Some recognition deep in her soul was unleashed as lips touched lips. *Yes*.

An aching flood of need washed through her so rapidly that she was swamped instantly. Hungers she had heard about but only dimly felt in the past were suddenly vivid and overwhelming. Her entire being yearned upward to the man whose mouth touched hers. Deep inside she felt a swelling, a pulsing, as everything slipped away except the moment and the man.

A deafening blast of thunder shocked them both back to awareness. The wind suddenly rushed down the gully, tugging at Gray Cloud's hair and whipping it around. They jerked apart, and some corner of Mercy's mind wondered why the mountain had gotten so angry over a little kiss.

For a long moment, ignoring the threatening thunder and scolding wind, Gray Cloud stared down at her. And then, as if shaking himself out of a dream, he pulled away and stood. Before she could start to rise, he reached down, grasped her hands and lifted her to her feet.

"Are you hurt?" he asked.

She shook her head quickly, feeling embarrassed. "No. A few bruises. Nothing important."

"Let's get going, then."

The kiss had never happened, she found herself thinking as she followed him up the side of the ravine. A meeting of lips that had been so brief and fleeting it had never occurred. Not really. Not where it mattered. Not in the heart or soul.

At least not in Gray Cloud's heart and soul, because it had been an earthquake in hers. The man was…irresistible. And that terrified her as much as anything.

If he turned to her right now and reached for her, she would go to him. She would do what she had always steadfastly refused to do: allow herself to be used. Because that brief contact had made her want him so badly that she doubted even her very strong instinct for emotional self-preservation would be enough to save her now.

She had tasted the forbidden fruit, she found herself thinking. Had tasted it so briefly and found it so very sweet.

She was all alone on a vast mountain with a reputed killer...and she wanted to make love with him.

"I am crazy!"

She spoke aloud without intending to, but the sound of her words penetrated the natural sounds of the wind and thunder in the most jarring way imaginable. Too late to snatch the words back, she could only scowl as Gray Cloud turned his head and looked down at her from a little higher up the slope.

"That makes two of us," he said.

Mercy didn't find that thought at all comforting.

The climb that had seemed to take forever had, in fact, taken only forty-five minutes. Not too far to climb every morning. Her base camp at the cave was not so close to the wolves that it would trouble them. She gave Gray Cloud high marks for his site selection.

The den was on a rocky slope; a small ledge protruded over the hole that had been burrowed into the hillside, and on the ledge slept a large gray wolf. It stirred a little as they approached, lifting its head to fix them with golden eyes. Mercy halted and hunkered down, trying to be quiet as she tugged the lens caps off her binoculars and raised them to her eyes.

A moment later she had the wolf in focus. "The alpha female," she whispered to Gray Cloud. The wolf was clearly pregnant, and in a wolf pack, usually only the alpha female ever bore young. Some researchers held that only the alpha male and alpha female ever mated; others had observed interference behavior that had the effect of limiting the mating of the other wolves in the pack, though not always eliminating it entirely.

The bitch stared at Mercy, tawny eyes blinking very slowly, measuring and gauging the potential threat. Gray Cloud hunkered down, too, and waited in perfect stillness as the moments ticked by.

"So beautiful," Mercy whispered on the merest breath. "So beautiful."

"She'll whelp soon," Gray Cloud murmured back. "Not much longer."

Mercy wished with all her heart that she could witness the event when it happened. It would *have* to be very soon, as Gray Cloud said. The wolf had remained at the den because she sensed the closeness of her own time, so the rest of the pack had gone hunting without her, in all likelihood, and would bring her back some of their kill.

Gradually the female relaxed and lowered her head to her paws once more. For a while after that she continued to stare steadily at the intruders, but finally her eyes began to droop closed, and she looked as contented and relaxed as if she were sunning on a warm summer day, instead of lying in the cold, stormy air halfway up a mountain.

And it *was* cold today. As soon as Mercy cooled off from the climb, she had to zip her jacket to the throat, and before long she was wishing for a hat of some kind to cover her ears. Instead she had to be content with hunching her shoulders up and promising herself that she would bring her stocking cap tomorrow.

The den was in a small, rocky clearing, a place that seemed to have carved out a peacefulness for itself. Here the storm didn't seem quite so threatening somehow, nor did the wind bite quite so hard. Perhaps,

Mercy found herself thinking, the mountain and wolves were happy together here, and that was what affected the mood.

Because it was a mood. The clearing had an unmistakable aura of serenity to it, a feeling of rightness. Here the mountain was content.

When her arms began to ache, Mercy reluctantly lowered the binoculars and glanced at Gray Cloud. He was sitting cross-legged beside her, his eyes closed and his head tilted back, looking relaxed and meditative.

In his own way he looked as much a part of the scene as the wolf did. And that left Mercy feeling like an intruder. Like someone the mountain *would* want to push away.

Uneasy, she tore her gaze from Gray Cloud and told herself that she would not succumb to the crazy thoughts that kept flitting through her head, thoughts about not being welcomed by the mountain, thoughts of how much she wanted to touch Gray Cloud, how much she wished he would touch her.

Something was definitely wrong with her brain circuits, she thought. Definitely something screwy in the way she kept thinking about the man beside her rather than her task here. Screwy in the way she kept falling into thoughts of the mountain as a being. The altitude had to be affecting her. Hypoxia, maybe? Wasn't that the term for lack of oxygen?

She was clutching at straws, and she knew it. Trying to find some way to explain strange events and her strange companion—and her even stranger reaction to him.

As she sat there telling herself not to look at Gray

Cloud but to concentrate on the wolves, her attention strayed upward to the sky above.

Her breath caught in her throat. The clouds no longer looked like gray storm clouds as they scraped the tree-tops. They had turned green and swirled malignantly, as if they had a life of their own. The hollow rumble of thunder continued at a distance, as if it came from else-where and bore no relation to the clouds overhead.

"Oh my God," she whispered as her hair began to stand on end. Her skin prickled all over, as if a million tiny bugs were dancing across it. The small silver friend-ship ring she wore on her right hand began to feel warmer than skin temperature. What was going on?

"Lie down."

She turned her head toward Gray Cloud in astonish-ment. "What?"

"Lie down," he demanded roughly. Even as he spoke, he was stretching out flat on the ground and tugging at her arm. "Lightning's going to strike."

It took a moment, just a moment, to click. And then she realized why her skin was prickling and her ring felt warm. A huge potential electrical charge was building right here, and at any moment...

She lay down as flat as she could get on her stomach and had the presence of mind to set the binoculars aside. Her ring. It was growing warmer still, and she yanked it from her hand, afraid she would get burned.

The ground hummed, as if the rocks were vibrating with the building power of the electrical charge. It was an eerie sound, almost like the whine of an electrical transformer, but it was coming from the ground, and all the more frightening for its origin.

Cheek on the cold, hard ground, she looked at Gray Cloud and saw his black hair spreading and standing on its own as the growing charge caused each strand to try to get as far from the others as it could.

The crawling sensation on her skin intensified, and she began to feel as if there were cobwebs all over her face.

I'm going to die. The thought was stark, clear. Lightning was going to strike this very spot, and if it didn't kill her, she was going to wish it had.

The humming sound grew until it seemed to fill the universe. The wolf howled, a lonely, eerie protest.

And then, with the suddenness of a thunderclap, there came the crack of a gunshot.

Chapter Five

The intruders intended harm. Evil emanations filled the air as the one with the tiny thunderstick moved toward the quiet clearing. Anger thrummed in the mountain, and it gathered itself to deal with this abomination. Power grew and focused, building until the mountain hummed its rage.

As soon as the sound of the shot faded, Mercy instinctively started to lift her head, but Gray Cloud shot out a hand and held her down. "Don't!" he snapped sharply.

Of course. She would make a target of herself. And the building charge in the ground... Her ring, which she had dropped on the dirt before her face, was vibrating visibly. The ground thrummed and hummed, a growing threat.

Another gunshot.

And then the world disappeared in a flash of white light so intense that it hurt Mercy's eyes as it washed away all color and contrast. The crack of the accompanying thunder was so loud that the concussion was more felt than heard. She saw Gray Cloud's lips move briefly, but she couldn't hear him.

After a few moments she realized that the humming of the earth had lessened slightly but hadn't entirely quit. Gray Cloud's hand was still resting on the side of her head, and his dark eyes warned her to keep down.

Her heart was hammering so hard that she couldn't catch her breath. Worst of all, though—worse than the terror of both lightning and the person with the gun— was the sense of hopelessness. Helplessness. There was nothing at all she could do but lie here and await the outcome of events.

She hated that feeling. Hated it so much that she twisted her head a little, trying to see anything at all besides dirt and Gray Cloud.

The humming was growing again, she realized, and the cobwebby feeling was intensifying. More lightning. She wondered if the man with the gun was lying down, too. And if Thunder Mountain was trying to kill him. Or her. Or all of them.

A wolf howled, probably the female, and then lightning snapped to the ground again, blindingly bright. Almost immediately there was another, and then another, and one of them struck so close that Mercy felt its heat sear the back of her neck.

Then the sky opened its floodgates and released a deluge that soaked them to the skin almost immediately.

But the terrible humming of the ground was gone, and the cobwebby feeling had vanished. Mercy dug her fingers into the earth and gave a huge sob of relief as she realized that she was safe from the lightning at least.

But that left the person with the gun.

"Don't move," Gray Cloud said quietly. "I'm going to circle around to check for the gunman."

Concerned, she reached out and caught his hand, staying him. "No!" she whispered sharply. "You could get hurt."

He silenced her with a shake of his head. "We need to know if he's still here. I'll be careful."

Moments later he was slinking away into the gray mist of rain in complete silence.

Leaving Mercy to lie on the ground and wonder why she didn't just go home and forget this insanity.

Just then the wolf howled again. A beckoning, beautifully lonesome sound. A moment later another howl answered her, and then another, and another, until Mercy couldn't tell how many voices responded as the harmonies built.

Grabbing the binoculars, she wiped the damp lenses on her sleeve and put them to her eyes. The alpha female was crouched before the den, her head tilted back so she could give her full-voiced cry. And it looked— oh, God, it looked as if she were bleeding. Had she been shot?

Without thinking, Mercy started to rise but caught herself before she got to her knees. The gunman might still be out there, and he might be inclined to shoot anything that moved...except that he wasn't shooting at the wolf right now.

Again she started to rise, needing to help in any way possible. Just then Gray Cloud entered the clearing, walking upright, and headed straight for the wolf. The female crouched, hackles rising, but she didn't flee, nor did she bare her fangs.

Even over the steady rush of the falling rain Mercy could hear Gray Cloud talking softly, a soothing singsong chant of some kind as he approached the wary wolf.

The female hunkered even lower but remained where she was, not even backing up as the man drew closer and closer.

When he reached her, Gray Cloud knelt beside her and began to gently check her side. As if sensing that he meant to help, the wolf relaxed her posture and rolled onto her side, giving the man access to her wound.

Mercy wanted to charge up there and help, but she held herself back, realizing that she would only frighten the wolf and disturb the tentative trust that had formed between man and beast. Best to stay back.

Taking care to keep quiet, she pulled a notebook out of her pocket, bent over it to keep the rain off it and began to hastily scribble her impression of all that she was seeing: the den, the wolf, the man, the interaction between them.

At some point she realized that pairs of tawny eyes were looking into the clearing from the edges of the forest all around. The pack had gathered and was staying back while Gray Cloud was with the female.

Moving slowly, careful not to startle, Mercy tried to count the wolves in the pack and find a distinctive marking on each one by which to identify them. Packs could grow to as many as thirty members, though they seldom did. This one, unless she had miscounted or had failed to see some of the wolves, numbered six, including the alpha female, a typical size.

A soft sound beside her alerted her, and she turned her head to see the black wolf that had twice visited her standing a few feet away, staring straight at her. She was sure it was him because of the light-dark markings over his eyes, unlike the other wolves of the pack.

And he had come to her again. The awe she had felt before became something almost reverent as she realized she was developing some kind of bond with this wolf.

And his tail was up, she realized. Only the alpha male and alpha female carried their tails straight up.

Oh, how she wanted to reach out and touch him, just to be sure he was real. But as soon as the thought crossed her mind, the wolf turned and vanished into the rain. Moments later she heard his howl, then heard it answered by the rest of the pack.

Turning, she saw all the tawny eyes vanish as the wolves pulled back from the clearing. Only the alpha female remained, lying docilely beneath the reassuring touch of Gray Cloud's hand. A minute or so later he rose and turned, walking away from the wolf as steadily and calmly as he had approached. Behind him, the female rolled onto her belly and watched his departure.

"Is she all right?" Mercy asked when Gray Cloud reached her.

"Seems to be. She's got a small score in her side. I can't tell if it was a bullet graze or something else."

"You think the gunman was shooting at her?"

He shook his head. "I don't know. Probably. I don't think you ought to come up here by yourself."

Mercy couldn't have agreed more, but that presented a serious problem. "There's no reason to think he'd hurt me."

"We've covered this ground—" He broke off abruptly, tilting his head and closing his eyes as if he heard something. Long seconds ticked by, and then he said, "All right."

Mercy waited for explanation and, when none was forthcoming, asked, "All right what?"

His eyes snapped open. "The wind says to let you do as you wish, Tomorrow Woman. That you must do as you intend for it all to come out as it has been ordained."

Mercy gaped at him, astonished past speech. When she could manage to speak, all she could ask was "Who's Tomorrow Woman? And what's been ordained?"

"You are Tomorrow Woman. Thus the wind has named you. As for what has been ordained…" He gave a noncommittal shrug. "We'll find that out, I guess."

Mercy looked away, not sure how to react to this. She wasn't sure which was harder to accept—that the wind had named her or that events were ordained. She was an avid believer in self-determination, and she was a long way from believing the wind spoke, let alone named things.

Doubt me not, Tomorrow Woman.

The whisper seemed to come from the trees, and as soon as she heard it, Mercy felt ice run down her spine. She was imagining things! She had to be! It was just the power of suggestion, after hearing Gray Cloud speak with such conviction about what the wind was saying.

Lie to yourself, Tomorrow Woman. The truth will triumph.

Ice touched the base of her skull as a new kind of terror took her. Could she really be losing her mind? Hearing voices was the sign of the worst kind of insanity. If she thought the wind was talking to her…

Shivering, she shook herself mentally. No. She had to concentrate on the wolves. Concentrate on what had *actually* happened in the real world. Her mind was just playing tricks on her, that was all. Not enough sleep. Too much tension because of the gunshot and the lightning. Overload.

This time no voice responded to her thoughts, and she allowed herself a brief sense of relief. All she had to do was focus on the task at hand…and figure out how to avoid trouble with the gunman.

She turned to Gray Cloud. "We need to tell the rangers that someone is shooting up here. You can't shoot in a National Forest, can you?"

"A person who shoots at an endangered species hardly cares about the rules."

"That isn't what I meant. I was thinking the rangers would do something about it."

Gray Cloud looked impassively at her, indicating nothing at all.

Yeah, right, Mercy found herself thinking. What *would* the rangers do about it? Looking for one man— or even a couple of men—on this mountain would be extremely difficult. But still, they ought to know.

The problem was, she didn't want to go down the mountain now to tell them. She would miss the birth of the wolf pups if she did, and as a consequence would miss an important part of her study of this pack's existence and behavior.

But if the gunman roamed unhindered here, he would have more opportunities to harm the wolves.

She turned toward Gray Cloud. "We have to do something to stop them."

He tipped his head just a fraction of an inch but never took his eyes from her.

"We can't let them hurt the wolves, Gray Cloud! We need to do something to prevent it!"

Even as she spoke, it struck her that perhaps it was ridiculous to align herself with Gray Cloud this way. What did she have as a basis for trusting him, apart from his assertion that he was here to protect the mountain, and apart from the way he seemed to be taking care of her? It wasn't much…but perhaps it was enough.

Just then a long, low moan drew their attention back to the pregnant wolf. She had risen to a squatting position, and even at this distance she appeared to be agitated and breathing hard. Mercy snatched up her binoculars again and peered through them.

"She's whelping!" This was the last thing Mercy had expected to see in the open. She had expected the wolf to retreat to her den.

The bitch stopped moaning as soon as she saw her first pup, almost as if once she understood what was happening, her contractions no longer bothered her. Instead she settled down to licking each newly arrived pup, washing away the placenta, and then tucking the newborn to her teats until the next delivery began. Seven pups in all were born during the next four hours. At some point the alpha male had returned and paced a patrol as his mate produced the litter.

During a pause in the delivery, Mercy was struck by a thought and looked at Gray Cloud. "What happened to the gunman? Why would he take one shot at the wolf and then disappear?"

"The mountain drove him away."

She was tempted to let that pass, because she knew she wasn't going to like the answers to any questions she asked. Curiosity, however, wouldn't let her ignore it. "How?"

"The lightning. You felt the power of the mountain."

Sometimes in life a fundamental shift in perception occurred. One of those shifts struck her now, with all the force of an earthquake. All her attempts to rationalize away her feelings came to an abrupt halt. As if she had abruptly been hurled hundreds of feet into the air to look down on her place in the world, she suddenly saw all that had been happening from a different perspective.

She was the mountain. Massive, towering above everything around, trees furring her slopes, sheltering animals so small they were nearly invisible. And she saw the intruders, troublesome as lice, threatening the natural order.

Yes, she thought, the mountain could take action, but whatever action it took would be on its own scale, destroying much more than its target. Rock slides, once set in motion, would carry away trees and animals, as well as the intruder. The lightning would strike in the area where the charge had built, but within that area were potential victims other than the intruders. The wolf, for example, could be hurt.

So the mountain restrained itself and took action only reluctantly. But when it acted...

Mercy shivered and was suddenly back in her own time and place, perceiving things from her own perspective. She couldn't possibly have really touched upon the mountain's consciousness, could she?

Gray Cloud regarded her steadily from enigmatic eyes. *The mountain drove him away.* She found herself believing that it was possible. The lightning would certainly have been a good tool for that, yet not precise enough to avoid doing other damage by accident. Which meant she could have been hurt. Gray Cloud could have been hurt. The wolf could have been hurt.

And somehow the understanding of how those forces worked was even more terrifying than blaming it all on natural occurrences. She looked at Gray Cloud again and found herself sinking into his obsidian gaze. This time, though, she felt as if his eyes were a window, and she was gazing into the black heart of the mountain.

Beware, Tomorrow Woman. Beware. All is not what it seems.

The fire burned brightly, orange and yellow flames leaping in the pit in the cave floor. The night was chilly and damp, and the endless thunder rumbled angrily. The night was alive with threat, and Mercy couldn't deny it any longer. All her scientific training had gone by the wayside, leaving her facing a stark reality in a world that was alien to everything she had believed.

Aware now, whether she wanted to be or not, she could feel the vitality of the mountain around her. It was a cold vitality, far removed from the swift, hot responses of humankind. The anger it felt was not swift and thoughtless but righteous and measured, a growing determination not to tolerate desecration.

And in that awareness she found another awareness of the ecosystem. She found herself reaching out with all her senses to embrace the world around her, the world of Thunder Mountain, from the smallest insect to the tallest tree. It was a perfect world, each creature serving a purpose in an endless cycle of life, death and rebirth.

Until mankind had arrived. Mankind interrupted that cycle and disturbed the balance. And disturbing the balance had awakened the slumbering mountain to its role as guardian. The mountain would protect its inhabitants.

What if the mountain misinterpreted *her* presence here and perceived her as a threat? Gray Cloud hadn't answered her when she'd asked him that, and then he had vanished somewhere into the night to do whatever it was he did when he left her.

The feeling of being watched, which had never quite left her, seemed more ominous now than before. The mountain was watching her. How could she possibly escape being watched as long as she stayed here? And how could she do anything else when it seemed clear that someone was up to no good?

She couldn't leave the wolves unprotected, particularly the pups. And the wolves themselves wouldn't do anything to protect them from men. She wasn't even sure, at this point, if she dared leave the wolves unprotected long enough to hike down to park headquarters and alert the rangers. So that left her and Gray Cloud— if he was what he said he was.

But her quandary merely raised the question of *how* she could protect the wolves. This man might not be deterred by the presence of witnesses. In fact, he might just kill the witnesses.

What she needed to know, she thought, was the goal

of the person or persons with a gun. What did they really hope to accomplish, and at what price? But how could she possibly learn that unless she could question someone? And who would she question?

Ask the mountain. Ask the wind.

The thought twisted sinuously into her mind, rattling her with a sense that she had been invaded somehow. Something *other* was able to get into her head, to say things to her. The mountain watched her, the wind whispered to her, and the night was full of threat.

Drawing her knees up to her chin, she wrapped her arms around them and stared into the fire, trying to shake the clammy sense of foreboding that clung to her, trying to sort out all her mixed feelings about today's events.

And wishing Gray Cloud would return. No matter how her mind wanted to distrust him, her emotions trusted him implicitly. And since that brief almost-kiss earlier, part of her just plain couldn't stop thinking about how much she wanted him to take her into his arms, how much she wanted him to take her on a journey to the end of the rainbow.

That was dangerous. If her mind was clouded with desire for him, how could she correctly evaluate him and what he was doing? For heaven's sake, the man had been accused of murder. He lived as a recluse on the side of a mountain and spoke to the wind and thunder. Was this a man she wanted to give her heart to?

Her mind said no. Her heart said...maybe. Damn, couldn't she pick someone better than that? Someone with an unclouded past and a bright future? This man had nothing except his dedication to this mountain and his vision. Even if he wasn't the killer he was reputed to be, it was still a recipe for grief!

Hormones, she told herself grimly. That was all it was. She wasn't really interested in him as a person; she was merely responding to his masculinity. And he *was* masculine. A slow, secret smile curved her mouth as, for a brief time, she forgot all her worries and thought about Gray Cloud. Very masculine. And so completely different from the academics she was accustomed to spending time with.

He moved with none of the flat-footedness of the street dweller, none of the constrictedness of someone who was used to being hemmed in. He moved instead with a fluid, confident grace. And he was truly a beautiful man. Not handsome, not pretty, just...quintessentially masculine. Incredibly appealing.

But not someone to let herself get involved with.

With a stern mental shake, she forced herself to stop thinking about Gray Cloud and start thinking about the wolves. The seven pups wouldn't even open their eyes for another eleven or twelve days. Until then they would be able to do little but whine, eat and crawl short distances by pulling themselves along with their forelegs. They certainly wouldn't be able to leave the den.

In her research she had come across records of wolves who had been observed to move their litters from den to den during the critical first three months, but the earliest moves recorded had been about three weeks after birth. It was likely, then, that the wolves and the pups were pretty well tied to this particular den at least until then—which made them extremely vulnerable to anyone who wished to harm them.

And that meant she and Gray Cloud *had* to do something. But what? It would take days to hike down to park headquarters to report the gunman. It wouldn't take that long to kill all the wolves, particularly with the pups so helpless.

But anything she could think of doing to protect the animals would also interfere with them. They were wild animals, not meant to be penned in or shadowed everywhere. Continued human protection could create problems, too.

Sighing, she closed her eyes and wished Gray Cloud would return. What if the gunman came back here? She shivered again and tightened her arms around her knees.

If she had an ounce of sense she would head home and leave the whole mess to the park rangers. But she'd never in her life turned tail from anything except emotional involvement, and she wasn't going to start now. The mere thought of abandoning those wolves made her stomach turn sour.

"Mercy."

As soundlessly as a wraith, Gray Cloud stepped out of the wind-tossed night and into the cave. Mercy looked up and lowered her knees, feeling a mixture of relief and apprehension at the sight of him. He squatted beside the fire, taking care to keep it between himself and the cave mouth, and warmed his hands.

"Did you find out anything useful?" she asked.

"There's more than one *wasicu* on this mountain, and they're all working together."

"How...? How did you discover that?" She almost hadn't asked, then resigned herself to the answer.

"The spirits told me," he replied levelly. "Men, hired

guns. They're here to clear the mountain of problems. The wolves. Me. You."

"Me?" Mercy gasped the word. "Me? Why me?"

"You know about the wolves. You're with me." He shrugged a shoulder. "What does it matter? They see you as a problem. They were hired to remove any obstacles to the goals of their employer."

"Who hired them?"

Gray Cloud shook his head slightly. "I wasn't able to learn that. Just how many and what their purpose is."

"We need to do something!"

He lowered himself to the ground and sat cross-legged. His dark eyes, looking like bottomless pits, stared at her over the flames. "I tried to persuade the wolves to move. The pups are too young, but…" He shrugged again.

Mercy felt an icy tendril of panic grip her stomach, but she couldn't tell what caused it, whether it was the horrible situation or the man who faced her across the fire. "Umm…how did you try to persuade the wolves?"

He didn't answer, but his gaze never wavered.

Mercy looked away, her heart beating with uncomfortable rapidity. The world she knew kept slipping away, and it was getting harder and harder to get it back. She was sliding slowly into a place where men talked to wolves, blue fire danced in the air, and the wind whispered secrets. And it was getting more and more difficult to tell herself that these things weren't real.

The power of the mountain seemed to surround her, and the wind had spoken to her. She had seen the blue light that Gray Cloud called the life force. Was she going to doubt her own senses in favor of a lifetime of beliefs? Or was she going to accept the evidence of those same senses in the face of all that she had believed throughout her life?

"I take it," she heard herself say, "that the wolves aren't going to move."

"Not just yet."

"What are you going to do about it?"

He cocked his head, still staring steadily at her, as if she were an interesting puzzle.

"You *are* going to do something?" she insisted.

"What would you have me do?"

"There must be something! If they want to kill the wolves, it would be so easy right now, with the pups helpless and the pack tied to that one den."

"In the way of wolves, the pack will move on if something happens to the pups. They won't risk themselves needlessly to save the litter. You know that."

She *did* know that. The adults would move on and leave the pups to their fate. It made evolutionary sense, survival sense, but it appalled her nonetheless.

"You're viewing the wolves in human terms."

She was; she admitted it to herself. It was a little shocking to her to have to be reminded of that by a man who—to her way of thinking, anyhow—seemed to anthropomorphize even the rocks and clouds. "Are you saying we shouldn't intervene?"

"I'm saying the wolves are smarter than you give them credit for, and these men won't find them so easy to get rid of. Whether we should do something..." He shook his head. "If we can think of something constructive, yes."

Mercy made an impatient sound. "I can't stand this! I can't stand this feeling of not being able to prevent a catastrophe. What happens when they get rid of us and the wolves? They'll still need to deal with all those environmental concerns. People in general are becoming less and less willing to allow wilderness areas to be timbered. They won't accomplish anything useful with this...this murder!"

She felt foolish almost as soon as the words were out of her mouth. She knew better. Gray Cloud merely nodded noncommittally.

After a moment, Mercy let go of her tension and sighed. "Somebody has to help the wolves," she said finally, sadly.

Gray Cloud rose to his feet in one smooth movement. Leaning forward, he passed his hand over the fire. As he did so, the flames leapt and changed color, growing blue and cold looking. "Events have been set into motion. Powers that slumbered have been awakened. We will have opportunities to intervene. We may see some way to take action. For now... For now we wait. The forces that gather on this mountain have not yet come together fully. If we act now, we may prevent an important development."

Slowly Mercy lowered her gaze from his stony face to the twisting blue flames. They no longer seemed to leap randomly but to weave sinuously, like dancers involved in an intricate ballet. And within those flames she thought she could see faces, almost familiar at times, nudging at her memory like a word she couldn't quite remember.

You know.

The whisper seemed to reach out of the fire toward her, telling her to remember, that she already knew. That all she had to do was recall.

Disturbed, she wanted to look away, to ignore the whisper, ignore the feelings it evoked, but as if hypnotized by the flames she continued to stare into the heart of the fire.

One face appeared to grow larger, to move closer and separate from the rest. For eyes and a mouth it had only dark holes, yet it was familiar to her. She knew that face, and if she could just fill in the eyes, she would recognize it. The memory danced maddeningly out of reach.

With a whoosh the flames leapt to man height and then subsided, turning orange once again as they did so. Beyond the cavern walls, thunder growled angrily, then shook the ground with its fury. Gray Cloud remained standing, his eyes closed as he viewed some inner vision.

Around her, Mercy heard the whispers of the elements, mocking voices that seemed to tell her to run while she still could. Beneath her, she felt the stirring power of the mountain.

Gray Cloud was right, she realized. The powers were coming together; ancient forces had been awakened. And the mountain would not care if a few innocent beings were destroyed as it sought to save its denizens. Just as the wolves would sacrifice the pups for the survival of the pack, the mountain would sacrifice some for the survival of many.

An uneasy shudder ran through her. When the mountain reacted, anything that happened to be in the way would be crushed. The mountain didn't care.

Nor, she feared, did Gray Cloud.

Sometime during the night she awoke in a state of terror. Claustrophobia hit with all the might of a falling boulder, and in an instant she was locked in a state of breathless panic.

The night was impenetrable, dark as pitch. The fire had died hours ago, not leaving even the faint glow of embers for illumination. The rushing sound of the wind filled the cavern, creating the sensation of falling endlessly through space.

Guided by deep-rooted instinct, propelled by unthinking terror, Mercy struggled out of her blankets and scrambled on hands and knees toward where she remembered the cave mouth to be.

She had to get out of here. The weight of the tons of rock around her was crushing her, bearing down on her, slowly burying her alive. The mountain was asphyxiating her as surely as if it were strangling her by the throat.

Air! She needed air now! Her lungs dragged desperately, sucking in nothing, as she crawled frantically across the rough cave floor. There was no air. Somehow she had fallen into a vacuum and was going to die with her lungs laboring uselessly while her heart pounded frantically in her ears.

The mouth of the cave wasn't where she expected it to be. Crawling desperately, she ran up hard against a rock wall, banging her head painfully. Where had the cave entrance gone?

All of a sudden, in a moment of clarity that pierced her panic, she understood. There was no longer any cave opening. The mountain had sealed her off underground. Had buried her alive in a cavern deep within its bowels.

The cave where she had fallen asleep had become her tomb.

Chapter Six

Buried alive.

Locked in the maw of the mountain, time became meaningless. The desperate need for air increased her panic, which increased her need for air....

But finally, at some point, she calmed down. It was not the calm of peace, but the calm of desperation, as her mind and body recognized that her only hope lay in forced composure. And as she calmed down, she discovered that she could breathe more easily, though the air was dank and heavy.

But nothing made it possible to see.

In the dark she became a young, frightened child again. The night was easy to populate with all kinds of unsavory things, and who knew what creatures might inhabit a cave like this? Insects. Spiders.

And she didn't dare move again, because it struck her that she didn't know where she was. She couldn't be sure that there wasn't a ledge here somewhere, that she wouldn't fall into a pit and plunge hundreds of feet to a painful death if she crawled in the wrong direction, down the unexplored passage.

Oh, she was cold. Huddling against the rock, she curled up and wished that she hadn't struggled out of her blankets. Now she needed them desperately, and she had no idea where they were, no way to find them. Well, she might not suffocate to death now, but hypothermia would kill her in a few hours.

How had she gotten here? The last thing she remembered was staring into the fire while Gray Cloud spoke of forces awakening.

Gray Cloud! What if this wasn't the cave she had fallen asleep in and he had brought her here? What if he had hypnotized her in some way and then carried her off and left her stranded in this deep, dark cave? What a way to commit murder! No one would ever guess that she hadn't just gotten lost and died of exposure. Nor was there a doubt in her mind that Gray Cloud was physically strong enough to carry her however far he needed to.

But why should he do any such thing? Why? The question kept taunting her. Not for the first time, she wondered why he hadn't killed her at the outset, if killing her was his intent.

Shivering, she curled up as tightly as she could and wished bitterly that she could at least have answers to her questions before she died.

As if in response to her thoughts, she made a connection she had not made before, one that answered her questions and settled her doubts.

Gray Cloud was dedicated to protecting Thunder Mountain. He believed the mountain was a sentient being. Well, even Mercy herself had come to believe that. If the mountain wanted Mercy dead, Gray Cloud would do it, wouldn't he? What if the mountain had just decided she needed to be eliminated and had told Gray Cloud to bring her to this cavern?

He would have done it. Gray Cloud would have done it, because the mountain demanded it.

The sense of betrayal she felt was sharp and deep. She had been coming to care for the man, coming to trust him. Coming to want him. And he had become the pawn of a mountain. An insane mountain, if it didn't distinguish between threats and non-threats, but simply chose to destroy everything that was an outsider.

Oh, God! This was crazy thinking. Sheer insanity! The mountain didn't think. Gray Cloud might not have anything to do with her present situation. Anyone could have carried her to this cave and left her to die, including the gunman. All they needed was a chance to get at her, and that could have happened anytime during the night while she slept.

She didn't want to believe Gray Cloud had done this to her, and when she thought of how he had looked after her since he rescued her from the landslide, she found it even harder to believe that he might hurt her.

Unless the mountain told him to. The thought was an uncomfortable prod, a reminder that there was something Gray Cloud put above all else. A reminder that he was a fanatic. And fanatics were capable of anything in their attempts to serve their cause.

He could have left her here, whether she wanted to believe it or not.

And that hurt. Hurt terribly. Hurt with a pain that was far more than trust betrayed.

* * *

When the whispering began, she had no idea at all how much time had passed. At first she thought perhaps it was merely an illusion of the rushing-wind sound that filled the cavern. Susurrations at first sounded like almost-words, tickling the edges of her mind even in her preoccupation with her dismal circumstances. Gradually, in syllables, words began to emerge from the background noise, like a radio not quite tuned.

"*Mercy....*"

"*...away...*"

"*...gone...*"

Her mind, she told herself, was simply manufacturing words out of random sounds, the way in the perfect dark her eyes kept seeing brilliant flashes of light that weren't really there. The mind needed to fill the void with something recognizable, to make sense out of nonsense.

Sensory deprivation. The term floated to her out of a long-ago psychology class. If the mind was deprived of all sensory input, it would begin to manufacture hallucinations to fill the void. That was what she was doing: hallucinating.

Shivering and cold, she didn't want to lose her mind, as well. She didn't want to die insane. Squeezing her eyes shut, as if it would make a difference, she forced herself to ignore the words that seemed to be emerging from the background sounds and tried instead to focus her thoughts into a logically consistent evaluation of her present situation. Any kind of focus, she reasoned, should counteract the hallucinations.

But it didn't. Instead she found that the flashes of light

in the pitch-darkness seemed to increase, becoming tiny dancing blue sparkles, not so very different from the ones that had seemed to guide Gray Cloud through the storm the night he rescued her.

And the susurrations seemed to become louder, more demanding.

"...*wolf*..."

"...*man*..."

"...*beast of*..."

It was as if the mountain was demanding her attention. The sparkles grew more numerous, the whispers became louder, until they began to sound like broken voices. The more she tried to ignore them, the more they demanded her attention.

And that was *not* the way hallucinations behaved.

In that instant she became certain that the mountain was trying to tell her something. Understanding flooded her, halting her attempt to ignore what was happening.

Listen to the mountain. The whispery voice of the wind spoke inside her head. *Listen to Thunder. Listen.*

A whirlwind snatched at her then, spinning her around, lifting her from the ground, tumbling her headlong into the pitch of night.

"Mercy? Mercy, wake up!"

A low, masculine voice yanked her out of the frightening freefall, and her eyes snapped open. She was in the cave, the dim red fireglow silhouetting Gray Cloud as he squatted beside her.

"Wake up," he said quietly. "You're having a nightmare."

Nightmare? Slowly, shaking her head, shivering internally from a cold that had seeped into her very bones, she sat up. No, it had been no nightmare, she thought. No nightmare. The cold was too real. Her hands felt like ice, and her head ached where she had bumped into the cave wall. No nightmare. Fright made her heart throb.

"Are you okay?" Gray Cloud asked. "You were thrashing around like a fish out of water."

Lightning flared brilliantly beyond the cave entrance, and thunder cracked loudly, a deafening reverberation that shook the ground. *Listen to Thunder.*

"I, uh, was dreaming that I was buried alive." The words escaped her in jerky bursts. She had no one to turn to right now except Gray Cloud, and now that she knew he hadn't kidnapped her, she was ready to trust him.

He sat up abruptly, folding his long legs and leaning toward her. With the dying fire behind him, she couldn't see much except the glitter of his eyes. "Buried alive? How?"

"In a cavern. There wasn't enough air, even though I could hear the wind rushing noisily all the time...or a waterfall, I guess. But I couldn't breathe, and it was so cold. So dark I couldn't see anything at all, except finally there were these little blue sparks dancing everywhere...." She shook her head, wincing when it throbbed where she had banged it in her dream. "I knew I was buried alive, in a cave deep in the mountain. Don't ask me how."

"Such things are known in dreams. Tell me."

"I heard voices in the wind." She could see him nod slowly. "Just a dream," she said after a moment, though her body argued otherwise.

"Dreams are real," he said. "My people never dismiss

a dream. They come to tell us things. The spirits speak to us, give us guidance and warning. Dreams are real, Mercy. Never ignore them."

Listen to the mountain. Listen to Thunder. Listen.

She turned her head a little and looked past Gray Cloud to the lightning-ruptured night. Listen. Just what was she supposed to hear?

Then, as if in another dream, she felt Gray Cloud's arm slip around her shoulders, felt him draw her close to his side and hold her with an ineffable gentleness that made her throat ache. The warmth and solidity of his side against hers, the power of his embracing arm—they seemed to shelter her.

A corner of her mind rebelled briefly, feeling afraid of the comfort that was being offered, feeling afraid of long unmet needs and hungers. But after only the briefest struggle, need won, and she let herself soften and sink against Gray Cloud's strength.

It felt so good to be held!

And as she relaxed into his embrace, he seemed to relax, too. His hand began to knead her shoulder gently, a soothing stroking almost like petting. And little by little his touch filled her with a warm sense of security.

Not until that instant had she realized just how tense and afraid she had been for the last several days. Feeling safe for even a few moments was such a relief, such a release. It would have been so easy to let go of everything, just leave it all to Gray Cloud and forget the wolves, forget her mission, just...forget. Let someone else handle everything.

Such a seductive feeling, one she had never in her life given in to. But she gave in to it a little now. Just a little. Releasing a long sigh, she yielded, feeling as if she were melting into a soft, warm puddle.

Gray Cloud's arm tightened around her shoulders. When she simply softened more against him, a gentle pressure from his hand urged her to turn toward him. A touch from his fingertips brought her chin up, and the next thing she knew, he was kissing her.

It was a warm, soft kiss. A coaxing, reverent touching of lips. It conveyed gentleness, caring, hope…tentativeness. That tentativeness slipped past her last defense, softening her completely, tipping her head back in an unmistakable invitation.

Accepting it, Gray Cloud lowered her gently back onto her blankets, following her down with his mouth pressed gently to hers. "So sweet," he whispered gutturally, then took her mouth again in a deeper, harder kiss.

And she wanted more; she wanted it so badly that she opened her mouth without urging, inviting him deep inside her. His tongue traced her lips softly, then slipped within to tease gently at hers. Soft sinuous strokes led her farther and farther along a path of yearning and hunger.

Her arms lifted, closing around his broad shoulders, at last discovering how hard and powerful he felt beneath her palms. Just being free to touch him was enough to make her insides curl, but being held and kissed by him softened her and wrapped her in a warm, hazy glow.

The terror of her dream receded, as did the storm-tossed night and the hard cave floor beneath her back. Her entire being focused on the man who held her so gently yet securely, on the mouth that caressed hers so tenderly, on the powerful body that hovered over her.

A body she wanted to have pressed full-length to hers. Her hands clenched on his back, fingers digging in, trying to bring him closer. When his weight settled on her, she almost groaned with the sheer delight of it. Until this very moment she had never guessed how satisfying that feeling could be.

His hands slipped beneath her head, cradling it gently, as his tongue foraged deeper in her mouth, coaxing hers into erotic play. Her entire body arched, trying to bring him closer yet, and her insides turned liquid.

She wanted him. Oh, Lord, how she wanted him. She wanted the promise that was in every line of this man's body; she wanted the seductive promises of his oh-so-gentle mouth and strong but tender hands. She wanted the answers to mysteries older than time and hungers newer than today. She wanted the answer to her womanhood, and every instinct cried that he held the key.

Listen. To what? Listen to what? The driving drumbeat in her blood? The whirlwind of aching needs in her head? The yearning of her heart for its mate? Oh, she was listening, all right. Listening with every fiber of her being to the silent messages of her own body and soul.

Listening to the way her body yearned for other touches and twisted subtly in invitation. Touch me, her body cried, and she turned a little, begging for the caress of his hands on her breast. On her side. On her…

In a flash she lost her breath. Where before he had lain half-over her, all of a sudden he was between her legs, his hardness pressing against her softness in unmistakable demand. He wanted her. He wanted her as much as she wanted him.

But all sense hadn't been lost. The sudden intimacy

of having him between her legs, even fully clothed, shattered her mood, quelling her arousal. And with stark, embarrassing clarity, she saw the dangerous game she was playing. Her eyes flew open, and she found herself looking straight into his—dark, mysterious pools in the dim light of the dying fire. An instant later he rolled away, freeing her.

Neither of them said anything as the night crept back between them. Embarrassment welled in her, a sense of shame at the ready way she had welcomed him and encouraged him. He'd probably only meant to comfort her after her nightmare, and she'd taken it wrong....

Oh, damn!

Why, she wondered miserably, was it so hard in retrospect to remember exactly what had happened—who had been responsible for the rising passion of the embrace?

But maybe she couldn't remember because it had happened *between* them, for both of them. Maybe she hadn't been alone in her shamelessness.

What did it matter, anyway? She wasn't going to do it again or encourage it to happen again. For heaven's sake, she didn't know anything about the man except that he'd been tried for murder and he believed that mountains were alive! And what kind of recommendation was that?

Listen.

The whispered word twisted sinuously into her mind, driving back other concerns with its cold breath.

Listen.

Listen to what? She wanted to groan in frustration, to demand an answer from the source of that maddening whisper. Listen to what?

Beyond the cave mouth, lightning leapt from cloud to cloud, splitting into six or seven blue forks before vanishing. Moments later, thunder rolled through the air and the ground, causing the world to tremble.

In the moment after the thunder died, in a stillness as even the wind seemed to hold its breath, came the howl of a wolf.

Mercy's scalp prickled, and she sat up abruptly. Gray Cloud did the same. Something was wrong. That howl was…different.

Gray Cloud rose to his feet in a single swift movement. "I'm going to check on the pups."

"I'm coming with you." The thought of that climb in the dead of the stormy night was daunting, but she couldn't just sit here and wait. Something was wrong.

The ground was slippery and treacherous from the rain. Smooth rocks became icelike, and the mud was every bit as bad. The little sparkles of blue light danced in the misty, wet air—guiding them, it seemed—and Mercy no longer questioned what her eyes were telling her. Whatever those little lights were, they were illuminating the way.

Gray Cloud never strayed from her side, keeping a hand at her elbow or back every step of the way. More than once, when she started to slip, he caught her and kept her from falling. She quickly grew accustomed to having his powerful arm snatch her about the waist and steady her.

She couldn't imagine why he wasn't having the same difficulty keeping his footing, but he appeared to be having no problem at all. Like a mountain goat.

Another howl rent the night, a sorrowful sound, and

what troubled Mercy more than anything was that there was no answering howl. What had happened to the rest of the pack? Had they abandoned the bitch and her pups? Or had one of them gotten injured and been left behind?

They surely couldn't have abandoned the den—not yet, when the pups had just been born. Something was very definitely seriously wrong.

Another howl, this time more of a low groaning sound than a true howl. It made Mercy's hair stand on end, it was so unnatural, and even Gray Cloud paused a moment, tilting his head back as he listened to it.

"Damn!" he muttered.

"It's hurt, isn't it?" She knew in her heart there could be no other explanation for that anguished, sorrowful sound.

He grunted acknowledgment as he urged her up the side of the ravine. She slipped again, but this time when he caught her, he didn't release her once she was steady. This time he kept his arm clamped around her waist.

"It's the bitch," he said.

"How can you tell?"

"I just know."

As usual. The wind had probably told him. She would have felt frustrated, except that she was far too worried about what could have made the wolf howl that way. Had a pup died? Was she sick in the aftermath of giving birth?

Where were the other wolves?

Listen.

Yeah, right. Listen. To what? That pained, painful, moaning howl? What the hell good would listening do? Something was wrong, and *listening* wasn't going to fix it!

The last bit of terrain was steep enough that Gray Cloud climbed up first, as he had earlier, then turned to reach down and give Mercy a hand up. She could have climbed it alone, but it seemed important to him to help, so she let him. Besides, arguing would only waste time, and they didn't have any to spare, to judge by the wolf's cry.

At last they came over the rise that concealed the den from them. The first thing they saw was fire.

Gray Cloud swore viciously, and Mercy cried out. Someone had built a fire at the mouth of the den, and the bitch was standing a few feet away, blocked from her pups by the flames, howling helplessly.

Gray Cloud released Mercy and loped forward toward the den. She was hard on his heels, not at all certain what she would do, but knowing they had to do what they could.

The wolf turned on them as they came running up. Squatting in a threatening posture, she growled and bared her fangs, warning them away.

Gray Cloud ignored her, brushing past her as if she were no more than a flea. Mercy halted and held her breath, expecting the wolf to leap at the man. But the bitch didn't. Her snarl faded swiftly into an expression of perplexity, and then she tipped back her head and howled again, the same sorrowful, anguished sound. Mercy hurried past her to help Gray Cloud.

Gray Cloud waded into the burning brush and wood as if he were wearing asbestos, with total disregard for his safety. He kicked the fire apart, scattering burning brands this way and that, clearing the door of the den. No sooner had he opened a path than the wolf darted past him into the tunnel.

The burning wood sizzled in the rain, and the flames began to die as the wood scattered. The wolf reappeared a short time later with a pup in her jaws. One after another she went back for them and laid them all just beyond reach of the scattered fire.

When she had retrieved the last of them, she sat on her haunches and looked up at Gray Cloud. The man stared back down at her. "I think," he said after a moment, "that she'll let us move the pups."

"Then let's do it."

Mercy's scalp prickled again as she watched the eerie interaction between man and wolf. Their eyes met and held, hers so yellow, his so dark, and silent messages seemed to pass between them. Gray Cloud removed his jacket slowly, but the wolf appeared to be confident that he meant no harm. When he squatted and spread his jacket on the wet ground, she merely moved to one side to allow him to pick up the squirming, whining pups and put them on the jacket. She waited patiently while he tied the arms together and made a sling, nosed at them once just before he picked them up, and then stood back, tail high, to allow him to lift her litter.

"Let's go," he said.

Whoever had set the fire at the mouth of the den had intended to suffocate those pups. The fire would have drawn all the oxygen out of the den and prevented any more from getting in, and the litter would have died from suffocation. The method of execution showed a degree of intelligence that made Mercy's skin crawl even more. To not just crawl in and kill them, to not just be content to kill the bitch and let them die from starvation, but to do it this way...

It was disturbing to see the way the wolf responded to Gray Cloud, as if the two of them could read minds, as if they had spoken together in some silent language and reached an agreement about the pups.

He really was a medicine man. The thought struck Mercy as she followed him back down to the cave. It was ludicrous, but until this very moment she had refused to consider what that might mean about him. He was a medicine man. A practitioner of arcane arts who believed in powers she couldn't even imagine. Someone who caused flickering blue lights to dance in the rainy nighttime woods to illuminate their path. Someone who could evidently talk to wolves and mountains.

This was no primitive mythology that Gray Cloud practiced, but a potent understanding of very real powers. That wolf wouldn't have offered her pups to just anyone, and offer them to Gray Cloud was exactly what she had done.

Getting down was, if possible, even more difficult than getting up had been. The slipperiness of the wet ground caused problems, and Gray Cloud had his hands pretty full with the pups. From time to time he would ask Mercy to hold the sling while he climbed down ahead of her, and then he would reach up to take it from her. The wolf grew uneasy every time the exchange was made, growling softly at the back of her throat, but then calmed down as soon as the litter was back in Gray Cloud's care.

Mercy felt bruised and scraped nearly everywhere by

the time they reached the cave and was glad to give up the struggle to stay upright on the treacherous ground.

The wolf seemed to have no qualms about following them into the cave. As soon as Gray Cloud settled her pups off to one side, safely away from the fire, she curled around them and nudged them to her teats before settling herself to watch her human companions.

Gray Cloud threw some more wood on the dying fire and proceeded to start a pot of coffee in Mercy's tiny tin pot. He was right, she thought; nobody was going to sleep now. Pawing around in her knapsack, she produced some trail mix and offered it to him.

"The pups would have died," she said.

He nodded.

"What *really* troubles me was the way he chose to kill them. There are so many other ways that wouldn't have required…well…"

"That wouldn't have displayed quite so much intelligence," Gray Cloud said heavily. "Only an educated person would know that the fire would suffocate the pups."

"And that required *thinking*," Mercy said. "Someone really *thought* about how to kill them. That bothers me more than if someone had crawled in there and shot them." She hesitated. "That sounds dumb, I guess."

He shook his head. "It strikes me the same way."

"Thank God we heard the howl." She looked at the wolf and shivered a little at the way the bitch's eyes seemed to glow with golden fire. These animals were far more intelligent than anyone wanted to believe, she thought. Far more intelligent. It glowed in their strange eyes in the same way it glowed in Gray Cloud's.

"This isn't good," she said suddenly. "Not for the bitch or her pups. It's not healthy for her to trust people."

Again he nodded, saying nothing as he stared into the fire and waited for the coffee to brew.

"I just don't know what we can do! We have to protect them, but we can't risk them coming to trust us. What if they trusted the people who want to kill them?"

"That's a problem," he acknowledged at last.

"So what do we do?"

"Wait. Powers are gathering. Any action now would be premature."

Frustration welled in her, and she made an impatient sound. "Damn it, you're always saying we should wait! What if we'd waited tonight? Those pups would have died."

Several heartbeats later, he lifted his gaze from the fire and looked directly at her. "Do you know how many people are out there? Who sent them? What their orders are? Without knowing these things, how can we make a plan that will be of any use?"

She drew an annoyed breath. "We *have* to do *something*."

He nodded slowly. "*Reconnaissance* is the word, I believe. We need to learn as much as we can about our foe. Scout the enemy. Only when we know exactly what we're up against can we be sure of taking appropriate action."

It made sense. It also made her uneasy. Later, lying on her blanket as the sky began to lighten with dawn, she remembered the fire in front of the den, remembered that Gray Cloud had been out of the cave until just a short time before the wolf howled.

He could have set the fire.

She tried to brush the thought away, but it clung like porcupine quills, keeping her awake and uncomfortable. He could have set the fire. He could be involved in the trouble, which would certainly make him reluctant to take any action. He had planned to go up after the pups alone. What if she hadn't followed? Would he have come back to say the pups had died and there was nothing he could do?

She should have been trying to sleep as dawn brightened Thunder Mountain, but all she could do was stare up at the cave ceiling and wonder if she was being completely and deliberately misled.

The wolf showed no desire to move herself or her pups. The rest of the pack found her without any apparent difficulty, and came and went throughout the morning, bringing her nourishment and checking on her, as it seemed to Mercy, who noted everything she possibly could and then proceeded to name all the wolves.

The alpha female she named Stripes, because of the pattern of colors on her snout. The alpha male became Eyebrows because of the markings over his eyes. Eyebrows didn't stray very far from his mate that morning and was there every time she stirred.

Mercy was painfully conscious of two things all morning: One, that she was observing the wolves in unique circumstances and, while informative, those observations would not be as illuminating as those made of the creatures in their natural habitat. The other thing she couldn't forget was that Gray Cloud was out there somewhere, supposedly scouting, but possibly arranging another threat against the wolves.

Or against her.

Almost as if he picked up on her thoughts, Eyebrows lifted his head from his paws and looked straight at her.

"Aren't you going to leave?" Mercy asked him. "You leave every time Gray Cloud returns, and he said he'd be back by noon."

The wolf's ears pricked forward, but other than that he showed no reaction.

She was losing her mind, she thought, turning her head so she could look out at another stormy day. A nightmare of being buried alive had managed somehow to leave her feeling physically sore even this morning— she must have gotten restless enough during the dream to crack her head on something. Hearing voices on the wind that kept whispering *Listen,* as if there was anything to listen to besides the wind. Hanging around with a man who had been accused of murder, distrusting him...

If she really distrusted him, she asked herself, why didn't she just pack up her stuff and move? Leave. Climb down from this godforsaken mountain and report that she'd found wolves and leave it at that. Let someone else come up here and figure out what was going on.

If she really distrusted Gray Cloud, what had she been doing when she fell into his arms last night?

And the memory of that made her *ache.* Why couldn't she feel that way about someone who was nice and safe, like one of her colleagues? Why had it taken an accused murderer on the wild side of a mountain, a man who evidently had no home and no job other than a mystical mission to protect a mountain?

She sat there, staring out at the dark pines, staring into the deep shadows beneath them, trying to remember what had seemed so important to begin with, why she had felt it necessary to come up here and find these wolves. Gray Cloud had been right about one thing: announcing the presence of the wolves might be detrimental to them. But not as detrimental as whatever the person who had built the fire at the den had intended. That alone was enough to convince her that the wolves were a serious target for some reason. That hadn't been a random act; it had been planned.

Well, obviously, she thought, realizing that her thoughts were running in circles. Round and round she was going, traveling the same ground in hopes that she could find some clue, some key—anything to help.

But Gray Cloud was making sense—they had to scout the situation before they could take any useful action. What *she* needed to do was keep an eye on Gray Cloud, as well, to be sure he wasn't the problem.

Because she couldn't stand the thought of anything happening to the wolves. In principle she sympathized with the desire of the Indians to keep their sacred places untouched, but from her perspective, the wolves and the environment were equally important. Perhaps more so. Merle had never understood her affinity for living things, whether plant or animal, or why she could get so upset about timbering or strip-mining. Yes, she used paper and drove a car and all the rest of it, but she was convinced there were better ways of providing these things than raping the environment for the fastest, largest profit possible.

Now the wolves were being threatened because they might stand between some company and its desire to make money from Thunder Mountain.

It was hard to believe Gray Cloud could be any part of such a conspiracy, but it *was* possible. What better cover than pretending to be here to protect the mountain?

She was never certain at what point she began to feel as if she were being watched. At first the sensation was mild, not quite as annoying as the buzzing of a lazy fly. But the feeling grew until it burst into her awareness with discomforting force.

She was being watched.

Her neck crawled with the sensation. Instinctively she looked toward the wolves, but Stripes was dozing with her pups, and Eyebrows was staring out the cave opening at the same shadows she had been staring at.

As she watched, his hackles rose and a growling began deep in his throat. Slowly he rose to a crouch, never taking his attention from the woods.

Mercy needed no more convincing. Rolling to her side, she lay on her stomach and began to inch toward the cave mouth, hoping to get a glimpse of whoever—or whatever—was watching them.

Listen.

"Listen to what, damn it?" she muttered under her breath as she eased her way to the entrance. Listen. Listen. Useless piece of advice!

You know him.

The whisper in her head stopped her cold. She knew him? Knew who? Gray Cloud?

God, was she listening to voices in her head?

By the time she reached the cave mouth and could see a broad expanse of the forest, Eyebrows had crept up, too, and was watching the woods guardedly.

Where was Gray Cloud?

Her breath jammed in her throat as she saw movement in the shadows beneath a tree. Someone standing there and watching the cave? An animal?

A low growl emanated from the wolf, and she decided it was no small animal stirring over there. Eyebrows wouldn't be reacting this way to a raccoon. Someone was in those shadows, and she had no reason to trust anyone on this mountain after what had happened to the wolf den last night.

For the first time in her life she honestly wished she had a gun. Damn it, Thunder Mountain, she found herself thinking, you're supposed to be protecting yourself and these wolves, the trees...

A rumble, at first hardly detectable, began to shake the earth beneath her. The trees swayed as if caught in a forceful wind, while the ground bucked and heaved beneath them. And the earth sound, the horrible moaning of the tortured ground, chilled her spine.

Earthquake.

As she watched, the ground undulated like waves on the water. Even the rock beneath her seemed to ripple. Eyebrows began to howl, and when she dared to glance his way, she saw he was pacing nervously, unwilling to abandon his mate and the pups, but wanting very badly to get out into the open.

And that was what you were supposed to do in an earthquake, Mercy remembered. Get outdoors, where falling debris was less likely to kill or injure you. But the pups...

Galvanized, forcing herself to ignore her own terror, Mercy crawled back into the cave to get the pups. When she reached the litter, she found Stripes hovering nervously over the squirming mass of whining pups.

"We'll get them out of here," Mercy told Stripes. Rising to her knees, she tugged her jacket off and spread it on the floor of the cave. Just as she reached for the first of the little wolves, thunder began to roll down the mountainside, shaking the earth in a different way. The undulations of the earthquake were a counterpoint to the hammering roar of falling rocks.

Mercy hesitated. This cave might be a death trap, but rock slides were just as deadly. Perhaps it would be safer in here.

And where the devil was Gray Cloud? At this moment she would have given a great deal not to be alone in the face of a world gone mad. Without the comfort of another human presence, death looked a lot more terrifying.

She had looked death in the eye before, when rock climbing, and by itself, death did not terrify her. But the thought of dying on a lonely mountainside, without another human being nearby to know or care, *did* bother her. She didn't want to die this way. Not this way.

"Gray Cloud..."

She spoke his name with yearning, as rocks began to tumble down in front of the cave entrance. Her defenses began to crumble, too, and she whispered his name again as she scooped up the pups. They had to get out of there before the rocks sealed off the cave. They would have a better chance in the woods below.

Gray Cloud.

In a moment of yearning so intense it beggared description, she called his name deep inside her soul and felt it wing upward and outward, a silent cry of the heart. And at that very moment the hail of rocks became a torrent. With horrifying speed, the mouth of the cave was sealed shut by fallen rocks.

She was trapped.

Chapter Seven

Gray Cloud.

He heard Mercy's cry in his mind in the same instant that he realized the mountain was taking action against the intruders. In a flash he understood the danger the woman and the wolves were facing. Forgetting the deserted campsite he was investigating, he turned and began to run in the direction of the cave.

Time seemed to become mired in mud. No matter how hard he ran, stretching his muscles to the utmost, racing at a speed that caused his heart to thunder in his chest, he didn't seem to be moving at all. Not at all. It was a nightmare come true, as the air seemed to grow so thick he felt as if he were running through molasses.

Gray Cloud.

But then he burst from the obscuring forest on the slope below the cave mouth…just in time to see a river of rock slide off the side of the mountain above and seal the mouth of the cave.

"Mercy!"

His shout was drowned by the roar of the falling rock. He stood there helpless to prevent it as boulders tumbled down before the cave mouth. Some kept going, rolling into the trees below, driving animals ahead of them, but enough rocks remained that Mercy and the wolf pups were trapped.

Her nightmare had come true.

His first instinct was to race up and start burrowing a hole in that tumbled wall of rock. All that held him back was an awareness of the mountain's anger, an awareness that his interference might arouse that ire even further and cause more harm. Without the mountain's forbearance, he couldn't be absolutely certain of getting Mercy out of there.

There couldn't be much time. There was some air in the cave, but not enough. The small tunnel leading off the back only came to a dead end.

A few hours, he thought. He had only a few hours to get her out of there. And each minute of those hours would be sheer terror for her. She was buried alive.

But first he had to appease the mountain, and his medicine bundle was back at his camp. With time being of the essence, he had no choice but to scan the surrounding area for items he could use to make an altar. No buffalo skull or painted sticks were available here, but there were plenty of rocks and earth. He would call on the Stone People to help him, and hope that *Tate* and *Wakinyan,* the Wind and Thunder, would aid him.

He needed stones, large unique ones. One as smooth and round as nature could make it, representing the harmony of the world. Another cracked and uneven, to represent the power of the mountain and earth. And finally, one perfectly flat stone to represent the sky above all. Finding them, he laid the stones out carefully, in a triangle, each separated from the others by a distance equal to the length of his forearm. It humbled him to measure himself against the mountain, and that was good.

He stood before the altar, closing his eyes, and extended his arms. Usually, when he prayed, he beseeched the mountain to hear him. Today he was angry. Fury shimmered in him, a force he could not quite control, as he railed at the mountain's willingness to sacrifice the wolves and the woman to its purpose.

There were those on these slopes who were a serious threat, but the woman and the wolves were not among them. Yet Thunder Mountain had shown no compunction about harming them, had not attempted to protect them in its drive to clear the intruders from its slopes. In seeking to drive away the men below who were plotting to kill the wolves, the mountain had been willing to kill the wolves itself.

And that infuriated Gray Cloud.

Today his chant had an angry sound to it, reflecting the outrage he felt. He had served this mountain for most of the days of his life, protecting it from the encroachments of those who could not understand the mountain's power or its sacred nature. Now the mountain was seeking to protect itself without regard to the cost, and this offended Gray Cloud.

He felt betrayed.

For a while it seemed that the mountain would not respond to him, that it was going to ignore him because he was angry. They were both angry, he and the mountain, but he was just angry enough to refuse to accept being ignored.

Answer me! The demand seemed to roar out of him, though he spoke the words only in his heart. *Answer me!*

And finally the mountain replied. *The intruders have moved back down lower. Why are you angry, little man?*

Gray Cloud was used to the mountain's detachment, but today, for some reason, it bothered him, fueling his anger. "What does it matter if you drive the intruders down lower, if you also kill the wolves?"

The wolves matter little. In time other wolves will come. The mountain must be preserved so that they can *come.*

"And the woman? What about the woman? She only came to study the wolves, not to hurt the mountain."

She is nothing. The world crawls with her kind.

Nothing. The world crawls with her kind. The intense heat of rage Gray Cloud felt at that dismissal blinded him to the danger inherent in confronting the mountain, made him forget the vision that had called him to protect this mountain, made him forget the sacred nature of the being with whom he dealt.

"Mountain!" he argued. "Her kind may be one of many, but *she* is unique, and she does not deserve to be killed simply because she was in the way!"

The earth trembled and shook beneath his feet, and the stones he had found moved a little, breaking the symmetry of the triangle. Gray Cloud stood his ground, prepared to face the mountain's ire.

"I am here," he continued as the ground bucked again, and another hail of rocks fell from above. "I am here, and I will free the wolves and the woman. If they are of no consequence, then they may as well live."

The mountain shrugged. Another torrent of rock

spilled down the slopes, but when the clatter died away, no more was forthcoming. Gray Cloud gathered up the stones into a pile, then turned toward the rocks that blocked the cave. He didn't know if he would be able to dig the woman and the wolves out in time.

He could only try.

No light filtered into the cave. Mercy huddled near the wolf and her pups, listening to the pups whine, and shivered from the cold. Another shudder of the earth shook debris down from the cave roof.

Buried alive. It was even more terrifying than her dream last night had been, perhaps because she knew that this time she couldn't wake up. This was *real*.

The pups wouldn't stop whining, and they squirmed back and forth between their mother and Mercy. They were blind and deaf so soon after birth, and had no way of knowing the world had turned dark and threatening. But they could feel the rumble of the ground and could probably smell the fear on Mercy and Stripes.

Eyebrows had vanished. Mercy hoped he hadn't been hurt or killed in the rock slide.

Stripes moaned low in her throat, an unhappy sound. Without even thinking about it, Mercy reached out and touched the wolf, digging her fingers into the thick fur and tugging gently. Stripes shivered and then moaned again, accepting the touch.

There was a flashlight in her pack, if she could find it. She crawled around in the dark on the floor of the cave for a while, realizing with a vague sense of shock that the cave was bigger than she had realized. Either that or she was crossing and recrossing her own path again and again.

Ah! Her pack. Memory told her the flashlight was tucked into a back pouch. Feeling carefully, she found the long aluminum cylinder and pulled it out. With an eager push of her thumb, she threw the switch and then watched in dismay as a thin, yellow beam gleamed, flickered and died. The batteries were gone.

Despair welled in her, nearly choking her, and she had to battle it for long moments, but finally she was able to shove down the impending tears and start thinking again.

The tunnel at the back of the cave crossed her mind, but she quailed at the thought of climbing into its narrow confines when the earth was shaking. If it collapsed...

It didn't bear thinking about.

Her heart was still hammering in her chest, and she was still gasping like a sprinter near the finish line, but adrenaline had cleared the panic-induced fog from her brain, and she was thinking again.

Without light she didn't dare try to dig herself out. Even with light, she might precipitate another rock slide, right into the cavern. *Think, Mercy! Think!*

Licking her finger, she held it up and waited, but could detect no movement in the air. That meant the tunnel at the back didn't lead to the outside, so there was no point in exploring it. That left the sealed cave mouth as her only hope of escape.

And it was no hope at all.

Closing her eyes, she turned inward, seeking some glimmer of an idea, seeking what clarity and strength she could summon to help her deal with her impending death.

Because she believed she was going to die. The mountain had won.

The mountain seethed, but so did Gray Cloud. He had dedicated his life to protecting this mountain, and in theory he understood that sometimes individuals must be sacrificed to preserve the greater good. He even agreed with the idea—in principle.

Reality was a different matter.

Despite the damp chilliness of the day, he grew hot and sweaty as he strove to clear a tunnel into the cave. Anger goaded him, as did an inexplicable sense of betrayal. Troubled, his mind ran over events again and again, trying to find the reason in what had occurred. He knew that in the larger scheme of things, a single life was insignificant. That an individual being was less than the single blink of an eye in the span of a lifetime. He knew this.

He also knew that all life was sacred, and while killing was sometimes necessary, life deserved more respect than to be dismissed as utterly insignificant.

But what really disturbed him was the uneasy sense that the mountain and the developer were both using the same reasoning. After all, didn't the developer tell himself that a few Indians were insignificant, that for the greater good the mountain must be timbered and mined and developed?

Did the end truly justify the means? That question had haunted him ever since he had taken a man's life. The taking of life was sometimes justified, yes. He believed that, and would kill again if necessary. But it was not justified to take an innocent life simply because it was inconsequential and was in the way.

When he cut willow branches to make a sweat lodge, a man should ask the forgiveness of the willow. When he cut a tree to make a lodge pole, he begged the forgiveness of the tree.

Life must be treated with respect and never ended with wanton indifference. The mountain evidently felt differently, and the mountain was an ancient and powerful being with much wisdom. Gray Cloud, who had promised to serve the mountain, wrestled with himself as he tried to come around to the mountain's way of thinking, as he tried to accept that perhaps the mountain was right.

As he faced the possibility that his role of protector might require him to harm the innocents who got in the way.

As he wondered yet again if Mercy was as innocent as she appeared.

The timing of her arrival was suspicious, coming as it did at the same time as the arrival of the men who had killed the deer and tried to kill the wolves. The men working for the developer who wanted to rape the slopes of Thunder Mountain.

Perhaps she was one of them, despite her concern for the wolves. Perhaps she was helping them. Perhaps the mountain had known what it was doing when it sealed the cave and drove the men below farther down.

If she was one of them, she would have to die.

The ground seemed never to be quite still. It quieted from time to time, but then the mountain would stir again, shaking loose more debris. Stripes howled each time the earth shook.

The air was growing stale. Mercy forced herself to remain as calm and motionless as possible to conserve air. She had to believe that someone would try to rescue her, that Gray Cloud was even now trying to dig his way into the cave.

And beneath her she felt the heartbeat of the mountain. In the dark, with the earth moaning and rumbling all around her, she felt the power surrounding her, felt the touch, however faint, of an alien mind.

The mountain lived.

At times Gray Cloud believed the mountain was not going to let him rescue the pups and the woman. Each time he thought he must at last be making headway, Thunder Mountain would rumble and tremble again, and rocks would cave in on the tunnel he was so laboriously digging. When he looked back, he could see how far he had come. When he looked forward, he could see only how much of his work had been undone.

The mountain was annoyed with him. The Stone People whispered sibilant warnings, the Wind murmured of dangers, and Thunder tolled an alarm overhead. What did the woman and the pups matter in the larger scheme of a world billions of years old?

But while the Stone People and Thunder seemed to chastise him, the Wind sided with him. *Tomorrow Woman listens,* the Wind murmured. *She hears.*

Hears what? wondered Gray Cloud as he lifted yet another boulder with aching, exhausted arms and felt his back twinge a sharp protest. What did the woman hear?

Another rumble of the ground started to shake rocks loose, and the rein on Gray Cloud's temper snapped. Rearing up, he bellowed, "Enough!"

For the space of a heartbeat the universe seemed to hold its breath. Even Thunder grew silent, and the Wind stilled in the treetops.

And then Thunder Mountain began to rumble. From deep within came the creaking, snapping groan of rocks on the move. As the heap of fallen rocks beneath his feet began to tremble violently, Gray Cloud turned and scrambled down from them, acutely aware that the temblor could shake all those loose boulders into another landslide.

Rocks started following him down as he hurried toward safety. The mountain was going to teach him a lesson. He hoped against hope that his lesson wouldn't cost the pups and the woman their lives, if they hadn't already died. But if it did, he would have no one to blame but himself.

Small rocks had been the first to shake free, but soon there were larger boulders bouncing downward. He reached the bottom of the rock heap just in time to dart to the side and miss being struck by a tumbling boulder the size of a man's head. Others rolled down behind it, parts of the mountain on the move.

This tremor would probably fill in the entire passageway he had labored so hard to clear. Frustration filled him, causing him to grind his teeth and clench his fists in an attempt to avoid challenging the mountain again.

Another violent shudder shook the mountain, causing the earth to buckle and heave, and turning dirt into a liquid that swallowed some of the smaller rocks. Bigger and bigger boulders tumbled down from the heap as a new landslide was unleashed.

Despair filled him as he watched rocks from farther up begin to tumble downward, too. The woman and the wolves were going to be freshly buried, and there wasn't a thing he could do to prevent it.

The temblor started deep within the heart of the mountain. Mercy felt it coming, as did Stripes, who nudged her pups even closer to Mercy, as if the two of them shared the task of protecting the newborns.

It was going to be a bad one, Mercy thought. A very bad one. Some part of her seemed to feel the mountain's intent, and that was almost as unnerving as the tremor itself.

Listen.

Listen to what? She wanted to shout the question in frustration, but she was afraid any sudden loud noise in the cavern would bring more of the roof down on them. It was only a distraction, anyway, the frustration. Something to feel besides the fear that had plagued her for hours now.

At least, she *thought* it had been hours since the rock slide sealed off the cave. And now, from the sound of it, she was going to get buried even deeper. Not that she had long left to worry about it. The air was getting thicker—so stale it was difficult to breathe. Her heart was beating rapidly now, and her respiration rate had increased significantly as her body struggled for the oxygen that was getting rarer and rarer with each breath she took.

The trembling grew, shaking more rock chips loose from the ceiling. This time Stripes didn't howl. Instead she gave a small, brief moan and wrapped herself more tightly around her pups.

At that moment Mercy didn't know whether she would rather have the roof collapse and end it all swiftly or wait until suffocation put her to sleep. Either way, she would be dead, free of this awful fear. She wouldn't have to sit here any longer while the ground heaved like an angry beast and rocks pelted her head with stinging force.

Hope hadn't died, but the renewed earthquake came close to killing it. She couldn't imagine that the rock surrounding her and creating this cave wouldn't crack and rupture under the strain of being twisted this way. And when it cracked...

Another rumble, sounding like a subway train approaching the station, worked its way up from deep within the mountain and shook the cavern again. More rock rained down on her, and Stripes yelped sharply as something struck her, but she didn't abandon her pups.

The dark was endless, fathomless. Not a ray of light reached them. From time to time one of her eyes would signal a brilliant flash of light to her brain, but it was illusory. Beautiful, though, as brilliant colors momentarily decorated the endless night.

Despite the flashes, the darkness was as suffocating as the air. Her mind cried out for light in the same way her body cried out for fresh air. The darkness was confining, crushing. An almost palpable weight bearing down on her.

And behind it all was the sense of an alien presence,

of a mind so very different from her own that its merest touch was chilling. To that mind, she and the wolves had as much substance and importance as ants did to a human. She was negligible. Too small and ephemeral to be considered.

For the human mind, it was almost impossible to comprehend the perspective of a being that lived for aeons, a being as massive as this mountain. What she could understand, though, was that the fate of the wolves, and the fate of Mercy Kendrick, didn't matter a whit. And it was terrifying indeed to think of all that power unleashed, not caring what it crushed.

The ground shook again, more violently this time, and Mercy found herself clinging to Stripes. The wolf didn't try to shake her off but seemed to burrow even closer. More rocks shook free of the ceiling and pelted them, and a terrible clatter came from the rock slide that had sealed the cave mouth, as if the rocks there were falling, too. More rocks were probably falling onto them, sealing the cave ever deeper.

Mercy felt tears running slowly down her cheeks as she faced the most terrible helplessness of all. She couldn't save herself or the wolves; there wasn't anything she could do. And if Gray Cloud had been trying to help them, this newest quake would have defeated him, as more tons of rock fell across the cave entrance.

This was the end, she thought. Buried alive in a dank cavern, her entire life an unfinished story. In these final moments, the most important things had become the things she hadn't done. The true love she had never given, and the children she had never had, suddenly seemed of far greater importance than anything she had achieved in her career to date.

She was going to die on the side of a mountain in remote Conard County, Wyoming, and her only legacy would be a few dry and dusty scientific papers that only a handful of people would ever read. What a waste!

Thunder Mountain rumbled again, a violent upheaval that felt as if it were going to shake everything off its shoulders—every man, beast and tree. The hail of stones from the ceiling grew thicker, and Mercy curled up, folding her arms over her head instinctively.

Stripes unleashed a mournful howl and curled around her pups.

This was it, Mercy thought. The whole cave was going to collapse on them.

Thunder Mountain bucked violently, and Gray Cloud fell to his knees, unable to maintain his balance on the wildly heaving earth.

Angry. The mountain was angry, striking out at those who had annoyed it, uncaring what others it might harm. Just like the timber people, Gray Cloud thought. Uncaring, blind to all but a single-minded purpose.

His purpose and the mountain's were the same. Gray Cloud had known that all his life, but for the very first time a part of him grew doubtful about the wisdom of that. This mountain must be protected for all the generations to come, for it was a sacred place. And as the sacred places diminished, it became harder and harder for a man to find his vision, his purpose, the meaning of his life. And without meaning, a man had nothing.

No, he could not doubt the rightness of the mountain's actions. He must not. The mountain knew more, saw more, viewed the centuries rather than the years. The good of the many far outweighed the good of a few.

But he thought of the wolves and the woman and was saddened, for surely they were no threat. Or were they? Had the mountain perhaps seen what he had not?

It was possible. It was always possible. There could be some tie between the woman and these men sent by Stockton-Wells. At least, he *thought* the lumber giant had sent them, because that name was stamped on some of the things he had found at the campsite earlier. He knew of Stockton-Wells, of course. They were famous throughout this part of the West, employing thousands in their timbering and mining operations. They were a formidable foe, too big for a single man to take on, but not too big for Thunder Mountain to deal with.

But what about the woman? Could she be involved somehow? Was she an innocent pawn...or a scheming player? No, she had been too upset about the wolves to be one of the people who would hurt them. He doubted she could be that good an actress.

But perhaps Stockton-Wells was using her in some way? Perhaps there was some connection between her and the timber company that had aroused the mountain's ire? For it seemed to Gray Cloud right now that the mountain was angry at him, and at Mercy Kendrick. If she still lived within that buried cave, she must be terrified beyond belief as she experienced the full force of the mountain's anger.

If there were any answers to his questions, they lay in the cave with the woman. As the ground heaved beneath him, as the earth shrieked and rocks tumbled from above, Gray Cloud looked down at his hands, which were bloodied and bruised from trying to dig a tunnel into the cave.

He had to get her out of there. He had to. He had to know.

Just then, with a thundering roar of rupturing rock, the mountain bucked violently one last time, and a cascade of boulders poured down from the heap of fallen rock, racing downward like stampeding bulls.

When the last echo of falling rocks had faded, the day turned stunningly quiet and peaceful. The ground no longer trembled, and even the ever-present thunder was silent.

It was over. Gray Cloud felt it in that part of him that was attached to the mountain. It was over. Without a moment's hesitation, he measured the rockfall that covered the cave entrance, sighted the best location and clambered up the treacherous slope to begin digging again. There wasn't a moment to spare.

Suddenly he halted, going perfectly still, even holding his breath, not certain he had heard...

Yes! Long and low, muffled but recognizable, came the howl of a wolf from within the buried cave. If the wolf still lived, then perhaps the woman and the pups did, too. And if he could hear them, then perhaps this wall of rock wasn't all that thick everywhere.

The howl sounded again, faintly, and Gray Cloud cocked his head, trying to determine where it seemed to come from, so that he would know where to begin digging. Moments later he had chosen his location, near the top and to the side.

There was no time to waste. Ignoring the pain in his

hands, the ache of his back and his battered legs, he began once again to tunnel into the cave.

The wolf's howl was getting on Mercy's nerves. Even the quieting of the earth, which had come as such a relief initially, no longer seemed as soothing. But there was no way to silence the wolf, no way at all.

The air was getting still thicker, almost impossible to breathe. If only she could see where to dig, had some idea of how to start. She needed to do something—anything—to feel as if she were helping herself, but even the poor air hadn't addled her brains enough to make her forget that if she pulled the wrong rock or boulder off that heap she could cause hundreds of pounds of rocks to tumble right down on her. And she couldn't see.

But that no longer seemed terribly relevant. She was dying in here, slowly asphyxiating. Pulling a ton of rock down on her head would only be a little quicker, but at least she would be doing something to help herself.

Listen.

The whisper in her head caught her attention, dragging her back from the edge of her ragged, exhausted thoughts.

Listen.

Okay, she thought, almost belligerently. Okay. Damn it, I'm listening. What the hell am I supposed to hear?

Scrunching her eyes closed, she strained to hear whatever it was. And into her senses poured an awareness of the mountain's vitality. Beneath her, she could feel the deep, slow heartbeat of the granite, the pulsation of alien life, so real and so different.

Was that what she was supposed to feel? Was this sensation the power that made this mountain so sacred to Gray Cloud? How could this possibly help her?

Listen.

The wolf howled again, a long, low cry for her mate, for her pack. Listen?

And then she heard it, the sound of rocks moving, the sound of…someone digging. Gray Cloud! She was sure it must be Gray Cloud, trying to get her out of here. Opening her eyes, she listened intently, trying to locate the source of the sound.

Then she crawled toward it, as swiftly as she could, trying not to drown the hopeful sound of the digging with sobs and scrambling noises, because she needed the sound as if it were the breath of life itself. Someone was trying to save her!

Wisdom fled before imminent rescue. She clambered up the dangerous slope of fallen rock toward the sound of boulders being moved, and when she thought she was exactly opposite the sounds, she began to dig, too. Rocks bruised and scraped her hands and made her fingers ache, but hope was within sight and nothing could stop her. Nothing.

Stripes gave forth another howl, this one longer and more excited, as if she, too, sensed the possibility of rescue now.

And through her tears, Mercy saw a faint glimmer of light. They were saved.

With hands that were bleeding and sore, Gray Cloud reached into the opening and pulled Mercy out into the watery light of an overcast late afternoon. She was sobbing, tears making white trails in the grime on her cheeks.

Relief slammed him hard, with unexpected force. For a moment he couldn't even breathe. She was alive.

His first thought was to get her to safety, to get her as far from the path of the rock slides as he could, so the mountain couldn't harm her again.

He folded his arms around her, holding her snugly to his chest. Then, ignoring the shrieking ache in his back and legs from his labors, he rose stiffly and carried her cautiously down the unstable rocks toward the trees, where she would be safe for at least a few minutes.

"The mountain," she whispered hoarsely, through a throat so parched it felt cracked.

"What about the mountain?"

"It's alive...."

He glanced down at her, but her eyes were closed. She knew the mountain was alive. It was incredible to him that she realized that. She wasn't like some of the *wa-sicu* who came here and pretended to be Indians while they made up a mishmash of ceremonies culled from books. She showed none of that interest or disrespect for the beliefs of his people. Yet she had realized the mountain lived.

And he wondered, with an uneasy tingle at the base of his spine, just what she had been through during her hours in the darkness to bring the mountain to life for her.

He set her down among the trees, well out of the path of the landslides. If the mountain shrugged again, she should be safe. Then he turned, intending to go back and help the wolf bitch save her pups. He didn't really want to crawl back into that cave, though, because he no longer trusted Thunder Mountain not to crush him as carelessly as it had tried to crush Mercy.

If he got in the way, he would die.

But even as he hesitated, in that briefest of seconds as he faced his own growing doubts about the vision that had sustained him all his life, the wolf pack materialized from the trees as if summoned. All of them.

As Gray Cloud watched, they climbed in silence to the tunnel opening he had managed to carve out and disappeared inside. A short time later they emerged, one at a time, each carrying a pup in its jaws.

"I don't believe that."

Mercy's soft whisper caught his attention long enough that he glanced her way and saw her watching with awe as the wolves rescued the litter.

He grunted an affirmative and turned back to the wolves, who were now carrying the litter toward the man and woman.

Take her to the Sun Tree....

Gray Cloud closed his eyes, forgetting the wolves as he realized the mountain was speaking with him.

Take her to the Sun Tree....

The Sun Tree? Gray Cloud looked down at Mercy and wondered why the mountain should want her there, one of the most sacred places. The Sun Tree was the tallest of the lodgepole pines on Thunder Mountain, thus called because a tall lodgepole was used in the traditional Sun Dance, and this tree was the tallest of them all.

Why should she go there? She didn't belong there at all, in such a holy place of great power.

Take her...

The woman was exhausted; she didn't look as if she could walk that distance. Yet to defy the mountain could be dangerous. There had to be a reason why it was so insistent.

Take her...

"We have to go," he told Mercy. "To get away from here. The mountain is warning me."

She looked up at him for the first time without any skepticism at all. "Then something else is going to happen." Without waiting for an answer, she pushed herself wearily to her feet. "I just needed the air," she told him. "I just needed to breathe. I can't tell you how good this fresh mountain air smells after being trapped in that cave." Pine-scented, clean and fresh with rain. Chilly, but good.

Then she remembered. "My pack. I have to get my pack."

Gray Cloud hesitated, weighing the dangers. "There's something important in there?"

"My wallet, my notes, all my money and credit cards." She bit her lip. "Nothing worth dying for, I guess."

"I'll get it." The decision was made in an instant, encouraged by a sense that the mountain wouldn't tremble again immediately.

Mercy's hand shot out and grabbed his forearm. "No! It's not worth it. Truly, it's not worth it!"

He ignored her, shaking off her hand and heading for the tunnel. This was important to him, a way of testing the mountain's mood. If the mountain let him rescue the pack, he would know where he stood after his rebellion this afternoon.

He couldn't ignore the opportunity.

Mercy instinctively started to follow him, still protesting, but he waved her impatiently back. "You don't understand. Just wait."

Climbing up the unstable pile of rocks and boulders, he felt uneasiness run along his spine like icy little fingers. Crawling into the tunnel he had wrested from the rockfall, he was acutely conscious of how easily even a small tremor from Thunder Mountain could crush him. Each time he eased forward, the skin on the back of his neck crawled.

And then he reached the dark pit of the cavern. As he slipped forward on his belly, from the tunnel into the cave, his mind was filled with the awareness of how easily the mountain could entomb him.

But nothing stirred. The air was still stale, rife with the smells of the wolves and Mercy's fear, but breathable. Beneath his feet, even through the thick soles of his hiking boots, he could feel the faint pulsation of the mountain. *Alive.*

Just enough thin, gray light poured through the tunnel opening to make it possible for him to locate Mercy's pack. He almost stumbled on her flashlight, and scooped it up, even though it didn't work. The blankets he saved, too, because nights could get very cold on Thunder Mountain.

Moments later, aware that he had been granted a very special reprieve, he climbed slowly and carefully back out the tunnel, pushing the backpack and blankets ahead of him.

The mountain wasn't angry at him.

A minute later he was leading Mercy toward the Sun Tree, the most sacred of places on the sacred mountain.

Chapter Eight

"The Sun Tree," Gray Cloud told Mercy, "is believed by some to be the tree that was seen in the vision when the Sun Dance was first given to us."

"Is there something special about it?"

"It's a very tall, very straight tree that has branches only at the very top, and the way they droop down reminds some of the leather thongs that are tied between the top of the tree and the Sun Dancer's chest below."

"I've seen drawings of that dance," she said. "I think."

"Then you should see the resemblance."

The climb was steep, not something Mercy really felt like doing, but if the mountain wanted it, she wasn't going to refuse, not after what she had experienced today.

The transition from believing mountains had moods and personalities to believing that *this* mountain, at least, was a sentient being, was not as difficult as she would have expected. After lying for hours trapped in the maw of the mountain, sensing the power and strength all around her, she couldn't doubt that Thunder Mountain lived.

And if the mountain lived, then surely it would do as Gray Cloud said and act to protect itself and its denizens. She had to hope it considered her worth protecting, along with the wolves and Gray Cloud.

The wolves followed them. Not closely, but near enough that Mercy glimpsed them briefly. Each of them carried a pup, and she hoped that all this traveling wouldn't be bad for the litter, all of whom were far too young to be bounced around like this.

"There." Gray Cloud halted and pointed to a clearing just ahead.

Mercy, who had been watching the wolves disappear and reappear at either side of the trail as they wove among the trees, lifted her head and looked.

She drew a long, appreciative breath as she forgot for a moment her fatigue and soreness and her earlier fright. The clearing was large, an almost perfect circle around the base of a towering lodgepole pine, a tree so tall it reached well above the rest of the forest. And from its very crown drooped branches that, just as Gray Cloud had said, were reminiscent of the leather thongs used to tie the Sun Dancers to the tree.

Gray Cloud started to step into the clearing, but as he did so, one of the wolves darted in front of him, causing him to stumble and halt. Mercy, following, just kept walking, her attention fixed on the beautiful tree, and she tripped, falling to her hands and knees when a wolf darted in front of her. She swore softly and pushed herself back to her feet.

"Wait." Gray Cloud's voice was low and intense, and he reached out a hand and stayed Mercy as she started to move forward again. She turned and looked up questioningly. "The wolves are trying to tell us something."

That was when her fascination with the beautiful tree gave way to a recognition that the wolves had indeed acted oddly. Slowly she looked around and saw the pack gathered about them, each wolf carrying a pup, and all moving nervously. "Something's wrong."

Gray Cloud nodded. "Stay where you are." When she nodded, he took another step toward the center of the clearing. Immediately a wolf set down the pup it carried and darted forward, leaping up a little to snatch at Gray Cloud's sleeve with its jaws. When Gray Cloud halted, the wolf sat back on its haunches and waited. When the man started to take yet another step forward, the animal leapt up and snatched again at his sleeve.

Gray Cloud turned around and began walking back to the edge of the clearing. At once the wolf snatched up the pup and headed back into the woods with its fellows.

"We'd better get out of here," Gray Cloud told Mercy.

She never hesitated. It couldn't have been any plainer to her that the wolf had been trying to tell Gray Cloud exactly that. After this day, she wasn't inclined to question such things. If the wolf didn't want to go into the clearing, neither did she. Later she would have the rest of her life for trying to rationalize all these events.

For now, there was only an urge to heed the warning of the wolves.

She had barely gone two steps when a flash of light blinded her. In the same instant, it felt as if a giant hand shoved the back of her jacket and threw her facedown on the ground.

* * *

Gray Cloud turned onto his back and looked up at the flaming, split trunk of the Sun Tree. There wasn't a doubt in his mind that the mountain had intended to kill Mercy. And possibly him. He had been leading the woman like a sheep to slaughter. The thought sickened him.

Twisting, he levered himself to his feet and reached down to help Mercy up. "Let's go," he said roughly. "We've got to get out of here."

She gave him no argument as he guided her stumbling feet into the woods. "Was that— Was that lightning?"

"Yes." The Sun Tree had been destroyed. Anger simmered in the pit of Gray Cloud's belly like a pot over a blazing fire. A thing of remarkable beauty, something unique in the world, had been carelessly destroyed in an attempt to destroy something else. That infuriated him.

But at the same time, he was uneasily aware that the mountain knew what it was doing. Something was wrong in his perception of Mercy Kendrick, something was there that he, Gray Cloud, failed to see, but which the mountain knew. There could be no other explanation for the mountain's determination.

But he would have to find out on his own. It was not his place to question the wisdom of Thunder Mountain, nor would the mountain tell him. Certainly not now that he had defied it.

A chance, he said inwardly to the mountain, hoping it would heed him. *Give me a chance to understand and banish the threat.* He couldn't bear the thought of another loss such as that of the Sun Tree. Couldn't bear the thought that this sacred place might be carved up, either by *wasicu* businessmen or by the mountain itself. His vision was to preserve Thunder Mountain for his people, and he would do whatever was necessary, even if he must face the mountain itself.

Even if he must kill the woman. For it was clear to him now, so very clear, that she must somehow be involved with the problem. With Stockton-Wells.

Because this had been a deliberate attempt to kill her.

The wolves seemed to be leading the way, Mercy realized, and Gray Cloud was following them without any hesitation, as if he trusted their instincts.

Well, she supposed she did, too, after the incident at the Sun Tree. The wolves must have felt the building charge of that lightning bolt at a level well below human perception...although that certainly didn't explain why they had chosen to aid the humans, or why they had acted in such an incredibly intelligent fashion to make their point.

Gray wolves slinking through the dim forest depths, while another of the endless storms of Thunder Mountain built up over their heads. Slipping, sliding, gliding on soundless paws as they carried the pups in gentle jaws. From time to time, one would turn to look back at them, its eyes glowing eerily, like golden flame, in the shadows.

Where were they going?

Not that any answer anyone gave her to that question would have made much sense. They were going somewhere with the wolves, and right now she was willing to trust herself to the wolves' instinct for safety, since their instinct for danger had been so much better than her own.

"We're going to the cirque," Gray Cloud said abruptly.

"The cirque?"

"It's a hollow in the side of the mountain, left long ago by a glacier."

"I know what a cirque is. It's just that the way you said it, it sounds especially important."

"It is."

She glanced over at him. "How so?" He moved as soundlessly and as fluidly as the wolves, she thought, blending with the shadows as well as they did.

A couple of minutes passed before he answered, and he did so grudgingly. "It's the place of strongest power on the mountain. My people go there to pray, or cry for a vision. The wolves think we'll be safer there."

Great, she thought. Now he was talking to the wolves as well as the wind. "What'll we do there?"

"Figure out how to deal with Stockton-Wells."

"Stockton-Wells? *Stockton-Wells?*"

The way she spoke brought Gray Cloud to an abrupt halt, and when he stopped, so did the wolves, wraithlike among the trees. Like an escort, Mercy thought vaguely. The wolves looked like some eerie kind of escort.

"You know Stockton-Wells?" he asked her.

Dragging her attention from Stripes, who was watching with tawny eyes from the shadows, Mercy looked up at Gray Cloud. "Yeah, sure. Everybody knows Stockton-Wells. Unfortunately, I also used to date the heir to Stockton-Wells. What a...a turkey!"

Gray Cloud's eyes narrowed, becoming dark, mysterious slits. "Why was he a turkey?"

"Because he just was! Oh, he made me so mad!" Suddenly realizing how childish she must sound, she shook her head and calmed herself. "We met in graduate school. He was studying forestry, and I was in wildlife biology, and we had a few classes together. We both liked rock climbing, so we took some day trips together and finally some big ones to do faces like El Capitan at Yosemite. We kind of got emotionally involved. At least, *I* thought we did, only it turned out he was engaged already, something he didn't bother to tell me. I didn't like his politics, anyway."

"What were his politics?"

"Oh, he pretended to be conservation-minded and concerned about endangered species and all those issues, but I don't think he was. Not really. Couldn't have been. I hear he's his dad's right-hand man these days."

She glanced up, wondering what Gray Cloud's reaction to all of this was. His face revealed nothing, but she still had the feeling she had said a whole lot of wrong things.

And that upset her, she realized as they resumed their trek across the mountain's rugged shoulder. That upset her, because she wanted the things she was beginning to feel for Gray Cloud to be reciprocated. She wanted him to want her as much as she wanted him. Wanted him to feel those warm, soft, gooey feelings that kept sneaking up on her whenever she forgot to hold them at bay.

Wanted him to wonder if her hair felt as silky as it looked, the way she wondered about his. Needed him to wonder if...

Oh, Lord, this had to stop now! The way the man had just looked at her, he would as likely kill her as make love to her. And she had to remember that she still didn't know diddly about him. Being acquitted of murder could mean so many things, from being freed on a technicality to being absolutely innocent. Could she afford to believe what she wanted to believe?

Besides, she didn't want to get carelessly involved with anyone. If she ever gave herself to a man again, it would be with love in her heart and a future ahead of her. Gray Cloud didn't look like the type to want to settle down to home, hearth and kids. Nope. Any woman foolish enough to love him would have to give up all those dreams.

The afternoon was growing darker, and the day's exertions and scares had taken a toll on Mercy. She began to stumble occasionally in small ways, and her mind wandered to thoughts of a warm fire and a hot meal, both of which were probably out of the question unless she and Gray Cloud could find some kind of shelter in which to build a fire. The rain was beginning to fall again, just a light sprinkle, but that wouldn't last. Soon it would be a drizzle, then a downpour, and they would get the usual violent display of lightning and thunder, which wouldn't be very fun out in the open on the side of this mountain.

Suddenly Stripes halted right in front of them and set one squirming, whining pup down on the ground. Slowly, like four-legged ghosts, the other wolves appeared from the shadowy forest depths and placed the rest of the pups with their mother. She twisted herself around them, nudging them close until they found her teats, then settled down to nurse them. So lovely, Mercy thought, her throat tightening inexplicably. So absolutely lovely.

"Here," Gray Cloud said. "Here is where we stay to-night." He jerked his chin to the right, and for the first time Mercy noticed what appeared to be a hollow in a huge boulder a little way back in the trees. Not a cave, not by any means, but it might keep the rain off enough to make a fire.

It did better than that. There was enough dry ground for them to spread their blankets to sleep on, as well as build a fire. Gray Cloud fetched water from a nearby brook, and Mercy invited him to join her in some re-constituted, freeze-dried stew.

Night gathered around them, rumbling irritably with the secrets of Thunder. The wind moaned in the trees, a cold and lonely sound, and in the distance the rush of the brook could be heard. The sounds were so incred-ibly clear on the night air, Mercy thought, staring past the fire into the darkness.

A huge pair of tawny eyes blinked back at her, and she almost smiled. Well, her purpose in studying the wolves had been blown all to hell, she thought. These animals weren't exactly wild, though they were far from domesticated, and she wasn't doing a darn thing to help keep them wild. Nope. Instead she was cooperat-ing in the process of turning them into some kind of...of pet? No, that wasn't right, but then, neither was this. These animals should be avoiding humans, not hang-ing around the campfire like this. However, these ani-mals shouldn't be showing quite this much intelligence, either.

Oh, wolves *were* intelligent—incredibly intelligent, by all reports. But the notion of them recognizing the danger at the Sun Tree and saving two humans from being fried by lightning was, well, a little difficult to put into words, even though she'd seen it happen. It would certainly be impossible to include in her study. Anecdotal evidence was not scientific.

The tawny eyes blinked again and continued to stare straight at her. Eyebrows, probably. He seemed to like to watch her, for some reason.

Anthropomorphizing again, she chided herself. And that was the real reason her study had been blown out of the water, she admitted at last. These wolves had become individuals to her. They had become *people* to her. No scientific objectivity in that. No way could she settle back in a blind and watch these animals and coldly record their behavior.

So she was going back empty-handed, she guessed, except for the news that there was indeed a viable wolf pack on Thunder Mountain. Some other researcher would come up here and study them, and she would get a brief acknowledgment for having located them.

Unless she could find some way to see these wolves as quadrupedal animals again.

Sighing, she rested her chin on her knees and stared back at Eyebrows, wishing in the vain way of the tired and worn-out that life didn't have to be so damn complicated all the time. Why did she have to worry about the future when all she wanted to do was make love with Gray Cloud? Why did she have to feel like a failure because these wolves were so spectacularly unique in some ways? Why should she feel like a fool because she had named them?

Why couldn't she just turn her head and press her cheek to Gray Cloud's shoulder and say to hell with it all, just once in her life? Why did she have to be so damn responsible and aware?

Another sigh escaped her, and she forced the yearning away. All that could possibly come of it would be grief, she told herself. Grief. She had enough of that without asking for more.

Gray Cloud spoke. "Do you know anyone at Stockton-Wells right now?"

For some reason an icy trickle seemed to run down her spine. She lifted her head and turned it slowly to look at him. His eyes, always dark, seemed darker now somehow, and the flames of the fire reflected in them, dancing hellishly. Why did she trust this man? she wondered wildly. Why?

"No," she said finally. "No one. I never knew anyone there except Merle."

He nodded ever so slightly but never took his gaze from her. "So you don't have any idea what they might be planning on this mountain?"

Her chin snapped up as she realized the direction of his questioning. "No! Absolutely not! How could you even think—" She bit the question off and looked away, suddenly so mad she couldn't even see straight. "No! Just because I knew Merle Stockton doesn't mean I'm privy to the secrets of the company! Damn it, Gray Cloud!" Suddenly she turned and glared at him. "Guilt by association, huh? Maybe I should wonder if you really killed that man!"

His expression never flickered by so much as a muscle. Horror filled Mercy like rising river waters, portending a flood but climbing slowly. Oh, God, how could she have? She wanted to snatch the words back, but they hung on the air as if branded there in fiery letters. Her throat locked, so she couldn't even apologize.

But even as she scrambled for some way to defuse the moment, he spoke, his words dropping heavily into the night, like stones into a pool.

"Yes," he said. "I killed a man."

Just that, and not another word.

The night crowded steadily in on them, thick with threat. Mercy lay on her back beside the fire, a rolled-up shirt making a pillow, and stared up at the patterns the flames made on the overhang above.

No explanations. No excuses. Just "I killed a man." Didn't he feel even the slightest normal compulsion to explain? To excuse himself or his action? Didn't he feel any urge to claim self-defense or something?

With that attitude, it was a wonder he *hadn't* been convicted. And with that attitude, it was hardly any wonder that everyone hereabouts remembered he had been accused of murder and referred to him as the Renegade of Thunder Mountain. Lord, that kind of answer was about as belligerent as they came.

The wind made a lonely sound in the treetops, like the rushing of water, as the night air grew colder. Voices seemed to murmur at the edge of consciousness, and Mercy found herself drifting into fractured half dreams of distorted faces that whispered warnings she couldn't quite hear.

Stockton-Wells. Merle Stockton's face floated before her, too well remembered even after all this time. He was a handsome devil, but what had attracted her had been his insouciant attraction to danger. Her attraction to him, however, had worn thin when she had discovered that was essentially all there was to him. Merle Stockton didn't have a feeling, caring bone in his body...except toward himself. His devotion to environmental concerns had been superficial, she had discovered, merely politically correct camouflage he'd worn while in graduate school.

In reality, Merle's one great passion had been Stockton-Wells, Inc., the company he would inherit from his father. His one burning goal had been to make some grand coup that would bring huge profits to the company and establish Merle as a power in his own right.

Maybe Merle thought Thunder Mountain could be his long-sought coup.

Oh, she could see it, all right. He would be scheming and conniving for ways to get around the Park Service and environmental groups, determined to somehow get away with doing more than was really permissible, because that would be the victory, figuring out how to do an end run around the law.

Turning her head a little, she looked across the crackling fire at Gray Cloud, who was sitting upright and staring out into the night. "Why do you think Stockton-Wells is involved?"

"I found some things at a campsite. That name was on them."

"It wouldn't be surprising."

"No." He turned his head and looked at her steadily.

He was waiting, she realized. Waiting to see if she would volunteer anything. But after her reaction earlier, he wasn't going to question her. Nor did he trust her now. The fact that she knew Merle Stockton had driven

a wedge of distrust between them that was as wide as
the fire burning in the pit. He was no longer willing to
believe that she was nothing but a wildlife biologist
who meant no harm to either the mountain or the
wolves.

And that made him dangerous, she realized with a
shiver down her spine. All this time he had been giving
her the benefit of the doubt, allowing that she might be
exactly what she said.

But now he considered her connected to Stockton-
Wells and her margin of doubt was gone.

She shivered again and pulled the blanket up until it
covered her to her chin. "I know Merle can be ruthless,"
she said finally. "I've seen it. If he wants something, it's
dangerous to get in his way."

Gray Cloud nodded, absorbing this. "How ruthless?"

"He'd kill if he thought he wouldn't get caught." Another river of ice trickled down her spine as she thought
what an unnerving thing that was to say to a man who
had killed. A man she had believed herself to be in love
with. "In fact, I don't think there's anything he *wouldn't*
do if he thought he stood to gain enough. Thunder
Mountain probably looks like an incredible opportunity
to him. All this timber...."

She shivered again and dragged her gaze from Gray
Cloud, who was regarding her with a steely intensity
that was growing steadily more and more unnerving.
"Merle wouldn't stop at much," she said finally. "But
then, I guess neither will the mountain."

Gray Cloud felt the night close around him after the
woman finally drifted into troubled sleep. Ordinarily he

welcomed the night, but tonight it wasn't peaceful. Tonight there were hard things, uneasy things, in the darkness. And murder was in the air.

She had said Merle Stockton wouldn't stop at much and then had likened the mountain to him. That troubled Gray Cloud at a very deep level. The mountain could hardly be compared to a man who would probably sell his grandmother if the price was right, but... perhaps there were similarities, anyway, and those possible similarities hovered in the pit of his stomach like a sickness that wouldn't quite go away.

The mountain had tried to kill Mercy this afternoon at the Sun Tree. Gray Cloud thought of that and felt his innards twist with horrified rage. He had been used to take the woman to a place where the mountain intended to execute her.

Perhaps she deserved to be executed. She was connected, by her own admission, with Stockton-Wells. Perhaps she was more connected than she had told him, and Thunder Mountain had discovered that. But to use Gray Cloud in that way...

The man released a harsh breath and tilted his head back, listening to the restless night sounds and hoping the wind would bring secrets to soothe him.

He needed more, he realized. He needed more than the mountain's perception to guide him now. For the first time in all the years he had served his vision, he truly needed to separate himself from the vision long enough to make his own decision. He needed to find out what was happening, who was really involved, and what they intended. He could not be blindly obedient this time. Not this time.

Glancing over at Mercy, he saw that she still slept. He had killed before, and if it was necessary, he would do so again, but he didn't want it to be this woman. He needed far more than the mountain's perception of matters to allow any harm to come to her.

The feeling made him uneasy, and he looked away, not wanting to admit his own yearning for the warmth of a woman's body and, more importantly, for the warmth of a woman's smile. He'd been alone far too long, but that was the way of the road he had been given. Few women these days had any desire to live on the side of a mountain with a medicine man.

He was alone and would remain alone, but being alone hadn't stolen from him an awareness that he owed something to his fellow man, at least as much as he owed this mountain and his vision. That debt required him to learn what was really happening here. To figure out whether Mercy Kendrick deserved the death the mountain seemed determined to inflict on her.

He could not stand idly by and just let it happen. Not without understanding why it was necessary.

So he had to learn his foes, and discover what it was they were after, what they intended to do. He had to discover the depth of Mercy's involvement. And then, for the sake of every living thing on this mountainside, he had to try to find a way to prevent Stockton-Wells from triumphing, so the mountain would not have to act again.

Because when the mountain acted, the innocent died. Gray Cloud didn't want to see one more thing die, not even the smallest raccoon. Everything sheltering on this mountain was to be protected, according to his vision, and right now the best way to do that was to handle the problem himself.

Out in the dark, he saw the strange golden glow of wolf eyes. The big male had come to look upon them again. Strange behavior for a wolf. Protective.

Why did the wolves of Thunder Mountain seem so protective of Mercy Kendrick? What did they know that the mountain didn't? Or did they know something about the mountain that Gray Cloud didn't?

The fire had died to a few glowing embers; the wind sighed through the tops of the trees like the voices of lost souls. The night was dark, unrelieved by even the faint glimmer of starshine. The tops of the tall trees were merely darker shadows swaying against shadows.

Something moved out there.

How Mercy knew that, she couldn't have said. She came wide-awake in an instant, filled with an absolute certainty that something out there was moving in some sinister fashion. Not a wolf or any other creature of the night.

Something else.

For long moments she lay paralyzed, straining to hear some sound that would identify whatever was out there, doubting finally that she had heard anything at all, but unable to convince herself that she hadn't.

Listen.

The whisper in her head seemed almost friendly now, and she heeded it, no longer trying to convince herself there was nothing out there. Listen. Straining to hear, she held her breath and tensed....

And caught the merest whisper of sound. So faint it

was almost beneath the threshold of audibility. But it was there. Her scalp recognized it, prickling as her hair stood on end. Something was moving. Either some small creature too tiny to make any appreciable noise, or something that was attempting a surreptitious approach.

Something that didn't want to be heard.

Her heart pounded in her chest, and she weighed her limited options. Sitting up abruptly would startle whoever or whatever was out there. That might either send them into flight or precipitate an attack. But what else could she do? Any movement or sound might alert whatever was out there.

Turning her head, she tried to see Gray Cloud on the other side of the very faintly glowing coals of the fire. The little bit of red light that was visible was just barely enough for her to make out the contours of his face.

"Gray Cloud…" She whispered it so softly that she couldn't hear the sound herself. Too softly, she thought, and opened her mouth to try again…when his black eyes snapped open and reflected the faint red glow.

"Don't move." His whisper was slightly louder than hers, just enough to reach her ears.

He had heard it, too, she thought. Now what? An eternity seemed to pass as they both lay there, eyes locked, ears straining.

The sound came again, still almost too faint for her to be sure it was there, still unidentifiable. But Gray Cloud had heard it, too. Of that Mercy was sure, for he tensed and shifted slightly beneath his blanket. Getting ready for whatever was coming, she guessed.

It had to be a person, she thought. One of the Stockton-Wells people must be closing in on them for some reason. No bear would approach this way, wary of detection. Someone intended to kill them both.

Again the faint sound. A twig bending? Something being crushed under a stealthy boot? Her heart scrambled right up into her throat as she realized the sound was growing more distinct, which meant it was coming closer.

Listen.

The wind sighed through the trees, then moaned softly. One of the wolves howled in the far distance. Where were the pups tonight?

And suddenly, as if stirred by some unseen hand, the coals in the fire pit suddenly brightened to a brilliant red glow, illuminating their shelter. Gray Cloud rose to his feet in one swift motion and darted into the darkness.

Mercy instinctively sat up, needing to know what was happening, but unable to see into the night beyond their shelter.

She heard a thud, followed by a sharp grunt...and then the sound of one pair of running feet as someone ran away into the dark woods. Moments later the world was silent, except for the normal sounds of night.

Gray Cloud must have been hurt. The thought chilled Mercy, but she could think of no other reason for the sounds she had heard, for the fact that someone had run off into the night and that Gray Cloud hadn't either pursued or come back to the fire. He must have been hurt.

Oh, God, could he have been killed?

What would she do if he were seriously injured?

Oh, God!

Scrambling to get out from under the blankets, she struggled at the same time to see into the impenetrable darkness and get some idea of where Gray Cloud was.

He could be bleeding to death out there. Concussed. Oh, Lord...

She got her feet beneath her and into her boots, then haphazardly tied the laces around the ankles so she wouldn't trip. Then she eased from beneath the deceptive protection of the overhang and into the restless night.

Lightning flickered in the distance, soundless, back-lighting the anvil of a thunderhead. The wind slipped through the trees, whispering of losses and woes in the dead of the night. Beneath her feet she felt the heartbeat of the mountain, a steady, almost imperceptible throb. Beyond that, the night was empty.

Just ahead. To the right...

The wind whispered to her, guiding her straight to Gray Cloud, who lay facedown on a carpet of pine needles. She could barely see him—he appeared to be a shapeless lump until she knelt beside him and bent close.

She could smell the metallic odor of blood, and then she saw the black stain on the side of his face. Reaching out with a tentative finger, she felt sticky wetness. Someone had bashed him in the head.

For an instant she froze, uncertain what to do. Every instinct cried out to her to help Gray Cloud, but she didn't have any way of evaluating the threat. If she went back to the fire and built it up so she could see, she might be exposing them even more to watching eyes. But she couldn't leave Gray Cloud there, and she couldn't do anything for him in darkness so thick she couldn't even evaluate the extent of his wounds.

With a queasy lurch of her stomach, she suddenly realized just how alone she was in the night, on the isolated side of this mountain. Alone. Completely.

Chapter Nine

Alone.

The whispered word mocked her from the forest's depths.

Alone.

Exposed. The night was alive with threat, a sussurating, taunting threat. The trees loomed over her, pressing in, crowding her, as they murmured of dire things. Thunder laughed hollowly in the distance.

Alone.

It was too dark to tell what lurked beneath the trees in the shadows. Too dark to gauge the threat or measure her safety. There was no one within shouting distance who she could turn to for help. No one at all except the person who had attacked Gray Cloud.

An urge straight out of childhood nearly overwhelmed her. She wanted to curl up in a tight little ball, hide her head in her arms and just be invisible until dawn. Her heart thundered like the hooves of a racehorse in sight of the finish line. Her lungs desperately dragged in air and couldn't seem to get enough of it. She was terrified.

But she had to do something. Almost anything at all would be better than sitting there waiting for doom to overtake her and Gray Cloud. She couldn't leave him unconscious in the open air like this. It might start raining at any moment, and hypothermia could kill him, even if his head wound didn't. She had to get him under the overhang.

But what if someone was out there? Watching. Waiting.

The icy river of fear trickled down her spine again, raising goose bumps all over. Her back felt mercilessly exposed, and even as the urge to look behind her grew until she could hardly stand it, she was terrified to turn her head for fear of what she might see.

Like a child, she hoped that if she didn't see it, it wouldn't see her.

Dumb. Really dumb. Get it together, Mercy, she scolded herself.

But her skin crawled and her scalp prickled with an awareness that couldn't be denied. She was exposed. Completely and utterly exposed, and her only defense was perfect stillness, perfect quiet. To become invisible to the predator by being motionless.

Only the predator was human, and motionlessness wouldn't fool him.

She was just beginning to shake her paralysis when a soft sound froze her again. Something had moved. The sighing wind snatched the sound and carried it away before she could identify it or locate the source, but she knew she had heard it. Her hair was standing on end.

Trying to hear anything over the cascading rush of the wind in the treetops was a hopeless proposition, but she tried, anyway, because instinct wouldn't let her do otherwise. How could she move unless she was sure she wasn't moving closer to the threat?

Listen...

She listened with all her might, straining to hear anything that might give her a clue.

Alone...

Yes, she was alone. Completely, utterly, terrifyingly alone. This aloneness was unlike anything she had experienced before. The vastness of the Wyoming night stretched around her, empty and comfortless...populated only by the person who had hurt Gray Cloud.

Tomorrow Woman...

Her head jerked around at the unmistakable whisper of the name Gray Cloud had said the wind had given her. Tomorrow Woman. Who else would know to call her that except Gray Cloud...and the wind?

She shivered violently. Not the wind. It couldn't be. But who else...?

Move...

Another sigh, but this one sounded like a command. And somehow, released from her paralysis, she bent toward Gray Cloud, thinking that if she turned him over she might be able to take him under his arms and drag him toward the overhang where they were camped. Once she had him safely away from the inevitable rain, she could think about what she needed to do.

Thunder crackled with sudden violence, a goad to action. A storm might break at any moment.

And if someone was watching her from the shadows, he could kill them as easily while she sat frozen here as he could if she moved.

Another sound, barely audible over the wind. Oh, how she wished that damn wind would stop for just a minute so she could really listen and figure out if she was truly hearing something.

A groan. This time unmistakable. Gray Cloud! Bending, she brought her face to within inches of his and called his name. She didn't dare say it loudly, afraid that she might attract unwanted attention. This night was full of the potential for such things.

Oh, how she wished she had listened to Sara Ironheart at the Conard County sheriff's office. Sara had urged her to bring a radio with her. She might have been able to reach the Park Service or a patrolling ranger for help. Instead she had shrugged off the suggestion because she was familiar with camping in the wild. Because she was confident she wouldn't get into trouble. Because she was always careful.

Because she was foolishly arrogant.

And now her isolation was absolute.

Move...

When she tugged gently on his shoulder, Gray Cloud stirred and moaned again. She whispered his name again, and he lifted his head.

"Can you hear me?" she asked. "Do you think you can get up?"

A few moments passed, then he answered, "Yeah. Yeah. I'm okay."

She seriously doubted that, considering he'd been knocked unconscious and was bleeding from a head wound, but at least he was conscious and coherent. "Let's try it, then."

She steadied him as they took it in stages, getting first

to their knees and then to their feet. He was definitely woozy, reeling just a little when he first stood, but then his head seemed to clear up.

Thunder growled a warning as lightning stabbed the clouds, leaping from thunderhead to thunderhead. A large, cold drop of rain splattered hard on Mercy's cheek, stinging, and the wind gusted restlessly. The air smelled scorched.

"Let's get to cover." Gray Cloud spoke rustily, but it was clear he was alert and thinking again. Relief nearly swamped Mercy, but another drop of rain slapped her cheek, prodding her toward their camp.

She felt chilled to the bone by the time they reached their bedrolls. Grabbing up blankets, she threw one around Gray Cloud's shoulders and another around herself, then sat beside him on the hard ground.

"We need to do something about your head," she told him. "You're bleeding. You might be concussed. You need to see a doctor."

"No. I'll take care of it."

She opened her mouth to ask how, but swallowed the question when he lifted his hand to his wound and began to chant softly. He was healing himself. Mercy's Western-educated mind rebelled, until she thought of the things she had sensed and felt during her time on Thunder Mountain. If a mountain could think, then Gray Cloud could heal himself.

In the dark, it was easy to see the faint blue shimmering that appeared around his hand where it touched his head. Easy to see it pulse and sparkle, dim as it was. The life force, he had said.

Several minutes later, the glow faded and he

dropped his hand. Then, without so much as a by-your-leave, he reached out with both hands, gathered Mercy to him and wrapped them snugly together in the blankets.

She should have rebelled. She should have snapped at him for his presumption and demanded he let her go. She should have been afraid.

Instead all she felt was a wonderfully weakening sense of security. The heat of his body was as welcome as the blast from a furnace on a frigid night. When he tucked her head into his shoulder, she gave up any thought of struggling. She hadn't felt this secure since early child-hood, and right now she didn't want to consider that she was in the arms of a man who had killed, a man who might well decide to kill her. Right now she just wanted to be in the arms she had been longing to feel around her for what seemed like half a lifetime. To forget for just a little while the terror that stalked them.

More childishness, but she gave in to it, promising herself it would be for only a few minutes. Just these few minutes.

"We've got to do something about this mess," Gray Cloud said. His voice was a rumble deep in his chest beneath her ear. "If that man had reached us while we were sleeping..."

He didn't finish. He didn't need to.

"What *can* we do?" Mercy asked. Funny, she thought, how only yesterday she had been trying to convince Gray Cloud that they had to do something, and now that he was saying the same thing, she couldn't imagine what it might be.

"Get down from this mountain and alert the Forest

Service and the Conard County sheriff. We've got something the sheriff can go on now. I was attacked."

"The wolves…"

"I don't want to leave them unprotected, either, but there's nothing we can do by ourselves. Nothing legal, anyway."

She almost tipped her head up to look at him, then remembered that it was too dark to see him, anyway. The sheriff, he'd said. Funny. She wouldn't have thought Gray Cloud a man to turn to the authorities, or to worry about whether his actions were legal.

But what *could* they do, short of killing someone? And if they hung around here, they were apt to get killed themselves. Gray Cloud was right: the authorities needed to know what was happening here. That alone would probably put a severe crimp in whatever illegal doings Stockton-Wells had in the works. It would do more to protect the wolves than she could. And Gray Cloud was right about another thing: they had more than the claim that something illegal was going on now. Now, with that gash in his head, they had proof of wrongdoing. Proof that someone had intended harm to them.

And certainly the authorities could do an awful lot more than she and Gray Cloud could to protect the wolves and the mountain.

"We have to act quickly," Gray Cloud said. "If we start to head down the mountain, perhaps they'll think they've scared us off and they'll relax. That'll give us some time."

"And maybe they'll realize we're running for the authorities."

His arm tightened around her shoulder. "That's a possibility. The mountain will keep trying to drive them away, but..." He hesitated.

"But other animals may get hurt," Mercy said for him. "Like the wolves that were trapped with me yesterday. Like me."

He didn't have to reply. Mercy shivered and turned her head to stare out into the restless, wind-tossed night. Stockton-Wells evidently wouldn't balk at killing them. The mountain apparently wouldn't hesitate, either.

"Talk about a rock and a hard place," she muttered.

A soft, unexpected chuckle escaped Gray Cloud. "The mountain and Stockton-Wells come close, don't they?" Then he sobered. "We'll leave at first light."

"The wolves—"

"Will take care of themselves."

Yes, she thought, they probably would. Heck, just yesterday the wolves had taken care of her and Gray Cloud. But how much could those poor little pups take?

The storm still hadn't broken at dawn. Gray light silhouetted the swaying treetops, and thunder growled almost ceaselessly, the way it always seemed to here on the mountain.

As they set out, Mercy again felt that brush of a strange mind, that touch of something not human. Thunder Mountain. It was watching them, she realized. She wished there was some way to tell if it objected or approved of what they were doing. She sure didn't want to end her life beneath a ton of rock.

Or any other way, for that matter.

Eyebrows showed up briefly, pacing them as they

trekked in the general direction of the Park Service headquarters. Mercy hoped the wolves were paying this much attention to the activities of the Stockton-Wells people. And briefly she wondered if Merle was here with his men or operating at a sanitary distance from the violence. Somehow she thought Merle might actually be part of this.

She wondered if he had learned about the wolves from old contacts at the university. If he had learned about her research proposal and perhaps followed her....

She couldn't bear the thought that she might have led him to the wolves.

Sheet lightning flickered, giving a surreal quality to the forest. Mercy tried to keep her attention on the path, to keep her thoughts from the fact that they might even now be followed by more than a wolf.

From time to time Gray Cloud paused and closed his eyes, listening. Mercy doubted he could actually hear anything over the restless rustling of the wind in the trees, but she didn't think he was listening with his ears. No, he was probably listening to the wind, and after what she'd been hearing, she didn't doubt the wind had plenty to say.

And then there was his head. The wound had scabbed over and looked as if it had happened several days earlier, not just a few hours ago. Another one of the inexplicable happenings of the past few days. The usual rules of reality evidently didn't hold here...or perhaps her view of such things had always been too narrow.

She shivered again, looking around at the shadowy forest, uneasily aware of just how many hiding places there were among the trees, boulders and ravines. An army could be hidden out there and never be spotted, let alone a few men bent on murder.

They traveled until midday without incident, though. When they halted for a lunch break, Gray Cloud left her in a relatively concealed place among some boulders and then circled out and away, looking for any sign that they were being followed. He moved as soundlessly as a cat, she thought as she watched him slip away. Even in boots.

The loamy ground was soft here, like a firm pillow, and she stretched out, deciding to catch up a little on her sleep if she could. Too many disturbed nights. Too much excitement. She was getting to the point where she honestly wouldn't have cared if Merle showed up right now, just so she could get this over with and get some sleep.

Damn, maybe she still had his picture in her wallet. If she did, she could give it to Gray Cloud in case he ever saw any of the men and could find out if Merle was among them.

At least it was something she could *do*. Pawing around in her backpack, she came up with a granola bar and her wallet. One of her failings was that she never cleaned out her wallet or her purse. Here was a grocery store receipt from…good grief, a year ago? And a credit card slip from last December…. A photo of her first college sweetheart.

And Merle. Sure enough, his handsome face was tucked in behind her insurance card. The problem with villains, she found herself thinking, was that they looked like ordinary people. The kind of people you met every day. Merle was no exception. You would never guess from looking at that rugged face that he had the instincts of a shark.

But after her initial infatuation with him had begun to ease, she'd noticed things that left her feeling vaguely uneasy. And later, when he'd become confident of her, he'd begun to poke fun at her. At the time she'd been hurt and confused, and too ready to forgive. In retrospect, she could all too clearly see the cruelty behind the barbs. She still wasn't sure that he'd intended to wound her with his remarks, but even if he hadn't, they said plenty about his lack of compassion.

And in retrospect, his attitude toward the mountains they had climbed together probably said a lot, too. Mercy had climbed because she enjoyed the challenge, enjoyed the mountains, enjoyed the backbreaking effort and the contest with nature. Merle had climbed to prove himself.

And proving himself was something he was undoubtedly trying to do here on Thunder Mountain. It had to be hard to be the son of an extremely successful father. Merle might never be able to meet or exceed his father's achievements, but there wasn't a doubt in Mercy's mind that he would do anything he considered necessary in an attempt to prove he could.

And the more she thought about the probability of Merle's involvement, the more she began to feel that perhaps she had been used, probably to find the wolves that were rumored to be on the mountain. It absolutely horrified her to think that she might have led the person who built the fire right to the den. That Gray Cloud had trusted her enough to show her the wolves, and that his trust might have been inadvertently abused.

Shaking her head, she tucked the picture back into her wallet, this time where she could find it easily. She wouldn't show it to Gray Cloud, she decided. He would never believe that she wasn't involved with Stockton-Wells if she showed him Merle's picture after claiming to have broken off with him so long ago. No, Gray Cloud wouldn't believe she simply never cleaned her wallet. Heck, she would hardly believe it herself if someone else gave her a story like that.

Things were tense enough with Gray Cloud, and there was no point in making them any worse. Hugging her knees, she tilted her head back and watched the low clouds scud overhead. Such a gray and gloomy place, Thunder Mountain. And what if the mountain believed she was still involved with Stockton? How would the mountain come to such a conclusion, anyway? Because Merle had followed her...if he had?

If the mountain figured she was part of the attack on the wolves, or responsible in some way for it, that might explain why she'd come so close to being buried alive. Or did the mountain even think in those terms? Had it just struck out, catching her and the wolves in the slide simply because they happened to be there? Or had it struck at her deliberately?

Would she ever know?

Thinking like this was enough to make her head reel. There couldn't possibly be any answers to questions like those. Heck, she couldn't believe she was even asking.

But she could feel the mountain around her, feel something more in the atmosphere than the raw chilliness of impending rain or the scent of the pine needles. Given a million years and a million words, she doubted she would be able to describe exactly what she sensed that convinced her the mountain was alive and aware. It just *was*. Like a crackle of static in the air, or an aroma so faint you couldn't quite identify it.

Life, she found herself thinking, had a sensation to it. Gray Cloud held blue sparkles in the palm of his hand and called them the life force. She felt something emanate from the mountain that told her at some primitive level that the mountain lived. Life force.

All of a sudden Gray Cloud appeared among the tumbled boulders, carrying some pine boughs. "Lie down," he ordered quietly. "We're being followed. They'll be here in a few minutes, and I want them to get past us without knowing we've stopped here."

He crawled into the crevice with her and pulled the pine boughs over them. Then he lay beside her on his back, cocking his head from time to time as he listened.

Mercy felt strangely secure there in the crowded crevice with the pine boughs over them like a tent. It was as if the mountain were cradling her protectively in its arms like a baby. As soon as the thought crossed her mind, she stiffened, wondering how she could so quickly forget that just yesterday this same mountain had tried to kill her.

Cautiously, she turned her head and looked at Gray Cloud. He was staring up into the pine boughs and listening for the sounds of their pursuers. What were they going to do now? she wondered. Followed already. It wouldn't be long before the Stockton-Wells people discovered Mercy and Gray Cloud were no longer ahead of them and backtracked. How could they be sure of getting a big enough lead to escape?

She wished she could just turn and curl into Gray Cloud's arms the same way she was curled into the mountain's embrace. Stupid way to feel about a man who might decide she was a problem that needed eliminating.

Gray Cloud tensed beside her, and Mercy instinctively held her breath, listening intently. They weren't being very quiet, probably because they weren't worried about being heard. They were far enough behind where they believed Gray Cloud and Mercy to be that noise wasn't a significant problem. They were even talking in low voices, and Mercy strained to make out a word or two, without success.

Gradually the sounds of the men faded into the normal background sounds of the forest, the wind and the thunder. They were once again alone in the clearing. As they waited, Mercy's thundering heart slowed down to nearly normal.

"There were four of them," Gray Cloud said quietly.

"How could you tell?"

"Four different voices."

They waited a few more minutes; then Gray Cloud pushed the boughs away and rose cautiously. "Okay," he said finally, and reached down to help her up.

"It won't be long before they discover they've lost us," Mercy said as she picked up her backpack. "What are we going to do?"

Gray Cloud hesitated only a moment. "Head higher up the mountain, to my home."

It shocked her to realize that she had never wondered where Gray Cloud lived. It was as if she had assumed he lived in the open, like the wolves, without a roof or any of the other comforts. Yet he was dressed decently, and was clean; if he had been living as she assumed, he would not have been.

Heading higher up the mountain would surely confuse their pursuers, she thought. The only problem with that was whether she and Gray Cloud would be able to get the help they needed. Could he possibly have a phone? No, not on the side of this mountain. No way.

"Do you have a radio?" she asked.

"No. No radio, no telephone."

"Then maybe going to your place is a mistake. We could get trapped there."

"I'm going to send a smoke signal."

For a heartbeat she couldn't even absorb what he was saying. "A—what?" The words came out on a nervous laugh.

"A smoke signal. I'm going to burn some trash in my wood stove and make enough smoke that the rangers will investigate."

It sounded like a good idea. "But that will alert the Stockton-Wells people, won't it?"

He shrugged. "Maybe. It's our best chance."

Mercy nodded reluctantly, admitting he was right. It seemed like an awfully slender thread of hope, but there wasn't another one in sight. "I just can't imagine why they should want to kill us. Not really. I mean, it seems like such an extreme act. Maybe they just want us to get out of the way."

Gray Cloud shook his head. "Human life is cheap compared to the millions and millions of dollars of timber on this mountain, compared to the potential for development. You think human life is precious, beyond price, but I assure you, that's not how others see it. Killing one or two people is simply a minor inconvenience, no more significant than moving a rock out of the way of the roads they'll have to build."

"In short, we're simply obstacles." Somehow she found it easy to believe that Merle thought that way. An obstacle. She was an obstacle to Merle's plans for this mountain. And that thought, striking her for the first time, sent chills running down her back. She knew how Merle viewed obstacles.

The climb was rugged, and Mercy suspected Gray Cloud had chosen a difficult path to slow their pursuers and make them harder to track. Rain started falling, a cold drizzle that slowly soaked them. Her hair hung limp and dripping around her face, and for the first time she genuinely wished she had worn a hat.

Too late now, she thought, shivering as the cold began to penetrate her jacket and jeans. She was just trying not to think about how they were headed up the side of the mountain, away from help. Trying not to think about how they might actually be trapping themselves.

She wondered what his home was like. A tepee wouldn't be much protection, but given Gray Cloud's attitudes and his role as medicine man and protector of Thunder Mountain, she wouldn't have been surprised at all if he had chosen to live in a traditional dwelling.

What she hoped for was a log cabin, something with walls thick enough to stop bullets. Of course, that could be burned down around their ears. Well, then, how about a stone fortress?

She almost giggled, and that was when she realized she was getting hypothermic. Woolly-headedness and loss of coordination were both warnings, and she was stumbling over her own feet now. Gray Cloud frequently had to shoot out a hand to steady her.

And his touch affected her like electricity. Sparks zinged from his fingers on her arm, even through all the layers of clothing she wore, and shot straight to her womb, filling her with an impatient tingling, a restless need to be touched and caressed.

She wondered if he felt anything at all for her. Anything at all.

Long ago, someone had built a large log cabin on the side of Thunder Mountain. Four rooms and a shed, all tightly chinked with mud. Gray Cloud had taken over the cabin when he had come to the mountain to live, had fixed it up a little, cleaned it up a lot, and turned it into a comfortable place where he could work and sleep.

The furnishings were all rough-hewn, handmade. Minimal. But the walls... Mercy turned in slow circles, drawing one awed breath after another as she drank in the surprising beauty of Indian blankets and rugs, of beadwork and leatherwork crafted by patient, talented hands.

And the shields. Beautiful leather shields decorated with feathers and beadwork were lined up along one wall—more than a dozen of them. She looked at Gray Cloud questioningly.

"I make the shields," he said almost grudgingly. "My friends made the other things."

Such talent! Mercy squatted before one of the round leather shields and touched it. "You do it all?"

"Start to finish, from rawhide to beadwork."

"You're very talented."

He shrugged dismissively. "It keeps clothes on my back."

Sensing he was uncomfortable with her admiration, she rose and forced herself to turn to other things. There would be time later, she promised herself, to learn more about this enigmatic man. "You live here alone?"

He nodded.

"What about family? Do you have any?"

"A sister." He scowled faintly. "Why?"

"Just curious about you. Aren't you curious about me?" Her heart hammered a little with nervousness. If he said he wasn't, she would be crushed.

But he didn't answer. Instead he turned away and began to close heavy wooden shutters over the windows, barring them in place. Next to a stone fortress, she thought, this cabin would certainly do.

Window by window he locked out the fading afternoon. A gust of wind moaned around the corner of the cabin, muffled by the thick walls, and rattled noisily in the stovepipe. When Gray Cloud squatted before his wood stove and opened the door to the firebox, there was a hollow sucking sound as wind skimming the chimney top created a vacuum.

He arranged kindling and split logs, then, with the flick of a match, ignited the fire. The draw was good, and in no time at all a bright blaze was burning. The stove door had a glass window in it, and Mercy found herself hypnotized by the dancing flames. She was tired. So very, very...tired. Moments later, she nodded off.

* * *

It was dark when she woke, the only light coming from the fire in the wood stove, a bright orangy glow. Gray Cloud sat before it, his back to her.

"Hungry?" He asked the question without turning to look at her. She wondered how he had known she was awake and decided there must have been a change in her breathing.

"Yes, I am." Hungry. Tired. Lonely. Achy. Too many things she didn't want to think about.

"I'll make some sandwiches." He stood, still without glancing at her, and headed toward the kitchen.

"Can I help?" Mercy called after him.

"No, thanks."

Somehow she had gotten to the couch, and a pillow had been tucked under her head. She must have sat down here just before she dozed off, but she sure didn't remember it. The last thing she remembered was standing in the middle of the room while Gray Cloud lit the fire.

"Do you think anyone saw your smoke?" she called.

"I hope so. Fire danger isn't exactly high right now, but the rangers usually keep an eye out, anyway. It should have been spotted from one of the fire watchtowers."

"And they'll come to investigate? Wouldn't they just fly over to make sure there isn't a forest fire?"

"They'll come because I sent the smoke up in puffs. Anybody would recognize that someone was signaling."

A smoke signal indeed, she realized. A smile touched the corners of her mouth, the first smile she had really felt in what seemed like a lifetime, though it couldn't have been more than a couple of days.

Gray Cloud returned with sandwiches for both of them—thick turkey, lettuce and tomato.

"How do you keep food up here?" she asked him. "You don't have electricity, do you?"

"Ice. The old-fashioned way. That shed outside is an ice house."

"Oh!" Lord, she couldn't imagine that, even though her own mother had told tales of the icebox when she was a little girl. This man was self-sufficient, and there was no reason to be surprised because he had an ice-house and knew how to use it. He probably hunted a lot, too. "Do you get into town often?"

"Often enough." He was sitting on the floor, watching the fire while he ate, but now he turned around and looked at her. "I go in every couple of weeks. I sell my stuff and buy whatever I need."

"Where does your sister live?"

"She's in Rapid City now."

"Did she used to live here, too?"

He averted his face for a moment. "She used to be married to Cal Witherspoon, who owned a ranch just east of here."

"I know the place. Wasn't he murder—" Too late she realized and bit her tongue, wishing she could snatch the words back, miserably aware that she couldn't. For a long time the only sound in the room was the dull pop from the fire, muffled by the fire door on the stove.

"I killed him," Gray Cloud said presently.

He had killed his sister's husband. Mercy sat transfixed, sandwich forgotten. The fire popped and flames leapt, and outside thunder rumbled until the cabin shook. Finally she found her voice. "There was... There was a reason, wasn't there?" And she suddenly thought she knew what it was.

"There's never a good reason for killing."

He spoke with flat condemnation, offering no apology or explanation. But Mercy stared at the back of his head, thought of what she knew of him, and would have bet right then that he had killed Cal Witherspoon because Witherspoon was abusive. "He beat her, didn't he?"

Gray Cloud's head jerked minutely. Seconds ticked by in utter silence before he turned his head and looked straight at her. "I knew he'd been beating her, but she wouldn't admit it."

"That's common enough." Hard to believe, but true. "An awful lot of abused wives keep it secret. Was it...? Was it really bad?"

His eyes looked almost hollow, dark pits in his face in the uncertain light. "I caught him beating her with a crowbar."

"My God!"

"I pulled him off her, and he came at me, and I...killed him."

And now she knew why he'd been acquitted. Self-defense was a strong justification, one she could readily accept. And she couldn't imagine that any person worth his or her salt could have stood by while that kind of abuse was going on. No way.

"How—how's your sister now?"

"Recovering. She still has some paralysis of her left side, but other than that, her worst problems are the scars on her mind and spirit."

"I'm so sorry, Gray Cloud. So sorry."

Thunder boomed again, rattling the walls despite their thickness.

"I don't think our pursuers will get here tonight," he said. Changing the subject, Mercy realized. He'd given her a view of his guts, and he wasn't comfortable about it. "It's going to be a bad storm."

Mercy offered a quiet sound of agreement and let the subject of his sister go. She knew now the kind of man he was, and she wasn't sure it gave her any comfort at all. He was capable of killing in the right circumstances. Perhaps he was capable of killing to protect Thunder Mountain. What if he decided she was a threat?

But it was hard to hang on to such concerns when the fire was warm, the night was deep and the wind howled beyond the door. It felt cozy in here, safe. She could feel herself softening and melting, sinking into a state of comfort she hadn't felt in a long, long time.

And all she wanted was to share it with the man who sat cross-legged on what was probably an extremely expensive Navaho rug. She wanted to melt into his arms and feel his strength surround her. She wanted to know how his body would fit with hers and how it would fill hers. She wanted to know him.

And he knew it. He turned his head, and it was as if he could read her mind. His eyes seemed to flare like brilliant flames of jet, and then he rose to his knees, facing her.

"Come here," he said.

Chapter Ten

The orange glow of the fire gilded the room. Outside, a storm raged, but inside the world had grown still, caught between breaths of anticipation. Slowly, feeling as if she were moving through molasses, Mercy rose from the couch and took the two steps that carried her to Gray Cloud. When he reached up for her hand, she dropped to her knees facing him.

He lifted both hands and cradled her face gently in his palms. Black eyes looked down at her, as dark and deep as the night sky. Eyes she could fall into and drown in gladly.

"I want you," he whispered. "I want you."

She couldn't find air to answer. It took the greatest effort to nod her head. Her muscles felt syrupy, her head heavy; nothing wanted to move. She simply wanted to melt until she became one with Gray Cloud.

As if he understood, he slipped his hands to her shoulders and then to the bottom of her forest green turtleneck. Slowly, so very slowly, he raised the hem.

She wore no bra. Her breasts were small and firm, and a bra was an unnecessary encumbrance when camping and hiking. For an instant she was almost embarrassed, realizing he would find out that she was naked under her shirt, and then she thought how silly that was....

His appreciative look told her he was glad he hadn't found a bra. He liked what he saw and lifted his head so he could smile at her. "Pretty," he said in a husky whisper.

He couldn't have chosen a better word. It was the only one she could almost believe. Did his hands tremble just a little as they tossed away her shirt and then gently cupped her breasts?

She stopped wondering as the electric shock of his touch ripped through her. So good. So warm and dry and welcoming. She ought to be embarrassed or nervous or something, she thought hazily, but she wasn't. Not at all. Her entire being had yearned for this moment, and now that it was here, it felt so right. So very, very right.

A wispy sigh escaped her, and she leaned into his touch, savoring the gentle kneading of his fingers on her tender flesh. Little rivers of warm sensation seemed to flow through her to her core, heating her, making her weak and restless all at once.

Gray Cloud leaned forward and lightly brushed his lips against the side of her neck. A delightful shiver ran through her, and a soft moan was drawn from her. Again and again he brushed his warm lips against her soft skin, sending wave after wave of pleasure through her.

Everything inside her was growing soft in the most delightful way, as surrender filled her.

"So sweet," he whispered. "So sweet..." His lips

trailed up the side of her neck to her ear, and then he electrified her by plunging his tongue inside. Another low moan escaped her, and her hips began a helpless undulation.

Carefully, so very carefully, never taking his tongue from her ear, he lowered her gently to her back on the rug. Coarse woven wool met the bare skin of her back, another stimulus, strangely delightful in its prickliness. When he reached for the snap of her jeans, she lifted her hips, silently beseeching him to hurry.

Her eyelids fluttered open in time to see his sleepy smile of satisfaction as he pulled her zipper down and then tugged her jeans over her hips. There was no doubting that he wanted her, and while some corner of her mind warned her not to place too much importance on that, her heart leapt, anyway.

At last she lay utterly naked before him. Kneeling between her legs, he let his eyes wander over her. Slowly his gaze returned to hers, and he gave her a warm smile. "Lovely," he said huskily. "Just lovely."

Joy bubbled up in her, filling her with a sudden happiness. She lifted her arms, reaching for him, and he lowered himself over her, covering her. He still wore his shirt and jeans, and she found the sensation incredibly erotic as denim rubbed against the soft skin of her inner thighs and the flannel of his shirt caressed her breasts and belly.

And then there was the absolutely exquisite sensation of his weight on her, holding her down, promising her so much more. A long sigh of happiness escaped her as he caught her head between his hands and held her steady for his kiss, this time a deep, plunging one that claimed her.

The world whirled away, fears and worries all forgotten in the warm blissfulness that filled her. It was as if his weight sheltered her from everything, as if his tongue had stroked her into purring contentment. Nothing else mattered.

As he kissed her, he began to rock his hips against her, a gentle, suggestive pressure that fueled the ache in her center. Her arms wrapped around his broad back, fingers digging in with delight. Closer. Every cell of her needed him closer, closer....

This is madness.... Some corner of her mind reminded her that she didn't fully trust this man, that she believed him capable of killing her if she threatened his precious mountain. Mercy brushed away the warnings with a soft sigh of surrender. She had lived long enough to know how rare were the feelings this man evoked in her, and she was old enough to accept that she would probably be hurt.

But the magic he cast about her was too fine and beautiful to deny. She wanted these moments and this man at any price.

There were no words of love, just whispered words of praise as he encouraged her in her surrender. He wasn't shy about letting her know that he approved of her, or reluctant to let her know what he liked. His honesty was an aphrodisiac beyond compare and elicited her own in return.

"Oh...yes..."

"Like that..."

"...please...oh, please..."

He slipped lower and took her breast into his mouth, the entire small mound vanishing into the warm, moist heat of him. A soft cry escaped her, and she arched into his touch, feeling consumed in the most delightful way. When his tongue swirled around her nipple, ribbons of sensation seemed to draw her tight on a rack of sheer pleasure.

Her hands tightened on his shirt, grabbing it and pulling it up, needing the feel of his skin against her palms. Needing to be skin to skin with him in the most intimate embrace of all.

His teeth nipped her gently, shooting exquisitely sharp pain-pleasure sensations racing to her core. Then he reared up and pulled his shirt over his head without unfastening the buttons. She reached at once for the button on his jeans, but his fingers were there ahead of her, working the zipper, helping her yank the denim down over his hips....

Everything stilled inside her, catching the moment in amber. Eyes wide open, she looked up at him, drinking him in with all her senses. He was magnificent in the ruddy glow from the fire, muscled and smooth and powerful. Her palms itched to run over him, to feel that sleek smoothness everywhere. Her body yearned to feel his weight bearing her down again. She needed him on her and in her with a ferocity that might have shocked her if she hadn't been caught so fully in its grip.

But he wanted to tease her, and tease her he did, with light touches of his fingers, first across her breasts, then down over her belly to her dewy core. Light touches, like the merest brush of butterfly wings, maddening touches that soon had her twisting and reaching, straining for harder and deeper touches.

Deep inside her, the heavy ache grew until it seemed

to consume her. She felt so open, so aware, so exquisitely filled with sensations...and she needed more. So
much more.

Reaching out, she caught his forearms and tugged. A
smile creased his face in response, and slowly, slowly,
he lowered himself onto her.

"Ahh..." The long, soft moan escaped her. Skin on
skin, no sensation in the world more exquisite or more
intimate. And then... And then the thrill of his penetra-
tion—that incredible, indescribable frisson of pleasure.

And when he was buried deep within her, he lifted his
head and looked straight down into her eyes. She would
never wonder if he knew who he was with, she realized
with an inward melting. It was Mercy Kendrick he was
looking at, and Mercy Kendrick he was loving as he
moved slowly within her, lifting her higher and higher
on an updraft of incredible sensation.

Her body took over completely, causing her to arch
up toward him so she could take him deeper, feel him
better. This was what she had been meant for. This moment, this place, this man's arms.

And almost before she was aware it was going to happen, she shattered in an explosive climax.

Firelight flickered faintly on the ceiling, and the red
glow filled the room. Gray Cloud's fingers brushed
lightly against her feminine curls, a soft, teasing, subtly
exciting touch. Her head was cradled on his arm, and
one of his legs was thrown across hers. He made her feel
as if he didn't want to let her go just yet, nor did she
want him to let go. The afterglow was sweeter than she
ever could have dreamed, and she didn't want it to end.

From time to time he kissed her cheek or shoulder, and when she turned her head toward him, he took her mouth in soft, sweet kisses. Surprising tenderness, she thought dreamily. The kind of tenderness she'd often wished for but had never found. Unexpected in this rough, wild man. So perfect she could have lain there forever and soaked it up like a contented cat.

But gradually passion began to build again. Contented movements began to grow restless, and she finally turned toward Gray Cloud, giving her hands the freedom his had taken. Smooth, sleek, warm… She reveled in the way he felt and loved the way he responded to her touch.

Hard and smooth across his chest, small pointed nipples that responded instantly to her lightest touch…that dragged groans from him when she lipped and nipped them gently. A smooth, flat belly that rippled and quivered beneath her fingers. Long, powerful thighs that flexed beneath her palms.

When she at last cupped his sex, the groan that escaped him sounded as if it had risen from his very toes. Exultation rose in her, strong and joyous, as he reached out and lifted her to straddle him.

"Take me," he whispered hoarsely. "Take me."

She did, deep and hard, with an instinct as old as the mountain below them.

Dawn crept around the edges of the shutters, a pale, rosy glow, surprising after days of grayness. Gray Cloud was up to see pink fingers stretch across the eastern sky as they reached for the western horizon. Beyond the open door where he stood, the shadows beneath the trees were still dark, pregnant with threat. They were safe for the moment, he thought. The mountain offered no warnings about intruders nearby, nor did the wind whisper alarms. All was peaceful for these few minutes.

Turning, he looked at the woman who slept naked beneath a quilt on the floor before the fire. She was a gentle, tender lover, eager to please, and generous. After the initial shyness had worn off, she had become a tigress of sorts. When he moved he could faintly feel the superficial scratches she had left on his back, and the awareness made him smile inwardly.

She was a woman fit for a warrior, he thought. *Tomorrow Woman.*

While it was safe to do so, he took a bucket out to the stream and filled it with fresh water. It would need boiling, of course. The *wasicu* had managed to spread parasites everywhere throughout the West, and the beavers, picking it up from human waste left too close to streams, carried it everywhere else. Water that had been safe to drink even twenty years ago was now rife with unhealthy organisms.

A disgrace, he thought as he carried the water back to the cabin. A disgrace. Nothing tasted sweeter than fresh, icy water from a mountain stream, flavored with minerals and moss.

He set the bucket on the porch and turned to look at the rising sun. There was a cliff a hundred feet from the porch, and the sudden drop opened a view to the east of Conard County and beyond. The sun was rising beneath the high overcast, bathing the world in a rosy glow. For once Thunder Mountain was free of the clouds that usually shrouded its peak, giving unlimited visibility.

That wouldn't last, he thought. Dipping his hand into the bucket, he sprinkled water with his fingers, scattering it in each of the four directions. Then, keeping his voice low so it wouldn't carry, he chanted a prayer to Tunkasila, the grandfather of the world.

"*Mitakuye oyasin.*" He ended the prayer with the ritual words *All my relations,* a reminder that all the world was one.

"That was beautiful."

At the soft whisper, he turned swiftly and found Mercy standing behind him in the open doorway. He hadn't heard her open the door, so involved had he been in his prayer.

There was a look to her this morning, he thought, a look of tenderness that could shred a man's soul, if he let it touch him. The rosy dawn light bathed her face, emphasizing her feminine softness, heightening the drowsy, just-awakened look that was both vulnerable and erotic. In a single instant he wanted to both make love to her and protect her.

Instead he looked away, toward the rising sun, and cleared his throat. "I was praying."

"I thought so. It was beautiful, somehow." She stepped out onto the porch and drew a deep breath of appreciation when she saw the view over the cliff. "Oh, it's wonderful! How can you ever bear to leave here?"

He didn't answer her, simply watched her drink in the morning's splendor. Then, reminding himself that he couldn't be sure that this woman wasn't assisting Stockton-Wells, he picked up the bucket and went inside.

As he walked past one of the chairs by the wood stove, the bucket knocked Mercy's backpack over, spilling some of its contents. He set the bucket aside, then knelt and began to gather up granola bars. And her wallet.

The wallet lay open, and Gray Cloud froze when he recognized a familiar face staring up at him from a color photograph. It was a face that belonged to one of the men he had seen at the Stockton-Wells campsite yesterday morning, just before they had moved out.

He stared at the photo, letting its significance resound through him. Then, swiftly, because he couldn't bear to look at the proof of her betrayal, he snatched up the wallet and jammed it into the backpack. By the time Mercy followed him inside, he was setting the steel bucket on the wood stove to start the water boiling.

You can't trust her.

The view from Gray Cloud's porch was breathtaking. The world seemed to be spread out below like a giant relief map. The air was so clear this morning that the valley looked close enough to touch. Mercy had seen views similar when she went rock climbing, but none had ever been quite this beautiful. She wondered if Gray Cloud saw this often, or if the habitual storm clouds usually concealed it from him.

The sun rose higher, and the rosy glow vanished as fresh storm clouds began to build around the peak. Even as she stood there and watched, swiftly racing patches of fog moved in, dripping strands of cloud as they coalesced and formed rapidly into storm clouds. The valley vanished, and Thunder Mountain was once again cloaked in a storm.

Sighing with reluctance, she went inside to ask Gray Cloud what they should do next.

She knew instantly that something was wrong. He didn't quite look at her when she spoke to him, and he seemed stiffer somehow. Surely she was imagining it?

But as he prepared fry bread for breakfast on the wood stove, she grew increasingly certain that something was the matter. Even when she had first met him, he hadn't seemed quite this distant. Nor had he seemed then to be avoiding her, and right now she got the definite feeling that he was avoiding her.

"Did something happen?" she asked him finally; when he passed her a tin plate loaded with bread, his eyes never lifting to hers.

"No."

Something had. The very fact that he didn't ask why she wondered was a giveaway. Something had happened, and he couldn't quite look at her. Last night, of course. He must be having second thoughts about it. Fears that she might expect a long-term relationship, which of course she didn't.

Did she?

The sinking sensation in the pit of her stomach told her that she was lying to herself. She wanted more, much more, from Gray Cloud than a one-night stand. It was folly, of course. Their lives would never mesh. She had to return to the university, and he wouldn't abandon his precious mountain. There was no future of any kind in that. None at all. He certainly realized that as clearly as she did, and that was why he couldn't look at her.

Wasn't it?

Uneasiness stalked her, making her stomach hurt and killing her appetite. She hardly touched the fry bread, even though it was delicious. He should have asked what the problem was. He didn't. Which meant that something was very definitely wrong.

He never lifted his eyes from his own plate as he spoke. "How long did you date Stockton?"

"Almost two years." Her stomach clenched hard, and knifelike pains radiated through it. Back to Merle, she thought. Gray Cloud might have made love to her last night, but he didn't trust her. And she didn't know how she could get him to.

Or even if she should try. He might decide she was a threat that needed eliminating. Maybe he already had. Maybe she ought to be running as hard and as fast as she could. He would do whatever he thought necessary to protect his damn mountain, and if he thought she was tied up somehow with Stockton-Wells...

Mercy jumped up and hurried toward the door, needing fresh air, needing to escape the miasma of suspicion that filled the cabin. She didn't trust him. He didn't trust her. The gulf between them had never been wider.

And maybe she ought to concentrate on that gulf. Damn it, Mercy, this man might decide to kill you! He might already have decided it! How could you have slept with him last night? How can you be so stupid now? He'd killed once; he could kill again! He was not the kind of a man she ought to be falling in love with.

He caught her at the door, his fingers biting into her upper arm, not quite hard enough to bruise, but hard enough that she felt his grip. It infuriated her, and she tried to yank free.

"Stop it!" he commanded in a low voice. "You can't go out there. Those people are bound to be on their way up here."

"Let me go!"

He gave an impatient shake of his head. "Not until you promise to stay here."

"Why should I? You think I'm involved with Stockton-Wells, don't you? You think I'd actually hurt those wolves, or help turn this mountain over for timber exploitation. Why should I stay with you when you believe that? So you can kill me?"

The gauntlet was thrown, the challenge thick in the air, as thick as the suspicion. He didn't answer her, and his silence confirmed her suspicions. He *did* think she might be involved with Stockton-Wells. Nor did he deny that he might kill her. Funny sort of honor, she found herself thinking, as everything inside her seemed to freeze into ice. He couldn't lie, but he could kill.

And then she realized what was really happening. He had no intention of ever letting her go. She was his prisoner.

Listen.

The day dragged endlessly. Gray Cloud sent up another smoke signal, burning pitch-soaked rags that must have produced huge clouds of black smoke. A forest ranger would surely have to investigate, Mercy thought. Soon. That smoke would be so anomalous that they couldn't overlook it.

But it would probably also alert the Stockton-Wells people.

The thought of a ranger showing up was comforting,

for it meant that Gray Cloud must intend to let her leave the mountain. He wouldn't be trying to get the rangers up here if he intended to kill her, would he?

But it would be so easy to kill her up here. Drop a rock on her head. Push her over that cliff out front. If he really intended to kill her, he would have done it already, wouldn't he? He wouldn't have rescued her after the rock slide trapped her in the cave, would he?

Would he?

But something had changed this morning. Something had definitely happened. This was not the man who had made love to her last night; this was a stranger with a hard face and cold eyes who didn't even want to look at her.

The time dragged. Noon crept up on them so slowly that Mercy felt as if days had passed. Thunder began to rumble again, promising more lightning and rain. The early afternoon darkened, and even though only one shutter was open, the change in light was enough to make it feel as if the day had passed into night.

Gray Cloud went to the window often, listening and watching intently, but no one appeared, and the forest seemed to remain undisturbed.

"They could have lost us," Mercy said finally, her voice cracking after hours of silence. "Maybe they lost us and never picked up on our new direction when they doubled back."

Gray Cloud shook his head. "They track too well. Anyone who could follow us as far as they did knows enough to find where we changed our direction."

"Merle always did talk about tracking like it was some mystical art. Maybe he finally learned how to really do it."

As soon as she spoke, she regretted it. Gray Cloud turned to look at her with eyes as cold as the depths of space. "Stockton."

"Yes, Stockton!" Her chin lifted, and she glared back at him, even as a corner of her mind warned her frantically that provoking this man could be a big mistake. "I told you I used to date him. Is that a crime?"

"You still know him."

"No, I don't! I haven't spoken a word to him in two years! He's a sleaze, and I never wanted anything to do with him again after we broke up!"

"But you carry his picture."

That explained it, she realized with a dull sense of loss. That explained the change in him. He had looked in her wallet. Damn it, she should have given him the photo last night instead of deciding against it, because any way you sliced it now, she looked guilty as hell.

And then anger ripped through her, as hot and fierce as a summer brush fire. "How dare you," she said in a low, angry voice. "How dare you snoop in my personal belongings! You are beneath contempt!"

For a couple of heartbeats it seemed as if he wouldn't answer. When he finally spoke, his voice was as cold and distant as his gaze. "I didn't snoop. Your wallet fell out of your pack, and I found it on the floor. Open."

"Right! While you're at it, try to sell me a bridge, why don't you! You snooped and pried and then leapt to conclusions, and you weren't even going to tell me! Just how the hell would it have been for you in your murder trial if the court had treated you the way you're treating me?"

Before she could say another word, before he could

respond in any way, thunder cracked and rumbled deafeningly, shaking the cabin and rattling the window glass in its frames. On and on it rolled, as if it would never cease, and Mercy's hands knotted into fists as she wondered if it was going to shake the cabin down around their ears.

Listen.

She wanted to scream, to shout, to tell the whisper to leave her alone, to get out of her head...or at least tell her what the devil she was supposed to be listening to. Her entire life seemed to be coming to an ignominious conclusion at the hands of a mountain and a fanatical medicine man, and she didn't want to riddle with the wind. Listen to *what?*

Thunder roared again, trumpeting angrily, shaking the world. The mountain replied with a rumble of its own, a deep shaking from within the earth and a groan of tortured rock.

Something was happening. Scared, aware of the power of the storm and the greater power of the mountain, Mercy forgot her anger and looked at Gray Cloud. "Wh—what's happening?"

He shook his head. "I don't know. Something's... wrong."

She could feel that herself. There was no escaping the sense that the storm and the mountain were crying out in outrage. Gray Cloud turned to look out the window again, and Mercy, forgetting her fear of him in the face of a stronger fear, hurried over to stand beside him.

The day was dark, almost bottle green, and fingers of deep gray cloud hung down so low they skimmed the treetops. It looked every bit as threatening as it sounded. Forks of lightning leapt from cloud to cloud, and some speared downward, as if seeking a target.

The ground shook again, and this time Mercy couldn't tell if it was the rumble of the thunder or the mountain moving.

As she watched, a doe suddenly leapt out of the woods to the right and dashed across the clearing as if it was being pursued.

"Something's definitely wrong," Gray Cloud muttered. "Damn it, what are those Stockton-Wells people up to now?" He turned abruptly, glaring down at her. "What are they doing?"

"I don't know!" Her anger at him seemed unimportant in the face of a world going mad. "I honestly don't know! Gray Cloud, I swear I haven't talked to him in years!"

"One hell of a coincidence that he shows up on this mountain at the same time you do!"

Mercy wanted to deny it—she even felt her jaw open on the words...but she couldn't make herself say them, not when the same suspicion had crossed her own mind. "He must have heard about my research grant. It's not a secret that I was coming to Thunder Mountain to look for the wolves."

"You told him."

"I did not!"

"You expect me to believe he just stumbled on it? How many research grants are made every year? Every *month?*"

"He has ties at the university. Lots of them! He took a graduate degree in forestry there. That's how I met

him. Any number of people could have mentioned my
grant. He has lots of friends there, damn it!"

He regarded her with steady coldness a moment before returning his attention to the forest beyond the
window. He didn't say anything.

"Damn it, Gray Cloud!" Mercy felt as if she were
fighting for her life, needing to convince him that she
hadn't been lying to him. "It's just a coincidence that
the wolves turned up on a mountain he wants to timber. If I'd found them on another mountain, he never
would have turned up. If any other biologist had come
out here, the same things would be happening. It
doesn't have anything to do with the fact that I *used*
to know him. Nothing at all! Believe me, I wouldn't
get involved in anything like that. I wouldn't. I
couldn't!"

He kept his face averted, his attention on the woods
outside. There was no way she could convince him, she
realized. No way at all. He would believe what he
wanted to believe, and if that meant he would believe
she was involved with Merle, she didn't stand a chance
in hell of changing his mind.

The pain she felt at that realization was crushing. In
that instant she realized just how much this man had
come to mean to her. Past reason, past common sense,
she had fallen in love with him. Oh, God, how could
she have been foolish enough to fall in love with someone who might actually intend her harm? Someone who
wouldn't hesitate to kill her if he felt it necessary.

She was crazy, she thought numbly. Crazy. Totally
and completely out of her mind. What she needed to do
was just give it all up, give up any hope of studying the

wolves or protecting them. Just get off this mountain while she was still in one piece and breathing.

The ground shook again, a violent trembling that was accompanied by the anguished groan of rock. Thunder cracked like a gunshot, deafening, and then growled angrily. Lightning stabbed at the ground, seeming to march toward them.

"Smoke." Gray Cloud spoke the word like a curse.

"Where?"

He jerked his chin to the right, and after a moment Mercy was able to see a haze of dark smoke against the dark sky. "Forest fire?" Wet as it had been, she couldn't imagine that the fire danger was any too high, but that didn't mean trees full of pine pitch couldn't burn.

"I don't know," he said. "Stockton wouldn't be stupid enough to burn down the forest he wants to cut, but it's a big forest."

"Controlled burns are part of forest management, aren't they? Maybe he's started a controlled burn. But it could be the lightning, too. Lightning starts fires all the time."

Gray Cloud shook his head slowly. "The mountain is angry. It wouldn't be angry if lightning had started the fire. That's a natural thing, part of the order of life and nature."

She kind of thought that herself. Which left only one conclusion. "Can we get out of here?"

At last he turned and looked at her. "Only by going farther up the mountain."

Which would trap them more, she thought. How far could they go up without limiting their options? She had a good idea how a tiger felt when the hunters began beating the bush to drive him out into the open. "There's no other way?"

He indicated the smoke with a jerk of his chin. "The only way to this cabin is along a ridge between two very deep gorges. It looks like they're burning the trees along the ridge."

There was no doubt in her mind that Merle could read a topographical map and see the terrain as clearly as if he were walking over it. She'd seen him do it. He would have recognized that ridge and its significance as soon as he looked at a map of the area. He knew he would be driving them upward, and he undoubtedly had some plan for trapping them.

"He's driving us into a trap," she told Gray Cloud. "I'm sure of it." She saw the distrust flicker across his face. He didn't want to accept her word without a fight, but there was no argument he could offer in the face of her greater knowledge of Merle Stockton. For now he had no choice but to accept that she knew what she was talking about.

But he didn't have to like it. He scowled at her and finally managed a reluctant nod. "It wouldn't be too difficult." He looked out the window again, toward the thickening smoke cloud and the threatening sky. "It's a good day to die."

Mercy found that the most chilling thing he had said yet.

Fire. A fire meant to kill, set by the men who wanted to rape the mountain. Anger grew until it was a seething fire in the mountain's belly. They must be stopped— at any cost.

And Gray Cloud…he who was chosen by Thunder protected the woman, and the woman was linked to the man who wished to rape the mountain. Even Gray Cloud…

There was sorrow, but there was even more rage.

No human could be trusted. Not one.

Gray Cloud filled Mercy's pack with dried foodstuffs and tied a fresh bedroll to it. Then he filled a pack of his own with more food and another blanket. He evidently thought they might be stuck in the wilderness for some time.

If they lived. Mercy was learning to ignore that qualifier, learning to ignore the chilly sense of unease that never quite let go of her spine, or the tension in the pit of her stomach that never quite let her relax. She hadn't really relaxed since the moment she had felt she was being watched as she climbed the mountain. With each passing hour it had only gotten worse.

Now they were setting out again, with Merle and his henchmen on their heels—or so she would be willing to bet—being driven into a trap of some kind. And as if that wasn't enough, they were going to climb the side of an angry mountain that at any moment might decide to smash them with a rock slide or zap them with lightning. She wished she had never wanted to leave the safety of her desk for the wild side of this mountain.

They left the cabin by a back entrance, slipping out into the forest's depths quietly. Just as long as no one was watching from nearby, they had escaped unseen.

Not that it would make any difference, Mercy thought. Merle wasn't stupid. He would have planned this carefully and probably knew exactly which way they would have to head. It would be a miracle if there wasn't already someone up above waiting to ambush them.

As soon as the thought crossed her mind, she voiced it to Gray Cloud. He merely gave her a short nod. "Wouldn't the mountain know if someone's up there?" she asked him. The absolute absurdity of the question struck her, but she was past caring whether she was crazy to believe the mountain was alive. The way things were going, she wasn't going to be around long enough to worry about such things.

"Yes."

"Well, wouldn't it warn you?"

Gray Cloud spared her a distant glance. "Perhaps not."

Perhaps not. Once again a chill seeped into her as she realized that Gray Cloud no longer trusted the mountain he served.

Chapter Eleven

It ought to be raining. It just ought to be raining. The air was so pregnant with the impending storm that it was thick, almost too thick to breathe. Perspiration from exertion soaked her and wouldn't dry, and finally she had to rip the bottom of her shirt to make a sweatband so she could keep her vision clear. Gray Cloud pulled a shoelace out of a shirt pocket and tied his hair back.

Thunder continued to growl and grumble like an irritable beast. The light turned so green it felt like they were walking underwater. Long fingers of cloud dipped down, looking as if they wanted to touch the ground. The lightning, though, stopped spearing from cloud to cloud, and from cloud to ground. It subsided to a flicker deep within the stormy sky, barely discernible despite the darkness of the afternoon.

And Thunder Mountain growled angrily. The ground never stopped vibrating, not quite strongly enough to make walking difficult, but enough that it was impossible to forget the mountain was angry and might at any moment lash out.

Before long, Mercy noted that Gray Cloud tended to avoid places where a rock slide might be a distinct danger—places where the slope was really steep, or the trees were really thin. Several times he skirted such places with evident caution, telling Mercy as clearly as any words that he was concerned about what the mountain might do.

And Mercy began to get angry. Very angry. It wouldn't do any good, so she bottled it up inside and chewed on her tongue to prevent the words from escaping. But what she wanted to do was stomp her foot and give the damn mountain a piece of her mind.

And the wolves. Where were the wolves? She and Gray Cloud had lost contact with them sometime yesterday. She assumed they'd gone to dig themselves a den somewhere for the pups and hoped they'd gotten well out of harm's way. But she was worried about them and wished she could at least catch a brief sight of Eyebrows.

But the afternoon waxed, then waned, and there was no sight of wildlife of any kind...which was really strange.

It was as if the forest was dead.

At some point she realized that they hadn't seen any living thing in hours, not a squirrel or a bird. Not a hint or sound of life. It was as if every living animal, bird and insect had vanished.

The silence echoed, and uneasiness stalked her. If the animals had fled...

She wasn't aware she had voiced the thought until Gray Cloud turned to her and nodded. "Very wrong," he said. "Something's very, very wrong."

Behind them, black smoke rose to meet the gray clouds, testament to Merle's willingness to destroy anything to get what he wanted. A doe had leapt out of the woods this morning, fleeing the fire. The ground trembled, but the animals of Thunder Mountain had in the past seemed used to that and unthreatened by it. This afternoon...perhaps they were scared by the fire, distant as it was, and had taken flight.

Or maybe they sensed that something else was about to happen. An earthquake? A really bad one?

They didn't pause long but continued the rough climb. Frequently Gray Cloud reached out to help her, and she wondered if he remembered last night at all, or if he had killed the memory ruthlessly. This morning he certainly seemed to believe her capable of consorting with Merle to destroy the mountain and using him callously in the process.

Suddenly Gray Cloud shot out an arm and motioned her to stop.

"What is it?" she asked in a whisper that was almost lost in the sudden gusting of wind through the treetops.

He shook his head, silencing her. With great effort she bit back her questions and waited, watching him as he tipped back his head and closed his eyes. It looked, she thought, as if he were opening his senses to the wind, seeking a sound or a smell that would tell him something.

Thunder rumbled again, a distant, angry growl. A large raindrop splattered Mercy's cheek, cold and stinging like an icy slap. The temperature was dropping, and it seemed likely that they might see snow, which wouldn't be unusual for this elevation even at this time of year...but would be absolutely miserable to hike through. She shivered and wished Gray Cloud would reach some kind of conclusion about the threat they were facing.

Where had all the animals gone?

Why had all the animals gone?

The wind whipped through the treetops with a sudden, ferocious moan. *Listen...*

A prickle at the back of her neck warned her. Forgetting Gray Cloud's injunction to silence, she whirled around and gasped as she saw a huge hawk perched on a low bough and staring straight at her with eyes that seemed to burn right through her. At her gasp, Gray Cloud spun around and saw the hawk, too.

It was watching them. It was watching them and following them. Mercy shuddered as frigid awareness seeped through her. There was no escape. Everywhere they went, they were being watched.

Gray Cloud muttered something she didn't understand. It didn't matter; she knew what she was seeing, and it didn't need a name. Those small, black eyes pinned her like twin knives, holding her motionless...almost helpless.

"Let's go." Gray Cloud clasped her elbow, dragging her out of the paralyzed state she had fallen into. For once she didn't mind a gentle tug that pulled her away, back into the real world.

If this world could be called real, she thought as she followed Gray Cloud farther up into the mountain. The hawk's eyes seemed to bore holes in her back even after the trees must have screened her from its view.

"It was watching us," she said. The altitude and exertion were making her breathless, and the words came out on small puffs of hard-won air.

"Yes."

"For who?"

"The mountain. The hawk is the eyes of the mountain."

She scrambled up a steep incline, scraping her knuckles a little as she grabbed handholds. The injuries didn't bother her; if such small hurts had mattered, she never would have become a rock climber. The back of her neck still seemed to burn from the hawk's gaze, and when she dared an upward glance at the stormy sky, she saw the bird above them, circling slowly.

The altitude must have been affecting her mind, because it was a while before she got to wondering why the mountain should be watching them. Gray Cloud, after all, was trusted by the mountain...wasn't he?

The possibility that the mountain had some reason not to trust him was awful to contemplate. She had seen some of what the mountain was capable of, and she suspected it was capable of far more than that. If for some reason it had come to distrust Gray Cloud...

The thought was chilling.

Just when her legs were turning to putty and she was beginning to stumble over her own feet, Gray Cloud called another halt. Sitting side by side on a low, flat boulder, they stared back down the way they had come. Beneath them the mountain continued to tremble, but so slightly it was almost possible to believe she was imagining it. For some reason her mind hopscotched to the seismograph the Forest Service kept on Mount Rainier. She'd seen it years ago, while taking a summer trip through the Northwest, and had been fascinated by the way the apparently quiet, lifeless mountain never really stopped trembling. Mount Rainier was a dormant volcano, and the seismograph was a reminder that the mountain could awake at any instant, that it merely slumbered.

Thunder Mountain was slumbering no longer. The entire Rocky Mountain area was seismically active, so it was hardly surprising that this mountain was rumbling and groaning as if waking from a centuries-old sleep.

But that wasn't all that was happening. Thunder Mountain was more than an accident of plate tectonics. A sleeping giant had been awakened by the threat of Stockton-Wells, and the more Mercy thought about it, the more likely she considered it that none of them would survive. Despite all the power and force contained within this mountain, she seriously doubted a surgical strike was within its capabilities. Everything that got in the way would probably be destroyed. The only hope she and Gray Cloud had of escaping would be to stay well away from Merle and his henchmen.

She turned to Gray Cloud. "Why is the mountain watching us? I thought you were its friend."

He turned slowly and looked straight at her. "I saved your life."

Her breath jammed in her throat as his meaning drove home. He was no longer the mountain's friend because he had dug her out of the cave. That must mean the mountain believed she was a threat, and if the mountain believed that...

"No!" She spat the word like an oath. "No, damn it, I'm not going to be hanged without a trial! Are you and this mountain both deaf and stupid? I came up here to study wolves, not to hurt one damn thing. I haven't talked to Merle Stockton in over two years, and his picture was in my wallet because I never clean my wallet, not because he's still a friend of mine! Don't you hear me?"

"I hear you." But the words conveyed no belief in what she was saying. None at all.

Right then, Mercy came as close as she ever had to committing an act of violence. The urge to swing at Gray Cloud, just to get his full attention, was nearly overwhelming. This man had made love to her just last night with a tenderness the mere memory of which made her breath catch, and yet now he was treating her as if she were a total stranger. He had convicted her on the basis of one lousy photograph.

And he wouldn't even listen to her explanation.

Tears pricked at her eyes, and she looked quickly away, trying to repress the sense of betrayal. She had trusted this man with everything that she was, had trusted him enough to open her body to him, making herself completely vulnerable. And instead of treating that gift with the respect it deserved, he had turned his back on her, choosing to disbelieve everything she had told him because of one stupid photo.

"You're worse than Stockton," she heard herself say. "You're even worse! What if I hadn't believed what you told me about killing your sister's husband? What if I believed you had made up a story that would make you look sympathetic and explain away your reputation! How would you feel?"

"That you were being wise and cautious."

Stunned, Mercy watched him rise and turn away.

"Let's go," he said roughly. "It's time. Something is brewing, and I want us to get up higher before it happens. There's a place where we'll at least have a chance if the mountain goes wild."

She wanted to scream and shout, to stamp her feet and insist that they weren't going anywhere until he listened to her, but even as she had the impulse, she was climbing to her feet and following him up the ravine. Screaming and shouting wouldn't change his mind. Nothing could do that except himself. If his mind was made up, no protest would alter it.

And that saddened her beyond words. She had given him her heart, and he didn't care. Not even a little bit. He had used her last night, that was all. Used her.

Listen…

The wind sighed the word through the treetops as evening darkened the sky even more. Gray Cloud settled them on a wide expanse of granite, a firm bit of ground that appeared as if it would resist buckling if Thunder Mountain shook harder.

For the mountain had never stopped shaking. The vibration was small, but it could be felt, and to Mercy it seemed as if something were building beneath them, like a pressure cooker. Some kind of explosion was imminent.

Dinner was a silent affair, a quick meal without even a passing word to lighten the atmosphere. The lightning began to play among the clouds, bright and colorful, beautiful but subtly threatening. Mercy curled up in her blankets and tried not to feel mercilessly exposed on the rock slab. More drops of rain spattered them, but not enough to make them wet. Just enough to remind them that they *could* get wet.

Gray Cloud defied the storm, standing tall and straight as he prayed, holding his arms up toward the clouds in supplication. Thunder had chosen him, she remembered. The Thunder Spirits had given him the vision that guided his life. He probably didn't fear the storm at all.

Lying on her back, she watched the wind toss his hair and whip it around him. With his hands turned palm upward, he seemed to be inviting the storm to come to him. Little blue sparks of light appeared in his cupped hands as they had once before, but this time, instead of remaining small little flickers, they grew until they filled his hands. And then blue light seemed to run along his arms, down his sides to his feet, until he was limned in glowing blue light bright enough to emphasize every detail of his face and body. She could see him as clearly as if he were standing in a bath of daylight.

And then, from his fingertips, the light reached outward, two strands of blue stretching up toward the clouds. Mercy held her breath, hardly daring to believe what she was seeing. She blinked repeatedly, but nothing made the image go away. Gray Cloud was bathed in lightning.

She cried out when a fork of blue lightning suddenly leapt down from the clouds and met the blue streamers flowing from his hands. She was sure he was a dead man then, that the lightning would kill him in an instant or burn him so badly that he would never get off this mountain....

But he remained standing, his arms upraised as he continued to chant his prayer. He was talking to the lightning, she realized, communing with the power of the storm. Speaking with the Thunder Spirits.

Her world had been turning topsy-turvy since she began her climb up Thunder Mountain, but now the last vestiges of her old reality slipped away as she crossed the threshold completely into the world of Thunder Mountain.

Into Gray Cloud's world. A world where thunder spoke and lightning touched on the power of life. A world where a medicine man could call upon the powers of nature to aid him.

For there was not a doubt in her mind that that was what he was doing. If the storm could aid them, he would ask it to. If the mountain hadn't condemned him, he would probably call on that, as well. And there was a sense that the light that bathed him was protective, that it would shelter him from harm. From evil.

Primitive instincts were awakening within her, and without realizing it, she rose to her knees. It could be harmful, she thought...or it could be helpful. And Gray Cloud was pleading for help.

He glowed with blue fire now, almost as if he were aflame, a brightness in the night that drove the shadows back. Slowly he turned toward her and reached out a flaming hand.

Her first instinct was to back up, run, get away. She could only be hurt by that blue fire.

Listen...

The wind dipped down from the treetops and

wrapped around her, the caress of the breeze catching at her short hair and lightly touching her cheeks.

Listen...

In spite of herself, her hand lifted and reached out for Gray Cloud's until their fingertips met. And as she watched, the blue light began to flow to her, to cover her fingers, then her hand, and slowly, slowly creep up her arm. She felt nothing at all except a very faint warmth. It was going to consume her just as it had consumed him.

Listen...

The wind curled around her as the fire slipped over her, and something inside her grew still with expectancy.

Listen...

Then wind and thunder claimed her.

The evil men were waiting above for Gray Cloud and the woman. They had laid a trap, and the mountain saw it all through the eyes of the hawk. Once they all came together, the mountain could free itself of the blight forever.

It was good.

The mountain settled down to wait, a mere blink of time until the sun rose again and the puny little humans on its slopes began once again to move.

It saw Gray Cloud speaking to Thunder, and saw Thunder take the woman in its embrace, and knew that Thunder would see through her to her heart and discover the evil there. Thunder would not protect her once it knew her.

Mercy didn't remember falling asleep, and when she woke to the first pearly light of dawn, she was astonished to find herself tucked up against Gray Cloud. When she moved, his arms tightened around her and tugged her even closer, so that her head was cradled on his shoulder. He couldn't be awake, she told herself. No way.

The last thing she remembered was watching the blue light crawl up her arm. She didn't even remember it reaching her shoulder. It probably had, though, because this morning she felt a subtle tingling everywhere, not so very different from what she had felt as the light crept up her arm.

She wished she understood what had happened last night. Wished she understood what all this meant. The rules of reality that she had been living by for so long were evidently meaningless on Thunder Mountain. Lightning had reached down from the sky and touched both her and Gray Cloud without harming them. Thunder had spoken to them, and she remembered it somewhere deep inside, though she couldn't remember what, if anything, she had learned.

What was different this morning, she realized suddenly, was that she no longer felt that she was running from something. Instead she felt that she was heading *toward* something. That she had a purpose.

Had Thunder given her a vision of some kind?

No. Her mind recoiled from the thought, not because she considered such a vision impossible, but because she wasn't the kind of person who had visions. Or a person who should receive such visions. Who was she that Thunder should talk to her? Nope. If anyone had had a vision last night, it would have been Gray Cloud.

But the lingering sense of rightness persisted, generated, she told herself, by Gray Cloud's arms around her.

From the start she had felt a sense of belonging with him, even when he was being his most critical of her. The rightness and peacefulness were illusory, she told herself, but that didn't keep her from soaking them up while she could.

But the sense of purpose that filled her now...that was harder to dismiss.

Listen...

Listen to the feeling? Why not? What difference could it possibly make, except to ease the next hours? If she continued this climb with a sense of purpose, that would make it easier to face whatever lay ahead. Why not believe that she had come to this point in time for a reason, that there was some cosmic scheme behind the horrible things that had been happening and would still happen? Would it really make any difference at all if she believed she had been guided here rather than that she had wound up here by accident?

Easier to believe that something had guided her. Easier to think about it when she remembered Jason Nighthorse from the anthropology department dropping in last autumn to mention the wolves he had heard about on Thunder Mountain...when Jason didn't have any interest in wolves. Then there was the way the grant opportunity had just fallen into her lap without a hitch almost before she had really started to think about seeking one. The way everything had come together to get her on this mountain at the same time as Merle.

A chill crept along her skin as she considered the size of that coincidence. Oh, it was easy to say Merle had heard about her research and followed her, but when she really thought about it...well, there were some awfully unlikely coincidences in the string of events that had put them both here.

If Merle was even really here. But she would have bet that he was. Merle was like that—he might hire a bunch of people to do the dirty work for him, but he would keep control for himself, and for Merle that meant being right there to superintend everything. Oh, she was familiar with that trait of his, all right. She'd even teased him about how awful it would be to work for him.

But that was neither here nor there. Some part of her knew he was on this mountain, and that for some reason or other they were going to have a final confrontation. She knew that as surely as she knew the sun was rising higher on the far side of the low clouds.

Listen...

She was listening. She wasn't sure what she was hearing, but she was listening. Inwardly, she knew this was all meant to be. That what was going to happen on the side of this mountain would affect the course of the future. That she would never again be the same.

Well, of course not. She had discovered that a mountain was capable of thinking and acting. That the rocks beneath her feet were sentient, and that the wind could whisper tales. She had discovered that the world was alive in ways she had never before imagined.

She had stepped out of the objective, impersonal Western world in which she had been raised and had entered a realm where the life force animated every molecule. She had stepped from her own world into Gray Cloud's.

No, she would never again be the same.

She tried to sit up but as soon as she stirred, Gray Cloud's arms tightened again and tugged her closer still. Instinctively she tipped her head back to see if he was awake and met the obsidian of his gaze. Not a single line of his face betrayed his thoughts. He looked as hard and forbidding as the mountain that surrounded them.

Then, without even the flicker of a muscle to betray his intent, his mouth swooped down and captured hers.

Joy erupted inside her like holiday fireworks. He wanted her. He still wanted her. And if he wanted her, perhaps he didn't entirely distrust her.

But did she trust *him*?

The question caused winter frost to creep through her. No, she didn't trust him.

As if he felt the chill strike her, Gray Cloud pulled away suddenly and in one swift movement rose to his feet.

Mercy watched him stride away into the woods and told herself that he had kissed her only because he'd been half-asleep and aware of nothing but the fact that there was a warm woman in his arms. That was all it had been. Any woman who had been pressed to him that way would have been kissed.

Sitting up, she ignored her stiff body and aching muscles and tried to find the calm that had been with her upon awakening. Matters were coming to a head.

Today everything would be decided.

Thunder was strangely silent that morning as they climbed up over increasingly difficult terrain. Gray Cloud paused often, giving her a chance to catch her breath in the thinner air, and checked things out. Or at least she assumed that was what he was doing when he tilted his head back and closed his eyes, appearing to listen.

Merle was waiting for them up ahead. Mercy wasn't sure exactly how she knew that, except that it wouldn't have been like Merle to start that fire until he was already in position to spring his trap when he drove his quarry upward.

"It has to be soon," Gray Cloud said finally. "Soon. If we get up much farther on this ridge, we'll be able to cut across and come back down the mountain. Our options will open up again."

"We could stay right here and wait for him. Pick our own ground." She was surprised when he gave her suggestion consideration and didn't say that she was simply encouraging him to do what Merle wanted him to do.

"Usually," he said, "picking your own ground is an advantage, but there's no good ground between here and the place where he's probably waiting for us. We'd be at a disadvantage everywhere, on the downhill side."

"Okay. It was just an idea. But if he really is already up there waiting for us, we're going to be at one hell of a disadvantage."

"He's up there," Gray Cloud said with conviction. "He's waiting."

"Shouldn't we make some kind of plan? Do something to try to save ourselves?"

He looked at her for a moment, then squatted and began to draw absent patterns in the dirt with his forefinger. "Thunder Mountain is a manifestation of Makan, the earth spirit, but it is not all-powerful. Thunder is more powerful. The wind is more powerful. These spirits are greater than the mountain." He glanced up questioningly, and she nodded that she understood what he was saying.

"I've asked *Wakinyan* and *Tate*, Thunder and Wind, to help us. We must trust that they will, and be ready to take advantage of whatever aid they give us. As for the mountain..." He shook his head. "I don't know what the mountain intends, but we have more to fear from it than we do from Stockton and his friends."

Mercy didn't like the sound of that at all. Not at all.

"I'm going to take you a little farther up," he continued. "There's a place there where you should be safe while I scout around and see if I can discover a way to take care of Stockton."

"I'll come with you."

He shook his head. "I can track more silently alone."

The thought of being left in isolation on the mountainside didn't appeal to her at all, but she couldn't come up with a good reason why he should take her with him. She didn't know how to track, and she certainly didn't know how to fight. She was a biologist, damn it, not a commando.

Feeling uneasy and grim, she had no choice but to follow Gray Cloud. Thunder rumbled uneasily from higher up, and the mountain trembled faintly. Forces were gathering, creating a tension in the air that was inescapable, a tension as palpable as that on a drawn rubber band, and to Mercy it felt as if something might snap at any moment.

The place Gray Cloud took her to was a table of granite surrounded by volcanic dikes that looked as if they reached to the very bedrock. "You'll be safe here," he told her. "Safe enough. The dikes will stop a rock slide."

So he thought there was a chance the mountain might try to kill her again. Mercy wanted to argue with him, tell him that he had to take her with him, but the words didn't come. Instead she sat on the table, surrounded by the bony fingers of upthrust rock, and watched him disappear into the dark, silent depths of the forest.

Alone, she listened...and heard nothing.

Chapter Twelve

The woman sat on the table of rock, thinking herself safe. Gray Cloud had underestimated the power of the mountain. With one shrug of its shoulders, it could send that entire table tumbling down to the valley below.

But not yet. The man who wanted to cut the trees and kill the wolves was closing in on the table. He would find the woman, and then the mountain could take care of the entire problem at once. Easily.

As for Gray Cloud... The mountain ruminated.

The day was growing colder as noon approached. Mercy watched the occasional snowflake fly and tucked her hands up beneath her arms to keep her fingers warm. What was taking Gray Cloud so long?

He was checking out a wide area, she told herself. The side of this mountain was pretty big, and rough terrain besides. Of course it was taking him a long time.

Standing, she hopped from one foot to the other, trying to build up some body heat inside her clothing. The pack was beginning to feel as if it weighed a ton, too, but it served to keep the wind off her back.

And the wind was beginning to develop a real bite, teeth of ice that nipped right through her clothing and were making her earlobes hurt. Roughly she chafed her ears with her hands and then covered them with her palms. What she needed to do was find something to tie around her head, she thought. Maybe one of the shirts tucked deep into her backpack.

Before she could slip the pack off, movement in the corner of her eye caught her attention. She turned swiftly but could see nothing in the woods beyond the table where she stood.

Something had been there. Something had moved. And it had been bright enough to snare her attention, which meant it probably wasn't an animal, which would have blended into the background.

Someone was out there.

For a few moments she allowed herself to think it must have been Gray Cloud, but when he didn't reappear, didn't emerge from among the trees and approach her, she knew it had to be someone or something who didn't want her to see them. One of Merle's people, perhaps. Or Merle himself. The unpleasant sense of being watched returned.

The hawk. Remembering the hawk that had followed and watched them yesterday, she looked around her, trying to find a large bird. *Hoping* to find a large bird, because that would explain the movement and the sense of being watched. But if the hawk was out there somewhere, she couldn't see it.

Where was Gray Cloud?

Thunder rumbled deeply from clouds that seemed to be closing in on her, curling downward around the trees, bringing the sky down to them. Lightning flickered, as yet not forking down to strike the mountain.

Feeling too exposed and too vulnerable, Mercy squatted down and hugged her knees, making herself as small a target as she could. If it hadn't been the hawk, then it was a person, and if it was a person, it was unquestionably Merle or one of his friends...and that was not good. Not good at all.

Scanning her immediate vicinity, she tried to see some way she could defend herself or escape if someone attacked. Running in the opposite direction was a simple option, but what if they came at her from *all* directions? And what if the mountain got involved? If the mountain struck out at the Stockton-Wells people, she would probably get caught in the cataclysm...which was why Gray Cloud had left her here, wasn't it? To keep her safe from another rock slide. These jutting dikes of basalt would unquestionably provide a shield against falling rocks from almost any direction.

But was a rock slide all the mountain could accomplish? Oh, God, she didn't even want to think about it. It was too much to contemplate. Her mind had absorbed so much strangeness in the past few days that it was getting balky. No more.

But not thinking about it wasn't going to change the reality, which was that Merle was stalking her and Gray Cloud, probably to arrange an accidental death for both of them so that no one would hear about the wolves, and any serious objections to his plans would be silenced.

Well, was she just going to sit here and take it? But what could she do? Keeping her eyes open, scanning the forest's edge continuously, she tried to think of some way to protect herself and stymie any attempt by Merle to hurt her.

And she tried not to feel as if she were the Judas goat set out to attract the tiger.

Because the longer she sat here, facing the threat alone, the more a small voice in her head kept saying that Gray Cloud had left her here purposely as a lure. That he had wanted to draw Merle out here for some reason, instead of meeting him some other place. That she was bait in the trap.

And bait was expendable.

Lord, it was getting so cold! Shivering inside her jacket, she considered what, if anything, she could do to draw the men out...and if she managed to draw them out into the open, what would she do then? Maybe the thing would be just to get up and try to walk away from here. If she moved before they were ready to act, she might have a chance, but the longer she stayed here, the more opportunity she was giving them to get ready to take her out. To make it look as if it was an accident.

There had to be *something* she could do, besides sit here and feel that she had been thrown to the predators by the man she loved.

Not that he loved *her*. Damn, he could hardly even bring himself to look at her today. Pain pierced her heart, an ache beyond description, as she considered what would never be. *Could* never be. How had she been so foolish as to give her heart to a man who didn't want it, a man who had set her out as bait in a trap and probably didn't care if she lived or died as a result? Well, the Judas goat usually died, didn't it, devoured by the tiger it had lured into the trap?

She shivered again and told herself it didn't matter. Nothing mattered. She had had a broken heart before; it wouldn't kill her. Nor was this the time to be moaning about that, not when her life might actually be hanging in the balance.

There was no more sign of movement from the woods, and it occurred to her that Merle could settle in just as well as she could, waiting for Gray Cloud to return so he could handle things all at once. There was no reason why he should act immediately. After all, his assumption would be that Gray Cloud would return to her, and it would certainly be less messy, and less likely to cause problems, if he killed them both in a single "accident."

But what kind? Shivering violently, she tipped her head back and looked around at the mysterious trees, the mountain slope rising away to her right, falling away to her left. A rock slide wouldn't be able to reach her very easily because of the upthrust basalt. Gray Cloud had been right about that.

So what other accident could happen here?

Beneath her, the ground trembled with suppressed power. The mountain was stirring again. The wind reached down and tugged at her hair.

Listen...

Giving herself up to the wind, Mercy forced her thoughts to quiet down and tilted her head back so the frigid air could nip at her unimpeded. *Listen.* All right, she would listen. To the wind. To the thunder and the lightning. And even to the mountain that might want to kill her.

Listen…Tomorrow Woman…listen…

She heard the earth groan and realized it was about to move again. This movement would be more than the small tremors that had been coming almost nonstop. This movement would be violent. An attack.

Deep within the mountain, stressed rock groaned and fractured, transferring its confined energy upward toward the surface.

Listen…

She heard the stressors, heard the anguish of the tortured rock and felt the earthquake push up toward her. The fingers of basalt that guarded her began to hum and vibrate as the shock wave deep within the mountain struck their buried bases.

Listen…

She heard the wind carry its warning along the mountain slopes to the small animals, herding them away from the epicenter.

Heard the wind whisper her name again. *Tomorrow Woman…run…run…*

The epicenter was beneath her. Directly below her. She saw it in a fractured moment out of time, as if the ground beneath her had become transparent, and she saw that the shock wave was racing straight up toward her feet.

Listen…

Thunder boomed hollowly, and the wind snatched at her hair, tugging.

Run…

Lightning forked down, dazzling her, terrifying her. She felt so exposed.

Run…

Lightning was trying to push her, she realized. Thunder was trying to warn her.

Run...

She rose from her crouch, ready to flee but not sure where to flee to. Barely had she reached her feet when the table of granite beneath her began to shudder violently. She teetered from side to side, finding it almost impossible to maintain her balance.

The upthrusting dikes of basalt trembled, too, shaking as if they were working their way out of the ground. The ground shrieked its agony now, crying out as it rent itself, severing ancient veins, tearing itself apart.

Run!

A crack opened at the edge of the rock table, and Mercy stared in horror as it widened, separating the table from the surrounding ground. Then slowly, so terribly slowly, the table began to tip.

Dread held her frozen, disbelief making it almost impossible for her to comprehend what was happening. The rock table was separating from the ground around it. The mountain was breaking it free, tipping it, trying to shake her off....

A sudden lurch tipped the table precariously. Galvanized by the same fear that only moments ago had paralyzed her, Mercy tried to scramble upward but slid backward as the rock tipped further. Looking behind her, she almost cried out. The ground back there had vanished, leaving a gaping hole. A cliff edge.

A nightmare place to fall into.

She had never forgotten the tale she had heard of the Alaska earthquake, had never forgotten the man who had seen a crevice open beneath his wife, had seen her fall in, had heard her cries as the crevice closed around her.

No, damn it, she wasn't going to die that way, swallowed alive by the mountain. No way!

Falling flat on the tipping table of rock, she used every one of her rock-climbing skills to edge her way higher. Handholds were almost nonexistent, but the surface of the rock wasn't perfectly smooth, either, and she was able to wedge her feet against small bumps, to claw a slippery grip on barely discernible ridges with her hands. In no time at all her fingertips were sore and bleeding, but she hardly noticed. It was reach the top or tumble into the pit behind her.

The attempt to survive demanded all her attention, but somewhere deep inside was the sorrowful, angry realization that Gray Cloud had left her here to die. He had indeed handed her to the mountain, like some sacrificial lamb.

An angry tear escaped, but she ignored it as she struggled upward on the violently shaking slab of rock. As soon as she felt her feet were braced securely enough that she wouldn't slide backward, she stretched her arms up and felt for handholds. More than once she slipped back a little, but more often she managed to inch upward.

Another strong tremor shook the rock, nearly shaking her off it. Just as she was sure she couldn't hang on another second, that she was going to slide backward into the pit the mountain had made, into the grave it had dug for her, the tremor let up and her grip held. Not even wasting a moment to allow herself to feel relief, she pushed upward again with her toes and then reached with her hands.

And felt the edge of the slab. For an instant she froze. What if all she found when she looked over the edge was another crevice…a deep pit that could swallow her as easily as the one behind her? What if there was no escape up there?

What alternative did she have? She should have run the instant the wind advised her to. The very instant.

Tomorrow Woman…listen.

To what? Oh, God, listen to what? Her breath was coming in sobs now, her fingers ached so badly from clinging to the bucking rock that they were cramping, and her thigh muscles were beginning to quiver.

Pull up!

The wind nipped at her ears, slapped her cheeks and forced her attention back to what she needed to do. This was no time for self-pity, no time to stop and moan. So what if her fingers cramped and her thighs ached? So what?

With her arms fully extended, she gripped the edge of the table and pulled with all her might. As if the rock realized she was close to achieving her goal, it shuddered wildly, like a horse trying to shake off a fly. That was what she felt like—like a fly plastered to the side of the rock—and about as significant.

Move!

She struggled, hauling herself up against all the resistance of gravity, against the friction of her clothing and body against the rock itself, inching higher and higher as her arms began to quiver and protest.

And finally she looked over the edge.

Into a crevice as black as night. Into the very maw of the mountain.

Jump!

Across a gaping hole five feet wide. How could she find a position from which to get stable enough to jump with any surety? What if she tumbled into that hole?

What alternative did she have?

Turning her head, she looked back down the slab of rock and saw the pit that waited there. It was far wider, far more of a threat, a sinkhole in the side of the mountain. At least she had a chance of jumping over the crevice.

Pulling herself up the last little bit, she clung for dear life as the rock bucked and shuddered beneath her. There had to be a place where she could stand just long enough to jump.

"Mercy, here!"

A voice from out of the past, a voice she had never wanted to hear again. Raising her eyes, she saw Merle Stockton standing on the other side of the crevice with a coiled rope in his hand. A vision from the past in woodland camouflage.

"I'll throw you a rope!"

She would have loved to tell him where to stick his rope. Although she was exhausted and scared, although it was likely she would die if someone didn't help her, she wanted to hurl his offer right back in his face.

But as soon as the resentment rose in her, it faded away, replaced by common sense. If he threw her that rope and she fell into the crevice when she jumped, there would at least be a chance he might pull her out. If he didn't pull her out...well, she wouldn't be any worse off, would she? And why would he throw her a rope if he wanted her to die? No, he must need her for some reason.

And that meant he would help her now.

She nodded her understanding to him, unable to speak as the rock shuddered yet again and tipped more.

"Catch it, Mercy!"

The earth shrieked again and trembled fiercely. Merle stepped back a little farther from the edge of the crevice and flung the coiled rope toward her. She shot out her hand but missed. Quickly Merle coiled the rope again, and again flung it out toward her. This time she managed to catch it and hang on.

"Tie it around your chest," he called to her. "Then stand up and try to jump. I'll stabilize you as much as I can when you get up."

She loosened her pack cautiously, watching Merle tie his end of the rope around himself, under one arm and over the other shoulder so he wouldn't asphyxiate if it yanked tight. She slipped a little as she shook her pack off her shoulders and watched it tumble down into the waiting pit. Then, wedging her feet as best she could, she wound the rope around herself, arranging it just as Merle had tied his end. She hesitated a moment, aware of the risk she was taking, aware that Merle could tumble her right into that crevice now if he chose.

But what choice did she have?

She tied the rope. When it was secure, she inched her painful way back up the shaking slab, feeling it tip even more, as if it wanted to turn over on her and bury her. When she reached the top again, Merle was still waiting.

"Ready," she called to him.

"Okay. Find a place to stand, and then jump. I'll brace you as best I can."

Which really wasn't bracing at all, since the rock slab had become as active as a bucking bronco. Time was running out, she realized. The mountain was going to turn that rock over with her on it.

Wedging one foot against the edge of the slab, she eased herself into a position where she would be able to rise and jump in one smooth, quick movement. The rock shook hard, and then steadied...just enough.

She shoved herself up and jumped.

The minute her feet left the ground she knew she wasn't going to quite make it. The chasm was just too wide, and it yawned beneath her like a hungry mouth. No, not quite, but she hit the far side with a thud that nearly knocked the wind out of her. At once her hands clawed for purchase on the edge of the crevice, seeking a hold to keep her from slipping down into the abyss below.

Damn it, why wasn't Merle pulling on the rope? Dirt crumbled beneath her hands, and she felt herself slip a little. The earth shuddered again, trying to shake her down into the crevice. She slipped a little more.

And then the rope around her torso tightened, and with a strong tug she felt herself being pulled upward. The earth groaned deeply, a sound of angry protest.

"Help me," Merle shouted at her from above. "The crevice is closing!"

Spurred on by the terror of being crushed to death in the maw of the mountain, Mercy managed to dig her fingers into the hard, dry dirt and pull herself upward a little.

"That's it," Merle called. "Keep it up, honey!"

She was past wondering why he should be helping

her, or why he'd call her "honey." The ground was shaking hard, and it was all she could do to keep from slipping downward. The rope around her was a reassurance, but she wasn't getting up the side of the crevasse fast enough. It could close at any moment, and she was willing to bet that was exactly what the mountain wanted to do.

"Come on," Merle called encouragingly, and all of a sudden, with a shove of her feet, a tug of her hands and the upward jerk of the rope, she got her torso up and over the edge. A few more seconds and she was out of the crevice and able to roll safely away from the edge.

Lying facedown, she gasped for air and hugged the shaking earth, grateful for its apparent solidity...a solidity that was frighteningly deceptive, as she'd just seen. Creeping coldly along her spine was the realization that the mountain could open another crack right beneath her, that if she held still long enough it could gather its energy and focus it in one place, and cause the earth to try to swallow her again. And it never stopped rumbling beneath her. Never.

Merle swore almost disbelievingly, and Mercy lifted her head in time to see the crevice close like snapping jaws. If she'd been in there...

She shuddered and watched the earth open again, this time as the rock table on which she'd been sitting heaved up a little more and finally tumbled over backward, falling into the sinkhole.

"My God," Merle said. "Let's get out of here. Now! It looks like this whole place is gonna fall apart."

He reached down to grab her hand, pulling her to her

feet. Together they ran uphill toward the trees, away from the bucking, buckling ground behind them.

In the thick pine woods, the ground trembled but didn't buckle and shake as hard. Perhaps the roots of the trees interfered with the shock waves, or perhaps the mountain didn't want to harm the trees. Whatever, it felt almost safe there, and Mercy had no qualms about falling to the ground to catch her breath. Merle didn't seem especially inclined to go any farther just yet, either. He fell to the ground beside her and drew breath raggedly. The air was thin up here near the tree line. Very thin.

"In all my days," Merle said finally, "I've never seen an earthquake like that. I've never seen *anything* like that."

That was because he'd never seen anything like Thunder Mountain, Mercy thought. But she knew better than to speak of such things to Merle. He'd made such fun of her for thinking mountains had moods, a purely artistic reaction to their shapes and colors. Or had it been? Maybe…maybe she'd sensed the life force in the rock even then. Even before Gray Cloud.

And what had happened to Gray Cloud? Not that it mattered, she told herself angrily. He'd left her there, and considering his relationship with this damn mountain, it was entirely possible that he'd conspired with the mountain to kill her.

"God!" Merle said. "That was incredible!"

Mercy suddenly remembered that she needed to appear ignorant about Merle's presence on the mountain. If she let him know that she'd been aware of his presence and purpose, he might perceive her as an even bigger threat. Certainly pretending ignorance was the only possible protection she had now. Sitting up, she reached for the knot of the rope wrapped around her and tried to look casual.

"Wherever did you come from?" she asked him. "I couldn't believe it when I heard your voice!"

"I came looking for you."

That answer astonished her enough that she forgot the knot she was untying and looked at him. She'd expected him to make their meeting sound accidental, not baldly say he'd been looking for her. Her heart began to beat uncomfortably as she realized that the only excuse he could have for being so blunt was that he was going to kill her, anyway, so it didn't matter what she knew.

"Looking for me?" Her voice quavered ever so slightly. "Why?"

Merle looked away. "You won't believe me."

"Try me." Damn, she thought, he was as handsome as ever. But now, when she looked at him, she could only think how pretty he was. Gray Cloud was much more...attractive. But Gray Cloud had tried to kill her. All because he'd seen Merle's picture in her wallet he'd been willing to convict her and sentence her to death.

Merle hesitated. "I haven't been able to forget you."

Mercy's jaw dropped. For a moment everything else was forgotten as she considered this man's unbelievable gall. "Oh, come on!"

He shook his head. "No. No, really. I told you that you wouldn't believe me. But the honest truth is, I haven't been able to forget you. Joanne and I are getting a divorce, and all I've been able to think about is you, and the times we used to spend together rock climbing and white-water kayaking.... Mercy, there isn't one woman in a hundred like you."

He was good, she found herself thinking, as she met his brilliant blue eyes. Oh, he was very good. Those eyes couldn't possibly be lying...except that she knew Merle better than that. "I'd have preferred to be one in a million."

He looked a little startled, and then a chuckle escaped him. "Well, I'm beginning to think you might be. I was a fool not to recognize it then. Mercy, you're exactly the woman I need, the woman I want to spend my life with."

A couple of years ago, she might have believed it. A week ago, under other circumstances, she might even have considered it. But too much had happened in the last few days. Too much. This man had been responsible—or so she believed—for the attempt to kill the wolf pups in their den. He would mow down the trees on Thunder Mountain, leaving this beautiful land denuded of all except a few seed trees. Perhaps he would be required to replant, but Thunder Mountain wouldn't look the same again for a century or two. All this beautiful old-growth forest would be gone. And with the loss of the trees would come the loss of so many animals and birds.

It wasn't that she objected to the timber industry. But she did object to clear-cutting, and she certainly felt that some areas ought to be left alone in their natural state as a legacy to the future. Let timber companies replant and harvest the same areas again and again. If that drove up the price of paper, so be it. Maybe there would be more recycling. But certainly this beautiful mountain ought to be left untouched for all the generations to come.

All Merle could see though, was all this pristine lumber. Not trees, but lumber. That was what he saw. And dollar signs. He wouldn't care about the wolves except as an obstacle, or about the owls and birds and mice and all the rest of the little creatures. He would come up here and cut away every last tree that wasn't jealously guarded, and would call it progress and profit. He would never count the losses.

So it didn't really matter whether he was telling the truth about wanting her. But she didn't believe he was. He was trying to manipulate her, to get her into his camp. He knew how much trouble he could save himself with a wildlife biologist on his side. Did he really think he could maneuver her so easily? Had she been such a wimp when they'd dated?

Probably.

And it would probably be best now to seem to believe him. If he thought he could control her, maybe he wouldn't be so eager to eliminate her. And the longer she survived, the more chance she would have to escape somehow.

So she managed to keep any trace of sarcasm out of her voice, and even managed to inject a trace of hopeful breathlessness, as she replied, "Really?"

Because she didn't believe him, it was easy to see the satisfaction in his answering smile. "Really," he said. "I know you'll need time to think about it, but honestly, honey, I've never been able to forget you. I think you're the primary reason I never made

Joanne happy…because I was always wishing I was with *you*."

She wanted to gag and looked quickly away, hoping the urge wasn't visible on her face. Hating every word, she forced herself to say, "I don't know, Merle. I mean…I hurt an awful lot over you. I cried for a long time."

"It'll be different now, I swear. Honestly, honey, I was a fool. I didn't know how lucky I was to have you, and I'd already made a promise to Joanne. I don't break promises, honey."

No, but you lie easily enough, Mercy thought angrily. What now? Trapped on the side of a murderous mountain in the company of a lying man who wouldn't hesitate to kill her if he thought it would make him a profit, abandoned by a man who had made love to her and then left her to be killed—a man who couldn't possibly love her, because he didn't believe in her basic honesty. No, he had used her. *Used her.* But anger at Gray Cloud wasn't going to help her deal with Merle.

She forced herself to bite her lower lip, a habit she had when she was undecided about something, a habit Merle had teased her about more than once. He would know what it meant, and it wouldn't occur to him that she was doing it deliberately to hide the anger and disgust she was feeling. And the fear. With everyone on this mountain determined to kill her and the wolves, how could she spare any emotion for anything else? But she did. She felt plenty of hot rage right now.

A flicker of motion caught her eye, and she turned her head a little, just barely managing to swallow a happy exclamation when she saw Eyebrows regarding her from deep within the forest shadows. He stared straight at her, then turned suddenly and slipped away. She had the strongest feeling that he'd been trying to tell her she wasn't alone.

"Mercy?" Merle was demanding her attention, the faintest trace of impatience in his voice.

"I don't know." She tried to sound truly doubtful but not skeptical. She hoped it sounded as if she really wanted to believe him. Oh, God, this was an impossible game to play! She was no actress. "I mean...if you'd really loved me..."

"Oh, honey, I did! I do! Just say you'll give me the chance to prove it to you. Just the chance."

She summoned a smile. "I think... I think I'd like that."

There was absolutely no mistaking the satisfaction in his smile now. He felt he had her, which was a comment on how easy she'd been for him the first time. There wasn't a doubt in his mind that he could exercise a little charm and that she would tumble like an overripe apple into his waiting arms. It might almost be interesting to actually do it, just so she could find out what he hoped to accomplish. Did he think she would be willing to claim the wolf pack didn't exist?

No, even Merle couldn't possibly be so mistaken about her. What he probably intended to do was kill the wolves and then have her testify to the fact that they were gone and that it wasn't likely any wolf pack would come to the area again in the foreseeable future. Yes, that would be within the realm of possibility. That was something she would be able to do without lying and compromising her conscience. With the weight of her reputation and university behind whatever he wanted her to say, it would be believed and not questioned too closely. No one, for example, would believe that she had colluded in the murder of the wolves, so whatever had happened to the pack would be assumed to be natural or accidental. No one would look too closely.

God, he was despicable! She shivered, feeling the ground shake with renewed vigor. "I've got to get off this mountain." That much was absolute truth.

"We will, honey. I promise we will. But first...well, I understand you came up here to study some wolves?"

Ahh. This was it. She managed a nod, but couldn't bring herself to look at him. Instead she seized on what had happened on the rock table. "Did you see the way that rock tipped up? Oh, Merle, I thought I was going to slide down into that pit!"

"I know, but you're safe now, honey." He slid over closer and started to put his arm around her, but just then Thunder Mountain gave a huge tremor, one strong enough that Mercy and Merle both lay back to ride it out rather than try to balance against it.

Mercy held her breath, hoping against hope that another crevice wouldn't open right under her. It was possible; she had seen what this mountain could do, and if it wanted to kill her and Merle both...

"Let's keep moving." The words were out of her mouth before she consciously formed them.

"You must be kidding! We won't even be able to stay on our feet!"

But the ground continued to shudder, and beneath her Mercy felt it buckle as if it were about to give way. Panic filled her, and she scrambled to her feet, swaying like a drunk as she tried to maintain her balance. "We've got to move!"

"Mercy, don't be stupid!"

The ground heaved upward now, doming beneath her feet, beneath Merle. That evidently connected in Merle's mind with Mount Saint Helens, because he scrambled to his feet, too, and stopped protesting. "Where?" he asked, as if she had all the answers.

"Anywhere. Anywhere away from here." Because it took the mountain time to act, and as long as they could keep moving, they might stay one step ahead of it.

They might survive.

Chapter Thirteen

They scrambled upward toward the mountain peak. As the trees grew thinner, the terrain grew steeper, and climbing became more difficult. Some corner of Mercy's mind wondered why she was heading upward instead of downward, why climbing seemed so imperative.

Listen...

Well, she was listening to something, she thought half-hysterically. Something was driving her higher up this mountain, and Merle was following without protest, probably because she seemed to know what she was doing.

Did she?

A different kind of thunder resounded from somewhere to the left; it sounded like a massive rock slide had been unleashed by the mountain's restlessness. Sobbing for oxygen in the thin high-altitude air, Mercy tilted her head and looked upward, afraid she would see some overhang or talus just waiting for the proper shake to set it loose. Much to her relief, there didn't appear to be anything that could easily be turned into a landslide.

But then she remembered the table, an apparently immovable, stable platform that had tried to tip her into a pit. Thunder Mountain had the power to do whatever it chose. No matter how stable and safe any portion of it looked, the mountain could turn it into a threat.

But she kept climbing. Running downward wouldn't make them any safer, and some instinct was demanding that she climb, that she get beyond the trees, if possible.

"Some friends of mine are up here a ways," Merle said breathlessly.

A corner of Mercy's mind registered his choice of words as odd. "Friends? You didn't come alone?"

"No. A bunch of us are, umm, camping out."

A small bubble of anger burst in Mercy. *Camping out* was a strange way to describe what these men had apparently been attempting to do. It infuriated her beyond speech to remember that fire set at the mouth of the wolf den. "I thought you came to find *me*."

"I did," he said as swiftly as his breathlessness would allow. "I did. But when I mentioned I was coming up here, a group of my pals decided to come along."

Right, thought Mercy. Right. Even for Merle, it was pretty damn thin. "How many of your pals?" That information might at least prove useful…if she lived long enough. Damn it, what had happened to Gray Cloud? She had a vision of him hiking happily down the side of the mountain while the mountain took care of all the problems, namely her, Merle and his friends. Another bubble of anger rose and burst within her.

"There are… There are four other guys with me," Merle said. "Good buddies."

Good murdering buddies, she thought bitterly. "Well, maybe if we all work together, we can get off this damn mountain." Hah.

"Yeah."

Just then, up ahead, she saw Eyebrows again. He stared straight at her and wagged his tail ever so slightly, as if he were greeting a member of his pack. Then he slipped away again into the shadows.

Climb...higher....

The trees were getting much thinner, and the barren slope above the tree line had just come into view when Merle reached out and stopped her. "Let's head south a little. That'll take us to my campsite."

Mercy hesitated, looking up the slope beyond the trees with something that felt very much like longing. Why should she want to get up there? There were fewer places to hide up there where nothing grew.

Listen...

At twelve thousand feet, the lack of oxygen was distinctly uncomfortable. Had they been flying this high in a small airplane, they would have been required to wear oxygen masks. She was sure the altitude was fogging her brain a little, and she hesitated for too long, looking from Merle to the slope above, unable to decide.

"Come on, Mercy, it's not far. Six of us together will stand a better chance, because we can help each other."

She wasn't sure about that, but there didn't seem to be an alternative. She couldn't argue without a reason, and her only reason was a sharp longing to get higher.

And somehow, without being aware of making any decision, she found herself traversing the slope behind Merle, heading toward his campsite. What was he going to do with her when he got her there? Keep up the pretense that he loved her? Make a prisoner of her? Or kill her?

The mountain shook, and thunder rumbled hollowly,

bouncing off the mountain and echoing through the canyons below, so that it sounded as if it came from everywhere all at once. With startling suddenness, lightning forked downward and hit a tree only fifty feet away. Blinded, Mercy stumbled to a halt as the thunderclap deadened her hearing.

The brilliance of the light seemed to have burned a hole in her retina. Everywhere she looked there was a black spot dead center in her vision, and she was afraid to move.

Merle swore savagely and reached out to hang on to a tree trunk as if he were afraid of falling. Long moments passed, and he just kept right on swearing.

When Mercy could finally see again, it was as if the world had been transformed. Black, roiling clouds had covered the sky, nearly turning day into night. Lightning flickered within the dark depths of the clouds, looking like the spluttering and spitting from a downed power line. Thunder Mountain's tremors had subsided a little, but the vibration of the ground beneath her feet was steady, a reminder.

They were greeted before they reached the campsite by one of Merle's "friends." Mercy took in the gun the man carried slung over his shoulder and recognized that it was no simple hunting rifle. These men weren't armed for deer, and it wouldn't matter, anyway, because it wasn't hunting season. The man looked from her to Merle in a way that made Mercy's skin crawl.

"My fiancée," Merle said, looking at Mercy with a smile. "At least, I hope she will be soon. Mercy, this is my buddy Vince."

She managed a smile. "Hi, Vince. Nice to meet you."

Vince didn't even bother with the smile. He nodded shortly and turned back to Merle. "Need a word with you."

The two men stepped away and spoke so softly that Mercy didn't have a hope of hearing. She pretended disinterest, turning away to look up through the trees at the barren slope above.

Listen...

She was listening. She was listening with every fiber of her being, trying to determine what she needed to do now. If she went to the camp with Merle, she might well be walking into her own grave. If she didn't...

Walk away....

The wind whispered the words to her, and she found herself walking slowly upslope, toward the tree line, away from Merle and Vince. Slowly, steadily, apparently unnoticed, she just kept going.

There was Eyebrows. He appeared again before her, staring straight at her with his strange golden eyes, and then turned, leading the way as if to encourage her.

Something was compelling her to get above the tree line. She wasn't sure what it was, or whether it was even the right thing to do, but she couldn't seem to stop herself. When finally she heard Merle shout after her, she was almost there, and she just kept going.

Listen...

Eyebrows glanced back, his tail high, his golden eyes mesmerizing. *Come with me,* he seemed to be saying. *Come with me.*

Beyond him she saw Stripes; the pups must have been left in a new den. And then the other members of the pack appeared like wraiths out of the thinning forest depths, standing to either side like an honor guard...or a gauntlet. As she advanced, they moved before her, always delineating the path, but never letting her get too close to them.

She could hear Merle behind her; he was hurrying to catch up, and the sound of his swift strides caused her to walk faster, too. Finally she broke into a run, her lungs straining painfully in the thin air.

The boiling clouds seemed to turn even blacker, and sparklers of blue lightning zipped through them. Stepping out into the open was going to turn her into a lightning rod, Mercy thought. She ought to stop right now....

No. Run, Tomorrow Woman. Run.

She ran, as fast as she could go, trusting the wind. Trusting the wind. The realization settled over her even as fear and worry propelled her. She was trusting the wind, the same wind that Gray Cloud spoke with. *Tate.*

A fork of lightning speared the ground ahead of her, but she kept running, urged on by the wolves and the whispers of the wind. Behind her, Merle shouted something.

Stop. Stop here....

She halted, nearly collapsing as her body shrieked for oxygen. Her legs trembled wildly, her lungs burned like fire, and every muscle screamed.

Merle shouted again. Mercy was leaning forward, hands braced just above her knees, gasping for air, but she turned her head and looked back.

Eyebrows came dashing back toward her, and when he reached her, he set himself between her and Merle, who came running up with Vince and three other men behind him. When the men approached, Eyebrows crouched and growled. One of the men leveled a gun at the wolf, but Mercy jumped in front of the animal, shielding it with her body. The man lowered his rifle.

"Damn it, Mercy, why did you run?" Merle said angrily. He approached but stopped a respectful distance back, eyeing the wolf warily.

"I don't know," she said. And honestly she didn't. "The wind told me to."

For an instant Merle was deprived of speech. He simply gaped at her before he finally said, "Honey, are you okay?"

"I'm just fine!"

"Then what do you mean, the wind told you to? The wind doesn't talk."

"Oh, yes, it does! And it told me to run. And you tell that friend of yours not to hurt any of these wolves! They're an endangered species, and this is the only known pack in Wyoming, and I'll make big trouble for anyone who hurts one of them!"

The change in Merle was astonishing. In an instant he went from concerned friend to angry enemy. She'd pushed too far, she realized. He wasn't going to try to cajole her over to his way of thinking on the subject.

"You won't be making trouble for anyone, Mercy. You won't be getting off this mountain alive."

Mercy opened her mouth to argue, then realized it wouldn't do any good. Merle had gotten her where he wanted her, and the gloves were off. She was about to die.

"Neither will you, Stockton."

At the sound of Gray Cloud's familiar voice, Mercy whirled around and saw him standing at the edge of the forest, blending closely with the dark shadows of a day turned almost into night.

Merle laughed quietly. "Thanks for turning up, Gray Cloud. I was sure you'd show your face once we got Mercy."

Mercy gasped, understanding. She had been everyone's bait. Now they could kill her *and* Gray Cloud, and take care of the wolves, leaving no loose ends behind.

But that was without reckoning on the mountain.

Eyebrows suddenly tilted his head back and gave a long, loud howl. He was answered immediately by the rest of the pack in their incredible harmony. Mercy instinctively looked around and cried out at what she saw.

She froze in shock and terror.

A crack was spreading along the ground toward Merle and Vince and the three other men who had joined them. Another crack was snaking steadily toward Mercy.

Jump back...

She obeyed immediately, without even thinking about it, jumping backward a foot. Merle looked at her oddly, then turned his head and saw the cracks that were creeping along the ground toward them. "What the hell...?"

"Thunder Mountain speaks," Gray Cloud said, his voice carrying steadily across the thunder, the wind and the sound of rupturing earth. "You have dared to threaten that which the mountain protects. You tried to kill the wolves. You want to kill the trees and countless small animals for your personal gain. The mountain will not allow it."

"The mountain doesn't have a damn thing to say about it," Merle snarled, but he didn't take his eyes from the cracks that were steadily approaching. Faster now, Mercy thought. As if the mountain had mastered the method, the cracks began to hurry toward them, gaining speed.

Eyebrows nudged at Mercy's knees, pushing her backward. She stumbled a little, but backed up, unable to tear her gaze from the accelerating cracks. Was the mountain going to try to swallow them? God, her worst nightmare!

The cracks weren't following a straight line, making it impossible to tell where they would intersect with the people...or which way she should go to avoid them. But they weren't big cracks, either, and when they arrived she would only have to step aside....

"Surrender now, Stockton," Gray Cloud called. "Tell your men to drop their guns and leave this mountain. You can still get off alive."

Merle snorted. "No way, Gray Cloud. You think a couple of cracks scare me?"

"You'll never timber this mountain," Gray Cloud said with flat certainty. Thunder rumbled in the boiling black clouds above, an angry, impatient sound. Lightning flickered faintly, almost as if it were waiting for some cue.

A restless flicker, Mercy thought. She dared a glance at Gray Cloud, then looked at the approaching cracks. They had almost reached them, she realized with an unpleasant start in the pit of her stomach. They didn't look deadly or even dangerous, but she knew the mountain better than to believe the cracks were innocent.

Step back.

She was long past wondering at the whispers in her head, long past ignoring them. She stepped back at once, just in time, it seemed, as a crack snaked in front of her, separating her from Merle. An innocuous little crack in the ground. Staggering only because of what it said about this mountain, what it revealed of the powers that dwelt here.

Another crack snaked between her and the men, right in front of Merle. He looked down at it and laughed.

Eyebrows nudged Mercy again, whining softly and pushing her away from the crack. She stepped back even farther.

"This is your last chance, Stockton," Gray Cloud said.

Another crack zipped along the ground, this time at a right angle to the one directly in front of Merle. It joined with another crack that had spread across the ground behind Merle and his men.

Mercy's heart seemed to stop. Didn't Merle see? Another crack, this one on the other side of the group. Sealing the square. Surrounding Merle and his men.

"Merle!" Mercy couldn't stand by and let this happen. Her conscience wouldn't allow it, much as she despised everything Merle was trying to do here. "Merle, for the love of God, get out of that square. Just step over here!"

Thunder roared suddenly, a furious explosion of sound, and lightning forked downward, stabbing at the ground nearby. Merle's henchmen were starting to look uneasy, but no one stepped out of the square the mountain had carved around them.

"Merle, please," Mercy begged. "Money isn't worth dying for!"

"The only people who are going to die are you and that redskin friend of yours," Merle snapped. "I'm bored with this crap. Shoot 'em!"

One of Merle's men leveled a rifle at Mercy; another pointed one in Gray Cloud's direction. But before either of them could pull the trigger, Eyebrows leapt, knocking the rifle from one man's hands and knocking the other man to one side. Immediately a third man fired at Eyebrows, but missed him.

As if the gunshots were a cue, the earth began to shake violently. As Mercy stared in horror, the cracks in the ground widened rapidly, in mere seconds becoming deep crevices, almost too wide to leap.

And from the depths of the crevices, flames shot upward. Suddenly a wall of fire stood between Mercy and Merle.

"Run, Mercy, run!" Gray Cloud shouted.

But horror held her frozen as she looked across a wall of flame at Merle. He and his men were surrounded now.

"Jump!" she shouted to him. "Jump across!"

"Mercy! Mercy, run!"

"Merle, jump! Jump!"

But the fire evidently terrified him too much, and he remained where he was, on the far side of a growing wall of flame.

"Mercy!"

Run...run, Tomorrow Woman! Before it's too late!

That was when Mercy became aware that another crack was zig zagging toward her, this one already a river of flame as it approached. Everywhere...everywhere she looked more fire-filled cracks were crisscrossing the ground.

"Mercy! Mercy!"

Eyebrows was suddenly there again, and this time he grabbed the sleeve of her jacket and tugged. As if released from a nightmare, she turned toward Gray Cloud....

And found he was on the far side of a wall of flame. She, too, was cut off, just as Merle and his men were. A scream came from one of Merle's men, but she didn't look. She was trapped by fire.

Jump through the fire.... Now!

But she couldn't. Fire terrified her, as it terrified most people. The heat of the flames felt as if it were singeing her skin without even touching her. Every instinct cried out to recoil...but there was no place to recoil to. She was trapped. Trapped.

A shriek from one of the men. Oh, God, how awful.... The bloodcurdling sound seemed to encase her in ice.

"Mercy!" Through the flames leapt Gray Cloud, appearing like some mythic warrior summoned by a wizard's spell. And suddenly he was there, holding her, squeezing her so tightly she thought a rib was going to pop.

"We have to jump," he told her. "We have to."

Some corner of her mind recognized the truth of it, but another part of her couldn't face the flames. She would be burned, and when it came to choices, she would rather be buried alive.

"Mercy, if we don't jump we're going to burn. Hold my hand. We'll jump together, and I'll make sure you don't get hurt."

She tilted her head back and looked up at him, thinking what a magnificent man he was. He had tied his hair down with a bandanna, which was the only way to keep it from catching fire, and he looked as much like a pirate right now as an Indian warrior.

"Mercy, we have to jump!"

Another scream from Merle's direction, but this one penetrated the fog that seemed to have paralyzed her mind. Yes, they had to jump. Refusing to look and see what was happening to the others, Mercy took Gray Cloud's offered hand.

"On the count of three," he said.

She nodded her understanding and tightened her grip on his hand.

"One..."

She reached inside her for the calm that helped her on the side of a cliff when she was rock climbing and there suddenly seemed to be no handholds above, no way to go.

"Two..."

When they got to the other side, the thing to do would be to roll on the ground, not wait to see if anything had caught fire, just roll to make sure that if anything *had* ignited it was put out. Focusing on the practical problem calmed her even more.

"Three!"

Somehow she was running straight toward that wall of flame as if it were an illusion to be ignored.

Jump, Tomorrow Woman. Jump!

She closed her eyes and jumped. Heat seared her skin, tightening it so that it felt it would peel off. Almost as soon as the blast furnace hit her, cool air replaced it. She opened her eyes just as the ground rushed up to meet her.

"Roll!"

She heard Gray Cloud shout the command, but she was already rolling, over and over, toward the woods. Toward what she hoped was sanctuary.

"Up!"

Hands pulled at her, lifting her to her feet, dragging her to the woods. Oh, God! Another wall of flame was zigzagging toward them. The mountain wasn't going to be denied.

"Keep running," Gray Cloud shouted. "Just keep running...."

Eyebrows suddenly appeared ahead of her and seemed to be beckoning. She ran. Hand in hand with Gray Cloud, she ran for the woods. Behind them, the screams stopped. Merle and his men were dead.

And the mountain had no intention of letting her and Gray Cloud escape. Another wall of fire zipped toward them, seeming to race along the ground like a burning fuse. When Mercy stumbled, Gray Cloud scooped her up, flung her over his shoulder and kept running. Mercy lifted her head and looked behind them. The entire clearing seemed to be on fire now.

And then they were in the trees. Little rivers of fire followed them for a bit, chasing and then stopping, as if the mountain were reluctant to set the forest ablaze.

A little deeper in the forest, Gray Cloud set Mercy on her feet and then wrapped her in his powerful arms, hugging her so tightly that she was surprised her ribs didn't crack.

"God," he whispered, "I thought I'd lost you!"

"Why did you leave me?" Struggling against his hold, she demanded an answer. "The mountain tried to kill me! It tipped up that table of rock and tried to dump me in a pit! Merle is the only reason I'm still alive!"

"I know. I saw." He shuddered. "I thought you'd be safe there. I really did. And when I came back and saw…" He shook his head and squeezed her harder. "I tracked you. I was so afraid Stockton would kill you before I could get to you."

"I thought—I thought you'd left me there to die."

He stiffened. In an instant he became as unyielding as rock. A moment later he released her and stepped back. "I see." He turned away.

"Well, what the hell was I supposed to think?" she demanded, torn between anger and tears. "You went off and didn't come back, and the mountain started trying to kill me, and Merle showed up and— Damn it, Gray Cloud, why were you gone so long?"

"I needed to locate all of Stockton's men so there wouldn't be any unpleasant surprises. They were scattered all over the place and—" He broke off abruptly. "What does it matter? Let's get out of here before something else happens."

The boiling black clouds overhead were as dark as night, and lightning speared through them threateningly. Nor had Thunder Mountain quieted. Beneath their feet the ground shook and heaved, but no fire spewed forth. The forest was safe from that, at least.

"The wolves," Mercy said. "I want to know if the wolves are okay."

"They're okay."

"How can you be sure? Eyebrows is the only one I've seen—"

"Eyebrows?" He interrupted her. "Who's Eyebrows?"

She was past caring whether she sounded stupid. All that mattered was that the wolves were okay and that she get off this mountain and never come back. "The alpha male. Because his eyebrows are different colors."

"Oh." He took several more long strides before replying. "I like it."

"Well, I want to know if they're all right, and I'm not going to settle for wondering. They helped me. All of them helped me right before Merle…got nasty. I'm not going to forget about them."

Gray Cloud halted abruptly and faced her. "All right," he said. "All right. I'll call them."

"Call them! You can't possibly—"

But he tilted back his head and let forth a perfect howl that caused the hair on Mercy's neck to stand on end. Chills ran down her spine as she listened to a sound she had never before heard issue from a human throat so perfectly.

Moments later another howl joined Gray Cloud's. Then another. Mercy couldn't tell how many wolves answered because of the deceptive harmonics, but in the end it didn't matter. In the end she was able to turn in a slow circle and make out pairs of golden eyes staring back from the forest's depths. They were all here, answering Gray Cloud's call, harmonizing beautifully with each other and the man.

Gray Cloud fell silent, while around them the wolves continued their full-throated song. "You see?" he said quietly. "They're fine."

Mercy nodded slowly, reluctant to let go of the moment, of the perfect beauty of the wolf pack's song, but she was aware that Thunder Mountain might attack again at any moment. Much as she hated to go, she had to. She had to get off this mountain before she died.

"Let's go," Gray Cloud said. "I have to calm the mountain."

The clouds remained so black and dense that it was impossible to gauge the time of day. Lightning continued to flicker, but it didn't seem threatening. The treetops swayed in the ceaseless wind, a constant rush of sound joined by the creak of bending tree trunks. From time to time an icy splatter of rain would fall.

Finally she was sure it must be sunset or later. Fatigue was making her stumble over her own feet, and the wind had developed a chilly bite. Even the black clouds seemed blacker. Just when she was beginning to think she couldn't take another step without collapsing, they emerged from the forest into the great bowl of the glacial cirque.

Mercy forgot her fatigue as she looked up at the peak of Thunder Mountain, bare and unadorned, the view unobstructed for once by the ever-present clouds. Tall and forbidding, a wall of gray granite rising to a peak as imposing as the Matterhorn. And down its side, from the glacier on its shoulder, ran a dazzling waterfall that plunged into the bowl of the cirque below.

Mercy understood instantly why this ground was sacred. Its beauty was breathtaking, but so was the bottom of the bowl, with its crazy tumble of boulders in shapes evocative of warriors frozen in stone, tall granite sentinels rising from a bed of the greenest grass and most dazzling wildflowers. Columbine and paintbrush vied for preeminence. And everywhere one looked there was a tall staff trailing a streamer of cloth—white and red, mostly, but some yellow, as well—left by someone who had come to pray.

It looked, Mercy thought, as if an army had been frozen in granite with their pennants still flying.

Gray Cloud began to chant, and Mercy turned to find him positioning three exquisite stones in a triangle, using his forearm as a measure of the distance between them. From a medicine bundle he took several other items and placed them in the center of the triangle. In the failing light she couldn't make them out, but it didn't matter. What mattered was the blue light that suddenly arced between the corners of the triangle, a dancing, flashing exhibition of vitality.

What mattered was Gray Cloud, standing over the triangle with his arms extended, palms uplifted. What mattered was that for the first time in days the mountain grew perfectly still and quiet.

Thunder Mountain listened.

The world grew silent, and even the clouds seemed to hold their breath. And a few minutes later, when Gray Cloud finished his prayer and bent to gather up all the items and wrap them securely in his prayer bundle, the world remained calm.

"It is finished," he told Mercy. "You'll be safe now."

"Just like that?"

"Just like that." He set the bundle down on the grass and sat cross-legged beside it. "We'll need to spend the night here. I'll take you down in the morning."

"I don't even have my pack anymore. No blankets."

"I'll keep you warm."

The offer drew her, and she settled beside him, nearly sighing when his arm wrapped around her shoulders.

After a while he spoke again. "I'll build a fire to keep us warm."

She watched, admiring his skill and economy of movement. He was a man comfortable in himself and in his world...and he wouldn't fit anywhere else. The thought filled her with sadness, haunting her with the awareness that their lives were worlds apart.

When the fire was burning brightly, driving back the darkness and casting warmth over them, Gray Cloud again settled beside her and drew her to his side.

"We need to get the Conard County sheriff and the rangers up here," he said.

Mercy was suddenly struck by a terrible thought. "Gray Cloud! What if they're not dead? What if one of them is only hurt?"

"They're dead." He said it flatly, with conviction.

"How can you possibly know?"

"The life force is gone from them. I felt it when they died. They're all gone, Mercy."

She ought to feel sad, she told herself. She ought to feel some kind of grief or compassion, but all she could feel was a horror at the terrible way they had died. It seemed like an awfully high cost for a mountain and some timber, yet it had been Merle and his men who had put that price tag on Thunder Mountain. They had been prepared to kill to get what they wanted. In the end, it seemed the mountain had played by their rules.

"Has the mountain decided I'm not a threat?" she asked him.

"The wolves like you."

She suspected that non sequitur was the only answer she was going to get. Thinking about it now, she got goose bumps remembering how the wolves had helped her more than once. Odd behavior from wild animals. "The wolves here are unusual."

Gray Cloud shook his head. "No. Wolves are extremely intelligent. Man has just been too blind to see."

"White men, you mean."

He turned his head and looked at her. "Not all."

There was something she needed to say, so she looked into the fire, squared her shoulders and said it. "I'm sorry I thought you wanted me dead."

"I never wanted that, Mercy. Never. But sometimes I wasn't sure I was going to be able to save you. The mountain sensed your connection with Merle. And I'm sorry I didn't believe you when you said it was over and done. I was jealous—not thinking clearly."

Jealous. The word hit her hard, depriving her of both speech and breath. *Jealous.* Could he really care enough about her to be jealous? Oh, but it could never work!

Could it?

Still not daring to breathe, she tilted her head so she could look at him. Firelight played in strange patterns over his face, making him look like a warrior out of time. Beyond him, the dark shadows of the granite warriors seemed to keep guard.

"I, uh, didn't want to admit I'd come to care so much about you," he said.

"Care?" She barely breathed the word, needing more, so much more.

He moved his head a little, looking very much like a man facing an unpleasant task. "Yes," he said finally. "Care. As in love. I love you."

She felt as if she had cartwheeled off the edge of the planet into a place of brilliant light and joy. But, oh, how afraid she was to believe it could be. That it could come to anything. Their lives were poles apart.

Listen, whispered the wind. *Listen to your heart.*

She listened. And what she heard was a love so shining and bright that it could not be contained. "I love you, too," she whispered softly. "I love you."

He turned, gathering her into his arms, onto his lap, cradling her as if she were the most precious thing in the world.

And he kissed her. Kissed her with love and passion and a need so strong that she felt it to her toes. It was cold, and without blankets he didn't want to expose her to the chill of the night air, so his hands slipped within her clothes to claim her, gentle touches that painted fire on every exquisite nerve ending. She felt so incredibly possessed and loved, and it seemed only natural when her body exploded into a climax so intense that she felt as if the mountain had erupted beneath her.

And then she was lying on her side with her back to the fire's warmth, with Gray Cloud's warmth sheltering her front, as he held her and gently stroked her, as he whispered soft words of love and yearning.

For a little while she simply basked in the glow of dreams come true, but she wasn't one to hide her head in the sand. There was no way their lives could be combined in any way that would make a satisfactory relationship. So when she walked down this mountain tomorrow, she would be walking away from Gray Cloud.

A long sigh escaped her as she realized she was going to lose what she had only just found, that she was going to have to sacrifice either the man she loved or the job she loved, because she could never have both at the same time. Unshed tears clogged her throat and made it hurt. She wanted to grab him and hold on to him and never let him go. But she couldn't give up everything she had worked so hard for to become a hermit on the side of a mountain.

Gray Cloud stirred a little. "I have fulfilled my vision."

For an instant what he was saying didn't connect. When she finally comprehended it, Mercy felt her heart stop. "What—what do you mean?"

"I've fulfilled my vision. What happened today—the rivers of fire—that was my vision. I saw myself needing to be there to aid the mountain against those who would harm it. I had to be there to save the wolf pups from those who would harm them. To save you from the fire."

Mercy caught her breath sharply. "You... You saw that?"

He nodded. "It was my vision, and it has come to pass. My vision is complete."

"So...what happens now? I thought you were going to protect this mountain forever?"

"I will. But not in the same way. I no longer need to live here all the time. Stockton was the threat I saw so long ago in my vision, and he's gone. I see no other threats in the immediate future. You'll tell the world of the wolves, and the mountain will be protected. Later— years from now, perhaps—there will be other threats. If I'm needed, I'll come."

Hope was beginning to grow in her, a beautiful hope that hardly dared to unfurl its petals and bloom. "And in the meantime?"

He drew his head back and looked straight into her eyes. "In the meantime I can make my shields and create ceremonial regalia anywhere. I would like to come here and stay on the mountain in the summers, but for the rest of the year...I can rest my head wherever you are."

She drew a long, shaky breath and closed her eyes, hardly daring to believe.

Believe, whispered the wind. *Believe.*

"Will you be my tomorrow?" he asked.

She opened her eyes and let forth a laugh of sheer joy, understanding at last the name the wind had given her.

And she dared to believe.